**Two brand-new stories in every volume...
twice a month!**

Duets Vol. #85

Talented Jill Shalvis first launched the
RED-HOT ROYALS miniseries in Temptation
with #861 *A Prince of a Guy*. The romantic regal
romp continues this month with a very special
Double Duets featuring *A Royal Mess* and
Her Knight To Remember. Jill is "fast, fanciful
and funny. Get ready for laughs, passion and
toe-curling romance," says *Rendezvous*.

Duets Vol. #86

Two talented writers make their Duets debut
this month—with a splash. Samantha Connolly,
who hails from Ireland, was an avid reader before
trying her hand at writing, with great results in
If the Shoe Fits. Dorien Kelly is still walking on air
after selling her first book, *Designs on Jake*, to Duets.
She's now hard at work on a second novel.
A welcome to this delightful duo!

Be sure to pick up both Duets volumes today!

"I'm going with the old-fashioned method."

Ha! C.J. thought smugly, switching the phone receiver from one ear to the other, now let's see how cavalier he is about baby making.

"Well, okay, that's fine," Jack said, after a moment's hesitation.

"What?" she said cagily.

"Look C.J., I'm ready to help, whatever it takes. To be honest I'd prefer to do it this way, as well. I figure that if you do have my baby we're going to end up facing a lot more testing situations than this. I want you to be able to trust me completely. It'll be fine, C.J. We're both adults. We'll go out for a relaxing dinner, have a nice bottle of wine and then we'll sleep together."

C.J. swiveled her chair from side to side, nodding to herself. She thought, but couldn't be sure, that he was smiling. Try to bluff a bluffer, would you?

"Okay," she said. "I'll figure out when I'm fertile and I'll give you a call."

"Perfect," he said, hanging up.

"What?"

For more, turn to page 9

Designs on Jake

"Jake, I think we should just be friends."

Well, damn. Was this really the woman who'd given him that all-out kiss the night before?

"Darlin', there hasn't been a man born yet who wants to be 'just friends.' In fact, we're genetically coded to bang our heads on a brick wall when a woman uses those words on us." Jake moved toward Rowan, and she backed away. "I don't know where we're headed, I haven't thought about your kids, but I'm pretty sure about one thing.... You don't want to be 'just friends.'"

"I don't?"

"Nope." Jake moved close enough to grasp her elbows and draw her the rest of the way to him. "Want me to prove it?"

Roman was staring at his mouth. "No."

"Liar," he said, then settled his lips over the pulse thrumming at her throat. She leaned into him and gave a sigh that did a lot for his self-confidence. "Need more proof?"

"Well, maybe just a little."

For more, turn to page 197

HARLEQUIN DUETS

ISBN 0-373-44152-5

Copyright in the collection:
Copyright © 2002 by Harlequin Books S.A.

The publisher acknowledges the copyright holders
of the individual works as follows:

IF THE SHOE FITS
Copyright © 2002 by Samantha Connolly

DESIGNS ON JAKE
Copyright © 2002 by Dorien Kelly

Visit us at www.eHarlequin.com

Printed in U.S.A.

If the Shoe Fits

Samantha Connolly

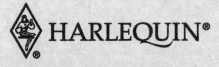

HARLEQUIN®

TORONTO • NEW YORK • LONDON
AMSTERDAM • PARIS • SYDNEY • HAMBURG
STOCKHOLM • ATHENS • TOKYO • MILAN • MADRID
PRAGUE • WARSAW • BUDAPEST • AUCKLAND

Dear Reader,

I was a reader myself long before I became a writer, so when I sat down to write this story I knew exactly the type of heroine I wanted to create. Someone feisty, who enjoys life and has a sense of adventure.

I admit that giving her a job as a shoe designer was pure indulgence, as was setting the book in New York. I once spent a summer there, working as a waitress, and absolutely loved the place, even though the pace of life was overwhelming.

Things are a lot more easygoing here in Ireland, where I live—in fact, where I was born—but we still appreciate the escapism of a good book. It has been a great thrill to have had a book published for the first time, especially as I am so far away, across the ocean. So, whether you're saving it for the weekend or grabbing a quick coffee break to read a few more pages, I hope you enjoy C.J. and Jack's romance.

I had great fun writing it, especially when I had to go out and try on lots of shoes—for research purposes!

Best wishes,

Samantha Connolly

For my mother, Denise
for her unflagging faith and support

and for my dad, Adrian
who, having read every other type of book,
now has to read a romance novel

1

"JUST A COFFEE, PLEASE," said C.J.

"Are you sure that's all?"

"Yes, thanks."

The waitress shifted her weight to her other foot.

"Our grilled cheese sandwiches are the best in town," she said chattily. "Best in all of Vermont, in fact."

C.J. picked up the menu and scanned it hastily. It was a single laminated sheet with a variety of breakfast and lunch specials laid out in pretty italics and bordered with pink and red roses.

C.J. couldn't imagine being able to eat but it was probably a good idea to order something. It would distract the waitress and it would give her something to fiddle with when Jack arrived.

Not something as messy as melting cheese, though.

"I'll have the toast and homemade jam," she said, eliciting a wide smile from the waitress.

C.J. watched her waddle away. Everywhere I go, she thought, I'm seeing pregnant women.

She exhaled slowly through her nose and rubbed the palms of her hands along her thighs. She surreptitiously pulled out a compact and checked herself. Her eyes looked wide in her face, filled with trepidation.

Calm down, she told herself. You are a successful businesswoman who speaks three languages and who hobnobs with famous actors and celebrities every week. This is just another business transaction, of which you've conducted hundreds, and there's no reason whatsoever to be nervous.

The waitress returned and placed C.J.'s coffee and food on the table in front of her.

"Thanks," said C.J., reaching for the milk jug. As she was trickling milk into her coffee, she became aware that the waitress hadn't left.

C.J. lifted her eyes slowly to find the waitress looking down at her, arms folded and head cocked speculatively.

"Aren't you C. J. Mathews?" she asked, narrowing her eyes at C.J.

C.J. smiled and gave a small nod.

The waitress squealed and clapped.

"I knew it," she said. "I just knew it. It took me a while to figure it out, because of your new hair and everything, but I said to myself, I definitely recognize her and if I just think about it for a minute, it will definitely come to me. You probably don't remember me, I was a few classes behind you."

She waited expectantly while C.J. wracked her brains to come up with a name.

"Are you Lisa?" she said hesitantly.

"Exactly!" exclaimed the girl, lowering herself into the seat opposite C.J. and leaning an elbow on the table, all without breaking the flow of her inquisition.

"You moved away to Europe, didn't you? My goodness, when did you come back? Are you back for something special? Have you come back for the Daffodil Festival? No, of course not, why on earth would you come all the way back for that? You probably have festivals all the time in Europe. Where exactly are you living? It's not Paris, is it? Oh, that would be so exciting. Have you been to Ireland? I told Pete that I wanted to go to Ireland for our vacation, but who's got time?"

She laughed and patted her stomach and then peered into C.J.'s eyes.

"It's not a family problem, is it? I know your mom had a touch of the flu over Christmas, but she's all right now, isn't she? We just haven't seen you around for a while. It must be something special to bring you all the way back. Nothing bad I hope?"

C.J. had given up hope of getting a word in, so she was startled by the sudden silence.

"Uh…no," she said. "I live in New York now, I moved there a few years ago. So it's just a short journey up. And my mother comes down and visits me all the time," she added, wanting to show Lisa that she wasn't some kind of neglectful daughter who just ran off and abandoned her family.

Lisa beamed at her.

"That's great," she said. "So now you can come and visit your mom anytime you want, you don't need an excuse."

"Mmm," agreed C.J., willing herself not to blush. "So are you working here full-time now Lisa?"

"Oh, I don't just work here, we own the place. Mr. Brown was retiring and this burger chain wanted to buy the place, but I told Mr. B. that he could have breakfast and lunch here for free for the rest of his life, and he said he'd be able to have that anyway if he sold out to a burger place, and I said sure, if you want to eat in the company of teenagers necking and playing video games. So Pete bought it and I did it up," she said, looking around proudly.

C.J. was honestly impressed. The diner was clean and well kept with brightly colored curtains and small vases of fresh flowers on each table.

"It's lovely," she said, "and I see congratulations are in order, is this your first?"

Lisa let out a peal of laughter.

"You are behind the times, this is our third. Well, it's my third. Technically speaking, it's only Pete's second."

"Pete...?" said C.J. searching her memory for a face to go with the name.

Lisa laughed again. "You got it, Pete Ledden. Lord knows I tried to get away from him, but he hooked me in the end. I guess you can't fight true love. Are you married?"

C.J. smiled and shook her head.

"Never mind," said Lisa, reaching over to pat her hand.

C.J. felt a spurt of irritation. She wanted to snap that being single was, in many ways, preferable to being tied to Pete Ledden for life, but one look at Lisa's open, friendly face and the urge fled.

She reminded herself that she'd been fortunate enough to make her own dream come true, and her life was exactly the way she wanted it to be, and just because someone five years younger than her was feeling sorry for her was no reason to be paranoid.

In fact, talking to Lisa had been just what she needed. A hefty dose of reality.

This wasn't New York, she couldn't go around making bizarre requests as casually as she might go out and buy a new dress. She relaxed her shoulders, congratulated herself on a narrow escape and started to think about how soon she could get a flight out.

Lisa glanced out the window and started to push herself up out of the booth.

"Look, there's Jack Harding, do you remember him? Hang on, let me go call him."

Lisa bustled off in excitement.

C.J.'s heart had thudded against her chest at the mention of Jack's name, and now it fluttered wildly as she looked out at the man coming across the street. She had an overwhelming urge to fling herself under the table and hide until he went away. This was an awful mistake and now she was trapped. She held the menu up over her face and peeked around the side of it.

Jack was squinting against the sun as he crossed the street, and he raised his hand in a wave as a neighbor's truck passed.

He had the same relaxed stride as always, and his face broke into an easy grin as he acknowledged Lisa's frantic gesturing.

C.J. put down the menu and moaned inaudibly as they came into the diner. This had seemed like such a practical idea from her store office on Spring Street. She had no choice but to brazen it out now.

The last time she'd seen Jack had been three years before, at her grandfather's funeral. C.J.'s father had died when she was young, so C.J.'s grandfather had been the main male in her life as she grew up. She had felt very small and lost at his funeral and Jack had been there throughout, a quiet stalwart figure, sombre in a suit, who'd told her she could always come to him if she needed help.

The Jack approaching her now was unmistakably the Jack of her childhood, the one who'd knocked her off her bike, the one who'd gotten into so much trouble for driving his dad's car when he was only twelve, the one with the blond hair that was always in disarray, the one who always had oil streaks across the thighs of his jeans.

His jeans and T-shirt were clean today, but his hair was still unruly and his eyes were the same disturbing deep blue, staring at her now.

And he had the same mischievious smirk.

"Well, who is it?" demanded Lisa at his elbow. "Go on, you must be able to guess. Imagine her with mousy-colored hair."

Oh, thank you so much, Lisa, thought C.J., steaming quietly. She looked up at Jack, silently pleading with him not to announce that she'd arranged this meeting. It would be all over town if Lisa heard about it.

Jack frowned thoughtfully, his eyes gleaming.

"Isn't she that Mathews girl, the one who used to walk around in those fancy shoes?"

Lisa slapped him lightly on the arm.

"That's right! Got it in one. I'd forgotten about those shoes. Lord, you were a sight."

She shook her head.

"Sit down now, Jack, and I'll get you a coffee. My lunch people are going to descend on me any minute so C.J. could use the company."

"Would you mind if I joined you?"

"Of course she wouldn't," said Lisa, giving him a little push.

Jack slid his long legs under the table, bumping his knees against C.J.'s.

"Hope you haven't been waiting too long," he murmured, grinning at her.

C.J. glanced over to make sure that Lisa had moved out of earshot before turning her attention to him.

"It gave me a chance to catch up on the local gossip," she said.

"I like your hair," he said.

She automatically put a hand up to touch it.

"Wasn't it this color the last time we met?"

"Not quite that red," he said honestly.

"Oh, well, the sun brings it out," she said, grinning.

Lisa came back and put a cup of coffee in front of Jack. She gave C.J. a wink before moving off again.

"When did you arrive?" Jack asked.

"I came up yesterday afternoon."

"How's your mom?"

"She's fine. She's delighted to have me to fuss over."

"Well, I'm glad you called, it's good to see you."

C.J. leaned her chin on her hand and smiled at him.

"You, too," she said.

The nervousness, which had subsided at Lisa's bossy

interventions, was starting to seep back into her veins again.

She felt her mouth beginning to dry and she looked out of the window to calm herself.

"How's the plane?" she asked.

He looked crestfallen. "It's grounded at the moment. I had a bit of a crash."

"Oh, no," she said, upset for him. They had talked on the phone soon after he'd bought it, and Jack had been overflowing with enthusiasm about the acquisition of the year-old Sukhoi.

"What happened?" she said.

"I had a bird strike and the engine got messed up. I had to make an emergency landing and damaged one of the wings. So, I hope you haven't come looking for a flight. But I'll have it fixed in a few weeks, so I could take you up then."

"You're fixing it? Do you know how to?"

"It's pretty similar to auto work. I've picked it up as I go along."

"Hmm," she said, thinking, *not in a million years am I going up in that.*

The conversation dried up again and C.J. sought for another subject.

"How's your family?" she asked.

"They're all fine. Allison is doing her internship in Boston, she says she's having the worst year of her life but she barely has time to notice it because she's so tired all the time. It's hard work and we hardly ever see her but I know she's loving it. I still can't believe it sometimes, my little sister, the doctor. And Eddie and Donna's kids are really growing up fast. Didi's nine now and Eddie Jr. was six last month. They're both brilliant. Mom and Dad are well. We've given up on Dad becoming used to retirement, he still scours the papers every day and takes his theories down to the station."

As he spoke, C.J. took the opportunity to study his face. She was used to glamor and perfection, some of the most beautiful people in the world came through her shop, but she had never managed to get Jack Harding's face out of her mind. Watching him now, she thought that perhaps the secret was that he just didn't know how handsome he was.

From the dark blue eyes, framed by long black lashes, to the strong jawline, he was simply a pleasure to look at. His skin was lightly browned, a natural outdoor tan, and blond stubble gleamed on his chin.

And he wasn't wearing a wedding band.

It was time for that first all-important question.

"What about you?" she asked casually. "Any special woman in your life?"

He ducked his head and smiled.

"No, no one at the moment. Still haven't managed to find anyone who will take second place to an airplane."

C.J.'s heart leaped but she kept her face impassive.

"I know, women are funny that way aren't they?" she said wryly.

He laughed.

"How about you? Managed to hook yourself a man yet?"

"Oh, not you, as well," she exclaimed in exasperation.

He raised his eyebrows at her.

"Sorry," she smiled. "Lisa was just sympathizing with me for still being on the shelf at the grand old age of thirty-three. I don't need to hear the same thing from a crusty old bachelor like you."

"Well, I know it must be by choice. Any man would be lucky to have you."

She looked up, but there was nothing in his eyes but avuncular affection.

That's for the best, she told herself. I don't want attraction or anything like that to go messing up this arrangement.

She clasped her hands on the table between them and gave him her best sales smile, trying to quell the tremors in her stomach.

"Anyway," she said brightly, "there was something I wanted to ask you."

"Yeah?" he said, looking at her with interest.

"Sort of a favor," she said, folding her arms and leaning on them. Her stomach was doing flip-flops.

His face became serious and he looked into her eyes.

"Of course, ask me anything."

She opened her mouth but no words came out.

She looked down at the table, thinking that maybe she'd be able to speak if he wasn't looking at her, but she still couldn't form the words.

What on earth had she been thinking? This was an utterly stupid idea. There was no way she could ask him. It was time to back out.

"I...I'd like you to take a look at my mother's car, it's been really stubborn about starting and I'd really appreciate it if you could check it out."

She looked innocently at him as a blush spread across her cheeks.

His eyebrows pushed down into a frown as he looked at her. He didn't say anything, just examined her face thoughtfully.

She avoided his eyes.

"I'd really appreciate it," she said weakly.

He waited another moment.

'Why don't you try again," he said at last. He reached over and squeezed her forearm. "Come on, C.J., it's me. You can ask me anything, whatever it is."

She focused on his long tapered fingers. The fingernails were ingrained with car oil. They looked so much more capable than the pampered and buffed hands of so many city men.

She looked up at him and breathed out purposefully.

"Look, I think I've changed my mind. I don't have any right to ask you, it was a crazy idea. Can we just forget it?"

He frowned again.

"Why can't you just ask me? You know you can trust me, don't you?"

She smiled ruefully.

"I do trust you, of course I do. It's just that if I ask you, well, I'm afraid that you won't like me anymore."

He shook his head at her and smiled.

"Come on, give me some credit. I forgave you for the shellfish incident, didn't I?"

She winced in embarrassment. "Thank you so much for bringing that up."

The corners of his mouth turned up and his voice took on a cajoling tone. "I promise I won't suddenly stop liking you, whatever it is. I want to help you, but if I can't I'll just say no, there'll be no hard feelings, right? Besides, I'm intrigued now, you can't just leave me hanging here."

She sighed.

"You're one of my oldest friends, Jack. I know we're not bosom buddies or anything but I still feel we're friends—"

"Of course," he said.

"—so, that made me think I could come to you with this. But I don't want to lose you over it."

"You won't, I promise." He lightened his tone. "You need money? You want me to dispose of a dead body for you? You want a major organ? Just say the word and I'll sort it out."

He pretended to look worried. "It isn't one of those, is it?"

She chewed at her lip and quirked an eyebrow.

"What if it was?"

A cold wave swept over Jack's heart. He'd never had any tolerance for helpless females, women who brought their cars into the garage with imaginary difficulties and then stood too close, leaning over the engine with him, oohing and aahing over everything he said. Perhaps it was because C.J. had always been so self-reliant and independent that his feelings of protectiveness toward her were so exaggerated. The thought of her in trouble brought the same pain to his chest as if it was his sister or niece.

C.J. looked up at him, expecting to see him smiling but his eyes were filled with concern.

She rushed to reassure him.

"No, no, I'm kidding, it's nothing like that."

"I think you'd better just tell me what's up, you're starting to scare me now."

C.J. put her elbows on the table and put her face into her hands, muttering, "I'm sorry, I've made a mess of this. I went over it again and again in my head and I had it all planned and now I've just made a mess of it."

She raised her head again.

Lisa was standing over her, looking fascinated.

She refilled their coffee cups, barely able to take her eyes off C.J.

"You guys want some pie or anything?"

"I'm fine," said Jack, smiling up at Lisa. "C.J., you want some pie?"

"No, I'm fine, thanks," said C.J., blushing.

"You want an aspirin?" asked Lisa.

"No thanks, Lisa," said C.J., glaring at Jack who was biting back a grin.

Lisa gave her one last dubious look before moving off reluctantly.

C.J. waited until Lisa was occupied with two men at the counter before she met Jack's eyes again.

"It must have made her day when you first came in," he said. "But I think that little display made her whole week."

C.J. plopped her chin into her cupped hand and stirred her coffee.

"Now I remember why I don't come back here so often," she said. "In Manhattan I'm the epitome of style and decorum. I get invited to exclusive parties and I cut a swish through the fashion world, but here in Ashfield I'm just that geeky kid who wears weird shoes and makes a fool of herself in the coffee shop."

Doesn't that just sum it up, thought Jack. I really liked that kid. I'd never met anyone quite like her and I never have since, but it turns out that was because she was a big-city career woman who didn't belong here in the first place.

He scolded himself for being so maudlin, they were still friends, weren't they?

"Well, we country folk sure do 'preciate ya'll taking the time to come and see us," he drawled.

She looked up and they smiled at each other.

"Okay," she said, glancing over to make sure Lisa was still at a safe distance. "I'll tell you why I'm here. I realize now that I should have arranged to do this in a bar and made sure you were pretty loaded first, but here goes. I just want to emphasize that we're talking about a business transaction here and you're quite free to say no, of course, but I'd really like you to think about it for a few days before you make any decisions."

"You got it," he said, mimicking her serious tone, even though his eyes were twinkling.

"Jack, I want to have…I want you to impregnate me."

There was such a heavy silence that C.J. imagined she could hear Jack blinking. She swallowed dryly.

"What?" he said at last.

"I know, it sounds crazy right? But I've put a lot of thought into this. I want to have a child and there's no man in my life. I guess I always assumed there would be by now, but there isn't, so I have to start thinking about getting this organized by myself.''

She knew she was babbling but she didn't want to give Jack the chance to speak.

''And it might seem like I've got years yet to fool around with, but I actually want to have two or three kids and I'll have to leave a couple of years in between each so I've really got to make a start. I guess you think that sounds kind of cold and clinical, but it's just biology and it's not the way I foresaw having a family but...''

She trailed off weakly.

''I don't understand,'' said Jack quietly. ''What exactly is it you want from me?''

C.J. thought it was self-evident, but she understood that Jack was probably in shock. After all, she'd already been thinking about this for over a year.

''I want you to be the father,'' she explained patiently. ''I could go to an insemination clinic but then I started considering other possibilities and I started thinking about the men I knew and I thought if the father was a friend of mine, someone I knew was a good person, then that would be better.''

''So I won the competition, did I?'' he said sarcastically. ''Or did you just put all the names in a hat and mine came out first? Or am I halfway down the list, but all the others said no?''

She had anticipated that he would laugh at her or simply refuse with amusement but she hadn't expected him to get so angry.

She'd thought that implying she'd picked him from a pool of suitable candidates would ease the pressure on him, unlike telling him the truth, which was that it had taken her a whole year to screw up the courage to ask him because he was the one man she wanted to father her child. She knew she couldn't have gone through with a clinic insemination unless she'd asked him first, that she couldn't have gone the rest of her life knowing she could have asked and didn't.

But he made her sound so emotionless and calculating.

"Sorry," she said simply. She felt tears springing to her eyes and she looked out of the window, embarrassed and angry with herself.

"I told you it was a stupid thing. I'm sorry I bothered you with it, I didn't mean to make you feel awkward."

Jack was leaning back in his seat, arms crossed.

"It's okay," he said. "It's just not what I expected. I guess I'm glad at least that you aren't in any trouble."

He fell silent and C.J. felt utterly miserable.

She forced herself to speak lightly.

"Well, what are the chances that we could just forget about this and go on from here?"

He looked up at her but let his eyes drop again immediately, then looked out the window.

Yeah, that's what I thought, she said to herself.

"Sorry," he said. "I just…"

"Hey, don't worry about it," she said, flicking a hand in the air. She slurped back the last of her coffee and began to rise.

"Um," he said, "I'm sure you know what you're doing and I don't want to be a pest, but I have to question the wisdom of going around asking all these different men out of the blue—"

"It's not different men," she snapped, her unhappiness overwhelming her and leaving her tongue unguarded. "Don't you understand? It was just you. You are the list. It's a list of one. Just you, and you said no. Fine, can we just forget it?"

She turned away from his surprised face and walked calmly to the door, even giving Lisa a cheery wave as if everything was okay. She held back the spill of frustrated tears until she was outside the door and she walked to her car, half hoping to feel a hand on her shoulder, but it didn't come.

2

JACK CURSED under his breath as the top of the small bolt sheared off. He decided it would be smarter if he avoided doing delicate work for the moment, he would be better off doing something like repaneling, something that would involve hitting a sheet of steel repeatedly would just about suit his mood.

"Jack! Hey, you in there?"

Jack put down the wrench and walked out to the garage courtyard. His brother was gazing admiringly at the pickup that Jack had been working on earlier in the week.

"Don't even think about it," said Jack.

Eddie ran his hand lovingly over the hood of the truck.

"You said you'd tell me the next time a fixer-upper came in," he reminded his brother.

"This one's already spoken for, get your greedy mitts off it. Besides, you know you can't afford to run another car. You can always borrow a truck off me, what do you want one of your own for? It's just something new to worry about, another hole in the ground to pour money into."

Jack shoved his hands deep into the pockets of his overalls and stood scowling at the truck.

Eddie looked at him.

"Thanks for taking away my fantasy world, Jack. Thank you for bringing me down to earth with a thud. You want to tell me what that was all about?"

"That's exactly it," continued Jack. "That's my point.

Having another car is just a fantasy for you. You've got kids now, responsibilities, and you have to forget about buying a car just for fun, all your cars have to be functional.''

Eddie looked over his own shoulder, at some imaginary person behind him.

''I don't know who you're talking to, but do you think you could take time out to have a look at my functional squad car? The front left light got clipped.''

Jack sighed and looked over at Eddie's car.

''You mean you clipped it. I really look forward to the day you learn to drive.''

Eddie clapped him on the shoulder.

''Well, my life may be functional and I may be burdened with responsibilities, but the fact remains that I can drive around as fast as I want whereas you, ordinary mortal, have to stay within the limits, or suffer the wrath of the law.''

A small smile cracked Jack's face.

''You want me to fix it or not?''

''Can you do it right away? I got roped in for a double tonight.''

Eddie went into the garage and came out a few minutes later with two cans of soda.

''Where's Tom?'' he asked.

''Mrs. Harris left her lights on all night again, he's gone to juice the battery.''

''And your unpaid slave?'' Eddie was referring to Billy, a local boy who spent all his free time in the garage.

''He's at school. And I don't treat him like a slave.''

''So you say. All I know is that any time I see him, he's working. I think he runs the place.''

''He likes working.''

''And you don't let him talk either.''

''He's just shy. He talks when he has something to say.''

Jack took the broken lens off Eddie's light and checked the bulb before putting on a new lens, fixing it tightly into place.

"There. Try and make this one last more than a month."

He took a soda from Eddie and leaned against the car.

"How's Donna?" he asked.

"Great," said Eddie. "Didi got bumped up to first reserve on the swim team so I rarely see her without goggles on these days. Eddie Jr. wants to be a bug exterminator. He's got the idea that he can train up some armies of superbugs to go in and wipe out the other bugs. Says it's an environment-friendly solution."

"What about the bugs he sent in?"

"I think the plan is that they all regroup afterward, you know, shower off, go home to their little bug wives before their next tour of duty."

Jack started laughing and his drink went down the wrong way. Eddie clapped him on the back until the coughing fit subsided.

"So, you doing anything tonight?" asked Eddie.

"Nothing planned."

"Would you come over? I won't be home till late. Keep Donna company?"

"Home-cooked food, are you kidding? No problem."

They drank in silence for a few minutes more, Eddie swatting at some early mosquitoes.

"So, you going to tell me what's up?"

Jack drained the last of his soda.

"It's nothing," he said. "Just got a bit backed up with work here, just a bit tired."

He squinted up at the sun.

Eddie laughed. "Since when has work put you under any pressure? Are you sure it doesn't have anything to do with a certain prodigal daughter returning to town for the weekend?"

Jack looked down, shaking his head wryly.

"Lisa doesn't lose any time."

"Lisa's a good citizen, keeping her neighborhood cop informed of pertinent occurrences."

"Who needs a surveillance camera, right?'

"Stop changing the subject."

"Hey, I didn't want to bring up this subject in the first place. In fact, I'd like to drop it right now."

Eddie was intrigued. Usually it took days to shut Jack up after he'd met C.J., or even after he'd talked to her on the phone.

A light dawned in Eddie's head.

"Oh, man," he said sympathetically. "She's getting married, isn't she?"

Jack gave a hollow laugh.

"You'd think so, wouldn't you? But not C.J. Oh, no, she has to go about things her own way."

Eddie's radio crackled and he growled.

Jack looked at him blandly.

"Aren't you supposed to be working?"

Eddie strode over to the car.

"I'll tell Donna you'll be over about eight, and this conversation isn't finished. I want to hear all about it."

"Forget it," said Jack under his breath as Eddie drove away.

JACK LOOKED DOWN at the vision that greeted him as the door swung open.

A small girl with big eyes looked up at him hopefully from under a crown of blond hair, which was decorated with multicolored braids. There were twin streaks of blue glitter across her freckled cheeks.

"I absolutely love your hair," he said gravely.

She beamed up at him.

"I can do yours if you like," she said chattily as she followed him into the kitchen where Donna was efficiently deboning a chicken.

"Uhm, I don't know if it would really suit me," he said.

Donna looked up at him and grinned.

"Oh, go on, Jack, all the surfers have them."

"Well, that does make it sound appealing."

Didi squealed with joy and ran off to fetch her reams of colored thread.

"I can take them out afterward, right?" said Jack worriedly.

"I don't think so," said Donna. "I think you either let them grow out or you cut them off."

Jack nodded. "She does know that I work in a garage, right? I mean, she does realize that I have to deal with large, beefy men all day long."

"I'm not sure," said Donna. "I think we might have told her that you run a roller disco."

"Oh, there are those child-rearing skills I've heard so much about."

Donna pushed a bunch of carrots toward him.

"Get peeling," she growled.

Jack was halfway through the second carrot when he glanced up to see Donna peeking at him out of the corner of her eye.

He put down the carrot and peeler.

"Oh great," he said. "He told you."

"Of course he told me," she said. "But don't worry, I'm not going to poke my nose in. You don't have to tell me anything you don't want to."

"I don't want to tell you anything. I don't even want to talk about it. In fact, I just want to forget all about it."

"Fine," said Donna, implacably rolling chicken pieces in seasoned flour.

Jack picked up the carrot again and resumed peeling until he had reduced the carrot to a pile of shavings. He looked awkwardly at the sliver remaining in his hand.

Donna chuckled.

"I think I'll make some coleslaw," she said kindly.

She turned at the sound of clicking on linoleum that heralded the entrance of Gypsy, the family collie, and Eddie Jr.

"Can I go over to Mark's house? I want to show him this blue leaf beetle."

"No, sweetheart, dinner's going to be ready soon. You can show him tomorrow."

"I'm not hungry," insisted Eddie Jr. "I don't want dinner."

"Okay, would you do me a favor and take Jack out of my way, show him where you keep the other blue bugs."

"It's a beetle. And I don't have any others. This is the first one I've captured. That's why I have to show Mark now."

"I could drive Eddie Jr. over to Mark's house. We'd still be back in time for dinner," suggested Jack, pleased with himself.

Donna met his eyes.

"But I don't think Mark's mum would be too happy about having her own dinner interrupted, do you?"

"Oops, right," said Jack. He looked down at Eddie Jr. "Well, buddy, it looks like we're going to have to make sure blue leaf gets first-class treatment tonight so he'll be ready for his big day tomorrow. Let's go sort out his accommodation."

"Good save," said Donna, giving him a smile as he scooped Eddie Jr. onto his hip. Jack turned to find Didi standing in the doorway, hands on her hips.

"Oh, yeah," he said. "Let's get started."

JACK HELPED DONNA wash up after the kids had reluctantly been dragged off to bed. They settled themselves gratefully in front of the television, Jack on the floor with his head against Donna's knee as she painstakingly worked the threads loose from his hair.

"I don't know how you do it," he said. "I love them

with all my heart, you know that, but wow, they're exhausting."

"Stop moving," she said. "They only wear you out because you're a novelty. That's your job as an uncle, to give them your undivided attention at all times. It's different when they're your own kids. As you can see, Eddie Jr. can hardly wait to scoot off to someone else's house."

She tilted his head to one side and started work on another braid. Her hands were gentle on his head and she gave his scalp a rub every time she tugged at the hair. Jack closed his eyes. It had been a draining couple of days. The last couple of hours had been the first time in three days that he'd managed to get C.J. out of his head, and now the touch of gentle hands had brought her back again, in full Technicolor.

He let out a heart-weary sigh.

Donna's hands stopped working and she bent over to look down at him.

"You sure you don't want to talk to someone about it?"

He pushed himself up from the floor and sank into an armchair. She curled her legs up under her on the sofa and waited.

"I don't know if I can tell you. I really don't want Eddie to know, I mean, he'd just have a field day with it. But I don't want to ask you to keep secrets from him...."

Donna didn't say anything. She could see that Jack was twisting himself up over something but she wasn't going to make false promises to him.

He looked up at her and smiled.

"Okay, here it is. You know C. J. Mathews was in town the other day and we met for coffee. I don't know how much Eddie's told you, but C.J. and I were in school together and we've always kind of been friends, even after she moved away to Milan to study. She moved to New York a few years ago, and we've always kept in touch. Christmas-card friends, that sort of thing."

Donna nodded. She hoped she didn't look too eager. Jack was only talking to her because she looked so indifferent, even if she was mentally drooling with curiosity.

"So she said she needed a favor and I said, sure, no problem, and it turned out she wants me to...she wants my..."

Donna wanted to reach over and choke it out of him.

"Just say it," she said calmly.

"She wants me to make her pregnant."

Donna's mouth fell open and a loud gasp escaped before she could stop herself.

"Holy cow!" she said, having long since trained herself out of using bad language when there were children in the house.

Jack looked at her, aghast.

"I knew it," he said miserably. "It is weird, isn't it? I thought maybe I was just behind the times, but it is a weird thing to ask someone. I knew it was."

"What did you say?" said Donna leaning forward, abandoning all pretence of indifference.

He looked at her in confusion.

"What do you think I said? No, of course. It's ridiculous."

Donna leaned back. "Just like that? Without even thinking about it?"

"Wait a minute, you just agreed it was crazy. What is there to think about?"

Donna frowned. "I didn't say it was crazy. It's a shock, of course, but that doesn't mean you couldn't think about it."

"I can't believe I'm hearing this," said Jack. "From you, of all people. I thought that surely you would be against it. You know what it means to have kids, you know the kind of responsibility involved, and now you're telling me you think this woman is sane?"

"Oh, calm down," said Donna. "You're right, I do

know what it means to have children and I know how much I wanted to have a family. I was lucky, I fell in love with a wonderful man who loves me back. Things don't always work out that way for everyone. Bearing in mind that I know absolutely nothing about this woman, I still think that you should talk to her about it, find out what her plan is. I mean, she could have just bought sperm in a clinic, it was obviously important to her to ask you. It was so important that she risked making a huge fool of herself, and I just think that you should give her more than a half hour in a coffee shop, that's all.''

Jack furrowed his brow in thought.

"But there's really nothing to talk about. I don't want kids, not yet anyway. I like my life the way it is. Sure, someday I'll want them, but not yet and not like this, like some kind of business deal.''

Donna bristled. "Yes, but unfortunately women don't have the luxury of waiting around until they're fifty years old before having to make decisions like this.''

Jack slumped back in his chair.

"Look, I'm just going to forget about it. I'm not going to call her, and I'm not going to father her child, and I'm not going to talk about it anymore. The subject is closed.''

3

C.J. STOOD OUTSIDE for as long as she could, gathering her composure. You've just had a lovely weekend in the country, she reminded herself, a lovely noneventful weekend and now you're back at work, situation normal. She put on a smile, ostensibly pleased with the window display, and went into her shop.

The only other occupants of the large open-plan shop were two women, both over six feet tall and weighing about one hundred pounds between them. They were obviously models, but C.J. didn't recognize them. More importantly they didn't recognize her, so she was ignored, to her great relief. She wasn't up to handling any schmoozing this morning.

"Welcome back, did you have a good time?" said Anoushka, her store manager. "A couple of late nights in a row, maybe?" she added diplomatically.

No, thought C.J. bitterly, just one big sleepless one, that's all it takes these days to really bring out the red in your eyes and the gray in your skin.

She smiled wanly at Anoushka and made for her office.

"Is Lex in here?" she asked.

Anoushka nodded. "He's been in there all morning with Kerry. They're speaking the international language." She rolled her eyes.

C.J. paused at the door.

"Sex?" she whispered with bemusement.

Anoushka barked a laugh.

"Numbers, C.J. Computers. My, how your mind works."

"Very funny," muttered C.J. She couldn't help it if that had been the main preoccupation of her weekend.

She took a deep breath as she opened the door. She wasn't too happy that Kerry was already here. She'd hoped to have an hour or so to prepare herself before she told Kerry about her big failure of a weekend.

Kerry Dawson was her best friend. They'd met three years before, when C.J. had hired her to design the Web site for the store. Expecting a nerdy computer geek, C.J. had been pleasantly surprised by the arrival of the vivacious and gregarious Kerry. Kerry had quizzed her thoroughly about her requirements for the store's Web site and had answered C.J.'s many queries patiently. C.J. had been delighted with the resulting site and the two had become friends.

Kerry had a six-year-old son, the product of a blissfully happy marriage that had ended in tragedy when Kerry's husband had died of leukemia at the age of thirty-six. Brian, their son, had been less than a year old at the time. Having effectively raised Brian on her own, Kerry was strongly supportive of C.J.'s decision to become a single mother.

She had thought that the decision to go ahead with artificial insemination was final, so she had been caught by surprise when C.J. announced she was running home for the weekend to ask an old school friend, whom she'd previously only ever mentioned in passing, to father her child.

Kerry thought it was wonderfully romantic and was absolutely dying to hear all about it.

She looked up now at C.J.'s pale face, hoping the tiredness was due to a late night in this guy's log cabin. She had some bad news of her own to impart and she didn't want it following on the heels of a former woe.

"Hey, guys," said C.J. "It's always the same, I leave

town for a couple of days and the two of you are in here, playing "Tomb Raider" or something equally worthwhile."

She looked at the reams of paper strewn about her desk. Kerry was looking crossly at the screen and Lex was running a pen down a column of figures, muttering and making notations.

"At least, I hope that's what you're doing because otherwise it looks like you're taking over my business."

She dropped her bags with relief and collapsed onto the long couch that ran along one wall of the office.

"Did you have a good time?" asked Kerry, pausing in her typing long enough to peer intently at C.J.

"I had a great time," said C.J. She leaned back and threw her arm across her face. "I'm stuffed with home cooking and worn-out from long country-road walks." She was hoping that Kerry had somehow been hit on the head and suffered short-term memory loss.

Specifically, last Friday.

Fat chance.

At least Kerry couldn't say anything with Lex in the room. C.J. closed her eyes and enjoyed the period of grace.

"So what's been happening here?" she asked.

There was silence and she uncovered her eyes to see two worried faces looking at her.

"I'm afraid the Help virus got you," said Kerry. "Luckily, your incredibly intelligent business manager called me straight away, so I was able to stop a complete spread but we still lost quite a bit. On the bright side, sort of, it was a global attack, so I think your clients should be pretty understanding. And Lex has a hard copy of all orders up to two weeks ago, so…it's manageable."

C.J. looked at her blankly, the meaning yet to sink in.

"Help virus?"

Kerry nodded. "A real nasty one," she said, unable to quite disguise the admiration in her voice. "An e-mail sent with the contents' tag, 'Thanks for your help.' Who's not going to want to open that? And then bam, virus escapes, memory wiped out, virus sent on to all the names in your address book, etcetera, the usual.''

"Thanks for your help," said C.J. in a small voice. She felt a deep weariness settle on her, as if someone had thrown a heavy wool blanket over her shoulders. Her bottom lip started trembling. She was exhausted, she'd irretrievably ruined her friendship with Jack, her mother had been hurt and disappointed by her sudden departure and now her business, the one thing she had in the world, was being taken away from her, as well, by some idiot hacker.

She let her head droop and a big fat tear plopped into her lap.

"I shouldn't have got it," she said, hiccupping on a sob. "I'm no help to anyone." Another sob escaped, and then her shoulders started to tremble and she couldn't hold back the flood of tears.

Lex's face crumpled in sympathy and he stood beside her, wringing his hands, until Kerry bundled him out the door.

"Go on, run the shop. No one comes in, got it?"

"I'll get her a chamomile tea," he said.

She's going to need something stronger than that, thought Kerry.

She closed the door and sat beside C.J. on the sofa, handing her tissues and letting her cry herself out. She paid no attention to C.J.'s mutterings. "I'm so stupid, I wish I could crawl into a box and die, I'm gonna move to Alaska, I hate kids anyway, I'd be a lousy mother."

She had just reached the shuddering breath stage when they heard a tentative knock. The door opened a few inches and Lex's arm deposited a steaming mug on the floor before the door was pulled gently shut again.

C.J. laughed tearfully and blew her nose.

"He's such a sweetie," she said.

Kerry brought her the cup of yellow tea.

C.J. looked down at it. "Chamomile," she said with a distinct lack of enthusiasm. "That's not going to do it."

"I didn't think so, either," said Kerry, pulling C.J. to her feet. "Let's get out of here."

"A BROKEN HEART is the best reason for drinking in the daytime," said Kerry. "Come on, neither of us has had a decent excuse to break down in ages."

"It's only two in the afternoon," argued C.J.

They were standing on the corner of Mercer Street and Howard, trying to decide if lunch was going to be liquid or solid.

"Hey, I've been stuck in the office with Lex since seven this morning. As far as I'm concerned my day's work is done and, let's face it, you're already good for nothing."

C.J. had to admit her reasoning was persuasive.

"Let's at least go somewhere where there's the possibility of food," she pleaded.

They settled on Mulligan's, an Irish bar they'd ducked into one night in order to avoid an ex-boyfriend of C.J.'s.

C.J. had gone back the following day to collect a wrap she'd left behind and had been pleasantly surprised to find that, without the crush of raucously singing Irishmen, the little bar was actually quite pretty and comfortable. The bar and booths were made of old oak, and the velvet cushioning on the seats was clean and colorful. The amber windows and lights threw a sepia glow around the room and the single bartender, although prompt about serving, generally passed his time reading his paper and quietly ignoring his patrons.

One of C.J.'s secret passions was to sneak off to an afternoon screening of a movie. She loved the darkness and the no-phones rule and the whole illicit escapism of it.

Mulligan's had the same effect on her. It was a place

where you could escape for a couple of hours, no one could find you and no one bothered you.

Kerry went to get their drinks and C.J. slid into a booth, leaned back and relaxed.

Jack would like it here, she thought absently.

A pain, like a band of steel, gripped her chest, as she realized she'd never be bringing him here, or anywhere.

How long have I been doing that, she wondered, making a little checklist in the back of my mind of all the places I'd like to show Jack, things I'd like to tell him about?

Kerry slid into the seat opposite her, and put a glass of beer and a toasted cheese-and-tomato sandwich in front of her.

"Now, from the beginning, please," said Kerry.

C.J. gave her a clinical review of the weekend's events, but Kerry couldn't help but notice the despondency in her voice and the droop of her shoulders.

"Look, babe, you've hardly ever mentioned this guy before. I thought you'd made a definite appointment at the fertility clinic and now, all of a sudden, you're an emotional wreck. What is it with this guy? What haven't you told me?"

"I just told you the whole story," insisted C.J. "I guess I'm just upset because I messed up a perfectly good friendship. I got so used to life here, the green-card marriages, the models' eggs up for sale, that I became accustomed to the idea that I could just go out and arrange my life the way I wanted. And now he thinks I'm crazy."

"So what's the big loss?" asked Kerry. "He sent you birthday cards, you talked on the phone maybe twice a year, you won't be missing out on much, will you?"

She watched her friend carefully as C.J. struggled to find the words.

"He was just always there. If I was having trouble at work or if I had a particularly horrible weekend or anything, I could call him and he'd cheer me up. I wouldn't even have to call him, you know, just the thought that I could was enough. He's the reason I'm not afraid to get phone calls at three in the morning. I don't automatically assume it's trouble, or bad news, because sometimes it's him, calling because he can't sleep or he just got back from a lousy party or something dumb like that. Now he's never going to call me again and I can't call him. I blew it.''

She waved at the bartender who brought them over another two drinks.

''I have just one question for you,'' said Kerry. ''How come you're not with this man, how come you're not married to him?''

C.J. sighed.

''It's not like that. We're friends. He just thinks of me as a little sister or one of the guys, that sort of thing. I mean, you should have seen how horrified he was when I brought up this whole baby thing.''

C.J. couldn't help but smile. The beer was giving her a pleasantly giddy feeling.

A snort of laughter escaped her, and then another.

She put her hands up to her mouth but she couldn't stop the erupting giggles.

Kerry watched her, bemused, until she, too, couldn't help laughing.

''Oh, boy,'' said C.J., leaning back at last and shaking her head.

''So,'' said Kerry, taking firm charge of the conversation and hustling it along the right path. ''What are you going to do now? Did you really make an appointment at the clinic?''

C.J. looked shamefaced. ''I canceled it.''

''Oh, they're going to be delighted to hear from you again,'' said Kerry.

C.J. fiddled with a napkin.

"I'm not sure about calling them. Maybe I should think about it some more, the whole having-a-baby thing."

Kerry narrowed her eyes and looked at her shrewdly.

"You've thought about nothing else for over a year. I thought you were decided."

C.J. didn't look at her.

"So maybe it wasn't a baby you wanted after all," said Kerry kindly. "Maybe it was Jack's baby."

There was a long pause. Kerry waited.

Eventually C.J. set her jaw and looked up.

"That's not true," she said firmly. "I do want a child. I admit I've been upset by this weekend. It was a traumatic experience, okay? But I'm feeling better already, and after a good night's sleep I'll be one hundred percent again, so you can just go and find some other little guinea pig to practice psychiatry on."

"Okay," said Kerry, raising her glass. "Wanna go see a movie?"

THE NEXT DAY C.J. immersed herself in work. Her label, Sabres, was already high profile, but then a famous actress had worn a pair of C.J.'s shoes to the premiere of her latest movie, and C.J.'s summer orders had doubled in quantity. She was running behind schedule on the designs for her fall collection, and now her records were in a mess because of the computer virus.

She had to phone and e-mail clients and delivery services to confirm which orders had been sent out already and which payments had been received.

She was almost grateful for the attack of the virus. C.J. was painfully organized. She made countless lists, she posted reminders to herself on her fridge and she color-coded client details. She had five separate Rolodexes, she always knew what she was going to do and when she was going to do it. Even Lex had been impressed when he'd started to work for her. He was obsessively orderly himself, a highly desirable trait in a business manager and he liked working for someone who had an appreciation of his organization skills.

So even though C.J. was sometimes overloaded with work, she was never swamped.

Kerry had explained vividly that the computer virus had the same effect as someone pulling out the drawers of an upright filing cabinet and flinging the files and folders to the four winds. C.J. had secretly been pleased by the picture. I might even have done this to myself, she thought wryly, momentarily tempted to carry out the vandalism on her own hard-copy files, just so that she could sit on the floor and sort pages, one by one, just so that she wouldn't have a single second to herself to dream.

AFTER FOUR DAYS things were back on track. Most records were restored, she had a satisfactory collection of first-draft patterns for the fall, and she had almost rebooked her appointment at the fertility clinic. That is, she had the number written on the top of a clean page on a fresh notepad in her drawer.

On Tuesday morning, after making sure that everything on her desk was aligned symmetrically, she took the notepad out and put it in front of her. She underlined the number and slipped on the phone headset.

Before she had a chance to dial, the phone buzzed loudly in her ear.

"Darn," she muttered. It had taken her so long to screw up her resolve and now she was going to have to start all over again.

"Hello?" she said, tapping her pen impatiently on the notepad.

"Hi, it's Jack."

Her hand froze.

"Jack?"

He laughed at her incredulity.

"Jack Harding? Remember me? We went to school together?"

"Yes, Jack, I know who you are," she said wryly. "How are you?" She hoped the question didn't sound as inane to him as it did to her.

"I'm fine, C.J. I just wanted to call to see how you are. I mean, did you get home okay?"

She couldn't believe he'd called.

"Um yes, fine, fine. Did you?"

She scrunched up her eyes in embarrassment.

"Yes, I did," he said after a pause. "I got home fine, too."

"So..." she said, her mind a blank. She couldn't remember ever feeling so uncomfortable, especially not with Jack. They'd always been able to make each other laugh, it was one thing she had depended on, and now they were like strangers. For the whole week she'd been wishing he'd call, just to clear the air, and now she realized how impossible that really was.

"Listen, C.J., I was talking to Donna—"

C.J. frowned before remembering that Donna was his sister-in-law. Great, someone else to add to the list of people who thought she was a lunatic.

"—and it kind of made me look at things in a different light, and made me think maybe I dismissed your idea too quickly."

C.J. was flabbergasted.

"Really?" she managed to say at last.

"Yeah," he said. "And I've been thinking about it and it's not so crazy. It might even be a good idea, and I just wanted to let you know that I'd be willing to help."

"You're kidding," she blurted.

"No, not at all. I know you've thought this out and I want to help. You can let me know what to do, I can come down to New York or you can let me know if there's a clinic here or...whatever. I don't really know the procedure.''

C.J. couldn't believe he had changed his mind so easily. The decision that had taken her a whole year, he had come to in a couple of days. How much could he have really thought about it? She decided impulsively to throw a couple of obstacles in his path.

''Well, actually, I have decided against going to a clinic.'' She crossed her fingers. ''They're notoriously unreliable, always losing sperm and mixing up donors.''

Any minute now, she thought, a bolt of lightning is going to come through my ceiling.

''Really?'' he said dubiously.

''Oh, sure,'' she said. ''And of course, they're companies just like any other, motivated by profit, so they might bring me in for more than one treatment, charging me each time, if you know what I mean.''

She made a mental note to send a large anonymous donation to the clinic's charity of choice.

''Wow,'' said Jack.

''So,'' she continued, ''I'm going to go with the old-fashioned method.''

There you go, she thought smugly, let's see how cavalier you are about it now.

''Well, okay, that's fine.'' he said, after a moment's hesitation.

She frowned.

He couldn't be agreeing to this.

''What?'' she said cagily.

''We'll do it that way. I'm sure you've done more research in this than me, you're the expert.''

She thought, but couldn't be sure, that he was smiling.

''So you have no problem with that?''

''No problem at all.''

They breathed down the phone line at each other, a stalemate reached.

"Uh..." said C.J., at a loss.

"Look, C.J.," he said. "I put some serious thought into this before I called you. I'm ready to help you, whatever it takes. To be honest, I'd prefer to do it this way, as well. I figure that if you do have my baby, we're going to end up facing a lot more testing situations than this. I want you to be able to trust me completely. It'll be fine, C.J. We're both adults. We'll go out for a relaxing dinner, have a nice bottle of wine and then we'll sleep together."

C.J. swiveled her chair from side to side, nodding to herself. Try to bluff a bluffer, would you, she thought. Huh, I'm no shark but I've played one or two hands of poker in my time.

"Okay," she said, "I'll figure out when I'm fertile and I'll give you a call."

"Perfect," he said, hanging up.

C.J. felt dazed. She didn't even notice that Kerry had come in.

"C.J.?" Kerry said again.

C.J. looked up at her.

"What's up with you?"

"That was Jack on the phone," said C.J. She chewed at her lip to prevent the stupid grin that wanted to spread across her face.

"No kidding?" said Kerry. "Did he...? He did, didn't he?"

C.J. nodded.

Kerry sat down on the chair opposite the desk from C.J.

"Oh, honey, that's brilliant. Are you happy?"

C.J. nodded again.

Kerry looked at her curiously. "What is it?"

C.J. swallowed and met Kerry's eyes, wondering how exactly to put it.

"He wants to...uh, carry out the...uhm, the procedure... himself. I mean, with me, ourselves. He thinks we should do it ourselves."

She dropped her eyes and busied herself with the contents of one of her drawers.

Kerry folded her arms and tilted her head to one side.

"He wants to have sex with you?"

"Uh-huh," said C.J. absently. She closed the drawer again and looked up, her eyes darting to the left.

"We've agreed that it's the best way to do it, you know, just cut out the middle man to save time and…" She trailed off weakly.

"It was Jack's idea," she added defiantly, thinking, when on earth did I become such an unashamed liar?

"I think he was squeamish about the idea of the clinic, you know men, so, anyway, we've decided on this."

She coughed and rubbed her nose.

Kerry decided not to say anything. If Jack had talked C.J. into agreeing to this, then who was she to talk her out of it? She, who knew better than most that life was sometimes short and that it was better to take chances than let them go by.

She forced herself to keep a serious expression.

"He's probably right," she said. "You'll have enough to think about, trying to synchronize your own schedules without trying to keep appointments and all that, as well." She waved her hand vaguely in the air.

"Exactly," said C.J. "It's simpler this way. Next time I'm fertile I just call him and we'll go out for dinner, have a nice evening, have some wine and then we'll just spend the night together."

"Sounds like a plan," said Kerry, forebearing to comment on C.J.'s crimson face.

"And then in the morning, I'll be pregnant."

"Right," said Kerry. "Except, of course, in this case it'll be a good thing."

4

C.J. TOOK A DEEP BREATH, exhaled through her nose and then spoke in confident tones.

"Stop fussing, C.J., you look absolutely gorgeous. Just go down and have a lovely evening, just be yourself. It is only Jack after all, and everything will be just splendid."

The butterflies in her stomach seemed to calm down for a second before resuming their fluttering with even more intensity.

"I must be crazy," she whispered.

She turned to look at a view of herself from the back and then checked her front again and then stood helplessly on the spot, trying to find something else to delay her exit from the hotel room.

The simple fact was that there was nothing more to be done.

She had left work at midday and flown into Bennington Airport and from there it was only a five-minute taxi ride to the Excelsior Hotel, the meeting place they'd agreed on.

Jack was going to drive down and they had arranged to meet at eight, in the hotel bar.

So C.J. had had the whole afternoon to prepare and, by golly, she'd made use of the time.

Not for nothing had she suggested the Excelsior. The hotel boasted a full complement of services for the woman embarking on a romantic tryst. She'd spent two hours in the beauty salon being exfoliated, covered in mud, toned and scrubbed, massaged and lightly steamed.

She'd had her nails and makeup done and her hair styled to perfection in an artistic chignon, piled high on her head with the requisite tendrils falling in perfect curls about her neck and face.

Then she'd returned to her room and begun the arduous task of clothing herself. The concierge hadn't even blinked when she'd carried in two suitcases for her overnight stay, and these she lay on the large king-size bed and opened with a flourish. One contained lacy underwear and shoes, and the other was full of dresses. One good thing to be said about the fashion industry was that it perpetuated the tradition of bartering. She gave away free shoes and she got free dresses.

She closed the curtains and switched on the light to simulate evening and proceeded to dress herself. The layers had to be built from the skin up, mindful that Jack would be seeing each layer.

Skin, underwear, dress, shoes.

She modeled garter belts and lacy hold-up stockings, demibras, push-ups and ruthlessly tight basques. She tried on long, flowing dresses and skimpy little ones, backless dresses and slinky sheer ones that were cut recklessly high on the thigh. She slipped in and out of gowns, mixing and matching with different shoes, until she fell on the bed in exhaustion.

She finally decided on a sheer satin Ben de Lisi of emerald green with a deceptively simple cut that lengthened her waist and flowed seductively over her hips. Under it she wore a strapless demibra that pushed her breasts up, straining against the material. She forwent the garter belt in favor of a shimmery pair of hold-up stockings and a miniscule wisp of lace that passed for a pair of panties.

She wore a pair of her own shoes, suede with three-inch heels, in the same verdurous shade as the dress.

As soon as her transformation was complete she had to decorate the room. First, she had to hide the two suitcases so Jack wouldn't realize she was completely crazy. Then she placed strategic candles on the bedside tables and put a small bottle of massage oil into one of the drawers.

Then, at last, she was perfect, the room was perfect and there was nothing more to be done.

It was a quarter to eight.

She checked herself in the mirror again. She pulled a curl of hair back from her forehead.

She gave herself another spritz of Ghost and checked her teeth for lipstick.

Her eyes strayed to the minibar.

She brought them resolutely back to the mirror.

"No," she said firmly. "Not a good idea."

"Besides," she added encouragingly, "it's only Jack. You're friends, there's no reason to be nervous."

The flutter started in the pit of her stomach and ascended with tortuous slowness until it escaped her mouth as a low, tremulous moan.

There was no two ways about it, she was nervous, desperately nervous.

Now that she was here, she couldn't believe she had thought this would be easy and straightforward.

This was going to change everything, and she was almost sick with a mixture of dread and anticipation. She looked at the minibar again.

"But they're really expensive," a feeble voice in her head told her. "They charge an arm and a leg for those."

Huh, she thought, that's not much of a deterrent to someone who has already spent a month's pay on beauty treatments.

She strode over and popped the seal on a little bottle of vodka. She mixed it with a tiny can of orange juice and drank it down with a few long swallows.

She washed out the glass and hid the empties in her suitcase.

She picked up her purse and looked in the mirror. She

wasn't sure if the vodka had had any real effect, but at least now it was eight o'clock and she had to go downstairs, ready or not.

"ARE YOU SURE this is the only Hotel Excelsior around here?" Jack asked the bartender.

She smiled kindly at him. "It's the only one in the whole of Bennington," she assured him.

He glanced up at the clock again.

Relax, he told himself, it's only five after.

For a while, caught in the traffic outside Arlington, he'd been afraid he'd be late, but he'd made it, with time for a quick stop in the lobby flower shop before going into the bar.

At least he'd arrived before her. He sipped his drink and was about to check the time again when his attention was drawn to the door.

C.J. WAS RELIEVED to see that Jack was already in the bar, although it did mean she had to walk through the room in the full spotlight of his gaze.

And quite a gaze it was, too. Jack appeared mesmerized and C.J. felt a blush of pleasure rise in her cheeks. All her primping and fussing had paid off.

"Hi," she said.

"Hi, yourself," he said softly.

There was a long pause.

She raised her eyebrows.

He shook his head, smiling. "I'm sorry, I'm being an idiot. I'm just speechless. You look so beautiful, C.J."

He handed her the rose, grateful he'd taken the time to buy it. She took it, smelled it and thanked him.

"You look good, too," she said. "All dressed up." The last time she'd seen Jack in a suit had been at her grandfather's funeral and she hadn't been in the mood to enjoy the sight of him then.

Now she did. The suit flattered his broad shoulders and his blond hair looked even more golden against the dark material.

He smiled and ducked his head at the compliment, and they stood together for a moment, somewhat awkwardly, before Jack found his tongue again.

"Would you like a drink or do you want to go straight to dinner?"

"Are you ready to eat now?" she asked.

"I could," he said. "Or I could wait, whatever you like."

"I don't mind waiting if you want to finish that," she said, pointing at his drink. "Or I could eat now if you want to bring it in with you?"

A smile spread across Jack's face, broadening until dimples formed.

"Or we could just stand here all night, being polite and accommodating," he said.

C.J. laughed, meeting his eyes. "Let's go to dinner," she said.

"Good idea."

SINCE IT WAS MIDWEEK, the restaurant wasn't busy and they got a cozy table in a little nook. The menu was unpretentious and their waiter was friendly and helpful so C.J. began to relax.

Unfortunately, once the business of ordering was over, she found herself with time to think once more, to remember the real purpose of their meeting.

She looked up and caught Jack looking at her.

"How are you feeling?" he asked.

She was about to give him a reassuring platitude, but she changed her mind and smiled shyly.

"I'm a little nervous," she said.

He nodded.

"I know," he said. "This is a bit strange. I mean, it's

good, but it's strange." He looked up at her mischievously.
"Although it's the first time I've ever gone to dinner with
a woman where I've known for sure that I'll score in the
end."

He regretted the words as soon as they left his mouth,
even more so when she didn't laugh.

"I'm sorry, that was supposed to be a joke but it was a
crude thing to say. I just don't know how to act. I'm afraid
if I'm too attentive you'll be uncomfortable, but if I act
nonchalant you won't realize that I do want to sleep with
you, and I feel like you should know that."

She looked puzzled. "I know why we're here, I haven't
forgotten that. I already know it's established, you don't
have to tell me."

Jack fiddled with his napkin before looking back up at
her.

"Look, what I'm trying to say is this. I don't think I
can put on an act or pretend with you, C.J., I feel like you
can see right through me, you always have. The thing is,
I know this is prearranged, but I feel like I have to be
honest and tell you that I'm actually looking forward to
it."

He met her eyes and held her gaze.

"You look absolutely beautiful tonight and I'm only
human. I want to be with you. I'm looking forward to it
and I'm going to enjoy it."

C.J. was glad she was sitting down.

A heat spread in her stomach at his words, a feeling she
knew unmistakably as desire, pure and raw. Her lips parted
and she dropped her eyes, not wanting him to see.

"There," he said. "Now you know. Are you angry?"

She looked back up at him in surprise, the man she'd
known for over twenty years. She saw the boy he'd been,
in the crinkle of his eyes when he smiled and the unruly
lock of hair that fell over his forehead, and she saw the

man he had become in the firm line of his jaw and the wisdom in his eyes. She felt a fierce tugging at her heart.

"Of course I'm not mad. How could I be? It's flattering. And I'm glad you told me." She flashed him an amused look. "For a moment I thought you were going to say that you were dreading it."

He laughed.

"Anyway," she said, looking away shyly. "I'm kind of looking forward to it, as well, I mean, I'm only human, too."

"So you think I'm looking pretty good tonight?" he teased.

C.J. looked at the ceiling. "I suppose so."

"Just good? Or very good? Or gorgeous? You can tell me I'm looking gorgeous, I won't mind."

The waiter didn't flicker an eyelash as he placed their food in front of them.

C.J. pointedly ignored Jack as she began to eat.

C.J. HAD ONCE gone to dinner with a man who'd talked for twenty minutes about his preference for black pepper over white and she'd considered faking a choking incident except she didn't want to give him an excuse to put his hands on her. In contrast, she found herself inordinately interested in what Jack did or didn't like. She noted that he picked the kidney beans out of his salad, and that he liked to load his fork with different flavors, and that he tore bread rolls crossways instead of lengthwise.

They ate slowly and their conversation flowed naturally. The food was delicious and they'd ordered a fruity Beaujolais to go with it.

The blue of Jack's eyes deepened in the candlelight and she enjoyed looking at them, enjoyed having them look at her.

C.J. finished up the last bite of her pasta and pushed her plate slightly away from her.

Jack refilled their glasses.

C.J. looked down at the table. "I suppose I'd better tell you about the provisions I'm going to make, in case anything happens to me."

He looked at her curiously.

"My friend, Kerry, who has a son of her own, is going to be the godmother, so I'll want her to take care of the child if anything happens."

Jack frowned. "After me, you mean."

C.J. looked uncomfortable. "Well, no. I mean, you'll still be part of his, or her, life but I'll want Kerry to have custody. And I want you to promise you won't fight her."

"That's out of the question," he said calmly. "I will fight her. It's going to be my child, too, and I will be responsible for it."

"That's just the point," said C.J. vehemently. "I don't want him to be raised by someone who just feels responsible for him. Kerry will take care of him out of love."

"And I wouldn't?" he said coldly.

Looking at his face, C.J. was torn.

"I don't know," she said hesitantly. "I would want him to have a mother and I just assumed you could go on visiting." She looked away and shrugged. "What if you got married and had a family? Would you really want a ten-year-old or a rebellious teenager dumped on you, messing up your home life?"

He looked at her thoughtfully. "What if something happened to your friend? Would you feel resentful if you had to take her kid, have him messing up your life?"

"That's different," she said. "I love Brian, he wouldn't be a burden. I'd do anything for him."

"So how exactly is it different?"

She couldn't find an answer for him.

He reached across the table and took her hand.

"If anything happens to you, which it won't, I will raise

our child. If I have to fight for custody, I will, I guarantee it, so don't make me.''

She nodded, feeling a great comfort in the strength that flowed from him in the certainty of his words.

The waiter brought the dessert menu, which gave them the chance to lighten the mood again. That was one of the things she most appreciated about Jack. She was unafraid to broach any subject with him. There was just so much to think about since she'd decided to have a child, there were so many eventualities to prepare for.

Notwithstanding their first inauspicious meeting in the diner, Jack was consistently unfazed by anything she came up with. She felt like she could say anything to him and he'd never be shocked, or worse, disappointed in her. It was actually the kind of trust she hoped her child would have in her.

''Would you like some more wine or would you prefer coffee?'' Jack asked, breaking her reverie.

She noted with surprise that they had finished the bottle. She felt that coffee might spoil the pleasant glow she was feeling so she asked the waiter if they could have a half bottle of the wine.

He returned apologetically with the information that half bottles of that particular vintage weren't available.

''We'll just get another full bottle,'' said Jack, smiling at C.J. ''We needn't drink all of it.''

C.J. smiled back and started in on the exquisite sour-cherry-and-chocolate gâteau. So she was being a glutton. She didn't care. She would be working it off in an hour or so.

The thought made her giggle and she peeped at Jack. He was looking at her, a dark light in his eyes. She felt herself blushing under his gaze, unaware that the blood made her skin glow in the candlelight.

''You're staring again,'' she teased him.

"Hard not to," he said quietly. She laughed in embarrassment.

"You are such a charmer. How come you haven't been snapped up by now?" she asked impulsively.

He rolled his eyes and sighed theatrically.

"Who would have me?"

She tilted her head and gave him a shrewd look.

"Come on, Jack, you can tell me. Hasn't there been anyone special?"

He met her eyes for a moment before looking away casually.

"Of course," he said. "I'm thirty-three years old, not fifteen. There have been women."

He chewed his bottom lip absently. "Some very nice women." He looked up as a smile curved his lips. "And some very nice women who turned not so nice when they realized I wasn't kidding about not settling down."

C.J. forced a laugh.

"Well, don't worry. I've got that message loud and clear. And I've certainly turned down my share of men," she added with bravado.

He smiled. "Now, why doesn't that surprise me?"

He put his chin in his hand and regarded her speculatively.

"You know you should hold out for the best, C.J., you deserve it."

She snorted. "Like I'm really going to take relationship advice from you."

He reached over and snatched a forkload of cake in retaliation.

They lingered over the last glass of wine, exchanging stories about family and work, making each other laugh. The restaurant emptied slowly but neither of them wanted to move, wary of disrupting the easy companionship they'd reached over dinner.

Eventually C.J. excused herself to go to the ladies' room while Jack took care of the bill.

C.J. LOOKED AT HERSELF in the mirror. Her face was flushed and her eyes were sparkling.

Wow, she thought, if I look like this now, how will I look when...

"This is it," she whispered. "We're going to do it. I'm going to make love to Jack."

She bit her lip as a woman emerged from one of the cubicles. They met each other's eyes in the mirror. The woman put on a fresh coat of lipstick and winked at C.J.

"Enjoy it, honey," she said, leaving C.J. alone to smirk at herself.

THEY SHARED the elevator ride with two florid men in expensive suits who were arguing loudly about falling stock-market prices.

Behind them, Jack reached up and trailed the back of his hand lightly along C.J.'s arm, starting at her shoulder and moving down with tantalizing slowness until his knuckles brushed hers. She felt the skin around her nipples tighten as all her nerve endings sprang to attention. He moved his arm around her and rested his palm on the small of her back, the heat of it burning her through the satin.

The elevator stopped and the two men got out, their voices echoing down the hall as the doors closed behind them.

The pressure of Jack's hand increased as he turned her and pulled her toward him. She didn't resist as the gentle pull of his arms brought her tightly against his hard body. She could smell him under the faint scent of cologne and her thudding heart was making the blood pulse in her veins.

She put her arms around his neck, feeling powerful and desirable under his heavy-lidded gaze. The hair, the dress, the wine, she didn't feel like herself, she felt strong and sexually charged. Jack's lips descended on hers, a soft touch that grew more insistent as she pressed against him, feeling his arms mold to her back. Their mouths opened and tongues sought each other, hungry and fierce, devouring each other.

The elevator doors opened and Jack and C.J. pulled apart slowly, their breathing labored.

"I thought that first kiss might be awkward," said Jack in a husky voice, "so I thought I'd better just do it."

She nodded, her throat dry.

They stepped out and stood in the hall as the doors closed behind them, their fingers twined loosely.

Jack ducked his head to look at her.

"C.J.? Which room is it?"

She looked up at him, still feeling dazed from the kiss. "Oh, it's five-fifty-four," she said, leading the way.

INSIDE THE ROOM C.J. lit the candles. She was about to lie down when she noticed Jack fiddling with the radio. He stopped as the melodious tones of Billie Holiday filled the air. He took off his jacket and pulled C.J. to him again.

They started to dance. Jack put one hand up and touched her face, running his thumb along her jawline. She had one arm on his shoulder and the other on his back, playing her fingers over the ridges of muscle that bordered his spine. She felt dizzy with the overload to her senses, the smell and feel of him, the taste of him still in her mouth. She leaned her head against his chest, closing her eyes. Her breathing slowed and she felt all of her cares melt away as she sunk deeper and deeper into the pleasure of the song and their sensuous movement.

AT FIRST Jack didn't notice it, he was too busy enjoying the softness of her hair against his chin, but then it occurred to him that she was growing heavy in his arms.

"C.J.," he said with uncertainty, looking down.

Her eyelids flickered and she peered up at him, blinking.

"I'm a little dizzy," she mumbled. "I think I'll lie down for a minute…"

He half carried her over to the bed and pulled back the bedclothes before laying her down.

"Oh, Jack, yes," she murmured, her head falling sideways on the pillow. He sat beside her and waited hopefully for a moment before he noted that the steady rise and fall of her chest was probably indicative of an impenetrable sleep.

He took off her shoes, put her feet up on the bed and pulled the covers over her.

He considered undressing her but then decided that satin was probably comfortable enough to sleep in. Besides, it would be just his luck if she woke up in the middle of it and fixed those curious green eyes on him. He got a glass of water from the bathroom, put it on her bedside table and sat for a moment on the bed beside her. He brushed a lock of hair from her face and stroked her brow. Her cheeks were flushed and he smiled at the innocent expression on her face, remembering the kiss in the elevator. He blew out the candles and took a spare blanket from the wardrobe before arranging himself on the couch.

C.J. WOKE SLOWLY, gradually becoming aware of a constriction around her legs. Blankets, she thought, twisted around me. She made an effort to free herself before an ache sluiced through her head, freezing her on the spot.

She concentrated on breathing softly and evenly. The pain abated and she opened her eyes, relieved to find that at least she was in her hotel room. Another memory surfaced and she turned over to look in the bed beside her.

No sign of Jack.

She turned her head the other way and caught sight of the glass of water. Ah, lifesaver.

She pushed herself into a sitting position and sipped the water, trying to remember what had happened the night before. She remembered the meal. And there were men in the elevator. But had Jack come back to her room? Surely, after that kiss. A tiny shiver of pleasure ran down her spine at the memory. Had he come back? Had they...? And if so, where was he now?

As if in answer to her question, the bathroom door opened and Jack emerged, clothed in a fluffy white bathrobe.

"Morning," he said cheerfully.

"Hi," said C.J. in a neutral voice.

She snuck a rapid peek down at herself and was disconcerted to see she was still wearing her dress.

Jack came over and lay across the end of the bed.

"Last night was magic, wasn't it?" he said, quirking an eyebrow at her.

She hesitated, then met his eyes bravely.

"It can't have been that magic or I'm sure I'd remember more of it."

Jack sighed expansively. "It's okay, I remember every single minute, every tiny detail."

He rolled onto his back and gazed at the ceiling.

C.J. looked at him. "Nothing happened, right?"

She waited.

"Jack?"

He looked over at her with a hurt expression. "I hope it's okay, C.J., you said you wanted it. You said, and I'm quoting here, 'I want it bad.'"

Vague memories tugged at C.J.'s mind but she couldn't grasp them.

"Don't you remember?" he asked.

"Uhm," she said. "I think now is a good time for me to take the Fifth."

He rolled back onto his side and grinned at her. He reached over and tweaked one of her toes.

"Nothing happened," he said. "You fell into bed and passed out."

"Oh, no," she wailed, closing her eyes and letting her head drop back onto the headboard. "That's worse."

He waited until she looked at him again.

"How are you feeling?" he asked.

"A bit headachy, but I'm okay. Oh, Jack, I'm so sorry." She looked at her hands and decided to come clean. "I was nervous about meeting you, and the whole thing you know, so I had vodka here, and then drank too much wine. What a mess."

"It's not a mess," he consoled her. "Come on, C.J., it's nothing. We were both nervous. I drank too much, as well. Maybe we just built it up too much, we could have gone about it a better way."

She finished the water and looked at him.

"What do you mean?"

"I don't know if you remember but there was a kiss in the elevator—"

The color rising in her cheeks and her impulsive smile gave him the answer he'd been hoping for.

"—so there's nothing wrong with the chemistry, but I think we need to work on the comfortable stuff. Just get used to being around each other."

"How do we do that?"

"I thought maybe you could come and visit me some weekend. Just stay over some night, platonically. Maybe we could go to a movie or something."

"You mean, like a date?"

"I guess," he laughed. "But we could agree this time that nothing will happen."

She pursed her lips. "I think that's a great idea."

"Good," he said, getting off the bed. "Go, have a shower, you'll feel better."

She got out of bed, wincing.

She went into the bathroom and looked at her disheveled

self in the mirror. Mascara ringed her eyes, her hair was a toppling bird's nest and lipstick was smeared across her cheek.

Jack knocked on the door and darted in to grab his shaving kit.

"I can see what the problem was," she joked miserably. "I wouldn't want to sleep with me, either."

He paused and brushed a finger across her cheek.

"It doesn't take all this stuff to make me want to sleep with you," he said. "But I draw the line at coming near you with a hangover. You have a shower and we'll go get some breakfast, and then I'll drive you to the airport."

He went back out and she smiled and met her eyes in the mirror.

Then she remembered the two suitcases.

"Oh, great," she sighed.

5

"GIVE THEM THE ORDER of Miu Mius and tell Saks we'll have the kitten heels by Tuesday," said C.J.

She was looking over Lex's shoulder at the computer screen, trying to get as much as she could squared before her weekend with Jack. His plane was due in five hours and she had to get home and have a shower, wash her hair, put on something a little more conservative and remove the blue nail polish that Kerry had convinced her to try.

She didn't know what made her look up at the window, but the sight of Jack outside, peering in at the display, made her panic on the spot.

"Oh, no," she squeaked, instinctively dropping to her knees and crouching behind Lex's desk.

Lex rested his chin on one hand and make a few perfunctory clicks on the computer.

"What's going on?" he muttered sotto voce.

"The guy at the window, is he coming in?"

Lex looked out casually. "Oh, I hope so. Why?"

C.J. squirmed. "Man, my hair's a mess, look what I'm wearing, and this stupid nail polish, what am I going to do?"

"You want me to send him away?"

C.J. agonized in indecision. "Oh, no, I can't let him go wandering about town on his own."

"You could give me the rest of the day off, I'll show him around."

C.J. snorted.

"He's coming in," hissed Lex, moving his mouse around busily.

C.J. heard the swish of the door and suddenly realized she'd left her decision too late. Now she would either have to stay in hiding or else emerge from under the desk and pretend she'd been untangling the computer cable or something. She couldn't even bring herself to imagine how bad it would look.

"Hi, I'm looking for C. J. Mathews." She heard Jack's soft rumbling voice.

Courage, she told herself, smooth movements and calm conviction. She unfolded herself and stood up, holding an invisible object in her fingers.

"Found it," she announced triumphantly. "Oh, hi, Jack," she said with laudable surprise. "How did you get here?"

"Here's your lens," she added to the grinning Lex. "You'll probably have to go and wash it." She gave an imperceptible jerk of her head.

"Oh, no," Lex said with an evil smile, "these soft ones are great, just wipe it off and pop it back in."

He displayed his extensive mime skills with a little sketch entitled "Man putting in Contact Lens."

Then he sat back and looked up at Jack and C.J. with eager anticipation.

"I decided to drive down," Jack said, "I left this morning and it took me a couple of hours less than I thought. I left the truck in the parking lot at JFK, though, I hate driving in this city. So I thought I'd come and surprise you. I wanted to see the store, too, it's really something."

C.J. smiled. She couldn't help but be proud of the store. She had picked out everything personally, from the lighting to the cornices on the shelves.

"Come on then," she said. "I'll give you the guided tour."

"So nice to meet you," said Lex, springing to his feet and putting out his hand.

C.J. turned back resignedly. "This is Lex, my business manager. Lex, this is Jack, he's an old friend of mine, from home."

She couldn't help but feel pleased at the obvious admiration in Lex's face. She already knew Jack was handsome, she didn't need to see it reflected in someone else's eyes. But it still made her feel good.

"Jack's a stunt pilot," she blurted out, like some kid who's brought home a new best friend.

"Oh, you are not," said Lex, folding his arms and tilting his head coquettishly.

C.J. tensed. Lex inevitably became camp when he was flirting but Jack seemed to take it in his stride.

"Only on weekends," he said, grinning. "In real life I'm a mechanic."

Lex opened his mouth to speak again but C.J. tugged Jack away, leading him around the shop. Jack chuckled and shook his head as he examined some of the more outrageous designs.

"Some of these are pure works of art," he said. "They're amazing. I can't believe people wear these."

C.J. basked in his admiration. She slipped off her own shoes and unself-consciously modeled some pairs for him. She showed him the clever engineering and balance in a pair of pink silk five-inch platforms, feeling as giddy as the first day she'd opened the store.

"DO YOU MIND if we walk for a bit?" asked Jack, as C.J. lifted her arm to hail a cab.

She looked at him and he grinned. "I don't come down here that often, it's too busy for me, to be honest, but I like to look around and enjoy it when I am here. I guess that makes me sound like a tourist."

C.J. was delighted. "No, it's good. We can actually

walk to my apartment from here.'' Her eyes lit up. ''But if you're feeling adventurous there's something we could do....''

It was a relief to get back aboveground again, although C.J. had guiltily enjoyed being squashed up against Jack in the subway throng. The weather was warm but the heavy humidity hadn't arrived yet.

Jack looked around casually as they walked. They had emerged from the subway at West 72nd Street and C.J. led him into the park past Strawberry Fields.

She liked the way he loped along, unfazed by the activities around him and not embarrassed by his naive interest. He was very comfortable in his own skin and it made him comfortable to be with. She noticed him smiling and questioned him about it.

''I just love the way everyone has such an attitude here, even elderly people.'' He squared his shoulders and puffed out his chest. ''It's like, get outta my way buddy, I got things to do.''

C.J. laughed at his accent. ''We're not that bad, are we?''

''Oh, I'm not criticizing. I couldn't, because for every fast-moving, busy person there's also the opposite.'' He nodded toward the group of people on their left who were moving in unison through graceful T'ai Chi exercises. ''It's the variety that's so amazing. In one day I've been on Pier 86, looking out over the Hudson river, I've been in the center of SoHo, mingling with the trendsetters, and now here we are in the park.''

C.J. looked at him in surprise. ''What were you doing on the West Side?''

Jack shrugged playfully. ''I went to the *Intrepid*,'' he said. ''Just for an hour, to see if they'd got anything new.''

''The what?''

He looked at her. ''The *Intrepid*. You know, the old World War II ship with all the aircraft on deck.''

"Oh," she said, nodding in understanding. "The Sea-Air-Space Museum."

"Right." He stopped to admire a bronze statue of a falconer lofting a bird before eventually looking down at her again. "It's not just for kids, you know."

She nodded, keeping her face straight for three seconds before a smile spread across it.

His eyes twinkled as he held her gaze. "It's not," he said again, daring her to giggle.

"I don't think I've ever been in this part of the park before," he said, looking around as they passed Bethesda Fountain. He leaned toward her and said, with a slightly sheepish expression, "Are there usually so many people on skates? Are some of them couriers?"

She answered innocently. "Some of them are people going home." A woman in a pink leotard flashed by. "Some are exercising."

"Heads up!" came a shout behind them as a six-foot Latino with tightly cropped luminous-green hair swept by.

"And some," said C.J., as they made their way onto Literary Walk, "some skate just for fun."

Jack stopped in his tracks at the sight that greeted him. The avenue was a moving tableau of flashing color, people of all shapes and sizes skimming the path like iridescent bugs on a lake.

"You're not going to make me do this, are you?" said Jack.

C.J. laughed at his worried expression.

"Not this time. Let's get some food."

They made their way slowly around the throng of skaters, Jack's head swivelling like an owl's as each new character caught his eye.

C.J. got the food and they found an unoccupied bench.

C.J.'s eyes watered at the pungency of the sauerkraut as she bit into the heavily loaded hot dog. Mustard fumes rose and tickled her nose.

"Wow," said Jack, after the first bite. "You can practically feel it eating through the stomach wall."

C.J. nodded happily. "Delicious, aren't they?"

There was no need for further conversation. They contented themselves with sitting back with eyes wide-open, taking in the spectacle.

"Is this a regular thing?" Jack asked as they finished the last bites of hot dog.

"Every weekend," said C.J.

"Do you come here often?"

She smiled at the cliché.

"Now and again."

"Do you skate?"

"Sure," she nodded. "You can rent skates over there."

They both winced as a slender woman in baggy combat pants took a spine-shattering fall nearby. The woman took a deep breath and checked her palms before clambering to her feet with determination.

"Ouch," said Jack.

C.J. nodded sympathetically. "I had a few of those when I was learning. It was like being ten again with skinned hands and bruised knees."

They shared a complicit look before Jack found himself distracted by a pair of smooth tanned knees that had braked to a halt in front of them. His eyes drifted slowly upward until he had taken in the full glory of the amazon in a Wonder Woman costume who stood before them. She bent at the waist to give C.J. a hug, the muscles in her thighs rippling as she maintained her balance.

When she spoke it was with an unexpectedly sweet voice.

"Friday. I wore the silver blocks with the heart cutout. Darling, those shoes are so comfortable. And they got me in everywhere." She flicked a hand dismissively. "City was mine. Eighteen straight hours. Of course my feet had gone down a whole size by the time I got home, you can't wear leather and not sweat.''

She gave Jack a wink. "Who's this?"

C.J. introduced them and Jack found himself enveloped in a cloud of perfume as she bestowed a hug upon him before speeding away.

"Another satisfied customer," said C.J.

She didn't mind Jack staring, Lucy was an impressive sight, but she was still pleased that he returned his attention promptly to her. Albeit to discuss, in awed tones, Lucy's shoe size.

AFTER A COUPLE of hours and another hot dog for Jack, they made their way to C.J.'s apartment.

C.J. flicked through her mail, mostly bills, a letter from a friend in Paris, nothing that couldn't wait. She dumped her bag with relief and got two bottles of cold water from the fridge.

"What do you think?" she asked.

Jack shook his head. "It's like an Aladdin's cave." He corrected himself. "Actually it's like one of the rooms in Aladdin's cave, it's Aladdin's wardrobe, his shoe cupboard.''

She was pleased by the description. She had half-finished shoes everywhere, and samples of shiny materials, which gave an air of decadent opulence to the room. She had a number of wooden lasts, foot-shaped blocks that she used as molds on which to construct prototypes. Most prototypes were abandoned halfway as the first flash of inspiration came up against insurmountable feasibility problems, but she couldn't throw any of them out, hoping she would come up with a way to make it work or that the sight of it, out of the corner of her eye, might lead her to another shoe, later on. As a result many half-made shoes doubled as receptacles for spare change and subway tokens, or as wedges for doors.

Jack had picked up one of her plastic skeletal feet, expertly constructed with moving parts, and was walking it along the windowsill. He held it up and tilted his head questioningly at her.

"If you have to make something, it's helpful to know what the foundation looks like. Especially when it's so complicated."

He looked at the foot again, the multitude of small bones intricately interlocking.

He looked back at her, with something akin to wonder in his face.

"You're an interesting woman, you know that?"

She shrugged modestly, feeling absurdly pleased. People told her everyday that she was amazing. They brushed her cheeks with air kisses and told her she was a genius, a maestro, but she knew the difference between that and a real compliment. The real words made you feel proud of yourself, not just your work.

She had a workstation in one corner of the room, beside a window. There was a desk with her computer and a stack of flat sketching boards, which she rested on her lap or put up on the easel, depending on her mood. Jack had moved over to look at the framed photographs that adorned the wall above the desk. They were all pictures of shoes, every kind from the classic Cinderella slipper carved out of Italian marble to the magnificent Andy Warhol platforms.

C.J. had even reproduced some of the classic museum pieces, and these decorated the shelves of the apartment.

"Who came up with the idea of heels first anyway?" asked Jack.

"Shoes began to have heels around the end of the sixteenth century," explained C.J. "But only men's shoes. Women's shoes were plain and boring because they were all hidden under long skirts anyway."

"Why on earth do women wear them? You couldn't pay me to walk around half-crippled all day."

"It's a matter of taste. I know women who feel the same as you, couldn't be paid to wear heels, but they might enjoy wearing platforms, just for the added three inches. Besides, no one should be wearing really high heels continuously, that's definitely bad for you."

"This might be a dumb question," said Jack, "but don't you ever get bored with shoes? I mean, you're designing at home and you have shoes at work, don't you ever get fed up and think about going into clothes or something?"

She considered the question.

"I guess the thing that keeps me fresh is that so much of my working life is filled with actual graft work. I'm a designer, but I'm also running a business. I have to think about everything from raw materials to ordering the packaging. Those fancy boxes don't spring out of thin air, you know. Then there's staff and all the income and expenses to be balanced. So the designing is the good stuff, the fun part."

"But how do you keep designing the same kind of thing over and over again without running dry? I mean, how many different shoes can there be? They serve one purpose."

She looked up at him with a grin.

"How many different cars can there be?"

"Okay," he laughed. "You got me."

She continued teasingly. "You know what the theory is on why men like them, don't you?"

He shrugged. "Makes legs look longer, I guess."

She half turned and pulled the sarong away from her leg. She pointed her foot, stretching her calf. "When you wear a high heel it extends your calf which makes you resemble a deer running away. The sight of stretched calf muscles brings out the primitive side of a man, the predator in him. He sees stretched calves and he wants to pounce."

She pulled the sarong up to her thighs and walked away on her toes. Jack growled playfully.

"YOU WANT PIZZA or Chinese?" asked C.J. She had changed out of her work clothes and taken a quick shower, and was now standing by the phone.

Jack looked at her. "Couldn't we cook something?"

C.J. laughed. "I'll get pizza." She hit the speed-dial button and waited.

Jack wandered into the kitchen, which was merely a cooking area separated from the main room by a counter with tall stools lined up along it.

At first glance there seemed to be food in the fridge, but closer inspection revealed it was mostly condiments: mayonnaise, ketchup, Thousand Island dressing, salsa, chutney. The selection of things to put these sauces on included a shriveled lemon, half a cheesecake, a tub of butter, a couple of bottles of beer, a six-pack of soda, milk, a curly stick of celery and plastic cartons stamped with names like Benny's Pizza and Dok Suni Rice Palace. Jack checked the freezer hopefully, but all it contained was one Lean Cuisine and an ice-encrusted box of waffles.

He closed the fridge and glanced over at C.J. who was fluently reeling off a list of pizza toppings.

He checked the cupboards out of curiosity and found a myriad selection of cereals, a few rolls of greaseproof paper and tinfoil—although he couldn't imagine what on earth for—and jars of vitamins.

Jack shrugged. He supposed if you lived on a diet of cereals and sauces, vitamins became a vital necessity.

C.J. HAD PUT the phone down and he came out to join her on the sofa.

"You don't cook much, do you?" he asked.

She shrugged carelessly. "Now and again. But it usually ends up such a production because there's never anything in the house, so I have to go shopping and I end up with way more food than I need, so I spend the next week watching vegetables shrivel and leftovers go moldy before I can bring myself to throw them out. So I tend to avoid it.''

''You don't have a roommate to eat all your food and borrow your best clothes while you're out?''

She smiled. ''About three years ago I finally started earning enough to get my own place.'' She looked around with satisfaction. ''It's not huge but it's all mine.''

''So we're alone?'' said Jack, raising his eyebrows suggestively.

C.J. laughed, knowing he was teasing, but a devilish impulse in her told her to take up his offer and she held Jack's eyes a fraction too long.

The door intercom buzzed, startling her.

''The pizza,'' she said, leaping off the couch with alacrity.

JACK GAINED a measure of understanding when he saw the food that had been delivered. It was a magnificent spread, a gigantic pizza lush with toppings and bubbling cheese. There was also rich garlic bread and a multipocketed plastic tray with a selection of salads, curried rice and coleslaw.

C.J. brought them more water from the fridge and they dug in.

She looked at Jack out of the corner of her eye as she bit hungrily into a chunk of garlic bread.

''Just as well this is only a friend's night,'' she said lightly, pointedly chewing the flavorsome bread.

Jack nodded, equally casually. He hadn't missed the electricity that had sparked between them before the buzz of the intercom. In a way he was pleased C.J. had felt the need to reestablish the boundaries. It proved that it hadn't just been wishful thinking on his part, she'd felt it, too. Nevertheless, he took the image of her, naked and wrapped in his arms, and he pushed it firmly to the back of his mind, concentrating on eating and trying to keep his sideways peeks at her to a minimum.

C.J. had folded her legs up under her on the sofa. She was working on a thick slice of steaming pizza and flicking through the channels on television.

She caught his glance and said, "What?"

He smiled. "You look so casual. Just eating pizza like any old regular person."

She wasn't sure how to react.

"What did you expect?" she asked.

"I guess when I thought of you I always imagined you flitting around at fashion shows and cocktail parties, or rushing around busily in a tailored suit with a briefcase. I never pictured you at home."

C.J. was torn over which avenue of that statement to pursue. She wanted to find out exactly just how much time he spent imagining her but she was also wondering if he was disappointed by her ordinariness.

"I'm glamorous and busy most of the time," she said lamely.

"I know," he said. "That's my point. I can easily picture you like that, so it's nice to see this side of you. You look kind of cute actually."

Who wouldn't look cute, she thought, in new Gucci hipster drawstring pants and a rose-colored sleeveless cotton vest? C.J. was sure she would if those clothes weren't at this moment folded up in a shopping bag on the floor of her office. She wasn't sure if the same could be said of her in her genuine chill-out clothes, faded gray sweatpants and an oversize Tank Girl T-shirt—a present from Kerry.

"Cute?" she said dubiously.

"Sure," he said, "with your hair up in a messy bunch like that and a bit of cheese stuck to your mouth."

Her hand flew upward then came down slowly as she recognized the curl of his lips that accompanied teasing.

Well, he wasn't the only one who could get one over.

That cute messy ponytail had taken four tries to get just right. They finished up the food and C.J. stacked the empty containers on the counter. She came back to find Jack had slumped sideways on the sofa so that he was now lying the length of it, his eyes closed and his feet dangling over the edge.

She nudged his legs with hers.

"Move up," she said.

He sighed. "I can't. I'm stuffed. I'm bloated. I'll never move again."

She paused uncertainly and then moved toward the single armchair.

"Oh, okay, if you insist," he said, swinging his feet down and allowing the impetus to carry his body to an upright position.

She swaggered smugly to the sofa and collapsed next to him, throwing her feet up onto the sturdy beech coffee table and letting out a sigh of satisfaction. She hunted around for the remote control before spotting it in Jack's hand. She reached over but he brushed her off.

"Guest gets the remote," he said.

She was too full to fight him so she sat back and put up with his channel hopping, only resorting to protest when they'd watched over twenty minutes of sports.

"Okay," he said, getting up to use the bathroom and tossing her the remote. "See if you can find a movie."

C.J. flicked channels while he was gone and wondered absently if she was making a mistake by trying to bring sex into their relationship. The afternoon had been so easy and nice, and now they were settled down for a comfortable night in front of the television. Maybe the reason they'd never progressed beyond friendship before was because that's all they were supposed to be. Maybe she shouldn't be interfering with the natural order of things, trying to create something that wasn't there.

She flicked to a channel showing *The Long Kiss Goodnight* just as Jack came back into the room.

"Leave that on," he said. "Geena Davis is great."

He sat down next to her.

Friends, thought C.J., that's what we are. It's enough, isn't it?

Jack leaned over suddenly, his hand closing over hers as he tried to wrest the remote from her grasp. She put up a fight but he resorted to the dirty tactic of tickling her side and she had to concede the remote to him as she wriggled away from his hand, squealing frantically.

Jack settled back onto the sofa, tucking the remote behind his back. He returned her glare with a beatific smile then shushed her as Samuel L. Jackson appeared on screen.

Well, thought C.J., that answers that question. A few moments later she was still breathing erratically after the wave of desire had punched through her at his touch.

As THE CREDITS rolled, Jack looked down at C.J. who seemed to have fallen asleep on his shoulder. Her eyelids flickered as the commercials came on and she struggled upright, blinking awake.

"Oh, I'm sorry," she said. "I only meant to close my eyes for a minute."

"It's okay," he said, unoffended.

She rubbed her hands across her face, squinting at him. "I stayed up late all week trying to get extra work done so I could enjoy my free time with you. I'll have a cup of coffee and I'll wake up again."

"Don't be silly," he said. "C'mon, it's late. I'm worn-out, too. Let's go to bed."

She looked at him. "You sure?"

"Yeah."

He got up and pulled her to her feet.

She looked about her uncertainly.

"Uhm...I suppose maybe you'd better have the couch, if you want. I'll get some blankets."

He snorted. "'Forget it, I'd be more comfortable on the floor than on that." He pushed her gently toward the bedroom. "We should try getting used to sleeping in the same bed. I promise I won't ravish you in your sleep and if you want to ravish me, hey, I have no problem with that."

She stopped in her tracks to look around at him with a worried expression.

He held up his hands, palms upturned. "I'm kidding! I promise to stay on my side of the bed. Do you want the bathroom first?"

With C.J. effectively sidetracked to the bathroom, Jack went into the bedroom and took off his jeans and sweater. He waited until he could hear her coming and then he walked out, rubbing his hair absently as he passed her.

"I...I left some towels out for you," said C.J., trying not to stare too obviously at him.

"Oh, thanks," he said, only allowing himself to smile after he'd closed the bathroom door. His intention was to put her at her ease, to completely underplay the fact that they were going to be in the same bed.

When he went back out she was behind the kitchen counter, fiddling with some glasses.

"Do you want a glass of water?" she asked.

"No, I'm fine. I'm going to crash if that's okay with you. I think the day's caught up with me."

"Okay," she said as he disappeared into the bedroom. She waited a minute more before following him, switching off the table lamp on her way.

He was in bed and she noticed that unless she wanted to stand around awkwardly for the rest of the night she had no choice but to join him. She turned off the light and slipped off her sweatpants before getting into bed.

"Well, good night," she said, lying stiffly on her back.

He lifted himself onto one elbow and looked at her in the dim light.

"Is this a bad idea?" he asked. "Is it too uncomfortable for you?"

She was feeling shy and frustrated but she knew she'd feel a lot worse if he slept on her couch. Her discomfort was due to how much she wanted him here, rather than not wanting him.

"I guess we should be getting used to this," she said, wishing she didn't sound so disgruntled and ungrateful.

"Come here," he said, lying down again and pulling her toward him before she had a chance to protest. He put one arm under her head and wrapped the other loosely around her, over the blankets. He planted a platonic kiss on the crown of her head and snuggled his head into the pillows behind hers.

She lay awake, staring at the wall, but eventually the pull of sleep was too strong and it was too comfortable in the fold of his arms, so her eyes closed and she drifted off.

6

JACK WOKE as C.J. stirred against him, mumbling in her sleep. He thought she was waking up but she slumbered on, breathing slowly through parted lips. Jack loved how beautiful she was under her makeup. He could see the effects of the makeup when she put it on, the longer lashes, the fuller mouth, but there was something more touching about her naked face. She looked more vulnerable and familiar. She sighed and shifted again and Jack decided it was time for him to go for a shower. To at least get out of bed before she woke, or he'd be forced to walk around holding a pillow in front of him, very undignified.

When he came out of the bathroom, washed and dressed, she was sitting on one of the stools at the counter, sipping a cup of coffee. She was dressed in a fluffy robe and still wearing a sleepy morning face.

"Morning," he said. "Did you sleep well?"

"Isn't that my question to ask?" she said. "As the host?"

He smiled. "I'm just checking that I didn't take up all the bed or try to push you out or anything like that."

She smiled in response. "Well, if you did, I didn't notice. I slept like a log. You want some coffee?"

He came over to the kitchen and hoisted himself onto the stool next to her.

"This is breakfast, isn't it?" he asked sadly.

"There's cereal," she said. "Oh, but wait, the milk is probably—"

"It is," he said, wrinkling his nose in disgust. "I found that out last night."

"Sorry," she laughed. "I was going to go shopping before you came yesterday."

"Oh, I see. It's my fault you live like a Spartan. What do you usually eat for breakfast?"

She shrugged. "I usually get a coffee on the walk to work and then I have something to eat around midmorning, when I've woken up properly."

"And on Sundays?" he asked. "You just sit around drinking black coffee all day?"

"No, I don't sit around drinking black coffee all day. Actually, I like to go out and get the papers and spend the morning in a café."

His eyes lit up at the thought of real food for breakfast. "Let's do that, then."

She slid off her stool. "Are you sure? I thought you might want to go shopping or sightseeing."

"What am I?" he asked incredulously. "A tourist?"

SHE PEEKED at his feet as he walked around, looking for his shoes. *If I do have his child,* she noted with approval, *he'll have good feet.*

"Is that automatic?" he asked.

She looked up at him hurriedly.

"What?"

He sat on the couch, putting on his socks and boots. "Checking out people's feet."

She smiled. "I guess. Yours are good."

"Good?"

"I mean, they look good. That is, they look strong."

She fled to the bedroom to get dressed.

When they got to the café, they commandeered a table on the pavement and split the papers between them. Jack ordered breakfast while C.J. contented herself with a large cappuccino and an almond croissant. After an hour the table had a lived-in look. There were filleted papers strewn about as they passed sections back and forth.

C.J. paused in her reading to stretch her eyes. She yawned and lazily watched people walking past them.

"You know, I think this is one of the great underestimated pleasures of the twenty-first century."

Jack looked up.

"Just sitting on the sidewalk," she said, "reading the papers with a friend."

Jack looked around. He closed his eyes and stretched his face to the sun for a moment. Then he looked back at her.

"Can I have the comics now?" he said.

EVENTUALLY, reluctantly, they had to move. Jack had to leave if he wanted to make it home before the next day. He hadn't left anything in her apartment so they decided they'd say goodbye as she put him on a train to the airport. She made sure their walk took them past Dean & DeLuca where she bought him a picnic for the drive home.

At the subway she checked that he knew where he was going and that he had his sandwiches. She was pointing out his changeovers on the wall map until he eventually had to put up his hand and stop her.

"C.J., this is not my first time in Manhattan. And I did get to your shop without your help."

"Sorry," she said sheepishly, resisting the urge to reach up and smooth his jacket.

"Thanks for a great weekend," he said. "It was fun."

"I'm glad," she said. "Make sure you drive safely on your way home."

"I will. So, how about next weekend?"

She looked up at him, unsure what he meant.

"Next weekend?"

"Yeah, are you free? You have to come visit me. Although it probably won't be as much fun for you. I live in a shack."

"A shack?"

He shrugged. "Well, sort of. It's more of a lean-to. It's an extension at the back of the garage. Tom, the guy who owns the garage, used to stay there but he says he's too old to be slumming it now, so I moved in. It's not too bad, I did a lot of work on it but, you know, it's not exactly a house."

"Oh, now you've just whetted my appetite," she said.

He laughed at her expression.

"So, you'll come?"

She glanced up at him and then away, looking casually across the street.

"Or, now that we're comfortable with each other, I could come visit when I'm fertile and maybe we could, you know, give it a shot."

She let her eyes slide back to his face.

He was smiling at her choice of words.

"Give it a shot?" he said.

She blushed and gave him a light slap on the arm.

"Yes, give it a shot. What do you think?"

"Sounds good to me."

"Okay, then."

"Okay."

C.J. WASN'T SURE she had the right place. From the outside, Jack's house looked a disquieting prospect. It did look more like a shed or an army barracks than a place where someone could live.

She looked around her again.

Jack had been clear in his instructions, such as they were. Around the back of the garage, you can't miss it.

Well, here she was.

"Hello?" she called. Darn him, he said he'd be here. The thought crossed her mind that maybe Jack was working in a different garage now and hadn't mentioned it, assuming she'd know. She looked around indecisively.

She heard the sound of running water and after a minute Jack emerged from the side door of the garage.

A smile split his face when he saw her.

"Hey," he said. "I've been running out at every car that passed all evening and, of course, you arrive while I'm distracted. I wish you'd called me, let me pick you up."

"I wasn't sure what flight I'd get," she explained.

"I'm glad you made it, it's great to see you."

"I wasn't sure I'd got the right place," she said, suddenly feeling shy and awkward.

He raised his eyebrows. "Really? I didn't think you could forget your way around Ashfield that easily."

"No, I didn't. I just wasn't sure it…" She gestured vaguely at the garage extension.

He grinned at her wryly. "I know. I wasn't sure if I should really invite you here. I'm always wary of exposing this place to the critical eye of a woman but I decided that fair is fair. I saw your place. You should see mine. It's a lot better on the inside."

He darted forward and opened the door, beckoning her in.

She wondered privately just how many women had passed through this portal before her, then scolded herself. It was none of her business.

He was right, she was pleasantly surprised, but also wryly amused, by the interior. There was no mistaking that this was a bachelor pad. The door opened onto a surprisingly airy sitting room. There was a wood-burning stove to her right with two mismatched armchairs in front of it. A small television nestled unobtrusively in one corner and a low double bed occupied the corner farthest from the door, under a large window.

Bookshelves ran along the walls under the small front

windows and a quick glance revealed them to be stocked predominantly with car manuals and automechanic texts. Other books lay strategically about the room, a toppling bundle of paperbacks by the bed, some bookmarked aviation textbooks on the coffee table between the armchairs.

A multitude of engine parts, unidentifiable pieces of machinery daubed with oil, were scattered about the room like pieces of abstract modern sculpture.

On the back wall, the one adjoining the garage, were pinned complicated diagrams and aviation maps. A calendar of auto events was marked off with black *X*s.

Jack was standing beside C.J., surveying the room with her.

"Great," he sighed. "All day it's looked perfectly respectable to me but now that you're here I can see it's a pigsty."

She bumped her shoulder against his and smiled.

"No, it isn't," she said. "It's lovely. It's comfortable." She genuinely meant it. The room was clean and there was a welcoming smell of burning pine. She threw her coat on the bed, on top of the sweater already lying there, and made for the small door in the corner behind the fire.

"I'll just freshen up," she said, opening the door and finding herself in the kitchen.

He followed her in.

"This is the part I was dreading," he said.

She couldn't understand why. The kitchen was generously stocked with an array of tempting foods. There was a large woven basket full of vegetables: bright orange carrots, large onions, fresh cabbage. The door of one of the head-height cupboards was slightly ajar, revealing a selection of jars and glass bottles, as well as other cooking ingredients.

She looked up at him.

"What is it?" she asked. "Have you got a head in the freezer or something?"

"No," he said. "I meant, telling you about the bathroom."

"You do have one?" she asked worriedly.

"Yes, but it's in the garage."

"Hmm."

HE WAS IN the kitchen when she came back in.

"Isn't that kind of awkward at night?" she asked, standing in the doorway. "Having to go out there in the dark?"

He turned around to look at her.

"Well, it's all right as long as you watch out for the bears," he said, deadpan.

She tried not to smile but couldn't help a small one curling her lips.

"Fine," she muttered.

"And cougars," he said thoughtfully. "Got to watch out for those cougars."

"I said, fine." Her smile widened.

"Golden eagles are the worst, though. One of those could just swoop down the minute you step outside the door and that's the last we'd see of you."

"You're making me sorry I didn't let the cockroaches get you," she warned.

He met her eyes and grinned.

"You idiot," she said affectionately.

He held her gaze and she felt a heat spreading in the pit of her stomach. She looked away, feeling the heat rise in her face.

"So, are you cooking up something special?" she asked, her voice scratchy in her throat.

He turned back to the chopping board.

"I thought there would be less chance of you being snapped by the paparazzi if we stayed in," he said.

She had confessed to him that she wasn't telling her mother she was passing through town, just to keep things simple. And she had intimated that the less people he told, the better she'd feel.

"Plus, I thought it might be an interesting experience for you to eat food that you actually had a hand in preparing."

"Very funny," she said, grateful for his bantering tone. As comfortable as she was around Jack, the main purpose of her visit was at the forefront of her mind and her nerves were stretching.

"So, what's my job?" she said, coming into the kitchen to watch what he was doing and fighting to keep her voice as light as his.

"You'll find a potato peeler in there," he said. He half turned and reached behind her to open the cutlery drawer. His arm brushed her shoulder and she caught a waft of his scent, a mix of wool and masculinity. She couldn't help it. She jerked away from him in alarm, banging her side against the counter.

"Oops, you startled me," she said weakly.

He put down the chopping knife, put his hands on her shoulders and turned her gently toward him. Then he stepped back and leaned against the counter, folding his arms loosely. She took a step back and mirrored his pose, avoiding his eyes.

"I have a suggestion," he said gently. "We both know why you're here and it's making me nervous, too. Why don't we call a sort of amnesty on tonight? I had a really nice time at your apartment and I want you to feel relaxed here. There's no rush, is there? Couldn't we just have another platonic evening?"

C.J. kept her face impassive. Was he really trying to put her at her ease? Or was he simply not attracted to her? He said he was nervous but there was no evidence of him behaving like a cat on a hot tin roof. He had suggested an amnesty, as if that was the easy option. C.J. didn't think she could stand another platonic evening when her head was filled with such inflammatory thoughts. When she watched him chopping she wanted to rush up and slide her arms around him, press herself against the length of that hard, lean back. She wanted to grab one of his hands and hold it against her breast, feel the fingers caress its weight. And when he gave her one of those teasing smiles that lifted just the corners of his mouth she wanted to pull his head down and press that mouth to hers, to inhale his scent.

Her face betrayed nothing of the turmoil of her emotions.

"You've changed your mind?" she said in a small voice, looking up at him from under her lashes.

"No, I haven't," he said. His voice was sure and steady. "I just think you were wise to say we should spend time getting to know each other again." He grinned cheekily. "If you jump like that when I touch you in the kitchen, I'm worried that you might shoot through the roof when I touch you in the bedroom."

She raised an incredulous eyebrow. The arrogance of the man!

"So, are we agreed?" he went on. "You'll keep your hands to yourself tonight?"

Her mouth fell open in outrage.

"I promise I'll try and control my primal urges," she said sardonically.

"Good," he said. "Now, get peeling."

She fumed to herself as she worked her way through the small heap of potatoes. Some men actually do find me irresistible, she thought huffily, some men would have jumped me without even waiting for me to take my coat off. Well, it'll be a cold day in hell before he gets the chance again.

Jack went to work seasoning the meat, hiding his smile.

"DO YOU REALLY have to know all this?" she asked.

They were sitting in the armchairs, the plates of leftovers discarded on the floor behind them. Jack had added more wood to the small, cozy fire and had switched on the two corner lamps as dusk drew in.

C.J. was sitting on the squishier of the two chairs, her shoes kicked off and her legs curled up under her. She was flipping through Jack's pilot-training manual.

He looked over to see which page she was looking at. She covered it and turned away from him playfully.

"Let me test you. What is hypoxia?"

He answered promptly. "A lack of oxygen to the brain. Most people can cope up to about 10,000 feet, but the air gets too thin above that. The fun thing about hypoxia is that one of the symptoms is elation, or euphoria. So you think you're doing great but really you're getting more clumsy and drowsy, and eventually you pass out."

She was impressed. "You really have to learn all this?"

"I don't mind the health-and-safety rules so much," he said. "I found the law and air traffic much more difficult to memorize. All that biology stuff is interesting."

She looked up at him and said casually, "Maybe you should have become a doctor."

He gave her a level look.

"Maybe you should have got married and spent your life in the kitchen, cooking and cleaning."

She laughed. "Touché."

She looked down at the book again and her nose crinkled as she read another paragraph.

"What?" he said, watching her with amusement.

"This bit about G-forces making a pilot black out. I thought only astronauts had to deal with that."

"Heck, no. You go into a decent spiral dive and you can build up at least three or four Gs."

"Is that good?"

He considered the question.

"I guess it is if you want all the blood in your body to end up in your head, making your eyes explode."

"Jack!" she exclaimed.

"I'm kidding," he said.

She breathed out.

"You'd need at least five Gs before that happened."

"You're teasing me," she said doubtfully.

"A bit," he admitted. "A decent aerobatics pilot shouldn't let himself get into a situation where he's dealing with those kinds of forces. That would be bad news."

"Have you ever got into real trouble in the air?"

Jack's eyes grew distant. "Not really. I made mistakes when I was learning, stalled the engine and came out of spins the wrong way up, that sort of thing, but I always had an instructor with me. The most terrifying flight I had was my first time doing solo aerobatics. I came down and I was literally soaked in sweat." He smiled at the memory. "But this bird strike was my first real emergency."

"What was it like?"

"It was very frightening," he said, nodding his head. "But I think the difference was the years of experience I have now. I knew what had happened and I knew that I could glide it down. I was lucky enough to be flying over harvested fields at the time, so I knew it was just a matter of finding a spot and bringing her down."

"How is it now, have you got it fixed?"

"I'm working on it, slowly but steadily. Sometimes when you hit a bird—"

"You don't have to go into details," she said, wrinkling her nose.

"Okay. Sometimes there's just damage to the propeller outside, which is easy enough to fix, just a matter of replacing one of the blades. But other times the bird gets caught in the center, and the whole shaft and engine is damaged. That's my problem, so it'll be a while before I'm airborne again."

She smiled in sympathy.

"Would you like to go out to the hangar tomorrow, have a look at it?"

"Oh, I don't know if I'll have time. My flight's at two, I have to be back by the evening."

"No problem. You can see it some other time."

"Okay," she said happily. "Do you feel restless when you're grounded?"

He looked at her, surprised. "I do. I've taken friends' aircraft up a few times, but it's not the same as flying your own. And since we were on the subject of careers, I'd better tell you that I love the stunt flying and have no intention of becoming an airline pilot."

"Of course not," she said wryly. "Why have a highly paid secure job when you can risk your life for free?"

"I don't mind risking my own life, I just don't like to be responsible for other people's."

He'd spoken without really thinking about the words. He bit his lip as their full meaning registered.

She looked up at him and smiled reassuringly.

"It's okay," she said. "I understand. I read a quote once that stuck with me. It said 'Becoming a mother means agreeing to have your heart walk around outside your body for the rest of your life.'"

"Doesn't it scare you?" he asked.

"Sure," she said. She waved her hand around at the car manuals and flight books. "But it's like you feel about this. Some people might think it's crazy or pointless but you know it's worth it."

The simplicity of her explanation impressed him. He felt a depth of understanding that he hadn't before and he had the absurd impulse to give her a bunch of flowers, or pull down the moon for her. Something to say "you're amazing" without exposing him for the helpless fawning male that he was at that moment.

"You know, if you have...if we have a son I could teach him how to fly, teach him how to drive, too."

He mistook her forbidding gaze.

"It'd be safe," he said. "He'll learn to drive anyway— better he should learn from someone who knows what they're doing."

"But if it's a girl you won't bother teaching her any of that manly stuff, is that it?" she asked sweetly.

Oops, thought Jack. He opened his mouth to protest. "I meant a girl, too. A girl or boy, whatever."

She looked unconvinced.

He stood up and began to gather the plates and salad bowls.

"Of course I meant girls, too," he said casually. "It's just that girls are so squeamish about it all." He put on a squeaky voice. "Ooh, Jack, what if there's negative Gs and my head explodes?"

He escaped into the kitchen.

"You just lost your chance of getting help with the washing up, buddy," she yelled at him, sinking more comfortably into the armchair.

He put the dishes onto the counter, tossing the leftover salad into the garbage.

"You want some pie?" he called.

"Yes, please."

"It's in the oven," he said innocently.

She waited, but all she could hear was the sound of dishes being scraped and running water.

"Darn you," she muttered under her breath. "Now I really do want pie."

She got to her feet and padded into the kitchen. She ignored his smug smile and took two plates from the cupboard.

"Excuse me," she said, bumping him out of the way with her hip and getting a Tupperware container of whipped cream out of the fridge.

She spooned generous helpings of cream onto the warm

pie, emptying the container. Then she went over to the sink, where Jack was washing the last of the dishes.

"Sorry," she said, moving in front of him to put the container into the sudsy water.

She knew it was the devil in her but she didn't care. He'd been infuriating her all evening and she thought it only fair to tease him right back. She bent forward slightly as she rinsed the container, pushing her thigh against his. He didn't give any ground but she heard the break in his breathing and she flashed him a triumphant glance as she turned back to the plates of dessert. She was about to bring them into the living room when she felt Jack behind her, gently pinning her against the counter.

His arms reached up on either side of her head to open the cupboards.

"I think I've got some cherries in here somewhere," he said, his breath soft on the top of her head.

C.J. didn't dare move. She could have ducked out under his arm but that would mean moving her hips, which would bring them into more definite contact with his, which were brushing against her bottom, almost imperceptibly, as he searched the cupboard.

She could feel her heart thudding against her rib cage. She tried to keep her breathing even but her insides felt like she was standing in a rapidly descending elevator. She gripped the counter, willing herself to stay upright.

"There they are," he said. "At the back."

He leaned forward and there was no mistaking that their proximity was affecting him as much as it was her. Unable to help herself, she pushed back at the pressure of his body. She held her breath and all she could think was that she'd die if he moved away from her.

But he didn't. He brought his arms down from the cupboard and put his hands on her shoulders before stroking the length of her arms. He snaked one arm around her waist, spreading his fingers across her belly and holding her tight against him. With the other he stroked her collarbone, playing his fingers lightly over the hollow in her neck. Even if she could have moved she wouldn't, for fear of breaking the spell.

He lowered his head, his lips as soft as warm velvet as he dropped small, tender kisses along the most sensitive part of her neck. She moaned inaudibly, melting under his touch as warmth suffused her whole body. She pressed herself against him as if to meld into his body. She dropped her arms from the counter and put them on his thighs, unashamedly reveling in the feel of the taut muscles. He moved his hand down from her throat and ran it over her breast with a touch so light that she arched her back, straining out toward his hand. He cupped her breast in his hand, teasing the nipple between his thumb and finger until she was almost weeping with desire for him.

"Oh, please," she breathed. "Please."

He turned her in his arms, pulling her tight against him. Her body pulsed again when she looked into his eyes, dark with lust. He lowered his head and touched his mouth to hers. Emboldened by her overwhelming need for him, she put her hand up to his head, clasping the soft blond hair, and opened her mouth to him.

He needed no further permission. His mouth explored hers hungrily, his tongue probing her. She was almost frightened by it, this hunger that had exploded between them, but it was like a tidal wave, she couldn't fight it. All she could do was cling to him and hope that he would bring her to safety.

He put his hands under her bottom and lifted her effortlessly onto his hips. She wrapped her legs tightly around him, loving the feel of his hardness against her.

He carried her through the doorway and lay her on the bed. He pulled off his sweater and T-shirt together in one sweep and then stopped to look down at her again.

He opened his mouth to speak but she silenced him with

a look, opening her own blouse and unclasping the front
hook of her bra. The lacy garment fell away from her
breasts and he leaned forward hungrily to take a swollen
nipple in his mouth, teasing it with his tongue. She reached
for his jeans, and he for hers, until they were both naked,
their limbs entwined.

Her hands moved incessantly over him, she couldn't get
enough of the feel of his skin, the curve of his buttocks,
the strong sweep of his shoulders.

She opened her mouth, tasting the slight saltiness of his
neck, tugging at his nipples with her teeth, plunging the
depths of his sweet mouth.

He stroked her back and ran his fingers along the crease
between buttocks and thigh, making her tremble. His hardness strained against her. He reached down and gently
parted her folds, stroking himself even more intimately
against her.

She cried out with little gasps as the pressure built
within her until she couldn't bear not to have him inside
her. She moved under him, angling herself to welcome him
in.

He raised himself on one elbow and reached over to
open a drawer in the bedside table. She put her hand on
his arm.

"Uhm...no," she said, with an involuntary smile.

"Oh...of course, I forgot," he said, smiling back at her.

She looked into his eyes, heavy with desire, and her
longing for him increased, though she wouldn't have
thought it possible.

"I want you so much," she sighed helplessly, and then
gasped with pleasure as he pushed into her, filling her up.
She wrapped her legs around him as their bodies fused
together with wave after wave of passion. She cried out as
he drove into her with a shuddering climax and then she
held him against her as their breathing slowed to normal.

The fire threw a red glow over their bodies, highlighting

the pleasing definition of his muscles, glinting on his golden hair.

She gave a little meow of complaint as he started to move, but he only reached for a duvet that he pulled over them before wrapping his body around hers again.

C.J. closed her eyes and thought that she had never felt so safe.

7

C.J.'S FIRST THOUGHT was that the pigeons had got singing lessons. They were harmonizing, low bass notes and delicate melodic trills.

Then the smell of frying bacon assailed her nostrils and she remembered that she wasn't in the city and that what she was hearing was a choir of different birds.

She opened her eyes slowly and looked down at her naked shoulders emerging from under the quilt. Her mouth curled upward in a smile and she gave a long sigh of satisfaction. She stretched, luxuriating in the feel of the warm cotton sheets against her tired muscles. Jack had woken her during the night for a slow-motion replay of their first tumultuous union. She closed her eyes and recalled the feel of him in the dark, touching her, exploring her body with unabashed desire. With only a quarter-moon to light their bodies they'd tasted each other, delicious torment, until they fell sated as the first light of dawn crept in. C.J. shivered at the memory.

"I didn't have any cereal so I hope this will do."

C.J.'s eyes flew open. Jack was standing beside the bed, holding an overflowing tray and grinning down at her.

"What?" she said, scrambling over to the far side of the bed while trying to keep some semblance of modesty with the bedclothes.

"No cereal," he repeated. "So I brought a bit of everything."

He put down the tray and handed her a mug of coffee

before placing a selection of plates on the bed. She looked at the food and realized she was starving. Jack handed her an empty plate and before long she was munching happily on a piece of crispy bacon, interspersed with bites of a fluffy, buttered croissant, chunks of melon and satisfying gulps of coffee.

Keeping her mouth full meant she didn't have to talk.

She was slightly perturbed by the disparity in their attire. Jack had put on boxer shorts and a T-shirt and she was still naked, the quilt pulled up and tucked under her arms like the bodice of an overstuffed ball gown. Although Jack's cotton shorts were perfectly respectable they left little to the imagination and then, there was also the sight of strong brown arms emerging from a white T-shirt to distract her from her breakfast. She had to keep reminding herself not to stare, just to be satisfied with swift peeks.

She couldn't help feeling disgruntled that he wasn't still in bed with her. No, he was up and about and even half-dressed. Well, what did you want, she asked herself, for him to bring you breakfast in the nude? C.J. swallowed and coughed as a piece of croissant went down the wrong way.

Jack looked at her.

"You okay?" he asked.

"Fine," she nodded, concentrating on drinking her coffee and keeping her eyes on her plate. "This is really delicious."

He waited for her to say something else but it looked like her mind was fixed firmly on breakfast.

"I thought I'd let you sleep in," he said at last. "Your flight isn't for two hours so I thought it would be okay. I figured you could use the rest."

She handed him her cup. "Could I have a refill?" she asked lightly.

"Sure," he said, getting up and going into the kitchen, a small frown between his eyebrows.

C.J. clenched her teeth together so she wouldn't yell out some unpleasant words. She leaned over the edge of the bed and plucked her blouse from the floor, giving it a quick shake before slinging it on. Jack came back into the room and she resisted the urge to grab one of the plates, now bereft of croissants, and fling it at his head.

What did he think, that she was just going to lie around in his bed all day until he kicked her out? She was perfectly well aware that she had a plane to catch. The sex might have been mind-blowing but it hadn't wiped out her memory.

"Thanks," she said sweetly as he returned with the cup.

"Um...you want some more fruit or anything?" he asked, gathering up the plates.

"No, I'm fine," she said brightly. "I'll just go take a shower and I should be ready to go."

C.J. took extra care putting on her makeup, both to delay her return into the house and to give her extra confidence for facing Jack again. Eventually she had no choice, she had to leave the bathroom or he would be forced to come looking for her.

Jack was flicking through a magazine when she came back in. He closed it and jumped to his feet, then wished that he hadn't. He was acting like some nervous patient awaiting the doctor. He had put on his jeans and boots, planning to suggest that they go for a quiet walk before she had to go, but the sight of her put him off. She was wearing what he thought of as her professional demeanor. Her hair was brushed and tied back. She had covered up the sprinkling of freckles that had been brought out by the previous day's sun and her full lips sported a fresh coat of lipstick. She stood awkwardly in the middle of the room.

"I suppose I should say thank you."

To hell with this, thought Jack. He strode over and put his arms around her waist, clasping his hands loosely on the small of her back.

"You can say thank you all you want," he said gruffly, "but I don't think I'll really believe it unless I get a hug to go with it."

He tilted his head and smiled down at her, his eyes twinkling.

She laughed and slipped her arms under his and around his waist. As she leaned into him, he could feel the tension ease from her body. He put one hand up and held her head, savoring the smell of freshly washed hair and the warmth of her.

They stood together quietly for a moment and then she pulled back, just enough to lift her head up to look at him.

"Last night was good," she said softly, looking deep into his clear blue eyes.

"It was a little more than good," he said, his lips turning up in the smile that he hoped would make her do the same.

He lowered his head and kissed her, their lips touching with heartbreaking tenderness. He felt her fingers tighten on his back and she raised up on her toes to push herself against him.

Jack groaned inaudibly. Did she have any idea what it felt like when she lifted herself up like that to return his kiss? He could now feel her breasts pushing against his chest, it brought her thighs into contact with his and it caused friction in another place where he definitely didn't need it. His loins were aching and he wanted to press himself tightly against her. Heck, he wanted to pull her down to the floor and drive himself into her like some kind of animal. His legs trembled with the effort of standing still.

So he didn't know if he was relieved or disappointed when he heard the voice calling outside.

"Jack, hey, Jack, you in there?"

C.J. ended the kiss abruptly and looked up at him with startled eyes.

He looked toward the door and grimaced.

"Sorry," he said, looking back down at her. "It's Tom. I thought he was going to a rally meet in Brandon. I told him I might see him there this evening. My truck's outside...."

Jack looked so sheepish that C.J. might have laughed if she wasn't feeling so frustrated.

"Of course," she said reassuringly. "Go on, answer it, it's fine."

They slipped apart and he went over to the door. He put his hand out to open it, then stopped to look back at her as if a thought had struck him.

"I'm sorry," he said. "I wasn't thinking straight. Do we need to—" he pointed to the bed and lifted his eyebrows "—again?"

C.J. used all her willpower to push her mouth into a smile.

"No, it's fine. I'm sure last night did the trick."

Tom was knocking now and his calling grew more insistent.

"Jack, you in there? You still in bed?"

"Go ahead, open it," said C.J. through her plastic smile. "Or he'll think the bears got you."

Her blood had turned to ice water in her veins. She had been stunned by the force of the desire that shot through her from something as simple as a kiss. Maybe it was merely proof that she was ovulating—natural body chemistry increasing the desire to mate. Maybe if she'd paid attention before she would have noticed it. Whatever it was, it had every cell in her body crying out to be touched but Jack obviously wasn't suffering the same type of craving. His casual attitude was proof of that.

He grinned at her, searing her heart, and let Tom in.

C.J. HAD TO constantly monitor her speed as she drove to the airport. Her foot would press harder and harder on the gas pedal as her anger grew and then she'd suddenly realize she was doing over eighty and she'd lift her foot, breath out a big cleansing whoosh of air before the cycle began again.

"What am I, some kind of broodmare? Someone who needs to be given a proper servicing before she's sent on her merry little way again? Or maybe I qualified for the buy-two-get-one-free special that was on this weekend, I mean, why didn't he just give me a bottleful to take on the road?"

She banged the steering wheel and growled fiercely, then breathed out again in an effort to regain her composure. Then she resumed the invective and kept it up, even when it had merely subsided to muttering, because it was the only sure way she could prevent herself from bursting into tears.

One thing was for certain, she wasn't going to cry over Jack Harding.

By the time she boarded her flight, C.J. had calmed considerably. Memories of the night had filled her head while she was sitting in the waiting lounge, and a smile of delight kept tugging her mouth upward. She spent the flight back to the city gazing out the window. The azure sky and puffy clouds were a perfect backdrop for the daydreams she was having—warm golden skin, beautiful blue eyes, curving brows, strong hands.

By the time they touched down at La Guardia her anger had completely dissipated, and for one crazy moment she thought about staying on the plane for the return flight so she could go straight back to his house and his bed. She knew things were bad when she considered trying to hide in one of the overhead compartments.

On the taxi ride back to the city she caught herself smiling again, and letting out long sighs of satisfaction.

What on earth is wrong with me, she thought, I feel like I've been breathing happy gas. Ha, maybe it's hormones, maybe I'm pregnant.

She looked at her watch. Sure, she told herself, it's been twelve hours and already you're suffering a pregnancy hormonal imbalance. Then a curious thought struck her. In all the time since she'd left Jack this was the first time she'd thought of pregnancy.

ANOUSHKA AND Lex kept looking for hidden cameras. It was not that C.J. was normally taciturn or unpleasant or anything like that—in fact, she was very easy to work for—but she wasn't usually so giddy.

Lately however, she was bright and cheery in the mornings, a minor miracle in itself, and she kept breaking into little trills of song and, most disconcertingly, sneaking up and tickling them.

Lex had caught her humming "Secret Love" and had rolled his eyes at Anoushka with the muttered comment, "Secret? As if."

C.J. KNEW SHE WAS being totally transparent but for once in her life she just couldn't help it. Jack had sent her flowers and had called to make sure she'd arrived home safely and hadn't been too upset at Tom's inopportune arrival.

"Of course not," she'd assured him, crossing her fingers.

Best of all, she knew she was pregnant. Well, she must be, there was no other explanation for the change in her outlook. Colors seemed brighter and more vivid, food was tastier, the little absurdities of life made her laugh out loud and silly songs made sense. It must be a chemical imbalance. So she didn't care if Anoushka and Lex exchanged knowing smiles. Let them think her good humor was simply due to sex, she knew better.

"AND THEN, after all that, they decided they wanted the double hyperlink after all and they wanted me to…" Kerry trailed into silence as she registered C.J.'s vacant stare.

"Are you hearing a word I'm saying?" she asked crossly.

C.J. blinked and looked at her.

"What? Of course I am."

"Oh, give me a break," snickered Kerry. "You look as though you've only just realized I'm here."

C.J. gave her an apologetic smile. The euphoria of the previous week had worn off and she was feeling the effects of day after day of sustained energetic work.

She was also frustrated by her inability to concentrate on anything. The pregnancy books had warned her that her concentration would lapse, one had even charmingly told her that she would gradually become bovine, and she was beginning to believe it.

She looked at Kerry and decided she had been discreet long enough.

"I'm sorry I wasn't listening," she said. "I know I've been distracted—"

"It's okay," Kerry interrupted her with a reassuring smile. "I know what it's like. You can't think about anything except the feel of his arms, the touch of his hand, the smell of his skin. Believe me, I've been there. Hey, if you weren't my best friend I'd be jealous but don't worry, you deserve to be a little crazy in love, or lust, or whatever, for a change."

C.J. frowned. "It's not just that," she said. "I mean, it's not that at all." She shook her head for emphasis, then smiled and leaned forward conspiratorially. "I think it worked. I think I'm pregnant." She hugged herself and raised her eyebrows gleefully at Kerry.

"Really?" said Kerry in hushed tones. "Oh wow, are you kidding? Why didn't you tell me? When did you do the test?"

C.J.'s eyes darted to the side.

"Well, not yet," she admitted. "I have to wait for a few days after my period's due, to be sure, you know?"

"Oh, right," said Kerry, nodding. She drumrolled with her fingers on the edge of the desk and they grinned at each other.

"This is pretty exciting," said Kerry, still somewhat in shock.

"I know," said C.J., her eyes sparkling.

"So when was it due?"

"What?"

"When were you supposed to get your period?"

C.J. coughed and rubbed her nose.

"Uhm…tomorrow."

Kerry stopped rocking.

"What?"

C.J. made a great show of checking her calendar.

"Ahm…yes, it's due tomorrow."

She looked up and met Kerry's eyes.

"I know," she said firmly, "but I can feel it, Kerry, I'm sure of it."

Kerry chewed her lip. In the hour she'd been in the office, C.J. had broken into song numerous times and had snapped at her twice between bouts of excessive cheeriness.

Kerry looked pointedly at the empty box that had contained three donuts, none of which she'd eaten.

C.J. followed her gaze and grabbed the box. She flung it defiantly into the trash.

"You'll see," she said.

THE GOOD THING about best friends, thought C.J. the next day as she swallowed two aspirin with a cup of hot sugary tea, is that you can be obnoxiously self-righteous one day and you can still cry on their shoulder the next.

"You're not an idiot," said Kerry for the fifth time. "You just got a little ahead of yourself, got a bit over-excited. Don't worry about it."

She added the finishing touch to her toenail polish and stretched out her foot to admire it.

They were sitting in Kerry's spacious front room, with the sun baking in the large French windows. Brian was lying stomach down on the floor, meticulously building a Lego city.

Kerry looked up to see C.J. gazing dreamily at the boy.

"You're not going to go crazy now and try and steal my son, are you?" she teased.

Brian looked up briefly and gave C.J. a beguiling smile before returning to his work. It was a testament to Kerry's parenting skills that he was utterly unconcerned by such witticisms.

C.J. smiled at her.

"I'm sorry I was such a crank," she said. "I just convinced myself that it was inevitable somehow."

"Hey, it would have been weird if you'd hit the jackpot first time." Kerry stretched out both her legs and wiggled her brightly colored toes. She looked up at C.J. from under her lashes.

"You just have to resign yourself to the fact that you'll have to try again. You'll probably have to make many, many attempts before you succeed." She stretched out the words lasciviously, making C.J. laugh.

"There you go," said Kerry. "That's more like it. And don't worry about the crankiness, we know now you had a good reason and besides, the unceasing high spirits were getting a little nauseating."

"What?" yelped C.J.

Kerry raised an eyebrow. "Spare me the innocent outrage," she said. "You know what I'm talking about. I nearly entered you for Miss Perky Spirits of the Year, or I would have if there was such a thing."

C.J. shrugged. "That was only because I thought I was—" She flashed a look at Brian who was trying to build a skyscraper. "—because I thought I'd got into that club."

While mention of pregnancy might have floated unnoticed over his head, C.J. had inadvertently picked a substitute word that piqued his interest. He looked up.

"What club?" he asked.

"Oh, nothing interesting," muttered C.J.

"Is it the mile-high club?" he asked.

Kerry's head snapped around. "What?"

Brian looked up at her innocently. "I told Jacqui and Alicia that C.J. was friends with a pilot and they said she'd get a free pass to the mile-high club." He looked back at C.J. "Could you get me a free pass?"

"No, she can't," said Kerry. "And don't go asking anyone else, either. It's not a club for kids. I am going to have to talk to those girls," she added under her breath.

Kerry had bought the apartment with the insurance money after her husband's death but she liked to lease out an annex, as much for the company as to add to Brian's college fund. Alicia and Jacqui were the two students currently in residence. Kerry was beginning to wonder if she'd have to rethink her reliance on them as baby-sitters.

She looked over in puzzlement at C.J. who had her hands over her face. She was making a strange squeaking noise and her shoulders were shaking. It was a worrying moment before Kerry realized C.J. was laughing. Then C.J. dropped her hands into her lap and fell back onto the sofa, and Kerry decided that laughing was too weak a word. C.J. was in hysterics, guffawing until tears rolled down her face.

Kerry started to giggle and soon she, too, was laughing uproariously. Brian shook his head at them before returning to his Lego.

Their laughter petered out and they daubed at their eyes.

"Jack should get a kick out of that," said Kerry. "Have you called him yet?"

C.J. looked surprised. "No, gosh, I didn't think of it. I guess I should." She ran a strand of hair through her fingers. Her eyes grew thoughtful and a small smile crept onto her face.

"I guess it does mean we'll have to try again."

"I guess so," said Kerry laconically. "Hope he doesn't take it too hard."

It pleased her immensely to watch her friend trying, and failing, to hide the anticipation in her voice.

8

"PUSH IT UP!" demanded Tom. "Push it up farther. Now hold it there."

"I don't think—" said Jack.

"Just hold it!" said Tom, ensuring that each screw was correctly torqued before painstakingly moving on to the next.

Jack dug his heels into the gravel and shifted his back lower on the blade of the airfoil to maintain the pressure.

"Stop moving," scolded Tom.

Jack rolled his eyes at Billy who just grunted in response. He was bent almost double with his arms outstretched keeping the wing in place. He dropped his head between his arms and exhaled forcefully before looking up again with stoic determination.

All three looked over at Jack's truck as the sound of a phone trilling came from the front seat.

"Don't you dare," said Tom in a monotone.

Jack looked over his shoulder at the row of bolts that Tom had fitted so far.

"This side's practically done," he said. "I could just run over and get the phone and come back. Billy could hold it."

"No!" shouted Billy and Tom in unison, Billy's voice probably a little shriller than he'd intended.

C.J. PUT THE PHONE down with measured carefulness.

"Okay," she said calmly. She aligned her pens at the

side of the desk and put a pad of Post-its back into her left-hand drawer.

"That's okay," she said again. "I'll just call him later. No big deal."

She jerked in her seat as the phone rang out loudly.

"Calm down," she said through gritted teeth before answering it.

"You called?"

She smiled, pleased.

"How did you know it was me?" she said flirtatiously, swivelling her chair from side to side.

"Caller ID," he said.

She brought the chair to an abrupt halt and sat up straight.

"Right," she said. "Of course. Well, it's good of you to call me back."

He grinned at the change in her tone, then grew nervous when she didn't go on.

Oh, man, he thought, it's happened.

"Hello?" said C.J. quizzically.

"I'm here," he said, leaning against the car to disguise the trembling in his legs, "So?"

"Well, it didn't work," she said, more brutally than she'd intended. The words just seemed to blurt themselves out.

"Oh," said Jack. "I'm sorry."

"I mean, it just didn't work this time," said C.J. "First time and all, it's probably not such a surprise."

"Oh, okay," he said.

She searched his voice for any clues to how he was feeling. He certainly wasn't giving her enough words to go on. Was he relieved? He'd sounded relieved and now he was probably trying to find some way to tell her he wanted out. She berated herself for not telling him in person. She pressed the phone to her face, trying to read his mind, over two hundred miles away.

"So what do you want to do?" he said.

"What do you want to do?" she said, feeling childish and shy.

"Well, I guess we'll have to try again," he said.

She heard the smile in his voice and her face flushed as she was suffused with happiness. He wanted to make a baby with her.

"I guess so," she said, rocking in her chair.

"I sure wouldn't say no to another night like that," he said.

Of course.

He just wanted the sex.

She ceased rocking.

"What man would refuse?" she said coldly.

There was a pause.

"Were you very disappointed it didn't happen this time?" he asked, his gentle tone disarming her effortlessly.

She wound a strand of hair around her finger.

"I had the automatic disappointment, just said 'oh darn it'…but I'm not worried yet or anything."

"Hey, why don't you come up this weekend? We're having a barbecue and you could come up Saturday and go back on Sunday."

C.J. laughed, pleased and flattered.

"Ahm, thanks, but it won't be the right time yet—"

"Not for that," he interrupted her, laughing. "I'm just asking you up for a barbecue. You women, only one thing on your minds."

C.J. blushed again, shaking her head.

"Just for a barbecue?" she asked.

"Yes, C.J. I'm just asking you if you want to come up and have some burgers, a few beers, hang out with the guys, you know, like friends do?"

"All right!" she said. "I get it."

God, the man was frustrating. How could he make her

feel so pleased and so much of an idiot in such a short space of time?

"So you'll come?" he said.

"Sure," she said. "Why not?"

"Great," he said. "And you know, if you want to get in a little practice on that other thing we could..."

She left him talking to a dial tone.

"NEED ANY HELP?"

Donna looked up from the chopping and brushed a strand of hair from her face with the back of her hand. She smiled.

"I think it's all under control now," she said. "I just wish I'd got a little bit more notice about this barbecue, you know?"

She caught C.J.'s puzzled look and tried to cover her slip of the tongue.

"You know the guys, they just decide they want to do it this weekend and that's it."

No, that didn't sound right, either.

"I'm sure it was Eddie's idea," she said lamely.

C.J. decided to pretend it was all going over her head.

"I'll bring the bread out," she said. "And what's this? Waldorf salad? It looks delicious."

"Thanks," said Donna. "Try and distract people with it so they'll leave a steak for me."

"I want steak, too," said Didi, industriously removing the labels from the empty cans and squashing them for the recycling bin.

"You got it, sweetie," said Jack, coming into the kitchen on a beer foray.

C.J. gave him a complicit smile as she passed him on her way out to the garden.

He narrowed his eyes.

"You told her I'd decided to have the barbecue after I'd actually invited her up didn't you?" he accused Donna.

She kept her back to him, putting odds and ends of vegetables and cheese back into the fridge. He reached around her and pulled out a six-pack before she closed the door.

"I didn't say a word," said Donna, straightening up and looking out the window.

"She looks like she's enjoying herself," she said, hoping to distract him.

It worked. He looked out, too, watching C.J. as she walked around handing out French bread slathered with fresh butter and teased the men into adding more salad to their plates. A small breeze pushed at her dress, molding it against her thighs. She bent over to put the bread platter down and the back of her knee flashed provocatively at him before the gauzy cotton covered it again. He exhaled audibly, unaware of Donna standing beside him, her head tilted knowingly.

"I like her shoes," she said.

Jack backed away from the window and made for the door, annoyed with himself for being flustered.

"Uh yeah," he said, "I think she made them."

C.J. HAD FINISHED the steak and a generous helping of a gorgeous mushroom-and-pepper salad, and was now attacking a buttered corn on the cob.

She had settled herself in a prime viewing spot at the top of the stone steps that led down from the small fishpond at the end of the garden.

Eddie Jr. was sitting with Tom and Billy. With their soda bottles, the two boys were imitating the way Tom held his beer by the neck and hooked his finger around the top to take a swig.

Didi was demonstrating Gypsy's incredible obedience, commanding her sternly to "si-i-it" while she surrounded the dog with a circle of steak scraps. Gypsy whined piteously but didn't budge until Didi released her, then she whirled around like a tornado, snuffling up every scrap and earning an extra hot dog for her patience.

Eddie was dripping more barbecue sauce over the last few steaks and calling on everyone to get their third helping of chicken wings.

Donna was sprawled on a deck chair, fanning herself with a straw hat and staring ravenously at the sizzling meat, with Eddie reassuring her that it was almost ready.

Jack came up and sat down next to C.J. He put a fresh drink on the step by her feet.

She had napkins spread over her lap and was leaning out over her splayed legs to let the butter drip to the ground. She grinned at him with shiny lips.

Jack felt his stomach clench. He wanted to grab her and lick the butter off her mouth, to cover her whole mouth in a buttery kiss.

She reached down to wipe a streak of butter from where it had dripped onto her calf.

"Oh, look at me," she laughed. "I'm such a mess. I just had a T-bone and I got steak sauce all over myself, as well." She daubed at her chest, just above the gentle rise of her breasts.

"I hope I got it all off," she said, looking down at her cleavage.

Jack rolled his bottle of beer between his hands and clenched his jaw. Was she doing it on purpose? Now he couldn't stop thinking about her breasts, about unbuttoning the dress very, very slowly and tasting her skin, slightly salty with sweat, then a hint of spicy sauce residue, then onto the sweetness of her nipple.

He took a long swallow of beer and cleared his throat, trying to fill his mind with thoughts of carburetors.

C.J. glanced at him. He was staring determinedly into space.

Her little ploy with the food hadn't worked. What had she been thinking? Steak sauce and butter. Cream was what people licked off each other wasn't it? Or ice cream? Something sweet anyway, not steak sauce.

She felt foolish.

Ever since she'd found out that Jack had arranged the barbecue especially for her, she'd wanted to be able to thank him.

Such a simple thing. Just to be able to snake her arms around his waist and lift her face up to his for a kiss and say, "Thank you, sweetheart."

Except he wasn't her sweetheart, and it was even beginning to look like he wasn't all that attracted to her, either.

"I'm having a good day," she said at last, "thanks for asking me up."

"No problem," he said.

C.J. bit savagely into her corn.

SHE WAS WIPING AWAY the last of the greasy residue from her fingers when Didi came and stood near them, leaning against one of the pillars.

"You having a good time, honey?" asked Jack.

"Yeah," she said dismissively, concentrating on C.J.

"Jack said you make shoes," she said.

"That's right," said C.J.

"It's my mom's birthday next week," said the girl, "and I was wondering if you could help me make a pair of shoes for her?" The words came out in a rush.

"Uh," said Jack, "I don't think that's—"

C.J. shushed him.

"What kind of shoes?" she asked.

Emboldened by her interest, Didi answered enthusiastically.

"I have some pictures in my room. I did some drawings."

Jack was hoping C.J. would be tactful in her refusal but C.J. had jumped to her feet.

"Let's see them," she said.

Didi clapped twice quickly and raced toward the house.

"I'm going to show C.J. my room," she shouted at her mother who gave C.J. a smile before concentrating on her huge plate of food again.

C.J. WAS DELIGHTED with Didi's drawings. They had a typical nine-year old's disregard for practicalities of comfort, or even balance.

Within fifteen minutes they were both sitting on the floor with sketches strewn around them.

C.J. had done some line drawings of famous novelty designs like Arcofora's glass slipper made from an old champagne bottle and some of her own more outrageous spangled platforms and imaginative wedge heels.

Didi had been fascinated but had impressed C.J. by admitting wisely, "Those are shoes that I like but I don't think my mom would."

So they returned to simpler, sleeker designs, trying to decide between shoes or boots, deciding on a color "Red!" and finally, while C.J. peeked out the window and verified that Donna was still in the garden, Didi snuck into her parents' room and brought back a couple of shoes for C.J. to examine.

C.J. tried on right and left, comparing the length and width of Donna's feet to her own, before Didi scooted back and replaced them.

They were gathering up the sheets of paper when they heard a tentative knock and Jack peeped his head around the door.

"You girls going to stay up here all day?" he asked.

"C.J.'s going to make red shoes for Mom," said Didi, unable to contain her excitement.

She grabbed Jack's hands and squeezed them, staring up at him solemnly.

"You have to promise, swear on your life you won't tell. Cross your heart."

"I do," he said. "I do all those things."

"C.J. will send them to you and you give them to me. Secretly!" she stressed.

"I got it," he said, squeezing her hands back, "Secretly."

"Okay," she said.

She turned and, after a moment's hesitation, threw her arms around C.J.'s waist and gave her a breathtaking squeeze.

"Thank you so much, this is so cool."

She stepped back and took a deep breath, letting it out slowly through pursed lips.

C.J. and Jack watched her with amusement.

"Okay, I am composed," she said, smoothing down her T-shirt. "I am serene and composed."

She turned and dashed down the stairs with great thumping steps.

C.J. and Jack looked at each other.

"That was really nice of you," said Jack.

"It's no hassle," she said. "I'll have them done on Monday and I'll send them straight up."

Jack looked confused.

"Oh, wait," he said. "You don't have to do that. I mean, we can just buy a pair at the airport or something. It won't make any difference. I know you're too busy—"

"Jack, I'm making them. I said I would and I will. It's a done deal, okay? And if there's any problem with size or fit I'll take care of that, too. Okay?"

Jack looked at her determined little face.

"Thanks. And I'll pay you, of course," he said, wishing he had half a clue how much a pair of designer label shoes went for.

"Don't be infuriating, you will not. It's a favor for a

friend, that's all. You're doing me a favor and I'm doing you one, no big deal.''

She cringed upon hearing the words.

"Not really on the same scale, though, are they?'' he asked.

She was relieved to see his eyes were twinkling but she blushed anyway.

"I didn't mean—'' she said falteringly. "I just meant that—''

"Come here,'' he said, pulling her into a friendly hug. She buried her face gratefully into his chest.

"Tell you what,'' he said. "I'll take you up for a spin in return for the shoes, how about that?''

She looked up at him. He held her companionably around the waist, keeping her body close to his.

"You mean in the plane that you are repairing yourself?'' she said dubiously.

"You have to say aircraft,'' he told her. "Pilots call them aircraft, not planes.''

"Whatever you want to call it I'm not sure I want to go up in it.''

He grinned at her and mimicked her previous stern tone. "Okay then, that's that, it's a done deal.''

C.J. smiled up at him. Despite the fact that he was threatening her with a ride in a death trap she felt incredibly warm and safe.

She looked at his mouth and willed him to read her mind, which had only one thought streaming through it.

Kiss me, kiss me, kiss me.

Jack looked at her upturned face and his eyes darkened. She was pressed against him and her lips were parted. She hadn't moved away, but then she couldn't, could she, with his arms holding her. It seemed like she was inviting him but what if she wasn't, what if she was just waiting impatiently for him to let go?

He didn't want to mess things up.

"So...you're sure this weekend is no good for the other thing?" he said, trying to keep his voice light and joking. She desperately wanted to lie.

Yes, I'm fertile. Let's do it now, and tomorrow and every day after that. Or just forget about the baby and make love to me just because you want to.

She dropped her head.

"No," she said, barely audible, "not this weekend."

"Oh, well," he said, through gritted teeth. He dropped a chaste kiss on her head and gave her a brotherly squeeze before letting go.

"I'd better go discuss our flight plan with Tom," he joked.

She forced a laugh and followed him down the stairs.

A WEEK HAD PASSED since the barbecue and it was Donna's birthday. She had been dispatched to the bedroom with instructions to dress up for the occasion.

She tried on three pairs of tights before she found one without a run.

"Why do I put ruined tights back in the drawer?" she asked herself crossly.

She was about to throw out the two flawed pairs but couldn't. Some day, she said to herself, some day I'll need a pair urgently and I won't have them and I'll be able to cut the laddered legs off each of these and wear the two remaining legs as a pair.

She looked in the mirror and smiled ruefully at herself.

"Were you this much of a Girl Scout before you had kids?" she asked.

She couldn't remember. It seemed natural to her now, automatically preparing for emergencies.

She turned sideways and examined her reflection.

"Hi, I'm Donna. I'm thirty-five."

She slipped on a pair of black pumps, gave her hair a quick brush and put on some more mascara.

She stood before the mirror again. Maybe this wasn't such a dumb idea, this insistence of Didi's that she get primped up before getting her birthday presents.

She smiled.

"Hi, I'm Donna. I'm thirty-five and I look great."

She went downstairs, chuckling to herself.

"...HAPPY BIRTHDAY dear Mo-om, happy birthday to you."

Donna blew out the candles amid cheers and then was seated ceremoniously on the sofa.

Eddie Jr. handed her an envelope.

"All our presents go together, there is a theme," he told her. "Go on, open it, open it."

She ripped open the envelope, imitating his excitement and pulled out two reservations for the Lakefront Inn, a renovated Victorian mansion on the outskirts of town.

"Oh, wow, thank you darling," she said, pulling her squirming son into a hug. She smiled up at Eddie. "I'm beginning to see why I had to get dressed up."

He came over and knelt on one knee before her, making her giggle.

"May I present myself as your handsome escort for the night? We have eight o'clock dinner reservations at the hotel restaurant, followed by late-night jazz in the Green Room after which we shall be putting the Do Not Disturb sign up on the door of our hotel room."

"Which is where I come in," said Jack, "with my superlative all-night baby-sitting skills."

She reached over and squeezed his arm.

"Thank you guys, this is brilliant."

"Last, but not least," said Eddie.

Didi stepped forward and presented Donna with a flamboyantly wrapped parcel. Donna removed the bows and silvery paper amid much exhortation to hurry up.

She froze when she saw the distinctive electric blue box with the trademark "SABRES by jane" slashed across the top.

"Oh my goodness," she breathed, lifting the lid reverently.

She pulled back the tissue paper and touched the crimson shoes as if they were the last couple of an endangered species.

"When on earth did you get these?" she said.

Her family flashed conspiratorial smiles.

She kicked off the pumps and slipped on the new shoes carefully.

"They fit perfectly. Oh, wow, they're beautiful." She walked over to the door and turned, looking at her family on the sofa.

"I can't believe you went out and got me a pair of Sabres. This is amazing."

"And look," said Didi, handing her the box and pointing out the silver-embossed sticker on the side that showed the size, color and style.

Size: 6
Color: Crimson
Style: Didi

Donna looked confused. "I don't get it."

"I helped design them," said Didi proudly. "With C.J."

Donna looked at Jack.

"You never told me she worked for Sabres," she said. Jack laughed.

"C.J. is Sabres. She owns the company. Her name, C.J.? Catherine Jane, Sabres by jane? Get it?"

"Are you kidding me?" shrieked Donna. "I can't believe you didn't tell me this. Have you any idea how cool these are?"

"Uh…"

"I would have walked to New York myself, in my bare feet, to get these."

Jack and Eddie exchanged an amused glance, but Donna was ignoring them.

She reached down and pulled Didi and Eddie Jr. into a hug.

"Thank you for these gorgeous shoes and thank you for the hotel so I can go out and show them off."

She kissed them soundly, then stood up again, putting out one foot to gaze down lovingly at it.

"I'm going to go and fix my makeup again and I'm going to change into something short and tight." She gave her husband a long hungry look. "You've got yourself a date tonight, babe," she said, swinging her hips as she went out of the room.

"Wow," said Eddie, grinning from ear to ear.

"And we're going to have a party night," said Jack to the kids, earning himself smiles. "Food and video games and more food and anything we want."

And then I'm going to run up Eddie's phone bill, he said to himself, when I call C.J. and tell her just how great she is.

9

"YOU GET A great view from up here," said C.J.

Jack glanced over at her. "You think this is a good view?"

"Sure, being up this high makes quite a difference."

He looked at her, smiling to himself.

"What?" she said.

"Nothing," he said.

"Are we there yet?"

His smile broadened. "Nearly, only about half an hour."

They were in Jack's pickup, on the way to a location that Jack was being very secretive about. C.J. had had few qualms about abandoning work for the weekend. Her body temperature had risen and she had thrown together a weekend bag while calling Jack. She had placated her conscience by working on the figures for the fall projections on the hour-long flight to Burlington. However, when she saw Jack waiting for her in the parking lot, leaning lazily against the truck, all thoughts of work fled and she stuffed her files resolutely into the bottom of her bag.

Although Jack had refused to tell her where they were going, C.J. was enjoying the drive. The truck gave a much better view of the roads and she could see over the hedges to the surrounding fields.

She put one foot up on the dash and rested her arm across her knee, sliding down comfortably into the seat and smiled as she met the amiable gaze of a horse.

Jack slowed the truck and turned left onto a rough dirt road. It was bounded on either side by trees, so C.J. had no clues until they reached the end and Jack pulled up beside a large barn. There were three men sitting on small wooden crates outside and they waved at the truck. Nearby, a small white plane gleamed in the sunlight.

C.J.'s mouth fell open and a thrill of anticipation ran through her.

"Decided I couldn't wait to take you up," said Jack, grinning at her. "Frank Foley, the guy in the baseball cap, is loaning me his Piper. Today's your lucky day."

C.J. swallowed. Somehow she thought she'd have more time to prepare for this. She'd become used to thinking of the plane ride as an abstract, something to look forward to someday. But now that the day was here, she found her excitement was tempered with trepidation. She licked her lips, which had suddenly become dry.

"Where's the runway?" she asked, looking around.

"That's it," he answered.

"The field?"

"Yup," he said. "There's a mown section in the middle, of course."

"Of course," she said weakly.

They got out of the truck and walked over to the gaggle of men who greeted Jack like old friends and shot curious glances at C.J. Jack introduced them and C.J. listened with half an ear as they swapped stories.

Her eyes kept straying to the plane. It looked rather small for something that would be carrying her through the sky. She looked up. The sky was a brilliant azure blue and small clouds scudded across the wide expanse.

"You guys have fun up there," said Frank, tossing a small bundle of keys to Jack.

C.J. tried to give them a brave smile as she and Jack walked over to the plane. "You okay?" asked Jack.

She smiled weakly and shrugged. "I'm excited but I'm also kind of scared."

She was surprised by her body's reaction. Her stomach was knotting and her hands had grown slick. She took a deep breath and let it out slowly.

"There's no need to be scared," said Jack, pulling the chocks out from under the wheels. "This is going to be fun."

"This from the guy who crashed his own plane," she muttered. There, she'd said it.

He looked at her thoughtfully.

"Okay," he said. "I understand. Listen, bird strikes are very rare. But I can't guarantee it won't happen. Frank takes very good care of his Piper, but it's always possible that a piece of grit will clog the fuel line and we'll have a problem in the air. I'm ninety-nine-percent sure nothing like that will happen. I think we'll go up, have a great time and land with no problems. I'm ninety-nine-percent sure but I can't guarantee it."

He paused, his voice steady. "But I can guarantee you that if anything goes wrong, I'll know how to handle it and I will get us down safely. I've been flying for ten years and there's nothing that can happen up there that will catch me unaware. I promise you, you'll be safe, so don't worry."

He waited for the frown to clear from her brow.

"You promise?" she said.

"I promise," he said. He twisted the handle and slid back the canopy before adding casually, "Statistically you'll be in a hundred times more danger on the drive home." He gave her a winning smile.

C.J. SQUEEZED HER fingers and tried to contain her excitement. Watching Jack prepare for the flight had been very reassuring and her last vestiges of fear had fallen away in the face of his competence. He had even checked the plane and engine physically before they climbed into the cockpit. It was replete with unfamiliar gauges and switches but it still felt disconcertingly like sitting in a Volkswagen Beetle with wings.

Jack started the engine and the roar of it startled C.J., as did the vibration. They trundled slowly to the end of the runway where Jack did some final instrument checks and received flight information from the tower, which C.J. thought was a rather grand name for Frank sitting in a small two-story hut at the end of the runway.

Jack pushed the throttle in smoothly and the engine roared loudly as they moved down the grass runway with increasing speed.

C.J. gasped an intake of breath as Jack pulled back on the stick and the small plane lifted easily into the air. Jack reached out and switched the radio frequency and she listened to the babble of words in the background as she stared, wide-eyed, at the ground falling away beneath them.

"Victor Bravo climbing to two thousand feet on heading 3-7-0. We'll be executing aerobatic maneuvers in the Bradford area."

"Roger Victor Bravo. QNH 1-0-2-1, QFE 1-0-0-4, surface wind 350/12. You're cleared to five thousand feet. You've got nimbostratus about five miles to the south, but heading south, wind due to pick up later, keep us informed."

"It's completely different from flying in a jumbo," said C.J., when she found her voice again.

Jack grinned. "Do you like it?"

"I love it," said C.J. with genuine feeling. Flight in the small plane had none of the impersonal smoothness of a 747. C.J. could feel the buffet of the air in the occasional sideways jerk. It was as though they were trundling over a rough dirt road, but also strangely cushioned.

C.J. could hardly open her eyes wide enough to take in the sight of the countryside below them.

She grinned. "This is why you laughed when I said there was a good view from the truck."

He smiled at her and turned the stick to the left, putting the plane into a slow, sweeping arc while C.J. stared avidly out the window, hardly able to believe the evidence of her own eyes.

They continued for twenty minutes in this fashion, Jack describing gentle curves in the sky. C.J. even took the stick for a while, learning to feel the tiny adjustments needed to keep the nose firmly aligned just above the horizon.

"Ready to try a barrel roll?" asked Jack a while later.

"You bet," said C.J. recklessly.

Jack grinned at her newfound confidence.

"Why don't we do a couple of steep turns to warm up?" he suggested. He began to turn the plane to the left, keeping steady pressure on the rudder as he increased the angle through thirty degrees, through forty-five and into sixty degrees.

C.J.'s heartrate tripled. It felt to her as if the small plane was tipped precariously onto its side, with nothing but the glass of the window between her and the ground.

Jack eased the plane into level flight again and began a steep turn to the right.

C.J. instinctively gripped the seat under her as she saw the wing on her side flip straight up into the air. She was grateful that she'd never been prone to seasickness and could enjoy the feel of the pull of gravity. There was no denying that the mixture of thrilling excitement and vague terror was oddly seductive.

Jack pulled out of the turn and climbed the plane back up several thousand feet. C.J. noticed him check the instruments and look over to check on her. She eased her hold on the seat and opened her mouth to speak.

The words caught in her throat as Jack rolled the plane.

The horizon spun sickeningly in front of her and she grabbed frantically, one hand clutching at the seat and the other pressing against the window. She felt frozen as the world whirled around them and then slowly the horizon came level again and there was blue above and green below.

C.J. let out her breath with a whoosh. "Why didn't you warn me?"

"I thought I should get it over with."

"That's a habit of yours, isn't it?"

"How do you feel?"

Her face was flushed and her heart was thudding erratically.

"Wonderful," she said, bursting into laughter.

Jack put the plane into a climb and when the altimeter hit five thousand feet he reached over and squeezed her knee.

"Ready?" he said.

"Yeah, do it again," she said eagerly, ready this time to look around and take more in.

"This is different," said Jack. He eased the plane into a shallow dive to build up speed and then he pulled back on the stick, lifting the plane into a climb.

C.J. saw the horizon drop away as the nose of the plane swept upward. In the blink of an eye she was pressed back in her seat, then upside down and the next thing she saw was the ground hurtling toward them as the plan came out of the loop.

C.J. pressed herself into the seat and her breath came in short pants. Three seconds of flying directly toward the ground felt like thirty and C.J. was rigid with fear while Jack calmly let out the throttle and eased the stick back until they were once again trundling along on the straight and level.

"Give me a chance to recover this time," she pleaded.

He smiled at her. "You're doing very well," he said. "Do you feel nauseous at all?"

She shook her head. "My whole body has broken out in a sweat and I think I'm about to have a heart attack but I feel...totally exhilarated, actually." She grinned at him.

"Want to try some more?"

She nodded eagerly.

By the time they landed C.J. felt as though she'd run a marathon. No, she corrected herself, she felt as though she'd run a marathon and won.

She was buzzing with invigoration and her legs were slightly wobbly when she jumped down from the cockpit. Jack caught her and propped her up against the plane while he went about the business of chocking it.

JACK WAS DELIGHTED with her enjoyment of the day. He had taken most of his family and friends up with varying reactions.

Eddie, Donna and his mother adored it. Billy had watched Jack with his trademark studiousness as he tried to memorize the movements. Unfortunately, even with motion-sickness tablets, his father couldn't bear it.

But Jack felt something he could only describe as goofy pride at pleasing C.J. He looked at her, gazing at the sky and smiling to herself and he felt an ache in his chest.

"You look about twelve years old," he said impulsively.

She gave him an open smile. "I feel about twelve," she said. Her eyes looked into the distance. "I feel all giddy and sort of pleased with myself. Kinda silly, don't really care, got nothing to worry about." She looked over at him again and was clearly blushing.

"Well, it suits you," he said, walking over toward the hangar. He saw her take a last look at the plane before following him.

C.J. FELT SO PROUD when the men at the hangar expressed admiration for the array of moves Jack had put the plane through. She knew he hadn't attempted anything difficult or dangerous but she couldn't help feeling smug when he described her as a natural.

Jack told her that he'd usually stay with Frank Foley when he was in this area, but he'd wanted them to have some privacy so he'd booked them into a bed-and-breakfast.

A few miles down the road he pulled into a semicircular driveway. Although the house was large, it carried an air of coziness in the ivy-covered walls and lead-patterned windows.

A lady who was working on the flower beds in front of the house clambered to her feet and came over to greet them. She took off her gardening gloves and brushed a strand of gray hair behind her ear before shaking hands with them and ushering them into the house.

"Your house is beautiful, Mrs. Cooper," said C.J.

"Call me Peggy," urged the woman, shooing a tiger-striped cat out of her way. "We're not very big on formality here. Did you have a nice drive up?"

Jack talked politely about traffic as Peggy led them up the stairs. C.J. followed them silently. She couldn't understand it but she was suddenly feeling quite tired.

Their room was a welcoming sight. It was decorated tastefully in subdued rose hues with hand-carved pine furniture. There was a vase of peonies on the sideboard and a panoramic view of the wooded countryside from their window.

"Now, I'll be serving dinner in about an hour if you want to eat here, or there's a few good restaurants in town, about six miles up. Would you like some lemonade and cookies now to tide you over or would you rather not spoil your appetite?"

C.J. looked at Jack. All she wanted to do was take a nap. Jack flashed her a look of understanding.

"I think we'll wait for dinner," he said. "But be warned, we'll be hungry enough to eat a horse by then."

"We'll see what we can do," said Peggy, smiling.

As soon as Peggy had left the room, C.J. flopped onto the bed, closing her eyes. Jack kicked off his boots and lay beside her, resting on one elbow and looking down at her.

She opened her eyes and looked at him apologetically. "I don't know what's got into me," she said. "I just feel exhausted all of a sudden."

"Hey, don't apologize," he said, stroking her arm absently. "Flying takes a lot out of you."

"I don't see how, I was just sitting there. You were the one doing all the work."

"Yes, but I didn't have every muscle in my body tensed for the full two hours."

She nodded wryly, rubbing her hand on the back of her neck.

"A hot shower and some food and you'll be right as rain again," he said.

She looked up at him languorously.

"And then, after dinner?"

"Your wish is my command."

"Oh, yeah?" She raised her eyebrow. "What if I command you to rub my tired muscles now?"

"I would have to do it," he said, holding her eyes.

Without breaking their gaze she reached down and pulled his T-shirt out from his jeans. She slid her hand into the gap and splayed her fingers on his stomach, which tautened under her touch.

His eyes darkened.

"Maybe if your muscles had a workout we would be even," she said.

"But what would you do?"

"I would just lie here," she said, "resting."

His mouth widened in a predatory smile and she rolled onto her back, stretching like a sleepy cat.

"Which muscles, specifically, would you like me to massage?" he asked, helping her take off her T-shirt.

"Uh, my back," she said, rolling onto her front and stretching her arms above her head. He unhooked her bra and ran his hands over her shoulders and down her waist.

"Close your eyes," he said.

She obeyed and he got off the bed. She felt him get on again a few minutes later and straddle her buttocks. His warm hands moved gently over her back, molding the tired muscles like putty, warming them until the aching eased. Then his hands moved down her spine and over her lower back, stroking repetitively until her body felt as pliable as rubber.

He opened her jeans and slid them over her hips, pulling her panties off with them. He rubbed his hands along her bare thighs and she moved her legs, parting them imperceptibly. She felt the change in his touch and she welcomed it. He stroked his hands along her sides, his fingers dipping under her to play along the edge of her stomach and over her hipbones. Her body began to thrum as he continued his downward stroke, splaying his hands over her bottom, pressing his fingers into the flesh. His hands parted as he ran one down each leg, his thumbs trailing lines of fire along her sensitive inner thighs.

Her breathing became ragged and she pushed her buttocks against his hands. She could feel that his legs were naked against hers. As his hands snaked upward again she pushed her shoulders off the bed. His arms slipped under her, cupping her tingling breasts.

She turned under him and he dipped his head, sucking one nipple and then the other until she clutched at his hair, pulling his hot mouth onto hers.

She pushed him off her and rolled him onto his back,

giving him a lascivious look. He reached for her but she pinned his arms above his head and straddled him, squeezing his hips between her thighs. He watched her with dark eyes as she slowly lowered herself onto him, gasping as her burning heat enveloped him.

He watched her as she rose and fell slowly, tormenting him. He reached for her again but she pushed his arms down, smiling as she controled him. She ran her hands down along his arms and over his chest, finally playing her fingers over his stomach. His arms strained as he clasped the headboard, arching under her to push even more deeply inside her.

She gasped and let her head fall back, feeling the waves building inside her. He reached down and held her hips, pushing into her relentlessly.

C.J. reached behind her and grabbed at his thighs, holding them tightly as her back arched and her body shuddered. She fell forward as the waves of the climax shook through them and he wrapped his arms around her. Their mouths met and she sucked gently at his lips before letting her head fall on his chest as their bodies relaxed.

"THAT REST certainly seems to have done you a world of good," said Peggy as she laid an array of serving dishes on the table in front of them. C.J. busied herself spooning steaming vegetables and slices of lamb onto her plate so she missed the smile that Peggy gave Jack.

They ate slowly, both feeling satisfactorily tired after the day and content in each other's company.

"There's an air show coming up in the fall. It's an annual thing, gets a big local crowd. I'll be flying in it, at that airfield. You should come."

"You know," said C.J., swallowing a mouthful of baby carrots, "it bothers me somewhat that you refer to that place as an airfield. Haven't you ever been to a real airport? With tarmac?"

He smiled. "Don't let Frank hear you say that. That place is his pride and joy. He spent twenty years at Dulles in traffic control. He's one of the best in the country but he retired and now he's happy with his own little field and flying the Piper. And he holds this annual air show. It's getting bigger every year as more pilots come, but it still has a friendly feel to it. We take people up in turns all day, scare the pants off them."

"That I can believe," said C.J. "But I hope you're gong to take me up again before that. I think I've caught the bug."

"Sure," he said. "I'll give you a pinch-hitter course the next time."

"What's that?"

"Oh, just the basics. What to do if I have a heart attack and pass out, that sort of thing."

She looked at him and he smiled guilelessly.

"If you ever have a heart attack in the air, I won't have time to land the plane because I'll be too busy killing you."

"Oh, I'm not planning on having one anytime soon. Unless you want me to give you another one of those massages tonight, that might do it."

She glanced quickly at the other guests but they were all happily engrossed in their own conversations.

She looked back and met his eyes.

"We'll just have to see about that, won't we?"

10

C.J. WOKE BEFORE Jack. He was lying on his side with the sheet at his waist, his ribs rising and falling evenly. The skin of his back was a smooth velvety golden brown.

She put out her hand carefully and stroked his back, amazed at the warmth of his skin. She put her hand up to touch the back of his neck, running a soft strand of hair through her fingers.

Jack let out a huff of air like a contented dog, making C.J. smile. She ran her hand along his arm, trailing onto his back again. She let it drift under the sheet and to the small of his back, feeling the silky down under her fingers. She ran the backs of her fingers softly over the curve of his buttocks and then up again across the hardness of his shoulder blades.

It was impossible not to be aroused by the proximity of such a glorious body. She inched closer, trying not to wake him, and put her face close to his skin, inhaling with her eyes closed.

She put her hand on his back again and slid it down his side, letting it slide around his waist to trace the curve of his ribs. Jack sighed and stirred as she ran her hand down to his stomach, feeling his unmistakable arousal against her knuckles.

She moved over, closing the gap between them and pressed her body against him, molding her thighs against his. She was melting with warmth and a heady feeling of sensuality. Jack reached back and pulled her against him with a long, strong arm. She kissed the back of his neck with an open mouth, sucking softly at his skin.

He shifted in the bed, turning onto his back and pulled her onto him. He opened his eyes and his mouth curved lazily before he kissed her, one hand under her chin to pull her face up to his.

They made love with an exquisite tenderness, their limbs heavy with slumber.

C.J. WAS TEMPTED to stay in bed all day. Jack had dragged himself into the shower and when he came out she was still sprawled across the bed, tangled provocatively in the duvet. Jack sat on the edge of the bed, a towel around his waist and drying his hair with another.

"Don't you want breakfast?" he asked.

C.J. gave him a tempting look. She crawled across the bed, the duvet twisted around her like a toga, and clambered onto his lap.

The action had been prompted by lust. The sight of his gleaming body within her reach was too much to resist, but when he wrapped his arms around her and held her securely in his lap a different wave of emotion swept over her. She felt small and safe and cared for. She felt lucky and completely content. Jack planted a kiss on the tip of her nose and she didn't know whether to laugh or cry.

"Thank you for bringing me here," she said, to cover her confusion.

"Thank you for coming," he said, trailing a row of baby kisses along her jaw. He pulled back and looked at her again, the blue of his eyes dark and fascinating to her.

"This is fun," she said.

"And there's even more to come," he said. He rose to his feet and carried her into the bathroom.

That's not what I meant, she thought in frustration. I meant this; us. What about us, Jack?

He switched on the shower and unwrapped her from the duvet.

"After breakfast, we're going hiking."

"What?"

"Relax, it's just the technical term for going for a walk."

PEGGY WAS HAPPY to supply them with a picnic and she even dug out two old rucksacks from a cupboard. C.J. was still dubious about the whole idea of hiking but, as Jack pointed out, she went to the gym and she was supposed to be relatively fit. She wondered if she wasn't seeing a previously unsuspected sadistic side to him.

Luckily he wasn't militant about it and C.J. fell into step easily beside him.

"I used to walk a lot in Italy," she said conversationally.

"I bet you saw some beautiful countryside there," he offered.

C.J. laughed. "Oh, I don't mean pleasant walks through the vineyards or on the beaches. I mean whenever I could grab some time from work I'd walk through the city, just thinking or working off my frustration."

"Didn't you like it there?" he asked.

"Oh, yes, very much. But I was full-time in college, I was working as a hotel chambermaid plus working as a gofer for Versace. Miles from home, new people, a new language, trying to fit in my studies while working thirteen hours a day for a pittance. And Milan is not the place to live on a pittance, let me tell you."

She shook her head, smiling at the memory.

Jack looked concerned. "Was it that bad?"

"It was awful," she said, with a big laugh. "I was terrified of doing the wrong thing, saying the wrong thing, losing my job, failing my exams. But of course it was wonderful, too. I wouldn't have missed it for the world. I was in Italy, mixing with outrageously glamorous people. I made a lot of friends, I spent hours in museums, sketching, and I had tragic, short-lived affairs with tempestuous Italian men. It was an extraordinary experience.''

Jack laughed. "You sound like you're talking about a lifetime ago.''

"It feels like it,'' said C.J., tearing a leaf from a branch that hung out over the road.

"Do you miss it?'' asked Jack.

"Oh, no,'' she said. "I love where I am now. I'm very happy and it's nice to have the experience to look back on.''

"I guess you must think I'm pretty boring, never having traveled much outside the state,'' said Jack with uncharacteristic self-effacement.

She looked at him, feeling annoyed. "How can you say that? Of course I don't. You're one of the most interesting people I know.''

Jack looked unconvinced.

C.J. laughed and gave him a friendly slap on the shoulder. "Oh, stop with the sad eyes. You don't need to fish for compliments.''

He looked at her, eyes wide with innocence.

"You know what I mean,'' she said. "Everywhere we go people are falling over themselves to talk to you. Hey, Jack, how's it hanging? How're things going, Jack? Everybody loves you.''

She laughed at the color rising in his cheeks. "Are you blushing?''

"Do you blame me?'' he mumbled. "You're making me sound like Walt Disney, admired and beloved by all.''

"Well, you are,'' she said.

"Not everybody,'' he muttered.

Tell him, she urged herself, you won't get an opening like this again.

He went on before she could speak. "Who wants to be

loved by everyone anyway? Only people with no person-
alities are loved indiscriminately. I wouldn't mind being
disliked for some of my opinions as long as I believed I
was doing the right thing.''

She smiled at his earnestness. ''Standing up for your
beliefs is a very admirable quality, too, you know.'' She
gave him a cheeky smile. ''Makes me like you even
more.''

His blush deepened and he shook his head as they
walked on.

C.J. spotted a lake near the road and suggested they go
down to it for their picnic. He agreed and they found a
trail that led to the water's edge. When they reached the
shore, C.J. shucked off her backpack and sat gratefully on
a rock. A heron squawked in the distance and there was a
soft chorus of croaking frogs.

She looked up at Jack who was peering at a spot farther
up along the shore.

''What are you looking at?'' she said.

He beckoned her over. ''Look, see the boat?''

She stood beside him. There was a red flat-bottomed
skiff tethered to a small pier about fifty yards away. Behind
it, a small wooden house nestled among the trees.

''Let's go ask if we can borrow it,'' said Jack. ''Do you
want to wait here?''

''No, I'm fine,'' said C.J. ''I'm starving, but I'm fine.''

He helped her put the rucksack back on and she followed him, getting caught up in his spirit of adventure.

A yapping greeted them as they neared the house and a
small wirehaired terrier came rushing out of the under-
growth, frantically wagging its tail.

There was a weatherworn man on the porch, mending a
wooden chair.

Jack fell into easy conversation with him and the man
said they could take out the skiff as long as they took the
dog with them.

Maybe I've just lived in the city too long, thought C.J., maybe people just take to each other more easily in the country.

Or maybe it is just Jack, she thought, as she watched the dog scrambling playfully around his legs, begging for attention.

She settled herself on one of the seats and waved to the man as Jack rowed toward the middle of the lake. The dog scampered past her to stand on the prow, sniffing the wind.

At the middle of the lake, Jack threw out the anchor and they set about having a picnic.

Luckily Peggy had been generous with the food as it was impossible to resist the small dog's pleading brown eyes.

After they'd finished the last of the ham-and-cheese sandwiches and washed down the brownies with a thermos of iced tea, Jack slid off his seat and lay along the bow of the boat, lifting his face to the sun and closing his eyes. C.J. put the empty wrappings back into their rucksacks and pulled an empty potato-chip bag away from the dog.

"No, you've had enough," she said. "You'll only get sick."

There was a shallow basin in the boat, presumably for bailing, and C.J. rinsed it and poured some water for the dog.

"There you go," she said.

Jack watched her through half-closed eyes.

"You've certainly got the mommy behavior down pat anyway," he said.

She gave him a look. "That's a compliment, right?"

He smiled in answer and, after a while, said, "You know, sometimes I worry about you taking all this on, on your own. Don't you worry about being able to cope?"

She tilted her head, absently stroking the slumbering dog.

"I worry about it a normal amount," she said. "But

being on my own isn't one of my concerns. After all, my mother practically raised me on her own and I turned out okay.''

''You think?'' said Jack.

She grinned and aimed a small kick at his leg.

''Yes, buddy, I do.''

''How are you going to explain to him why his parents don't live together?''

She shrugged. ''I'll cross that bridge when I come to it. I'll just explain that we had wanted different things in life or something like that.''

''Sounds kind of weak,'' said Jack bluntly. He paused. ''Hey, maybe we should live together for the sake of the kid, give him some kind of family unit.''

C.J. gave a burst of laughter to cover up her ire. Why did he have to make jokes like that? It was all right for him, he didn't care, but they simply weren't funny to her anymore.

''Now who's being weak?'' she said scathingly. ''You sound like one of the broody males.''

''The what?''

''A broody male,'' she explained. ''Is a man who has reached midthirties or sometimes midforties and decides he wants a kid, or kids. Obviously it's much easier for a woman who becomes broody, she can go out and do it herself. Case in point,'' she said, before Jack could. ''So these men go out and latch on to a woman with kids or a woman in her late thirties who they figure will be getting desperate, without any real regard for the women themselves.''

''And you're saying I'm one of those?'' he asked in outrage.

''I just said you sounded like one, for a minute.''

''That's ridiculous,'' he said. ''I'm not thinking like that at all. Having a kid was all your idea. I didn't even want—''

He broke off abruptly and the silence that hung between them echoed back over the expanse of the lake.

"You don't want a kid, is that what you were going to say?" she asked quietly.

"I was going to say, I *didn't* want a kid," he corrected her. "But now...it's okay if I have one. I mean, if you have one."

Her expression was still cold.

"Besides," he rushed on, "you can't think about backing out now, you might already be pregnant."

"Exactly," she said in a flinty voice. "I might be. And how would you feel then?"

He looked at her steadily. "I'd be happy, C.J., I really would. I'd be absolutely scared out of my wits but I'd be happy."

He caught the hint of a smile on her lips and he pulled himself into a sitting position.

"In fact," he said, giving her a devilish look, "I'm going to prove it to you right now."

He stood up, legs planted surely as the boat swayed.

"Jack," she said, tensing and giving him a warning look. She put her hands out and held the sides of the boat.

"Don't," she pleaded.

The dog woke and jumped to his feet, yapping.

"Come here you sexy love goddess," Jack said, stepping toward her and causing the boat to rock even more precariously.

C.J. squealed despite herself.

Jack grabbed her arm and pulled her toward him.

"I must have you," he growled.

C.J. tried to pull him down and they ended up in a tussled heap at the bow, C.J. laughing breathlessly with relief.

"Ah, you think you're safe now, do you?" Jack murmured, sliding a hand under her T-shirt and around her waist.

She warmed instantly to his touch and their mouths met in a long searching kiss. She leaned into him but as he rolled toward her the boat dipped suddenly again.

C.J. yelped and clutched at the side, pushing Jack off her until the boat was floating level again.

Jack laughed and she looked at him apologetically.

"I really don't feel like a swim right now," she said. "I'm so warm and content and full of food. Please don't tip us."

"Come here," he said, lifting his arm to put it under her head.

She snuggled into him, her head on his chest, one leg draped loosely over his.

The dog had settled after the excitement and fell asleep again, his head resting on C.J.'s foot.

They dozed in the sun as the boat rocked gently over the wind ripples on the lake.

What is it, C.J. thought sleepily, about the proximity of another living creature, that is so comforting? The warmth of another body, the quiet thud of the heartbeat, the slow regular rise and fall of the rib cage. She could feel Jack's breath on her forehead, soft and warm.

An hour passed and the small clouds that had dotted the sky began to thicken. It grew shady and C.J. woke as the temperature dropped.

"What time is it?" she asked Jack.

He checked his watch.

"Four," he said. "What do you want to do?"

Stay here forever, she thought, just sleeping wrapped in your arms.

She shrugged.

"Is there any food left?" he asked.

She shook her head.

Jack lifted his arms above his head, stretched and yawned mightily.

"Are you hungry?" he asked.

"I will be in an hour," she said.

He brought his arms down around her again and held her in a hug, looking down at her.

"I don't want to move," he said, smiling.

She reached up to trace his cheekbone.

"Me, neither."

They kissed slowly. Jack smiled. "They'll find our two skeletons adrift and our names will go down in legend. Grandparents will tell stories around the fire of the couple who were too lazy to move."

They heard a squeaky yawn from the stern and looked down to see the dog stretch and shake himself so vigorously that his hind legs lifted into the air. His tail started to wag and he looked at them eagerly.

Jack and C.J. grinned ruefully at each other.

"So much for having a choice," she said.

He laughed. "Just wait until you have a baby."

She smiled at him, pleased at how easily the words flowed from his lips.

The dog yapped again, bored by their inaction.

They started to move, then bolted upright as the dog jumped overboard with a loud splash. He swam enthusiastically, the little head bobbing on the surface.

"Where's he going?" said C.J., watching him with some trepidation.

"Swimming for shore," said Jack. "Because you were too lazy to row."

She gave him a look and watched as the dog turned and headed back toward the boat.

"Come here, you mad thing," she said, reaching out to pull him in. She couldn't help but smile at the sight of the drenched dog, skinny as a rat under the wet fur. He wriggled out of her grasp and shook himself frenetically, spraying her with water.

"Just row," she said, as Jack snorted with laughter behind her.

AFTER DINNER Peggy invited them to sit out in the large garden at the back of the house, enticing them with the promise of live entertainment. It was a mellow evening, the sun a heavy orange ball in the royal-blue sky. Other guests drifted out to join them and they exchanged stories of their respective weekend activities.

One by one, as promised, the musicians arrived. At first there were only two men with a guitar and an accordian but the volume swelled as others joined them, each new arrival bringing their own unique sound to the widening circle. Eventually there was quite a healthy representation of instruments, from flutes and fiddles, to washboards and accordians.

The styles were also varied. They were treated to rousing Cajun tunes, evocative Gaelic ballads and impromtu fiddle solos. Even though it initially seemed like a free-for-all, C.J. could see that each musician took his turn to start up a melody and the others fell in with him, improvizing and harmonizing.

Peggy brought out hot drinks as dusk approached and switched on the tall garden lamps, creating a warm circle of light around the gathering.

It was impossible not to be swept up in the cheer of it. The musicians teased each other over dropped tunes and people got up to dance. Jack whirled C.J. vigorously in her first polka until she was breathless. When he held her in a slow waltz she closed her eyes and inhaled the night's scent. She felt her eyes mist over as Peggy sang a haunting love song in a crystal-clear soprano voice.

The night wound down slowly as the musicians tired. After the end of their second encore they laughingly packed away their instruments and told the guests they'd have to come back next week if they wanted more.

Jack and C.J. went to their room, C.J. still humming to herself. Jack switched on the bedside lamps while C.J. stood at the window, looking down on the last of the men as they snapped shut music cases and walked off, talking and laughing.

Jack came up behind her and she leaned back against him.

"Thank you for this weekend, Jack, it was amazing."

"I'm glad," he said. "We don't make such a bad couple, do we?" He was amazed at how nervous it made him to say the words out loud.

"No," she said softly. She turned in his arms and looked up at him.

"C.J.—"

"Jack—"

They both smiled and urged the other to speak first. Jack took a breath but was cut off by the sound of beeping from C.J.'s bag.

She looked down at it. "I must have a message, on my voice mail." She chewed her lip anxiously.

"Go on," he said. "You can check it."

She didn't move, just looked up at him, her forehead creased in indecision. "It must be something important," she said. "Otherwise no one would be bothering me."

He gave her a little push toward the bag. "Go on," he said, shaking his head in mock frustration.

He went to the bathroom and brushed his teeth while she listened to the message. He was relieved to see that she was looking happy when he came back out.

"Guess what?" she said gleefully, rubbing her hands in excitement.

Before he had a chance to speak she was talking again, blurting out the news. "*Vogue* are doing a spread on me, I mean, on my shoes. Eight pages! Can you believe it?"

"Of course I can, you're amazing," he said, making her laugh. She hugged herself and wiggled her shoulders triumphantly, her eyes shining. He smiled at the sight of her, she was glowing with happiness.

"It's great news, C.J.," he said.

"Oh, Jack," she said, regret rising in her eyes, "I'm sorry to do this, but I have to call Lex. He left that message hours ago and he'll be going out of his mind. We're going to be up the walls with this, every minute is precious."

He fought down the urge to fling the phone out of the window and gave her a supportive hug instead.

"We can have another weekend sometime," she said, in a tone that was halfway between hopeful and placating.

"Sure," he said. He smoothed the worried lines from her brow and gave her a reassuring smile before going to bed alone. He tried to stay awake until she joined him but the last thing he saw before sleep overtook him was C.J. curled up in an armchair, muttering softly on the phone and making notes.

11

"ARE YOU EVER going to throw these out?" asked Kerry, fingering one of the wilted roses gingerly. She pulled her hand back guiltily as another petal dropped off. "I'm sorry, but having a bunch of stalks on your desk is just not cool. They're going to start rotting soon."

"I know," sighed C.J. "Go ahead, you dump them."

"You should press some of the petals," said Kerry. "You can keep them that way."

"I already did," said C.J. "From the first two that wilted. Then I realized I was being obsessive and I quit it."

Kerry took the lifeless roses, snapped them in half and crunched them into the garbage.

"Thanks," said C.J. She closed her eyes and rubbed a hand across her face. She scrunched up her nose and let out a huge yawn.

"How's it going?" asked Kerry.

"I feel like I'm producing a movie or something, not just sorting out an eight-page spread. At the moment the problem is the photographer."

When she was first starting out in the business, C.J. would have been naive enough to believe that if the photo spread was about shoes, then shoes would be the main focus of attention. Her experiences since those days had taught her that any space in a fashion magazine was seen as a personal showcase by anyone involved, however peripherally. The models, the makeup artists and photographer were all anxious to display their prowess, to shine, their names to be noted and remembered. And the more well-known a model or photographer was, the more important it became that theirs was by far the most notable contribution to the spread.

"What's wrong with the photographer?" asked Kerry.

C.J. gave a martyred sigh. "They've set me up with Ally Fisher and I hate her work, all those out-of-focus shots, it's rubbish."

She slid a folder of photographs across the desk to Kerry.

"This one is pretty good," said Kerry, picking a color shot out of the bunch.

It was of a foot landing in a puddle, throwing up a bowl-shaped spray of water, which glinted with reflected light.

C.J. looked over at the photograph.

"What color is the shoe?"

"Mmm, green? No, brown. It's kind of hard to tell."

She looked up to see C.J. nodding, point made.

"What are you going to do?"

"Oh, it's simple. All I have to do is find a photographer whom *Vogue* will consider an upgrade from Ally, their flavor of the month. It's so annoying. I can think of ten unknowns who would do a better job than her but *Vogue* won't even consider them. I have to find a name who's willing to do me a favor."

They looked up as Lex came in.

"Salina Buñuel's agent called and she can give you two days. Should I get her foot?"

"That's brilliant, Lex, thanks. Book her for next week and tell Anna to do the boots."

He bustled out again and C.J. rubbed her hands together. "That's good news," she said. "There was a mix-up with the leather needed for a pair of nude boots and they sent me umber instead of biscuit."

"The nude boots are those really soft ones that are like stockings with five-inch heels, right?"

"Right," said C.J. "But you can't put umber on a pale-skinned girl, it just looks awful, so I had to get a new model and struck gold with Buñuel, she's a gorgeous Brazilian. So now we've just got to get the boots made in time."

She rubbed her neck. "All the other shoes are made, so no problems there unless we have to change models."

"You made them to fit specific models?" asked Kerry in surprise.

"Yes," said C.J. "There's nothing worse than looking at a gap behind the model's heel, it looks so shoddy."

"You are such a perfectionist," said Kerry. "Have you had a chance to see lover boy at all since your weekend in the country?"

"Don't call him that," said C.J., smirking to herself and glancing at her desk calendar.

Kerry reached across the desk and picked up the calendar, which had the next day circled in red.

"Dare I ask if this is D day?" she said.

"Yup," said C.J. "It's due tomorrow. And I have to say, even though I'm not thinking about it at all, that I have had no symptoms of PMS whatsoever."

Kerry looked up at her. "You're not thinking about it?"

"Not at all," C.J. assured her. "If it happens, it happens. If not, whatever, no big deal."

"No big deal because you'll get to sleep with him again right?" said Kerry, looking at the calendar.

"Not necessarily," said C.J.

Kerry didn't react, just continued to peruse the calendar.

"Well, yes," admitted C.J. She folded her arms and leaned forward on the desk, curious. "What are you looking at?"

"Ssh," said Kerry. Another moment passed and C.J.

was about to go back to her work when Kerry held up the calendar, facing C.J.

"You've circled tomorrow, right?" she asked.

"Well done," said C.J. "You can read dates."

Kerry pointed to a Sunday of the previous month. "And this is the last day you got it?"

"Uh-huh."

"So, you're waiting thirty days before you check?"

C.J. peered at the calendar. "No, that's twenty-nine days. I'm waiting twenty-nine days, just to be sure."

"No, tomorrow's the thirtieth day," repeated Kerry.

"What! That means it was due over two days ago. I should have checked this morning." She wrenched open a drawer in her desk and grabbed the pregnancy test. Kerry got up to follow but C.J. stopped her. "No, if we both go rushing to the bathroom they'll know something is up."

Kerry whined like a puppy before slumping back into her chair.

C.J. rushed out the door.

"Nope, not thinking about it at all," Kerry said to herself with a smile.

C.J. CAME BACK into the room with an absolutely blank expression on her face.

"Well?" demanded Kerry.

C.J. didn't say anything and Kerry glared at her as she walked toward her desk.

"Tell me, tell me!"

C.J. sat down and looked across at her with a placid expression.

"You are, right? You're pregnant? Or not? You're not? Tell me, tell me, tell me!"

C.J. spoke in a calm voice. "What's that phrase they use when they score in football?"

Kerry's synapses buzzed with lightning speed as she interpreted the question. Her eyes lit up. "Touchdown!" she roared. "Woo-hoo!"

"Ssh," hissed C.J., laughing.

"Are you serious?" said Kerry. "Let me see the test."

She recoiled as C.J. held out the little plastic stick.

"Eeuw, I don't want to touch it, just show it to me."

C.J. held it up, her hand jittering like crazy, while Kerry read the result for herself.

"Wow," she breathed.

"I know," said C.J. Her mind was a daze. "Do you want to feel it?"

Kerry played along, putting her hand on C.J.'s flat stomach. "I felt it kick," she squealed.

C.J. squealed, too, and then her shoulders began to shake.

"Oh, come here, honey," said Kerry, laughing.

C.J. buried her face in Kerry's shoulder as sobs wracked her. She lifted her head eventually and patted her pockets. Kerry pulled a packet of tissues from her bag and handed them to her.

"Better now?" she asked.

C.J. blew her nose and nodded as the last of the sobs shuddered through her.

"I'm so happy. I just can't believe it." She looked up at Kerry. "Do I look pregnant?"

"Yeah," laughed Kerry, taking in C.J.'s joyful expression behind the red nose and watery eyes.

"PUT HIM ON SPEAKER," said Kerry. "I want to hear it."

C.J. put down the phone and chewed at her lip. "I'm going to wait," she said. "I'm going to wait until I'm sure."

"No, call him now," urged Kerry.

"Stop it, you're supposed to be my friend." C.J. pushed the phone away from her. "I'm not calling him now. No way. I'm going to wait a few days and then go to a doctor. I'll have to be sure.''

"I guess," said Kerry reluctantly. "But promise me you won't tell him without me.''

C.J. gave her a level look. "Forget it, I don't want you leering at me during one of the most important moments of my life.''

"I know, you're right," said Kerry. "Can I tell Anoushka and Lex?''

"No, you can't tell them. In the first place, you can't tell anyone until I've told Jack and in the second place, you can't tell them anyway, they're my employees.''

Kerry pooched out her lip. "You're a mean mommy," she said, earning herself a glare.

"BILLY'S CONVERSATION these days," said Mr. Chadwick, "is so one-track. I've heard more about cars and airplanes in this past six months than in my whole life." He gave Jack a small smile then grew serious again. "The thing is, Billy's an extremely bright boy and my wife and I have always intended that he go to medical school and become a doctor. We feel he should be studying harder and cutting down on his extracurricular activities.''

The man looked down at his hands, twisting in each other. "I know this will be difficult for him and that's why I've come to talk to you Mr. Harding—''

"Please, call me Jack.''

"Uh, Jack. You understand that we want the best for Billy, and maybe it would be easier for him to give this up if you were to encourage him.''

Jack could see that the man's heart was in the right place, but he couldn't stand by and let Billy be steamrolled into something he didn't really want to do. He knew Billy would put aside his own wishes in order to please his parents, but he also knew that in the long-term it would only drive a wedge of resentment between them.

He had already had this conversation with Billy's dad on the phone but he had invited him down to the garage to make one last effort.

He led Mr. Chadwick into the corner of the garage where Billy had set up his own workstation. Well-oiled tools hung in brackets on the wall next to flight maps. The worktable was covered with pages and pages of calculations and diagrams.

"I'm not trying to tell you how to raise your son," said Jack, "but I just wanted you to see that being a mechanic these days doesn't necessarily mean being a low-paid grease monkey. Billy's one of the most natural drivers I've ever seen. He has that instinctive feel for it that can't be taught. He sits in and becomes part of the car, and if I were to teach him to fly it would be the same thing." Jack thought it best not to mention the lessons he'd already given the boy. "He has learned stuff that it would take years to teach others. And he's equally competent with the technical side of it."

Billy's father looked at the neat, organized desk, and at the textwork he couldn't understand.

"If you tell him to study medicine he will," said Jack, "and he might be a good doctor, but if you let him do this, I guarantee he'll be a leader in the field. He could be a designer or an engineer or even just a pilot."

Mr. Chadwick looked over and met Jack's eyes. He gave a small smile. "I guess my wife would be happy with 'just' a pilot," he said.

"WHAT WAS THAT ABOUT?" asked Eddie. He had driven into the yard as Billy's dad drove away.

"I think things might be better for Billy from now on," said Jack, folding his arms and inflating his chest with pride.

"Really?" said Eddie. "That's great. I'm getting kinda

used to having the little tyke around. You're not so bad at this dad thing after all."

Jack looked uncomfortable.

"What?" said Eddie.

"I don't know if I am," said Jack.

"Oh, don't worry. It's not that bad. By the time you get to the third you can do it blindfolded, I've heard."

When Jack still didn't laugh Eddie looked over at him in consternation.

"What's up?" He hadn't seen Jack looking this unhappy in a long time.

"This whole thing," said Jack, "It's gotten out of hand."

"What do you mean?"

"I'm not sure. I don't know how to explain it. It's just too much, or too little. It's just no good, I don't think I can go on with it."

"What? The baby thing?"

"All of it," said Jack, throwing his arms in the air. "I mean, it's crazy. I'm supposed to be making a child but not caring for it afterward. C.J. and I are supposed to be just friends but we're having sex. We're having sex but we're not supposed to be in love. The whole thing's a mess, and I can't do it anymore."

"I thought things had never been better with you, you've been walking on air for weeks. I don't get it."

"But what happens when she gets pregnant, what then?"

"Well, then you'll probably see her even more. You'll be tied together. Is that what's bothering you? Being tied down?"

Jack looked at his brother, trying to make him understand his frustration.

"No, not at all. Don't you get it? It's the not being tied down I can't stand. I want to be with her. I only want to be with her."

Eddie nodded, as if he'd known this was coming all along. "So when did you figure it out?"

"I don't know," said Jack. "Maybe just now, maybe always." He looked up at Eddie and shrugged. "It's a pain in the ass, frankly."

Eddie laughed. "Hey, it's nothing to get upset about. You had to bite the dust sometime. So, when are you going to tell her?"

Jack looked down at his hands with an air of sadness that hurt Eddie to see.

"What's the point? She doesn't care."

"What do you mean?"

"How much plainer can I put it? She doesn't feel the same way."

"And you know this for a fact, do you?"

Jack didn't look up. "Yeah."

"You're absolutely, one-hundred-percent sure she has no feelings for you?"

Jack looked annoyed. "Of course she has feelings for me. She cares for me, she thinks I'm a great guy, she thinks I'm highly qualified as a sperm donor."

They heard the phone in the office ringing. Jack didn't budge. "They'll call back."

A few moments later Eddie's phone trilled.

"Must be Mom," said Eddie, answering it.

"Oh, hey, C.J.," he said, widening his eyes at Jack who shook his head.

"Uh, no, I dunno where he is, did you try the garage?", he said, giving a thumbs-up to Jack who rolled his eyes.

"Well, maybe he's gone on a flight. I'll probably see him later, you want me to give him a message?"

C.J. didn't answer for so long that Eddie thought they'd been cut off.

"C.J.? Hello?" he said. "Oh…okay…sure, I'll tell him."

He hung up and met Jack's curious stare.

"That was a bit strange," said Eddie. "She said to tell you to give her a call but she said it's not urgent, and she said to make sure and tell you that it's not any major news. What's that about?"

Jack counted mentally and then nodded. "It means she's not pregnant." He sighed. "I guess that's that then. A clean ending."

"An ending? What are you talking about?"

"I'm going to call her and tell her I don't want to do this anymore. Just tell her the truth."

"You're going to tell her you love her?"

Jack looked mutinous. "She already knows that, she'd have to be blind not to. I'm not going to make a total fool of myself. I'm just going to end it. It's too hard for me this way."

"I wish you'd think about it some more. You're just getting an attack of cold feet, it's just a mood you're in."

"No, I think I've been lucky that she didn't get pregnant. I've realized that I couldn't stand it. It's bad enough that she's out there, walking around, and I can't have her but at least if I don't have to see her I can get on with my life. This is really hard enough, Eddie, I couldn't stand it if we had a child. What if she got married or something? No, I'm going to end it now, while I still can."

He got up and walked toward the garage.

C.J. PUT DOWN the phone. She hoped she hadn't betrayed herself while talking to Eddie. She wanted to hear Jack's reaction firsthand and she didn't want Eddie giving him any clues.

Darn him, anyway. She'd been planning this phone call for days, playing it over and over in her head. She was finding it harder to concentrate on work, the secret taking up all her brain, bursting to be told.

Then the phone rang and she picked it up hopefully.

"Hello?"

"Hi, it's Jack."

A smile spread across her face but she tried to keep it out of her voice. "You got my message."

"Yeah, Eddie told me."

"I'm glad you called," she said, still grinning. Now that she had him on the phone she wanted to delay the moment of telling him. She knew it would change things forever between them and she wanted to savor each moment before she imparted her precious news. She also felt very calm, sure of her love for him.

"So, how are you?" she said.

There was a pause before he answered. "I'm fine. How is your magazine thing going?"

"We're still in the middle of it," she said. "Total pandemonium as expected, but it will be worth it." She bit her lip to stop another giggle escaping. Enough playing around, she would have to tell him.

"There's something I want to talk to you about, C.J."

"What is it?" she asked, hoping everyone in his family was all right.

Again there was a pause and then C.J. heard him mutter, "This is harder than I thought it would be."

"Jack, what's wrong?" she said, a dark shadow of apprehension creeping across her heart.

"I've been thinking, C.J., about a lot of things, and I just don't think I can go on with this." He waited but there was no response from her so he blundered on. "I know you'll probably be mad, or upset, I don't know, but I just can't...do this. I know my doubts are just going to get bigger and bigger and ignoring them won't be any good for either of us. I'm really sorry, C.J., I hope you can understand."

C.J. felt as though someone was choking her. Her hand gripped the edge of the desk and she swallowed dryly. Her thoughts were in a tumult. Tell him, one voice urged, tell him it's too late for cold feet, he'll have to be happy anyway. I can't tell him, another part of her said, I can't tell him now.

Jack broke the silence. "C.J.?" he said softly.

"I'm here," she said.

"Are you all right?"

She didn't answer. Tears started in her eyes and she began to shake her head slowly. She put her hand up to cover her mouth.

"I'm so sorry, C.J.," Jack said again. "I'm just not ready. It just…it wouldn't work."

His words sank slowly, poisonously into her brain. He wasn't just talking about the pregnancy issue, he was talking about them. Her heart grew cold and the prevailing thought in her head was that she had to get off the phone. She drew in a breath slowly and, mustering every shred of willpower, she spoke evenly.

"I see. This is…this is a bit of a surprise but I appreciate your candor." Her lip curled in disgust at the words she was speaking. "I guess that's it then."

"Are you going to be all right?"

A shiver of pain ran through her. She almost told him about the baby, their baby, but a protective seed of anger held her tongue.

"I'm sorry, Jack, I have to go now, things are very busy here."

"I'll give you a call sometime," said Jack, cringing at the sound of the cliché.

"I don't think that's a good idea," she said coldly. She put the phone down and folded her arms, curling her shoulders and rocking in the seat as anguish overwhelmed her.

NOW THAT IT WAS DONE Jack couldn't believe that it was over so simply. His stomach was knotted and he felt slightly stunned, blindsided by the outcome. The hurt in her voice had bruised his heart and his instinct was to call her back but he decided it would only make things worse. He held the phone in his hand for a moment more before eventually putting it down.

12

_____

IT WAS RELATIVELY EASY for C.J. to avoid thinking about Jack for the first few months because she spent every spare moment sleeping.

She arrived home from work and collapsed on the couch for a nap that generally lasted until about ten o'clock, at which point she had something to eat, usually toast and marmalade, before going to bed.

Her doctor assured her this was normal, even though it was astonishing to C.J. who had never even considered that it was possible to sleep so much. She also had perpetually incipient morning sickness. She never actually got sick, just felt green about the gills all day.

Her breasts felt heavy and tender and, seemingly overnight, had swelled two sizes. She often got delayed in the bathroom in the mornings because she thought her voluptuousness in her regular T-shirts bordered on the unseemly.

She could only manage to eat fruit, soup or bread during the day. She automatically went off coffee and the smell of alcohol, which she thought she'd miss, made her stomach flip right over.

The *Vogue* spread was a huge success. C.J. had secured the services of Alex Rook, a young photographer and media darling by promising to make size-sixteen shoes for all his drag-queen friends. *Vogue* had been thrilled, Ally Fisher had been dumped, the models shone under Alex's touch and Sabres' sales figures had skyrocketed.

C.J. had to send a box of the specific edition to her

mother who wanted to give one to everyone she knew. It also helped to explain why she was too busy to visit her mother just at the moment.

And then one morning, just as the doctor and Kerry had promised, she felt fine. And not just fine, she started to feel all the things she'd been promised. She felt stronger and her skin was like a baby's, soft and creamy and elastic. Her appetite returned with a vengeance and she ate with impunity because she was supposed to be putting on weight. Delighted that she had her energy back, she spent every spare moment preparing for the new arrival.

So she was at home when Jack called. She was putting the last coat of varnish on an old crib she'd found in the junk room of an antique shop. After sanding off the thick layers of magnolia paint and staining the wood underneath she'd applied a decoupage pattern of flowers on the little headboard. The effect was very pleasing and she was chatting to her stomach about the possibility of decoupage shoes when the phone rang.

"Hello?" she said, absently tucking the phone under her chin and surveying her work proudly.

"Hi, what are you up to?" came the familiar tones.

Her heart seized as if he'd reached down the phone line and grabbed it.

"Uh...hello," she said. "Who is this?"

Silence followed and she bit her lip, thinking she'd gone too far.

"Okay," he said at last. "I'm going to assume I deserved that. Is there anything else I can say or do to make this easier?"

"Make what easier?" she asked warily.

"I'm trying to make friends with you again, C.J. I thought maybe I could just forget about us and everything and that would be the easiest, but...I don't want to lose you. This is exactly what we didn't want to happen, isn't it? Can't we get back to normal? Back to how things were?''

Elation flowed unbidden through C.J.'s veins. He wanted her back. He'd realized what a terrible mistake he'd made, her absence had revealed it, and now he wanted her back. Wow, was he going to be surprised at the news she had for him. But she'd have to lead up to it slowly.

"Back to how things were?" she said, wanting to hear him say the words.

"Yeah, back to where we started," he said. "We were friends, C.J. I know a lot happened and there's bound to be some awkwardness between us but can't we be friends again?"

C.J. stared, unfocused, at the wall.

"Friends," she said dully.

"Yeah," he said. "I thought maybe you'd like to come up for a day, go for another flight, and you know, the air show will be coming up—"

"I have enough friends," she said abruptly, hanging up.

JACK TOOK THE SOUND like a blow. He stared at the phone, considered redialing, then cursed under his breath and shook his head. He'd blown it. He'd been trying to be nonthreatening, trying not to pressure her and he'd ended up sounding like some pathetic teenager, asking the prom queen out.

Now, just like some young kid, his stomach hurt. C.J. didn't want him. She didn't need him. She'd just needed one thing and when he couldn't provide it, he was no use to her.

C.J. STARED AT the crib, clenching her jaw angrily. Kerry was always telling her about words that had been coined through use on the Internet, like *umfriend*, Kerry's favorite, a word for when people were introducing someone that they might or might not be sleeping with, as in "This is

Jay, my um…friend.'' To C.J.'s infuriation, Kerry used these made-up words in conversation and they were becoming stuck in C.J.'s subconscious.

The word that surfaced now was *anticipointment*. So much worse than garden-variety disappointment because you'd been anticipating something, actually wanting it so badly that it felt like a double blow, a fall twice as far when you didn't get it.

C.J. felt sick. She'd almost convinced herself that she didn't want Jack anymore, that she had, in fact, ended up with exactly what she'd planned all along.

A baby, and no strings.

Until he'd called and she'd felt the blood like fire running through her veins, making her heart ache for him.

She looked sullenly at the phone. She was glad she hadn't called him. She didn't care if he never found out. He didn't deserve to know. Let him hear about it from one of the neighbors, let him think it was someone else's baby. She didn't care. She hoped she'd never see him again.

UNFORTUNATELY, since C.J. was now in her second trimester and feeling human again, Kerry had decided it was time to redouble her efforts to persuade C.J. to call both her mother and Jack.

"I know you're scared,'' she said.

"Can we talk about this after class?'' said C.J., putting on a cotton jersey over her T-shirt.

"You always want to talk about it some other time,'' complained Kerry. "I can never pin you down.''

C.J. glared at her. "Well, I sure don't want to talk about it before yoga class, I can tell you that much.''

"I'm just saying this could be something you really regret when you look back on it, sometime when you're less hormonal—''

"I'm not hormonal! This is me, C.J., saying I don't want to see him. Now, let it go.''

She went out of the dressing room and some of the other women gave Kerry supportive grins.

"Just imagine what she was like before she started doing yoga," muttered Kerry.

The classes had been Kerry's idea, who had herself been convinced to start them when she was pregnant. The teacher kept an eye on C.J., telling her what postures she should or shouldn't do. There was one other pregnant woman in the small class of twenty and the sight of her in a shoulder stand with her huge belly hanging over her was something to behold.

In the beginning C.J. was mortified by how inflexible she was. She'd always considered herself fit but on the first day, as they all sat on their mats, she couldn't even bring her chest to her knees while others splayed their legs and lowered their torsos to the ground.

"Imagine having a pelvis that loose in the delivery room," Kerry had whispered.

C.J. had vowed to continue with the classes.

As the weeks progressed and she stuck religiously to her twenty minutes in the morning and evenings, she found herself becoming stronger and more supple without even thinking about it.

She loved being aware of her body as it changed. The yoga exercises helped her digestion and posture and it also amused her to look forward to the day when she could meditate like a smiling Buddha, with a big round protruding belly.

Although she kept a resolute face to Kerry, C.J. was in some turmoil over Jack. Sometimes she caught herself staring at the phone. Surely she had to tell him? He would find out eventually, she wasn't fooling herself that it would remain a secret forever, but she had a vague fantasy that maybe it could be avoided for a few years, until scars had formed over the wounds on her heart left by his sudden departure.

She almost didn't know which was more of a burden on her, that she hadn't told Jack, or that she hadn't told her mother.

For the first time in her life C.J. had become a procrastinator. Every few days she would tell herself that something had to be done. She would tell her mother and since her mother would spread the news proudly like wildfire, C.J. would have to tell Jack. And that's where her resolve crumbled.

As much as she told herself that his reaction didn't matter—after all, she'd always intended to go this alone—she couldn't stand the thought of his voice turning cold on the phone, or dutifully telling her he would stand by her.

She simply didn't know how he'd react and every time she tried to gather her courage she ended up throwing her hands in the air in dismay and telling herself she would, probably, handle it next week.

"PICK UP, PICK UP, PICK UP, I know you're there," the voice trilled from the answering machine.

C.J. blew her nose and reached over for the phone.

"Hi," she said halfheartedly.

"Well, how did it go?" asked Kerry.

C.J. squirmed. "Fine, she was very happy."

"Oh, you liar," said Kerry. "You didn't tell her."

"It's hard to find the right words," said C.J.

"What about 'Hi mom, I'm four months pregnant,' what about those words?"

C.J. sniffed and wiped her nose again. "I have a new idea. How about I tell her I just found out I'm pregnant and then when I have the baby I'll just say it's premature."

"Five months premature," said Kerry drily.

C.J. sighed and sniffed again.

"Are you crying?" asked Kerry.

"Oh, there's this commercial on television, the family forgot to let the dog in and it's started raining, he's getting all wet.'' Another sob caught in her throat and Kerry laughed heartlessly.

"Hey, can I come over? I mean, are you doing anything besides crying at bad commercials and screening your calls?''

"No, why?''

"Oh, I'm just bored. Brian's on a sleepover. I'll see you in a while.''

"Hey, Kerry?''

"What?''

"Will you call my mom for me?''

Kerry hung up and C.J. started crying again because the family had brought the dog in and were drying him with soft fluffy towels.

"I COME BEARING GIFTS,'' said Kerry, handing C.J. a large shopping bag as she came in.

C.J.'s eyes widened. "Oh, Kerry, you didn't have to.''

"Please don't start crying again,'' said Kerry. "It was on sale.''

"I wonder why,'' said C.J. as she pulled out an outfit made of black leatherette.

"It's a pregnant Catwoman suit, isn't it cool?''

"You're kidding me,'' said C.J.

"Try it on.''

"I don't think so.''

"I thought you were on the lookout for groovy clothes.''

"Clothes that I can wear outside, in daylight,'' said C.J., laughing as she settled herself back on the couch.

"How are you feeling?'' asked Kerry.

"Pretty good. Still getting a bit of heartburn sometimes but I'm sleeping well.''

Kerry put her hand on C.J.'s stomach. "Is she kicking much?''

C.J. smiled. She wouldn't let the doctor tell her the sex,

she wanted it to be a surprise, so she and Kerry alternated genders when they were talking about the baby.

"Mostly when I'm just about ready to go to sleep. Oh, and I'm getting that strange people-touching-me thing you were talking about. A lady in the bus yesterday started feeling me and said, 'Oooh, what is it?'"

Kerry smiled widely. "Tell me you told her it was a roast chicken."

"It was tempting," admitted C.J. with a grin. "But she was just being nice. I still find it weird when people rub me, though."

"I was the same," said Kerry. "But then when you're wheeling him around in the park you can't wait for people to stop and admire him." She looked seriously at C.J. "You have to call your mother tonight. I'll help you. This is really not fair on her."

C.J. met her eyes. "Pass me the phone," she said, squaring her shoulders.

C.J. HUNG UP an hour later. The conversation had been as draining as expected.

Her mother was initially elated at the news, even more so when C.J. had revealed Jack as the father but then confusion had taken over as the full story unfurled.

Four months! her mother had shrieked, unable to believe that C.J. had waited so long to tell her, leaving C.J. feeling overcome with remorse.

Then her mother had insisted that C.J. tell Jack. Although they argued about it for some time, her mother had eventually agreed that it was C.J.'s decision to make, but every word of praise she had for Jack only increased C.J.'s yearning for him.

Inevitably, the joy of the news prevailed over everything and C.J. quickly realized how much she'd missed out by not sharing the experience with the woman who'd given birth to her. Her mother had accepted the invitation to come to the city almost before the words were out of C.J.'s mouth. C.J. knew it wasn't like she had a choice in the matter.

It had been an emotion-laden phone call and C.J. was grateful that Kerry was there with her when it was over.

"What about calling Jack now?" said Kerry gently.

"Boy, you are one demanding woman," said C.J. "Haven't I had enough catharsis for one night?"

Kerry looked at her. "I just hate to see you carrying the worry of it around. Every day you don't tell him it gets a little bigger and heavier. Don't you think it outweighs the potential awfulness of his reaction by now?"

C.J. rested her head back, gazing reflectively at the candle flickering on the coffee table. Sometimes she didn't know whether she loved Kerry more for her crazy dress sense and smart mouth or for her compassionate perception.

"You know, I wish I'd listened to you a few months ago. I feel like it's too late now."

"I know. But you don't want to be saying the same thing two months, or six months, or a year from now."

"I wish I'd confronted him before I started showing. I wish I'd gone and met him and just talked to him. Found out what was really going on."

"Is he still sending flowers?"

"Not lately."

Kerry indicated the phone. "But you're still screening calls?"

C.J. smiled sadly.

"That's more of a hopeful ritual than anything else. He hasn't tried to contact me for weeks."

"Do you miss him?"

C.J. didn't speak. Her lip quivered and she stared at the table, fighting the tears. Funny thing about crying, she could bawl her eyes out at a sad movie but she was terrified of letting one tear fall for Jack because she thought if she started she might never stop.

"I feel like there isn't any way that he'll be able to see me now." C.J. tapped her finger on her breastbone. "I mean, just see me, C.J., by myself. That time is gone. To him, I'll only ever be the mother of his child. I can never ask him, Jack, how do you feel about me?"

"Sure you can, over the phone."

"Yeah, and what if he says he wants me and I turn up on his doorstep, barefoot and pregnant? I'll feel like I tricked him."

"I'm sure he'll be happy."

"And what if, on the phone, he says he doesn't want me and then I show up in Ashfield with a baby, I'll feel like some kind of blackmailer."

Kerry looked at her friend, gauging her strength.

"You might not get the relationship you want with Jack but you can't deny him his relationship with his own child."

C.J. closed her eyes and pushed her head back against the couch. Kerry could see the tendons in her neck twitching.

"I know," C.J. said quietly. "But not tonight."

HER MOTHER, having come for a week, stayed for six. C.J. was glad of the distraction and found that her mother integrated herself very easily into life in the city. They went shopping and spent time in museums. They went to movies and dinner, and her mother persuaded her to visit some of the sights that C.J., as a jaded New Yorker, hadn't got around to before. They talked late into the night, sharing pregnancy anecdotes and it was a relief to have someone around who kept the apartment clean on those days when C.J. just couldn't face it.

Like Kerry, her mother sometimes nagged C.J. to call Jack but, like Kerry, on that issue she was ignored.

THEN THE FALL was upon them and work took precedence again. C.J. was justifiably proud of her new collection after all the hours of painstaking work that had gone into it and she had the money to throw an extravagant show, which she enjoyed being the star of, even though she didn't go quite as far as wearing the plastic cat suit. Once again the orders flooded in and they got back to the day-to-day routine, leaving C.J. plenty of time to concentrate on the pregnancy.

"WE SHOULD CELEBRATE," said Lex. "We should all go out."

C.J. laughed and Kerry looked up in amusement.

"We should go out to dinner because Fran Drescher was in the shop?" teased C.J. "She didn't even buy anything."

Lex put his hand over his heart. "I think she'll be back. I can feel it."

C.J.'s smile widened. "Whatever you say, Lex."

"Oh, come on, we have to do something to mark the occasion. Let's go to dinner. C.J.'s treat."

Kerry laughed. "Thanks, C.J., I'm in."

Lex looked at C.J. "Say yes. You can pretend we're celebrating your rotundity if you like."

C.J.'s nostrils flared as she tried not to laugh.

At seven months she was really beginning to balloon, her waist swelled by the day instead of by the week, and the baby, be it boy or girl, definitely had a pair of athlete's legs. She had nearly become accustomed to the idea of herself as a single mother, though she'd become increasingly grateful for the strong support of her friends.

Kerry got to her feet. "It's a great idea. Tell Anoushka. Let's go somewhere posh and French."

"Ugh," said Lex. "Let's not. There's a fabulous new seafood place in the east village."

"No, seafood's out," said Kerry.

"Why?"

Kerry pointed at C.J. "She's allergic."

Lex looked over at C.J. indignantly. "You're allergic to seafood? How come I didn't know this, how could you not tell me?"

C.J. shrugged.

"Haven't you ever heard the shellfish story?" asked Kerry.

"What shellfish story?" asked Lex.

"We don't have time for it now," said C.J. with forced joviality. "Let's go if we're going."

"No, I want to tell it," said Kerry. "It's a great story."

C.J. looked weary. "Oh, I don't want to hear it again, it's not that funny."

Lex looked fascinated. "I want to hear it, I do."

C.J. busied herself with her coat while Kerry was speaking.

"It happened after some ball game or something when C.J. was in school, she was thirteen. Her mom couldn't pick her up so she got a lift with one of her friends, and the friend's mother said, come in for a snack and then I'll drop you home. So they go in and have some sandwiches and soda and the mother says, here are some mini crabcakes left over from dinner last night, try one."

Lex looked over at C.J. who was trying to look like she was enjoying herself.

"C.J.'s allergic to shellfish but she thought it'd be rude to refuse, so she decided to have one and then go to the bathroom and put her finger in her throat, and throw up before there's any harm done."

Lex wrinkled his nose at C.J. "Oh, right, that's so much more polite."

She poked the tip of her tongue out at him.

"Anyway," said Kerry, "she eats the crabcake and goes to the bathroom and tries to throw up but, of course, she starts having an allergic reaction, so she runs to the door but can't open it, so she starts banging on it. The mother comes running and opens the door to find C.J. on the floor, her face all swollen up.''

Lex was staring at Kerry, pop-eyed.

''So they whisk her off to the hospital and save her life, major drama.''

''Oh, you crazy person,'' said Lex, looking at C.J. She was staring down at her desk and didn't answer.

''Your friend must have been delighted,'' said Lex, trying to lighten the tension that had crept into the room. ''Keeling over at her mother's cooking.''

''His mother's cooking,'' C.J. corrected him quietly. ''It was a he.''

The look on C.J.'s face immediately told Kerry something she hadn't known before and filled in a blank.

''I didn't know it was Jack,'' Kerry said, cursing herself silently. ''You never—''

''It doesn't matter,'' replied C.J. She looked up and gave them a reassuring smile. ''I'm sorry. The old hormones are acting up again. Come on, let's go to dinner.''

''Maybe if you only had half a crabcake this time,'' said Lex as they left the office. ''That might be all right.''

She shoved him affectionately.

13

"ARE YOU SURE it's ready?" asked Eddie.

"Ready as it'll ever be," said Jack. "The airspeed indicator is still broken but I think I'll manage without it."

He rolled his eyes at Eddie's alarmed face. "I'm kidding, everything's fine. You sure you don't want to come up with me?"

"Forget it," said Eddie. "You're doing this one on your own." He wiped Eddie Jr.'s face clean of cotton candy and sent him running back to Donna, who had positioned their picnic blanket strategically upwind of the row of planes, which were running as pilots ran checks on their engines. There was a huge turnout of both pilots and spectators for the air show. It occurred to Jack that C.J. wouldn't have recognized it as the same little airfield, crowded as it was with families picnicking, food stalls and children running excitedly among the variety of small planes.

Eddie looked back in time to catch Jack scanning the crowd again.

"Are you looking for someone in particular?" he said.

"Very funny," said Jack.

"Did you even ask her to come?"

"Yeah, I called her about it last month and left a message. She doesn't seem to be answering her phone these days," he added drily. "Anyway, she didn't call back."

"Ouch," said Eddie.

Jack exhaled in frustration.

''It's like we've never even met now,'' he said. ''Actually, it's worse. It's like we've met and I sold her a bad car or something, she really seems to dislike me.''

''You can't mix friendship with love,'' said Eddie sagely. ''It's always a mistake, always going to result in disaster.''

He looked up to see Jack glowering at him.

''Funny how you didn't mention this in the beginning. In fact you seemed to think it was a good idea. And I bet if we were together you'd be taking credit for it.''

Eddie shrugged.

''You know, if you hadn't been dumb enough to tell her you couldn't see her you might still be together.''

It was Jack's turn to shrug.

''I really thought it would be easier in the long run.''

''And is it?''

Jack ran his hand through his hair, tugging at his scalp.

''I don't know. I'm always thinking about her, you know, she's just this constant presence in my mind. But she doesn't have two words to say to me. God, it makes me want to go and just shake the life out of her. She's still making me crazy and it's been over half a year, why can't I forget about her?''

''I still think you should go and see her,'' said Eddie, speaking with the calm assurance of someone who isn't directly affected by the situation.

''Oh, right,'' snorted Jack. ''That would really make me feel better. I can imagine myself standing in front of her like Oliver Twist. 'Please, C.J., can I have some more?'''

Eddie threw up his hands. ''Well, if you're not going to go after her and she obviously hasn't come here, could we just drop the subject? It's even starting to make me crazy. Now, are you sure this plane is ready? I mean, we can lose you but we really can't afford any lawsuits.''

''Thanks a lot. Relax, it's fine. I'll just be doing basic moves today, nothing tricky.''

"There's a big crowd," said Eddie.

"More than we expected," said Jack. "Got a few Cherokees up from Manchester and even with them I'm going to be taking people up all day, if I ever get this check over with." He looked pointedly at Eddie who was leaning against the fuselage, casting a lazy eye over the crowd.

"Have fun," said Eddie, patting the side of the plane before sauntering back to his family.

JACK SLID INTO the cockpit. Even though he was disappointed about C.J., it was good to have his Sukhoi in the air again. It was good to be among the noise and bustle of an air show, to be among friends and entertaining people by doing what he loved best. Maybe it would even be greedy to expect more from life than this.

He turned the magnetos and the engine fired into life. He slipped on the headphones and called the tower.

"This is Echo Foxtrot by the south-side hangar, request taxi for fifteen-minute test flight."

"Echo Foxtrot, good to see the old bird back, line up second behind the AA5A. QNH 1-0-2-3, QFE 1-0-0-4 and it's a right-hand turn out from runway 0-9."

"QNH 1-0-2-3, QFE 1-0-0-4, right-hand on runway 0-9," repeated Jack, setting his altimeter.

He pushed in the throttle and the plane trundled slowly toward the end of the runway.

Frank was keeping everyone moving steadily and Jack was cleared to take off as soon as he reached the end of the runway. He turned right in the middle of his climb, using the river below as a guideline and headed out over the dense birch forest, which bordered the airfield. The airfield was on an elevation so there was an increased feeling of the world falling away from him as he climbed to two thousand feet.

The usual feeling of peace came over him. Pilots used to ascribe this calm to the thinness of the air, but they'd come to accept that it was just the mere experience of being in the air, so high above the world and unattached, that lead to the feeling of freedom.

He went through his maneuvers without difficulty, the plane gliding through the motions. The flying conditions were perfect and the plane was performing well. He could feel just the right amount of resistance in the controls.

After about twenty minutes, satisfied that the aircraft's performance was at a maximum, he turned back toward the airfield and contacted the tower.

"Roger Echo Foxtrot, some nice flying out there," came back the lazy drawl. "A Cherokee has just left the ground, you should be able to see him in your two o'clock as you join, right-hand on 0-9. QFE 1-0-0-4. Call me on finals."

Jack spotted the Cherokee climbing away above him and he called the tower again when he was at 500 feet, lined up with the runway.

"Cleared to land Echo Foxtrot, surface wind 110/20 and gusting, watch those wings."

Jack repeated back the information and concentrated on landing.

He was approaching the numbers when he thought he saw C.J. at the edge of the crowd.

His heart skipped a beat but then his eyes narrowed. It wasn't her. Just a woman with the same red hair, flashing in the sunlight.

He checked his airspeed again. Steady at seventy. He lowered the second stage of flaps.

His eyes were drawn again to the woman as hope prevailed over hard evidence.

Okay, it definitely wasn't her.

He dragged his eyes back to the task at hand. Fuel pump on, second flaps, a tug on the stick as the plane bucked slightly.

"Echo Foxtrot," came a voice in his ear, "We've had a report of—"

Jack missed the end of the tower's warning because his plane suddenly lurched in the sky as if an invisible giant had reached out and yanked it downward.

His heart started to thud as he scanned the instruments. It could only be wind shear.

He had been flung off course and lost a hundred feet in the blink of an eye.

He raised the flaps one step, trying to cut down on drag while maintaining every foot of precious height above the ground. He swore as a strong gust tipped up under the right wing, tilting the plane to the left. He fought against the skid and applied more throttle.

He could imagine the alarm that would be spreading through the crowd. The small plane that had seemed so cute on the ground was a different prospect when the full weight of it was bearing down on you.

He eased back on the throttle, not too much, and turned toward the right, sweat breaking out on his back as he coaxed the plane back on course.

He gradually lined up with the runway once more but he still had to contend with the dangerously bucking plane, which was moving too slowly to rise and too fast to land. Jack saw the edge of the woodlands approaching rapidly in the distance and groaned.

He eased off the throttle and pushed at the yoke tentatively, trying to force the plane down. The nosewheel hit the uneven ground with an explosive bump and the plane bucked up into the air again.

Jack looked up at the trees looming large in the windscreen.

He gritted his teeth and closed the throttle completely, nudging the nose downward again.

The bounce was more forceful this time and he felt a terrible jolt as the nosewheel snapped off. The nose of the plane ploughed into the ground.

Jack spat an expletive as the plane careened into the
trees, his seat belt knocking the air out of him as he was
flung forward.

EDDIE AND DONNA had watched the erratic descent with
increasing alarm and Eddie had reacted quickly, jumping
into Jack's truck and racing toward the downed plane.

He skidded to a halt and leaped out of the truck. He
was able to see Jack in the cockpit. His head was lolling
on the headrest and there was blood trickling from his
mouth.

Eddie jumped onto the wing and scrabbled at the door
clasp with shaking fingers. He pulled back the canopy and
Jack opened his eyes to look up at him. His face was
chalky white but he was grinning.

"You're scrapping this bloody plane and that's final,"
said Eddie, his breath coming in gasps.

"No way," said Jack. "She's definitely a keeper. That's
twice she's brought me down alive." He reached up and
daubed at his mouth. "I think I cut my lip."

Eddie reached out and clasped his arm. "You're lucky
I don't kill you myself. What the hell happened?"

"Wind shear. I thought I saw C.J. in the crowd so I was
kind of distracted, and it just caught me out of nowhere. I
tried to pull out but I didn't have enough lift so...well,
here I am."

He grimaced. "I snapped the nosewheel." Eddie
grinned in sympathy. Only the most amateur pilots took
off the nosewheel in landing. Once the news got around
that he was safe he would have to contend with merciless
teasings.

"Now you're seeing hallucinations of her," scolded
Eddie. "If that isn't crazy and, evidently, dangerous, I
don't know what is."

Jack shucked off his seat belt and Eddie's eyebrows
creased in concern as he noticed Jack wincing.

"Are you hurt?"

Jack exhaled. "My shoulder."

"Did you break something?"

Jack was feeling his left shoulder tentatively. He gasped as his fingers found a tender spot. "I think I wrenched my shoulder with the seat belt."

"You're lucky that's all," said Eddie pragmatically. "C'mon, let's get you out of there."

They drove slowly back to the airfield, Jack moving his extremities and feeling his ribs for other injuries.

"So, did your life flash before your eyes this time?" asked Eddie curiously.

"I told you already, there's no time for that, I'm always too busy trying to land." Jack paused. "I did think of C.J., though. For one second I faced the possibility that I might never see her again, that felt terrible."

"And then you thought about how terrible it would be never to see me and Donna and the kids again, right?" said Eddie sarcastically.

"Uh…" said Jack.

"Oh, that's just great!"

"I only had one second to spare," said Jack unconvincingly.

"Well, now you've got a good reason to call her," said Eddie.

"And tell her what?" said Jack bitterly. "That I crashed my plane, yet again? That'll really bring her rushing into my arms."

"You're injured," Eddie reminded him. "Women love that. She'll want to come and take care of you, feed you and mop your brow."

Jack looked over at him, one eyebrow raised.

"Okay, maybe if I was in a coma or had broken about fifty bones I could see there being some shred of potential in the situation but if I call her and say 'oh, boohoo, I separated my shoulder,' she'll just think I'm pathetic."

Jack shook his head. "I think you spend too much time in that little fantasy world of yours, I really do."

He spotted Donna's drawn face as they pulled up at the edge of the crowd and he gave her a reassuring grin. She ran up to him as he got out of the truck and threw her arms around him, clasping him in a massive bear hug.

Sweat popped out on his brow.

"Get your wife off me," he said to Eddie through gritted teeth, "before I hurt her."

Eddie pulled Donna back gently, murmuring "separated shoulder" in her ear. She swiped at her eyes and put her arm around Eddie's waist, holding him fiercely to her.

"Jeez, Jack, you scared us," was all she could manage.

"He was too busy checking out women in the crowd to concentrate on landing, believe it or not," Eddie said gruffly.

Jack opened his mouth to protest, but Donna was gathering up their picnic stuff and the kids and bundling them all haphazardly into the back of the truck.

"Come on," she said, "We're going to the hospital to get you checked out."

"BUT WHY NOT?"

"Because I'm forbidding you, that's why," said Jack crossly. "Because it's a dumb idea and I don't want to do it."

"It's not a dumb idea and you don't have to do anything," said Eddie relentlessly. "I'm the one who has to do all the acting."

"Lying, you mean," said Jack.

Eddie raised his hands pleadingly to the ceiling. "Dear God, what more does he want? Jack, you'll never have such a perfect opportunity again. It's fate! C'mon, a redhaired woman causing you to crash. It's so obvious. This happened for a reason. To bring you and C.J. back together. Please let me call her."

Jack's eyebrows dipped in the middle, a sign that he was thinking about it and Eddie pushed forward the advantage. "She'll have to come and see you," he said persuasively.

"And what then?" said Jack. "What happens when she arrives and finds out I'm not hurt that badly after all?"

"By then the good will have been done. She'll have been so terrified at the thought of losing you that everything else will fall away."

"You sure?"

"Of course," said Eddie excitedly. "She'll be glad, Jack. She'll be happy you're alive and she'll have faced the truth of her feelings."

"And what if she doesn't come?" reasoned Jack. "What if she says, 'Oh that's awful, well, give me a call next week and let me know how he's getting on.'"

Eddie looked at him compassionately. "Then you'll know the truth of her feelings and you'll be able to get on with your life."

Jack didn't say anything.

"It's a win-win situation," said Eddie softly.

They locked eyes.

Jack shook his head and smiled. "Okay, do it, call her."

"You won't regret it," said Eddie, making for the hallway.

"Just try not to scare her too much," Jack called after him.

"She won't be scared unless she cares," Eddie called back.

14

"DON'T ANSWER IT," said Kerry, pushing the phone out of C.J.'s reach.

"Why not?" said C.J., laughing.

"Because I'm trying to explain this to you and I can't if you're going to keep answering the phone."

"I already know how to upload new pages," said C.J., trying to reach around Kerry.

"I beg to differ," said Kerry, blocking her again.

"Kerry!" said C.J., with mock severity.

"Fine," said Kerry. "Answer the phone, remain computer illiterate for all your life, see if I care."

C.J. was still laughing when she picked up, but the smile fell off her face as soon as she recognized who it was. She was puzzled to hear Eddie's voice but assumed it was another ploy of Jack's, an attempt to get her attention.

"Hi, Eddie," she said. "Is everything okay?"

It was an automatic question, asked with no real regard for the answer.

Kerry looked up at the mention of the name. This was an interesting twist. C.J. had promised Kerry that she would call Jack that evening but Kerry hadn't put any money on it.

She watched C.J. with open curiosity and her eyes widened in alarm when she saw the color drain from C.J.'s face.

Kerry wrote down the name of the hospital as C.J. repeated it, a fierce dread gripping her.

"Of course, I'll be there as soon as I can," said C.J. before she hung up.

"Jack?" said Kerry, knowing the answer already.

C.J. nodded and spoke as though she was discussing something she'd heard on the news, something she couldn't quite believe. "He crashed his plane. At the air show. The one I was supposed to go to—" her voice cracked before the air of detachment came back "—there were strong winds and he had to turn but he was too low or something. So he hit some trees and the plane was totaled and he's in the hospital. He's pretty beat up, Eddie said, and he's asking for me."

She looked at her desk with a slightly puzzled expression, as if she'd mislaid something.

"Why don't you sit—"

"I have to call the airline, get a flight," said C.J., her voice a level monotone.

She reached for the phone and her hand started to shake. Kerry was up out of her seat and around the desk as C.J. started to sag. She caught her as her knees gave way and she lowered her into a chair.

"Just breathe," she said, concerned. C.J. looked as if she had no blood in her. Kerry spoke as firmly as she could manage.

"Come on now, C.J., you're going to faint if you don't concentrate, come on, breathe in, big one, and out. In again, hold it, and let it out. There you go, that's better."

C.J.'s eyes focused again and she nodded. "I have to call the airline," she said to Kerry.

Kerry pulled a chair over and sat down opposite her. She took C.J.'s hands in both of hers. "They're not going to let you fly, not when you're this far along."

She felt C.J.'s grip tighten.

"I have to go. He has to know this."

"I know, I know," said Kerry. "I'm just saying you won't be able to fly."

"I'll drive," said C.J. forcefully. She tried to pull away from Kerry and stand up.

Kerry held her. She could see C.J. was falling into shock. Her hands were icy and she was shaking.

"I'll drive you, C.J. Don't worry, we'll get there. I'm going to get you some tea and you've got to try not to panic, okay?"

She left C.J. in the care of Lex while she collected her car. Luckily C.J. had a small emergency suitcase of clothes and supplies in her office in case of premature labor so they were able to leave within the hour.

The traffic was backed up, as usual, and Kerry kept flashing concerned glances at C.J., but C.J. had disappeared to somewhere inside herself and she just stared out of the window. Tears welled silently in her eyes and flowed, unheeded, down her face. Occasionally she mouthed a prayer.

"YOU'RE LOOKING BETTER," said Donna. She sat on the edge of the bed while Didi and Eddie Jr. climbed onto the foot of it. "Was it just the shoulder?"

"They're taking some X rays but generally I seem to be all right. They're just running routine tests, making sure there's no internal damage," Jack told her.

He and Eddie exchanged a glance.

"What are you guys looking so smug about?" asked Donna suspiciously. "What's going on?"

"You didn't see anybody familiar in the parking lot or in the waiting room, did you?" asked Eddie mischievously.

"No, why?"

Eddie and Jack gave each other another complicit grin, provoking a cross look from Donna.

"Oh, for goodness sake, tell me what's going on already!"

"I called C.J.," said Eddie. "I told her about the accident and she said she'd be right here."

"That was a couple of hours ago so we're expecting her any minute."

"Oh, that's great," said Donna. "It's about time you guys were talking again."

Eddie smiled proudly. "It was my idea. And it worked like a charm if I do say so myself. She heard old Jack here was rushed to the hospital and she said she was on the next flight out, simple as that."

Donna chuckled. "Rushed? That's a slight exaggeration isn't it?"

Jack looked sheepish but Eddie shrugged. "Well, we had to get her attention, didn't we? Had to make sure she was concerned enough to come."

"So what did you say?" asked Donna, with a slight edge to her voice.

The two brothers looked at each other.

"It was your idea," prompted Jack.

Eddie looked at his wife. "I just said Jack had been in a crash and had suffered…uh…some injuries…and was in the hospital."

There was a long silence. Jack shifted uneasily in the bed.

"You're kidding me, right?" said Donna.

"What?" said Eddie, with an innocent shrug.

"The poor girl! You've probably scared the wits out of her."

Eddie had the grace to look shamefaced, but he was still defensive. "So she's worried for an hour or two, so what? She'll get over it once she sees Jack is all right. I swear, you'll all be thanking me when they're back together."

Donna gave Jack a wry look. "You know she's going to kill you as soon as she sees you're okay."

"Really?" asked Jack worriedly.

"Oh, I guarantee it."

C.J. WAS BECOMING more and more irate as their journey progressed. Once the shock had worn off, the reality of the situation began to dawn on her and she had to fight to control her panic. Every time she tried to think of the world without Jack in it her mind went blank except for a howling of agony in her skull. Then she would have to remind herself to calm down again as the baby kicked inside her.

She couldn't stop the awful imaginings in her head. She thought Jack might die and then she thought that the pain of that would be so unendurable for her that she would lose the baby, the only part of him left. She moaned as despair gripped her again.

"Hang in there, honey," said Kerry. "How are you feeling physically?"

C.J. rubbed her hands over her belly. Her face was flushed and strands of hair were sweat-stuck to her brow.

"My head is aching," said C.J. "I can't think straight. One minute I'm on the edge of despair because I can't lose him and I think if I wasn't pregnant I could have flown and I'd be with him by now and then I worry about the baby and I'm mad at him because I feel like I shouldn't have to cope with this right now and then I feel like those bad thoughts might have harmed him even more and I just want to scream. I feel like I'm being asked to make a choice between Jack and our baby and I can't do that."

"You're not making a choice," said Kerry. "You're just coping with a situation that's outside your control. You've got to focus on yourself. Your thoughts can't hurt Jack but they can't help him either. You've got to stay as calm as you can for the sake of the baby, that's a situation you can control. We'll be there in about ten minutes."

"You're right," said C.J. "I'm so glad we're nearly there. This has been the worst part. I'll be all right once I can see him. It's going to be okay, it will. He's strong, he'll come out of this, he has to."

"COME ON, COME ON!" demanded C.J. as the automatic doors drifted open. She rushed up to the emergency desk, panting from the exertion.

"Where's the intensive care?" she demanded.

The nurse looked at her. "Are you in labor?"

C.J. waved her hand in frustration. "No, no, I'm fine. I'm looking for a patient. His name is Jack Harding, he was brought in from a plane crash."

"Oh, yes," said the nurse. "We're just about to let him go. He's down there, in Ward 3."

"Let him go?" said C.J., her voice rising in alarm. "What are you talking about? How long has it been?"

The nurse looked at her in confusion. "I'm sorry? Jack Harding, the accident at the air show? That's who you mean isn't it?"

"Yes," said C.J., almost weeping with frustration.

The nurse looked down at her notes again. C.J. gave a small cry and rushed toward the ward she'd already indicated.

Eddie heard the sound of hurried footsteps and stuck his head out the door of the ward only to see a hugely pregnant woman heading straight for him. He was about to ask her if she needed help when the familiarity of the face dawned on him. His mouth fell open in disbelief.

"C.J.! C.J., is that you? Oh wow, I don't believe this."

C.J. grabbed his arm and spoke in jerks.

"Am I on time? The nurse wouldn't tell me anything, she's got him mixed up with someone else. I got here as fast as I could, I couldn't get on a plane, Kerry drove me. Where is he?"

Eddie was transfixed by the sight of her. She looked like she was about to give birth right there in front of him.

He began to feel queasy and it showed on his face.

C.J.'s heart plummeted. "Oh, God Eddie, please tell me where he is."

Eddie looked guiltily toward the end of the ward.

"C.J., wait, he's okay..." Eddie began but she ignored him and rushed into the ward.

Jack was engrossed in a game with Didi so Donna saw C.J. first.

"Holy cow," she breathed as C.J. stopped in her tracks, stunned by the happy familial sight that greeted her.

Jack looked up and started to smile. It froze on his lips as he took in her swollen belly. For a split second he thought she was playing some kind of joke on him in retaliation for his deception, but the reality of her distress was all too evident.

"Jack?" she said, taking an unsteady step toward him.

He swung his legs off the bed and got to his feet, moving stiffly. "C.J., sit down. I don't believe this, why didn't you tell me?"

He reached for her arm but she shrugged him off brusquely, her eyes full of confusion.

"I don't understand. Eddie told me you were injured. He said there was a crash."

"There was," said Jack. He couldn't really pay much attention to what she was saying because he was so amazed at the sight of her. He reached for her arm again but she slapped him away, the crack echoing loudly around the ward.

"Let me get this straight. I just spent three hours going insane with fear and there's nothing wrong with you? Was this supposed to be a joke? I'm eight months pregnant, you idiot! Kerry drove like a demon to get me here, anything could have happened. We could have been killed."

She struck his chest, her eyes full of rage.

"I'm so sorry, C.J., I didn't know. Why didn't you tell me? I would never have..." Jack struggled to explain. "I did have a crash and I separated my shoulder—"

"This one, was it?" said C.J., thumping him across the shoulder.

Jack clenched his jaw and tried to ignore the fiery blaze of agony that reached to his fingertips.

Every other patient on the ward was engrossed by the unfolding scene and there was a collective intake of breath as C.J. snarled at Jack.

"I'm going to kill you. I am going to rip you apart with my bare hands!"

She wobbled on her feet again and Eddie, who had finally gathered the courage to join them, put both hands out to hold her shoulders.

She wheeled around savagely. "Back off," she spat, ferocious as a wounded animal.

She turned back to Jack, her face a mask of anguish. "How could you do this to me?"

Jack reached her in one step and he pulled her to his chest with his good arm, holding her tightly.

She struggled and gave his ribs another few thumps before slumping against him, burying her face in his chest. He kissed her head, murmuring softly, apologizing and whispering endearments.

Didi and Eddie Jr. started to clap and jump on the bed before Donna whisked them off guiltily.

C.J. lifted her face to Jack's. "I'll never forgive you for this," she said.

"I know," he said. "I don't deserve it, but I'm going to try and earn it anyway." He kissed her forehead and she gave him a ghost of a smile.

"Maybe your time would be better spent actually learning how to fly."

"It wasn't my fault," he insisted.

"Again it wasn't your fault," she said, her smile widening.

He led her to the bed and helped her sit down. Donna and Eddie tactfully brought the kids out to the waiting room for some snacks.

"When were you going to tell me?" asked Jack, sitting

down beside her. He couldn't take his eyes off her stomach.

"Never," she said. She gave a tired laugh at his expression. "I've been so confused, Jack. I didn't know what to do so I thought I'd just concentrate on this." She reached out and took his hand, placing it on her swollen belly.

He moved his hand over her slowly, speechless with wonder. Her eyes filled with tears. She had imagined such a scene many times but the beauty of it surpassed all her expectations.

Jack looked up at her, his eyes misty. "Were you going to call me for the birth?"

She grinned. "No, I thought the journey might be too strenuous for you so I decided I'd drive up here instead."

He reached up and stroked her cheek, brushing the hair back from her face.

"You may find this hard to believe," she said, fingering her lank hair self-consciously, "but I've actually been looking quite healthy and glowing for most of the pregnancy."

"Stop it," he said gently. "You know you're gorgeous. And I'm not going to let you go now that you're here. You're moving in with me today and I'm going to take care of you."

"But work—"

"No arguments. We'll get you a computer, you can keep in touch from here. I want you with me, C.J. I want to pamper you and show you off and just make up for all the time I've lost."

She looked shamefaced. "I'm so sorry Jack, I should have called you before."

"Don't be sorry. I don't blame you, I was an idiot."

She smiled at him. "You want me to call it even, don't you?"

He didn't say anything. He was trying to look supplicatory but his eyebrows curved up hopefully.

She pretended to consider it, before laughing and leaning over to kiss him.

"I'm going to make you so happy," he murmured, holding her face and touching his forehead to hers.

C.J.'s lip quivered and a sob hitched in her throat. She blinked and two wet trails appeared on her face. Another sob shook her and she crumpled against him.

Jack held her, trying to work out what was wrong.

"What is it, C.J.? What did I say?"

"I'm just so happy you're okay," she said between sobs. "I was so scared."

She closed her eyes and he held her until the crying jag passed.

She sighed heavily. "I am so tired right now. I feel like I could sleep for twenty-four hours straight."

"Come on," he said, helping her to her feet. "Let's get you home."

"I bet you have loads of nice food at home, too, don't you?" she said as they walked towards the entrance.

"You'll have anything you want," he said.

They walked out the doors and came face-to-face with Kerry who stopped in her tracks. She took in C.J.'s red eyes and tearstained face, and then looked at the tall blond man who was holding her. He looked remarkably like the man in the photos she'd seen of Jack. Maybe he was the brother.

Kerry's hand flew to her mouth in anguish.

"Oh, no, C.J., is he…?"

To her astonishment C.J. and the brother started smiling at each other.

"Uh, Kerry, I'd like you to meet Jack. Jack, this is Kerry."

Jack removed his good hand from C.J.'s shoulder and held it out.

"I've heard a lot about you," he said.

Kerry automatically shook his hand, though she still looked confused.

"I've heard some things about you, too."

"Uh..." said Jack.

"I'll explain in the car," said C.J.

"Wait for me," said Jack. "I'll just tell Eddie I'm going with you."

"Please don't hit me," Jack said as he came back to Kerry's car. C.J. was getting into the back seat and Kerry was looking at him crossly.

Her face softened. "I guess I can understand it. I tried to get her to call you."

"Will you please stop discussing me and take me home," came a plaintive voice from the back of the car.

Jack slid in beside her and looked at her worriedly as she breathed in sharply.

She exhaled slowly and smiled reassuringly at him. "Just indigestion," she said.

"Are you sure? Maybe we should get a checkup while we're here."

"Oh, can't we just go home? I'm so tired and it's nothing."

Kerry started the car and pulled out of the parking lot. She slowed to a stop and looked in the rearview mirror as she heard another quick intake of breath from the back seat.

C.J. rubbed her side slowly.

"It's just indigestion," she insisted.

"How could it be indigestion when you haven't eaten all day?" asked Kerry.

"All right then, it's hunger. Come on, let's go."

"The seat is wet," said Jack.

"No, it isn't," said C.J. "You're imagining it."

Jack met Kerry's eyes in the mirror.

"The seat is wet," he said again.

Kerry swung around the driveway and pulled up to the hospital entrance.

"No," wailed C.J. "I can't do this now, I'm exhausted." She bent forward over her stomach and grunted as another contraction gripped her.

"You couldn't have timed it better," said Kerry. "Go on, get out."

Jack got out and ran around to pull C.J. out, still protesting feebly that she wasn't ready.

"WILL YOU TEACH HER to fly?" asked C.J., her voice croaky.

"Of course," said Jack, gazing down at the tiny baby.

"She looks like you," said C.J.

"I think she looks like you."

"She's got your eyes, though, sort of almond shaped."

"Oh, so you wanted me for my eyes, did you?"

C.J. looked at him. They were exhausted and elated and C.J. couldn't believe she'd almost missed the opportunity to be with him at this moment.

"I was scared," she said quietly.

He raised his eyes from the baby to look at her. "I know. So was I."

"You were the only person in my life I'd felt that strongly about. I didn't know what to do. I wanted to be able to tell you how I felt but I was afraid it would get mixed up and swept away by the fact that I was pregnant and I knew that would have an influence on you whether you wanted it to or not."

"I remember a moment," said Jack, "when it struck me that if you got pregnant you'd be forced to see me all the time. That's kind of why I ended it, too. I decided my motives weren't very pure and I thought it would be more honorable or something to bow out. But I can't live without you, C.J., I love you, I want to be with you."

"I love you, too," she whispered.

"So you'll move back to Ashfield?" he said.

Her shoulders stiffened and he stroked her head. "I was kidding," he said softly. "You'll never have to change your life for me, C.J. I love you and I always will."

"What will we do?" she asked.

"We'll work something out," he said. "Lots of married couples have conflicting schedules, but they work it out."

Her eyes widened. "Married?"

"Of course," he said. "What did you expect?"

"I expect a formal proposal," she said haughtily.

"And give you the chance to back out? Forget it."

C.J. stared at him.

Jack looked down at their tiny perfect baby.

"Hey, kid," he whispered. "Will you ask your mom if she'll marry me?"

"Tell your dad I said yes."

How To Play

1. With a coin, carefully scratch off the 3 gold areas on your Lucky Carnival Wheel. By doing so you have qualified to receive everything revealed—2 FREE books and a surprise gift—ABSOLUTELY FREE!

2. Send back this card and you'll receive 2 brand-new Harlequin Duets™ novels. These books have a cover price of $5.99 each in the U.S. and $6.99 each in Canada, but they are yours ABSOLUTELY FREE.

3. There's no catch! You're under no obligation to buy anything. We charge nothing—ZERO—for your first shipment. And you don't have to make any minimum number of purchases—not even one!

4. The fact is thousands of readers enjoy receiving books by mail from the Harlequin Reader Service®. They enjoy the convenience of home delivery...they like getting the best new novels at discount prices, BEFORE they're available in stores... and they love their *Heart to Heart* subscriber newsletter featuring author news, horoscopes, recipes, book reviews and much more!

5. We hope that after receiving your free books you'll want to remain a subscriber. But the choice is yours—to continue or cancel, any time at all! So why not take us up on our invitation, with no risk of any kind. You'll be glad you did!

A surprise gift

FREE

We can't tell you what it is...but we're sure you'll like it! A

FREE GIFT!

just for playing LUCKY CARNIVAL WHEEL!

Visit us online at
www.eHarlequin.com

Find Out Instantly The Gifts You Get **Absolutely FREE!**
'UCKY Carnival Wheel
Scratch-off Game

Scratch off
ALL 3
Gold areas

YES! I have scratched off the 3 Gold Areas above.
Please send me the 2 FREE books and gift for which I qualify! I understand I am under no obligation to purchase any books, as explained on the back and on the opposite page.

311 HDL DNWZ   111 HDL DNWQ

FIRST NAME	LAST NAME

ADDRESS

APT.#	CITY

STATE/PROV.	ZIP/POSTAL CODE

The Harlequin Reader Service — Here's how it works.

Accepting your 2 free books and gift places you under no obligation to buy anything. You may keep the books and gift and return the shipping statement marked "cancel." If you do not cancel, about a month later we'll send you 2 additional novels and bill you just $5.14 each in the U.S., or $6.14 each in Canada, plus 50¢ shipping & handling per book and applicable taxes if any.* That's the complete price and — compared to cover prices of $5.99 each in the U.S. and $6.99 each in Canada—it's quite a bargain! You may cancel at any time, but if you choose to continue, every month we'll send you 2 more books, which you may either purchase at the discount price or return to us and cancel your subscription.

*Terms and prices subject to change without notice. Sales tax applicable in N.Y. Canadian residents will be charged applicable provincial taxes and GST.

If offer card is missing write to: Harlequin Reader Service, 3010 Walden Ave., P.O. Box 1867, Buffalo, NY 14240-1867

BUSINESS REPLY MAIL
FIRST-CLASS MAIL   PERMIT NO. 717-003   BUFFALO, NY

POSTAGE WILL BE PAID BY ADDRESSEE

HARLEQUIN READER SERVICE
3010 WALDEN AVE
PO BOX 1867
BUFFALO NY 14240-9952

NO POSTAGE
NECESSARY
IF MAILED
IN THE
UNITED STATES

Designs
on Jake

Dorien
Kelly

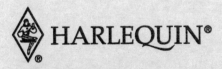

HARLEQUIN®

TORONTO • NEW YORK • LONDON
AMSTERDAM • PARIS • SYDNEY • HAMBURG
STOCKHOLM • ATHENS • TOKYO • MILAN • MADRID
PRAGUE • WARSAW • BUDAPEST • AUCKLAND

Dear Reader,

A while back, a vacant storefront in my hometown caught my writer's eye. I wondered about the people who lived in the apartments above the empty shop. I imagined what sort of place I'd open if I had the courage to start my own business. And I began to write *Designs on Jake*.

Soon after I finished, someone rented the space, and a dress shop appeared. Not a chain store, but a place filled with one-of-a-kind creations just like the ones my heroine, Rowan Lindsay, would design! I haven't snooped in the store's cellar or seen evidence of twins trapping customers outside, but I can't pass it by without smiling.

Writing is my new business, and like Rowan, I'm excited and sometimes a little frazzled. But most of all, I'm thrilled to have the chance to share Rowan's unusual path to love with you! Online readers can write to me at dorienkell@aol.com.

Wishing you all the best,

Dorien Kelly

To Tom, with all my love,
for your incredible patience.
To Sean, Cait and Erin for telling anyone
who will listen that their mom is a romance writer.
And to Barbara Caputo for encouraging me
every step of the way!

1

"YOU'RE TAKING A *WHAT?*"

Rowan Lindsay gave her best friend, Melanie, an I-dare-you-to-laugh glare. "You heard me—a Boy Vacation. No dinners, no dates, no disasters."

Melanie, of course, laughed anyway.

"Go ahead, make fun of me," Rowan said, before turning to dust a haphazard swathe through Lindsay's Antique Emporium. Over her shoulder she added, "But when you're done laughing, I'm sending you on a scavenger hunt. Find me one guy in the Detroit area who doesn't run screaming when he learns that his date is the mother of twin five-year-olds."

"Okay, I get the picture, but don't you think you're being a tad extreme—even for you?"

Easy for happily married Melanie to say. And it wasn't that Rowan didn't want a little romance. She craved it, actually. But considering her rocky record with the male side of the species, beginning with that first braces-locked kiss at age thirteen, the answer was a cinch. "Nope."

Heck, when faced with her own life, sometimes Rowan wanted to run screaming. She loved Abby and Mac with all her heart, but they were a handful. The past year had been tough on all of them. Rowan had coped by working hard, here in her aunt Celeste's store. And the twins? Well, when it came to trouble, they were now gold-medal contenders. She glanced under the oak drop-leaf table where they'd last been playing and found them...

Gone!

Even as the feather duster slipped from limp fingers, Rowan squelched the first wave of panic. "Mel, check for the kids in the back room and I'll look in here."

"I know the drill," Melanie answered in the resigned tones of a grizzled twin-capades veteran, then hustled off.

Dropping to her knees, Rowan stuck her head under the first in a row of dining tables. "Abby...Mac, the game's over. Hey, come on out."

Ducking even lower and resting on her forearms, she squinted through the forest of furniture legs. "I mean business, you two. If you don't—"

"Missing some kids?"

At the sound of the unfamiliar voice, deep and definitely male, Rowan froze. Still bottom up, she turned her head just enough to see a scuffed pair of black cowboy boots, one foot tapping a slow rhythm. On each side of those angry boots was a pair of worn red canvas sneakers, two little sets of tennies that she'd sent through the washing machine countless times. Relief warred with a distinct maternal sense of mischief afoot.

"Nine-point-five on the trouble scale," she muttered, briefly resting her forehead on the dusty wooden floor. It was then she realized that—like her children—she had put something other than her best foot forward. And that *something* wasn't what she considered her finest attribute. In fact, her every guilty caloric indulgence seemed to land right there. It was a blessing, she thought as she backed away from the table on all fours, that dignity had never been a big issue with her. Rowan stood and pinned on a smile.

"They're mine, all right," she said, not quite meeting his eyes. She had learned it was a bad thing, looking into the furious face of one of the twins' victims. All that hostility tended to make her scrape, grovel and babble.

The man held Abby and Mac away from his body, one thumb and index finger barely grasping each of their collars. He was doing his best to avoid physical contact, yet at the same time, keep the terrible twosome corralled. She bet he hadn't been this close to one child, let alone two, in his entire adult life.

"You can let them go."

"Sure thing." Then he took a giant step backward, looking relieved and almost tempted to wipe off his hands on his jeans. Or maybe shower in disinfectant.

"They might be a little grubby, but they're not contagious," she said, feeling compelled to defend the twins' honor.

He ignored her last comment. "Do you always let them roam the street? I found them out on the sidewalk. Want to guess what they were doing?"

Here was one game of Twenty Questions she was bound to lose. Rowan shook her head a silent no.

"They were wrapping string between a parking meter and the planter next to the front door, then trying to camouflage the whole mess with fallen leaves." He pulled a wad of twine from his back pocket and tossed the evidence into a plaster umbrella stand that eerily resembled an elephant's foot. "If you can't keep track of 'em, you might consider an armed guard."

Rowan frowned at the twins, but they kept gazing at their captor as if he were a superhero. "Earth to kids," she called, snapping her fingers a few times. The twins eventually noticed her. "All right, you two, explain, please."

"We were trying to catch Auntie Celeste some customers," Mac said. Abby nodded in agreement, her wild black curls springing up and down.

Rowan finally looked at the man they'd trapped and smiled in spite of herself. *Outstanding job, guys... stellar, in fact,* was her initial assessment. The stranger's dark brows rose slightly, as if he expected an explanation for her smile. Not that she had one, other than temporary insanity given her newly hatched declaration of Boy Vacation. But then again, she still could admire him as one would any museum-quality work of art.

His hair was longish and definitely unconservative. On most men, the style would be an affectation. On him it looked natural. Nope, no buttoned-down collar and snugged-up tie on this guy, unlike her rat of an ex-husband, Chip.

This man was muscled and just tall enough. Since she was barely five foot two, he still stood well above her. If they were dancing, her head would come about to his...

"You're staring."

He had a pirate's grin, teeth white against tan skin. Rowan realized that she liked men who looked as though they spent time outdoors. She hadn't given it much thought before. Just watching him, she could smell green summer grass and the salty tang of hard work. She could imagine him, shirt off, muscles flexing across his chest as he...

"You're still staring."

Truth be told, *staring* was too polite a term. She was gaping at him just as the twins were, but with a far more adult interest that had her heart drumming and her blood humming along to its hot little tune. She fumbled for something to say while fighting a losing battle with her overheated imagination.

"Oh, sorry…I didn't mean to. I really wasn't thinking about you at all." She winced as the blatant lie escaped.

He grinned. "So much for feeding my ego. You should have just let me think my looks struck you speechless." The teasing sparkle and obvious appreciation in his brown eyes were something she hadn't had directed at her in years.

Maybe never.

A sharp twinge arrowed through her. When it came to flirtation, she was rustier than Dorothy's Tin Man, and not nearly as brave as that lion.

She turned her attention back to the semisafe haven of her children. "How many times have I told you two that you have to stay in the store? You know that I—"

"As well-practiced as it might be, I think I'll skip the loving parental lecture. I've got things to do."

At the sound of his voice, smooth and rich as really fine chocolate, one last warm tingle danced through Rowan. He paused several steps inside the door, as if he didn't really want to leave. For an instant she didn't want him to, either. Then she recalled how her last gentleman caller had departed with his pant legs neatly trimmed to Bermuda length, courtesy of a certain artistic and very insulted five-year-old.

Boy Vacation. It was the best—and safest—for all involved.

Rowan nodded awkwardly. "Well, thanks again."

"No problem," he said over his shoulder on the way out the door. He sent a scowl in the twins' direction. They called goodbye anyway, friendly even when relegated to the status of nonpersons.

"Hey, Rowan." Melanie stood in the archway leading from the back room. "Does this Boy Vacation of yours extend all the way to men? Because, darlin', that guy you let slip away was one *M-A-N*." She spelled the last word with a bump and grind that would have done a professional stripper proud.

Rowan laughed to mask the mix of nerves and odd excitement that still had her reeling. "Don't be fooled, Mel. Underneath those tasty looks, he's still a *B-O-Y*," she retorted, omitting the hip action in deference to her mommy status. "Haven't met one yet who wasn't."

"That's because you chase them off before you can find out for sure."

Rowan flinched. After all, she had chased off Chip. Like the ghosts of old battle cries, echoes of their arguments rang through her head. *"You can't ever be like anyone else, can you? Not just one kid, but two! And those clothes you make for yourself. Why didn't you go see the personal shopper I hired for you?"*

She pulled back her shoulders and with a firm mental command of *Stay,* put the specter of Chip behind her. "No more men," Rowan proclaimed.

Melanie's little cupid's mouth turned downward. "For Pete's sake, you're only twenty-five years old. Are you planning on spending the rest of your life alone?" Her face brightened. "Dan says there's this new guy at the office, and—"

Rowan raised her hands to shield herself. Melanie's husband seemed to have a rotating stock of eligible friends, all of whom had been thrilled to meet her. That is, until the twins barreled at them, arms open and squealing one word at the tops of their lungs: *"Daddy!"* Their little game had run off more than one brave soul.

"No way, Mel. And I'm not exactly alone, you know." She pointed to Mac and Abby, who had their noses pressed to the front window, no doubt trying for one last glimpse of their new hero. "I figure I've got at least the next dozen years booked right there. And after that, hey, maybe some of those boys will have grown up."

"It just takes one, Rowan. Just one. And that man you chased out of here looked plenty grown-up to me."

Before Rowan was forced to refute the obvious truth, Melanie glanced at her watch. "Almost four! Hey, I gotta run." She paused on her way out the door. "I know you're busy, but tomorrow can we work on that dress you're designing for me?"

"No problem," Rowan said. Actually, she'd be willing to work on dress designs in the dark of an Arctic winter. Bare as a newborn babe, too. For the moment, dress design, in the buff or otherwise, would have to wait. Melanie was no sooner out the door than the twins corraled her.

Mac hopped up and down, tugging on her hand. "Wasn't that man funny, Mommy? We scared him, and he's so much bigger 'n us!"

"But we caught him," Abby chimed in. "Our trap really worked. Too bad he made us take it down. Hey, you should've made him buy something!"

Mac sidled closer. "Are we in trouble? You said we could go outside."

"I did no such thing!"

"You sort of did."

"How could I *sort of* give you permission to go out?" Rowan bent forward, hands on hips, waiting to see how he'd wiggle around this one. Brilliantly, no doubt.

When the twins were three, they'd shocked her by teaching themselves to read. She'd had them tested and found they were academically gifted. It was both exciting and scary, raising kids with supercharged minds.

"So, pal of mine, what's your answer?" she prompted Mac.

He frowned in concentration. Rowan bit back a smile; it was tough to be serious when looking into a perfect mirror of her own mannerisms.

"When we were going out the door I whispered—I was being real quiet just like you tell me to—anyway, I whispered that we'd be right in front of the store. And you nodded."

"I did?"

"Well, maybe you blinked," he grudgingly conceded.

She burst into laughter. "Mac Wilmont, you must think I was born yesterday. You're going to have to do better than that."

Mac screwed his face into a stubborn pout and stared down at his sneakers. Rowan turned her attention to Abby.

"Do you have anything to add, kiddo?"

"Nope, 'cept you weren't born yesterday, Mommy. You're real old—almost as old as Auntie Celeste."

"Teetering on the brink of senility," Rowan's aunt Celeste announced as she breezed in from the back room. Actually, Celeste was as sharp as they came, though her flower-child-meets-Victorian-lady mode of dress tended to put off some people. Not Rowan, who'd been known to wear stranger stuff herself.

Celeste waggled her magenta-tipped nails in the direction of the twins. "And how are you two wild things doing this afternoon?"

"Great! We went huntin' for customers and trapped one, too!"

"Yeah, but Mommy made us let him go," said Abby.

"We could hardly have kept him," Rowan supplied in self-defense. But he *was* a keeper. Her face warmed as she wondered how all that sleek hair of his would feel under her fingers.

"Just how did you trap a customer?" Aunt Celeste seemed intrigued at the concept.

"With string, of course." Mac nodded knowingly, as if every merchant would applaud the logic of this approach.

"Of course," Celeste agreed. "You're turning into a regular marketing genius! But now I need you and your sister to go back to your play area. Your mom and I have to talk."

As they scampered off, Rowan wondered what her aunt was up to. It wasn't like her to send the twins away.

Lifting reading glasses that hung from a chunky beaded chain, Aunt Celeste took a moment to flip through waiting phone messages and mail. "Rowan, I've found a tenant for the adjacent space and apartment above," she said as she paged through a catalog. "Never thought I'd rent that space again."

Head spinning, Rowan pulled out the first available chair and sat down hard. Celeste didn't look up from the mail.

"Privacy, the new tenant wants lots of privacy. He doesn't even want the entry connecting to this space left open, so workmen will be here on Monday to close it off. And quiet—he was incredibly insistent about quiet, too. He asked whether the folks in the apartment next to his— *you guys*—are noisy. I stretched the truth until it screamed and said you're as quiet as church mice."

Rowan nodded absently, looking through the archway at the small space Celeste owned, in addition to her shop. It wasn't much to speak of. The room had a musty smell to it and needed a new coat of paint and junk hauled out. But to Rowan, it couldn't have been more beautiful. After all, as soon as she got together the money, it was going to be the home of her own design studio.

At least, until twenty seconds ago, it was going to be. But she wouldn't give up on her dream without a good fight.

"So what does the new tenant do that requires all this quiet? Sounds pretty suspicious to me. Did you check him out with the police or the FBI or anything?"

Aunt Celeste made an impatient huffing sound and slapped down the mail. "He's the son of an old friend...a very good old friend."

No doubt what Rowan's conservative dad referred to as one of his sister's "Bohemian romances." Rowan knew she was treading on hallowed ground, fighting against the son of a "very good old friend."

"And he can afford the space," her aunt added. "I don't need to know anything more."

"That's pretty trusting. We're not on the farm in Hart, you know."

Celeste readjusted her glasses, as if she couldn't believe what she was seeing. Eyes narrowed, she frowned at Rowan. "Yes, I've noticed we're clear across the state from Hart. And geography aside, you don't see many folks like that back home." She gestured at a pair of biker dudes clad in black motorcycle leathers, standing hand in hand, looking in the front window.

"Rowan, I've lived in Royal Oak for the past thirty years. And for all that time I've run a good business *and* managed to continue to trust people."

"Message received," Rowan replied in a less than perky voice. "I'm sure it'll all work out."

Aunt Celeste sighed with exasperation. "I have no idea what's bothering you, and I know you'll never tell me."

"Nothing's wrong. Nothing at all. Just tell me what you want me to do." *Maybe stick bamboo slivers under my fingernails?*

"To begin with, you can quit acting as if the worst is about to happen. In your case it probably already has, if that's any comfort."

"As good as I'm going to get." Especially now that she'd lost the comfort of an imaginary store to plan.

"Cheer up," Aunt Celeste directed. "The new tenant isn't an ax murderer, and I don't think he's plotting the destruction of civilization. You might even like him, you know."

Rowan refrained from voicing the "fat chance" that fought to escape.

"Maybe you could even slightly bend the rules and go introduce yourself."

"Nope, not talking to boys anymore. Boy Vacation," Rowan announced from her perch on the edge of her aunt's favorite Stickley chair.

Celeste rolled her eyes heavenward. "You're a complete mystery to me, Rowan Wilmont."

"Lindsay. You know I dropped Chip's last name."

"Now if you could just drop the nasty baggage you let him settle on you," her aunt directed briskly. "And get off that chair!"

Not wanting to push her luck, Rowan stood.

"But on to the really big news...I've decided to leave town for a while—about three weeks, I think. A dealer I know in Seattle is going out of business, and I want to see what I can pick up. Then I figured since I have you here, I'll take my first real vacation since way back when at

Woodstock.'' Her aunt's brief, reminiscing smile had a naughty tilt to it.

Rowan's head spun. Three weeks anchored to the store with no one else to help? Three weeks watching the lost opportunity next door slip by? Those bamboo slivers under her fingernails were beginning to sound pretty good.

Still, her aunt had taken her in after the divorce, when she'd fled Chip, his mistress and all his gossipy Boston chums. Without Celeste, she'd be back under her parents' roof. She was their only child and loved them with all her heart, but moving home was like a public admission of failure. In a town as small as Hart, there were few secrets.

Rowan packed a wealth of hesitance but no outright refusal into two simple words. ''Three weeks?''

''Relax, fall business is always slow. Besides, this is an antique shop I'm asking you to watch, not a dynamite lab. All you have to do is post your hours on the door, and relax. *And* quit gnawing your fingernails!''

Darn, she'd been doing it again. Rowan dropped her hand from her mouth. She hadn't bitten her fingernails since Chip had left her. She needed to get a grip.

''Gotcha,'' she said to Celeste.

''Oh, and the new tenant… He has a lot of, ah, personality. Don't let him intimidate you,'' her aunt added before she swept out the front door.

''Not if I can intimidate him first,'' Rowan muttered, then plopped down in disgust on Celeste's precious Stickley chair.

JAKE ALBREIGHT knew he should celebrate. He had his retail space and even a place of sorts to live. He should be relieved to be taking another step down that torturous trail toward freedom. Instead, he felt more wary than content. And really, he had only himself to blame.

"Ambushed," he muttered.

Hot to flee the scene of his downfall, he slid behind the wheel of his pickup and tossed the newly signed lease on the seat beside him. A few weeks ago, he'd suspected Celeste Lindsay was up to something when she offered to rent him the space adjacent to her antique shop.

He'd known Celeste since he was twelve years old, back when she'd dated his long-widowed dad. Even after she and his dad broke up, she'd kept in touch. She wasn't quite a mom, but could be as meddling as one. Her recent, ever-so-casual mention that Rowan, her favorite niece, "divorced with two great kids," lived above the antique shop only confirmed that.

He wasn't in the market for a relationship, not after the nightmare with Victoria the money grabber. This was his time to howl and prowl.

To become involved with a woman who had kids was insane, anyway. Kids were like concrete blocks tied to your ankles, dragging you down with whining and neediness and endless responsibilities until you drowned. Heck, he hadn't even liked himself as a kid. He'd seen how raising him and his wild older brother had ground his dad down to nothing but an empty wallet and a worn-out temper. Jake didn't want to step into his old man's shoes.

Still, Celeste's price for the shop space was right, especially in an up-and-coming town like Royal Oak. With its art galleries, laid-back attitude and young population, this was the hot place to be. He had simply issued a few rules designed to keep his new neighbors at bay.

Today, though, he'd forgotten all of those well-laid plans. He had forgotten his name, and what he was doing in Celeste's shop with twin terrors in tow. In fact, he was lucky their mom had looked pretty floored herself because it had taken him a stretch of time just to remember how to breathe. He'd felt as if he'd been kicked in the gut when he saw her. Wide eyes like those of a forest creature, wild black hair, creamy skin and a mouth definitely made for kissing.

He'd made her nervous, and while he was sorry for that, he found it funny. He had tried to be polite. Really, he had. If he'd shown even a tenth of his sudden, almost inexplicable interest, she would have clutched those two little hellions to her bosom and run for the door.

He took an unwelcome pleasure from the fact she had noticed him, too. The startled intensity of her gaze had made him curious. It was almost as if she'd been unaware of her own interest. He wondered what it would feel like to be the one to wake her. He wondered what *she* would feel like.

Jake shoved aside the crazy thought. He'd dumped all the complications from his life a few months ago, when he sold his landscaping business for some major cash. He didn't want a woman, especially not a mother of two who appeared to survive on the kindness of others. He'd never allow himself to be used again.

He'd sat on both sides of the coin—rich and poor—and knew one thing for sure: Money had a way of messing things up. Sweet freedom was the name of the game, not his sweet neighbor.

2

ROWAN RAISED HER WINE in a toast. "Here's to me." After taking a sip, she balanced the glass on the edge of the bathtub, gave a blissful sigh and sank lower in the scented water. She'd survived seven wild days of running the shop, then sewing late into the night. This was her reward—a candlelit, midnight soak and a glass of good wine.

While she didn't miss Chip in the least, or much of the life she had left behind in Boston, she did miss a few of the creature comforts. Being able to afford wine that didn't come with a screw top quickly came to mind. Today, she'd splurged and bought herself a nice Californian Merlot. Chip would have sooner drunk hemlock than a domestic wine.

"Maybe I should have slipped you hemlock, Chip Wilmont." Her voice ricocheted off the chipped peach-colored bathroom tile, making her flinch. She hoped she hadn't awakened the twins.

No matter what she thought of Chip, she wanted them to have a good relationship with their father. Assuming he ever contacted them. Since he'd had the incredible gall to contest paternity as a ploy during the divorce proceedings, she wasn't betting on it.

Rowan pushed away the gloomy thoughts. "Hey, this is supposed to be a celebration," she reminded herself. "No tricks from the kids, no unanswerable questions about antiques, just silence.'' She swirled her hand slowly back and forth and relished the silken feeling of the warm water against her skin.

"Silence," she whispered.

The noise, more vibration than actual sound, started so low and distant that it took a second to register in her brain. By then it had gained in strength, rolling through the small two-bedroom apartment, filling the bathroom.

"Aw, come on! Three nights in a row? Obviously, Aunt Celeste didn't bother to ask him if *he'd* be quiet.''

The first night, the twins had shot from their beds with the sound, which had stood out even against the town's exuberant nightlife. But as soon as Rowan had explained that it was coming from next door, they'd allowed themselves to be tucked back in without so much as a peep. When it started last night, she'd crept in to check on them and could have sworn Abby was smiling in her sleep.

Rowan decided that tonight she'd stay in the tub and relax in spite of her neighbor. Even if he was growing louder. Her wineglass clattered and danced on its ceramic perch. She steadied it with one hand, not wanting it to skitter to the edge and land on the tile below.

Rowan frowned in concentration, listening carefully. "Didgeridoo!"

The noise was just like the sound from the aboriginal instruments she'd heard when watching the Travel Channel, while Chip was at one of his endless late nights at "work." Thanks to cable television and a husband who'd stuck to his vows for a time equal to the half-life of a fruit fly, Rowan had quite a list of places she wanted to visit. Unless her prospects improved, though, the closest she'd be getting to Australia was her neighbor's nightly concert.

"Maybe some sort of religious cult," she muttered. If

he was a cult leader, he was a dismal failure. She'd checked the back parking area for strange cars the first night. All the lot had held was her ancient Volvo wagon and the tenant's black Dodge pickup.

"A cult of one—small wonder," she said, then laughed at the picture she made, sitting in the tub and chattering away like a magpie with no one to hear but herself. The guy was making her nuts, and she hadn't even seen him. She was sure her list of grievances would grow once they met.

If they met.

He probably was some kind of hermit. Maybe his cult rules didn't permit communication with humans. With her luck, he wasn't allowed to bathe, either. She sniffed the air suspiciously, then laughed again.

"I don't know what you're up to in there, but you can bet I'll find out," she said, and got a long wail in answer— enough to rouse even the deepest-sleeping five-year-old.

Rowan wasn't waiting for the curtain call on this show. Dredging herself from the tub, she grabbed her towel. Tracking sloppy, wet footprints across the worn beige living-room carpet, she reached her target. A sharp thump on the common wall stopped the noise. Giving a satisfied sniff, she turned away. One last, mocking *"bla-a-at"* sounded, stiffening her spine.

As far as Rowan was concerned the gauntlet had been thrown. She stalked to the bathroom. In moments she had wrenched on an oversize tie-dyed sleep shirt. She snatched up her wineglass and marched back to the living room. Standing between the sunshine-yellow, slipcovered armchair and a formerly three-legged coffee table, all part of her rejuvenated discards decor, she faced her neighbor's apartment.

"This is war, buster!" She downed the dregs of her wine and saluted the wall with the empty glass. "Hope you're up for it."

THE OPENING SALVO sounded at 6:00 a.m. Unfortunately, it wasn't Rowan's, and it seemed to involve both power saws and drills. Muttering an old Scottish curse involving ill will to sheep and fallow fields, Rowan dragged her too-long bangs out of her face and sat up in bed. When she'd shaken the sleep from her brain, she saw the twins standing bedside, wearing matching expectant expressions.

"Can we go next door? We wanna see what the man who makes funny noises is doing." Apparently, Mac was the mouthpiece today.

"Not a chance, kiddo. You know he's off-limits."

"But *why-y-y-y?*" The whine rang out in stereo, almost as shrill as the power tools it competed with.

She resorted to the traditional maternal power play. "Because that's just the way it is."

"That's always your answer," Mac groused.

Rowan didn't like the stubborn set of his jaw, or the determined light shining in Abby's eyes. "I'm not kidding, you two. There'll be no uninvited visits to our new neighbor. Aunt Celeste said no, and when she does, she means it. And so do I. Understand? Besides, you've got a great day ahead at school. You don't need to waste your time with the goofy noises next door."

Twin chins still stuck out mutinously. In response, Rowan put on her best frown.

"Okay," they finally echoed in skeptical voices.

Rowan knew she was pushing it, too. A rousing kindergarten chorus of "Itsy-Bitsy Spider" had nothing on the full-tilt construction boogie taking place next door. But every now and then, Mommy actually managed to rule. Through diversion, mostly.

"Go get dressed, and since we're up so early, we have lots of time for a pancake breakfast before school starts. Sound good?" Rowan asked unnecessarily. Pancakes slathered with jelly were the twins' favorite food. Yep, there was nothing like starch and sugar to buy some peace. Now if she could just figure out the best way to make some war with Mr. Noise.

A few hours later, Rowan concluded that a career as a CIA operative was a definite no. Trying her best to be unobtrusive, she strolled up the sidewalk, looping past the hardware store, the magic shop and the potter's studio. Slowly, she headed back to her starting point and zeroed in on her target.

Cool and casual, she told herself, glancing at the new neighbor's storefront. Not much of a fan of publicity, she decided. Every square inch of window was covered from the inside with white butcher paper. A well-planned incursion was the only hope.

Acting as though it was no big deal to peer at a solid sea of white, she nonchalantly moved closer. The first thing that struck her was the relative quiet. The friendly human chatter and automotive symphony of Main Street still played out behind her, but it wasn't matched by anything behind that paper. Sometime while she was walking the twins to school, Mr. Noise had actually managed to knock it off. She noticed the small brass plate to the left of the door. Engraved in stark roman script was J. Albreight.

Rowan permitted herself a brief smirk, though generally it didn't do to gloat in victory. She had the guy's name, or at least part of it. Emboldened, she pressed her nose to

the glass, slitting one eye shut and squinting with the other.
Just a fraction of an inch or so to the left, and she'd...

"So whatcha looking at?"

Rowan jumped, bumping her nose hard enough to have
it go numb. "Ahhh..." she stammered, rubbing at the tip
of her nose. "I was, uh..." She turned around, and once
she did, even the confused stammer was too tough to work
up.

Oh, the man looked tasty, all right. Possibly even better
than he did when the twins had trapped him. His faded
blue chambray shirt set off his tan, and those black jeans
fit to decadent perfection. Realizing she was slack-jawed,
Rowan closed her mouth with a snap.

Hooking his thumbs into his back pockets, he rocked
back and forth on his cowboy boots and gave her a smile
that made her nerve endings zing.

"Sooo?" He drew out the question long and amused.

"Window shopping... I was window shopping," she
repeated with more conviction.

"Really? See anything you like?"

She did, and it wasn't the sheaves of paper. It was the
solid strength and confidence in front of her, just close
enough to touch. *Bad thought, very bad.* Rowan leaned
against the window, pressing her sweaty palms against its
cool surface.

"Okay, so I was snooping," she said, resorting to absolute, embarrassing honesty. She never performed well
under pressure. And fighting the impulse to trace that tiny
cleft in his chin with one fingertip was big-time pressure.
"Somebody new just moved in and strange things are going on...noises and, ah..."

His dark brows arched in surprise. "So instead of knocking on the door and introducing yourself, you're doing some sort of cloak-and-dagger bit?''

"Okay, so it sounds pretty crazy, but I have my reasons. And there's no telling what might be in there. Like…like…"

With a grin, he filled in the gap. "Ghosts of Prohibition rumrunners? Extraterrestrial life?"

"You never know!"

He didn't bother to hide his laughter. "Now I see where your kids get it from."

"Get what?" What she was doing wasn't *that* crazy. And only she was allowed to acknowledge that Mac and Abby could be somewhat south of angelic.

"Guts, chutzpah. I like that—in adults, at least."

And she liked him. A lot. Rowan could feel her heart opening, softening, and it scared her. But he thought she was a woman with chutzpah, and she could never, ever admit fear.

He nodded toward the sidewalk. "Got time to do some real window shopping? Maybe a coffee?"

Rowan repeated her mental chant: *Boy Vacation.* It had a snappy ring to it, her new mantra. Snappy and safe from hurt.

"I can't," she said, tugging a key ring from her pocket. "I've got to open the store soon."

"Then maybe another time, supersleuth." He strolled off, giving Rowan a view of broad shoulders, fine butt and attitude. Attitude she liked.

Giving in to impulse, she stuck out her tongue at J. Albreight's paper-covered windows. Not the most mature gesture in the world, but fitting. "You could learn a thing or two from that guy, pal."

A DAMN LOT HAPPIER than he'd been in a long time, Jake rounded the corner from Main onto Fourth Street. He strode over the railroad tracks and waved to the old guy in the Tigers baseball cap who always sat on the bench by the crossing. Maybe he was a vagrant, maybe a millionaire. That was the cool thing about this town—you just never knew.

One thing he did know—gutsy Rowan liked the way he looked. He couldn't believe that scientists had bothered to conduct studies to learn whether a person could feel someone staring at them. He'd felt her gaze on his back all the way down the block. And it had felt good.

Running into her had made an awesome idea pop into his head. Maybe Jake Albreight, his fat bankbook and all the hassle and uncertainty that wealth brought could stay safely in hiding. Meanwhile, in the guise of the anonymous guy off the street, he could arrange a few "chance" meetings with his delectable neighbor. It was a win-win deal.

Raising two kids on her own couldn't be a whole lot of laughs. In fact, with the hours kids ate and the way you could never just pick up and take off if you wanted, it sounded like a prison term to him. The twins' warden could use a few innocent distractions. With dual identities, he wouldn't have to get in deeper than he wanted. And Rowan could have twice the fun.

"No harm…no foul," Jake said to himself just before he swung open the door to his favorite breakfast joint. "And one helluva good time."

SETTLED IN FRONT of the sewing machine she'd set up in the corner of the shop, Rowan zipped through the dress for Melanie. Stitching away, she conducted an internal debate on the pros and cons of Boy Vacation. Maybe her decision had been a little hasty, a little ill-advised. After all, some great guys like the twins' former captive still roamed the earth.

On the other hand, there seemed to be tons of men like the nutcase next door. Rowan sighed. That was the worst of it. She had begun to doubt her ability to tell the good from the bad.

Though she still talked a bold game, these days it was pretty much that—talk. Chip had managed to strip away too much of her confidence. That was why she had never asked Aunt Celeste for the space next door. And why she spent too many nights awake worrying about her next failure, instead of grabbing for her next success. Still, Mr. Gorgeous on the street thought she had guts.

Rowan brightened. She did have guts, or at least she could again. Glaring at the new drywall patch where a doorway once had been, she decided not to let one small setback ruin her plans. She'd dealt with worse in her day. Rowan snipped the last threads from Melanie's dress, hung it in the armoire she'd appropriated for her personal use, then pulled out her sketch pad. She'd have her success, and savor it all the more because she'd earned it herself.

The afternoon stretched out quiet and still until Rowan's least favorite customer appeared. This was the woman's third visit to admire a mahogany dining set. Each time, she had lingered just a bit longer, running her dagger-tipped nails over the smooth surface of the table with an almost sexual pleasure. Today, she looked ready to make an offer.

"It's a beautiful set," the woman purred.

"Yes, it is."

Rowan noted the diamond only slightly smaller than a Ping-Pong ball sitting on her customer's left hand. The customer pursed her lips in a cute little pout that had probably pried lots of trinkets loose from her doting spouse.

"So the price is firm?"

Rowan then estimated the cost of the woman's designer wear and found she couldn't work up an ounce of sympathy or much of a discount, either. She opened her mouth to answer, but was drowned out by a loud blast of horn not usually heard outside the Swiss Alps.

"I—" she began again at the first available break, then clamped her jaw shut as the din resumed.

The customer stared curiously in the direction of J. Albreight's domain. "What's going on over there?"

Rowan raised one index finger in the universal sign for "hang on a minute," and marched toward the offending wall.

"Figures the guy would have the lung capacity of a marathon runner," she muttered under her breath. "My one big chance to make a sale, and this bozo's going to blow it for me—literally!"

She began to pound on the wall, fists slamming in unison. Framed Victorian prints rattled in time. The blast of horn was replaced by male laughter. Deep, loud and oddly familiar, the sound passed through the common wall. Rowan wanted to crawl right through and squash his nasty, smirking face.

"Jerk," she growled. She slammed the wall harder and the laughter amplified. A really awful cherub print flew from the wall and landed at her feet. The angelic little face gazed up at her in surprise. Rowan stared down at it, her breath coming in hitches.

She stood frozen, her hands poised on either side of her head like twin hammers. She was losing it, and in a big way. Slowly, she lowered her fists and impersonally noted that she was shaking. Not a genteel tremble, either. This was a full-fledged, rage-inspired tremor. She clasped her hands together in an effort to still them and turned to face her customer.

The woman stood, mouth agape, purse clutched to her chest.

"Yes, the price is firm," Rowan replied with a polite smile, as though no break in the conversation—or her sanity—had occurred.

"It's a very fair price, too." The customer's voice had climbed an octave. "I'll take the set."

"Fine." Rowan smoothed out her hair. She knew there wasn't much she could do about the crazed look she probably still carried in her eyes. "Let's not forget the sales tax, either."

The woman's sleek haircut bobbed up and down as she nodded her head in alarmed agreement. She wrote out a check and shoved a driver's license at Rowan without being asked. Rowan tried for a gracious smile.

As her customer hurriedly stuffed the identification back into her purse, Rowan asked, "You'll call with arrangements for pickup?"

"N-naturally."

Before Rowan could even thank her for the sale, the front door slammed shut, its bells clanging their objection to the rough treatment.

Rowan eased into a wing chair and examined the check in her hand. The sum made her smile with mercenary glee. Rage could be quite profitable. She could have given up a good fifteen percent on the set's marked price. Not that this customer had been in the mood to dicker. She probably felt lucky to have escaped with her life.

Rowan's gaze traveled to the rough patch of wall separating her from her neighbor. If he kept up with stunts like today's, Mr. J. Albreight was going to be lucky to escape with his life, too. As if he sensed her thoughts and found them pretty darned funny, that almost-familiar laughter started again.

3

JAKE COULDN'T STOP LAUGHING. He leaned his shoulder against the wall and just let the humor roll. For the first time since those randy days of early adolescence, he wished for X-ray vision. His powers of imagination weren't up to the task of picturing that sassy little mommy letting loose and pounding on the wall for all she was worth.

"Priceless," he murmured, then wiped the tears of mirth from his eyes. When he was more or less back under control, he wandered over to his latest piece.

Several months ago, on a rare day off work, he had visited one of his favorite hangouts, the Cranbrook Institute of Science. Cranbrook had been featuring an exhibit on peat bogs, including photos and recordings of a pair of *lurs,* ancient instruments unearthed in Danish bogs. The horns' sinuous lines attracted him—no big shock considering his eye for curves of one type or another.

He had decided on the spot that mastering one would be his next project. He'd returned to the museum a dozen times and listened to a recording of the *lur* before he got the tone just right. He grinned. The payoff was the rise it had gotten from his also nicely curved neighbor.

In the background the phone rang, a shrill annoyance. Three people had his new number. His dad was fishing in the Florida Keys and his older brother never called anyway. That left Victoria, who'd conned the number out of his dad.

Jake let the answering machine do the dirty work. On the heels of his terse recorded greeting, his ex-girlfriend's smooth voice echoed through the mostly empty shop.

"Jake, I know you're there. Pick up the phone. It's childish to ignore me like this."

He chuckled at that one. His evasive behavior was no more childish than Victoria's daily tantrums on his answering machine.

"I just want to make sure you're all right." She'd schooled her voice to a conciliatory tone, as if she were talking a jumper back from the edge. Too late. He'd taken the leap months ago.

"I stopped by, but you've got the windows covered. I'm worried about you."

He snorted. He'd been with Victoria long enough to know what "worried" meant. She was suffering from Empty Bed Syndrome and didn't know how to flat-out say she wanted sex. Victoria had never really worried about him. About polishing his rough edges, making sure he didn't make an ass of himself at one of her company parties, maybe. But about *him?* Never. He hated to admit it, but the thought still hurt.

"Call me, Jake."

"No way, Vicki."

She'd dumped him the second he told her about his plans to open a shop. It was okay for a hotshot auto exec to live with someone who had barely found time to finish high school. That is, so long as he owned one of the largest landscaping companies in the state. It was something else if he was unemployed.

Appearances meant everything to Victoria, and she'd

cultivated his down to the smallest detail. She'd educated him in the smooth business manners he lacked, and after a while, he'd come to resent her for the lessons. The more polished he became, the larger the business had grown. So big that it had almost eaten him alive. He'd ditched it, and Vicki ditched him. Now she was having second thoughts.

Well, he wasn't. Or only a few, which was why he refused to take her calls. Sometimes when it was late at night and he was feeling lonely, he'd wonder if he just might be stupid enough to allow her to come back. But more than he hated being alone, he hated being wanted for his money. Really, cold cash was all Vicki had wanted from him. That and hot sex, so long as it didn't mess up her hair or her business schedule.

The kicker of it was, he had more money now than he'd ever had when he was with Vicki. The best part of selling Greenworks was an agreement called a Covenant Not to Compete. The purchasers of his company weren't too keen on the idea of him opening a new landscaping business right away. For the next two years, he was being well paid to do nothing. Not bad work—if you could find it.

He set aside the horn and moved on to his workbench. Its surface was covered with whistles, drums and panpipes, made of everything from rosewood to PVC. He'd always made stuff like this, giving the instruments to family and friends, even selling a few to strangers. The best, though, he'd put aside, maybe with a half thought of someday doing just what he planned to now.

Victoria's friends had called his creations "art." Back then, he'd scoffed at the idea. It was just a hobby—sawing, painting, pounding on metal, a way of relieving stress.

Now, Jake didn't give a fat donkey's behind whether his work was art or therapy or both. When he got this gallery together, he'd round up his old business buddies, together with some of those bored, rich folks he'd met through Victoria. Then he'd throw one hell of an opening bash.

After that, with luck, he'd make enough cash from his hobby to call it a job. If not, when the Covenant Not to Compete ran out, he'd start a new company. And this time he'd have the brains to stop growing it before it killed him.

Jake took a good look around his new workplace and gave a resigned shake of his head. Even after he ripped up the carpet, a patchwork of 1970s shag samples, he'd still be quarts of cleaner followed by gallons of paint away from an opening. Still, there was only one way to start.

A few hours later, lopsided shelves had been demolished and chucked in the Dumpster. Beneath their camouflage of grunge, the walls were a putrid shade of aqua that reminded him of his great-aunt Bernice. Every room in her house had been this color. Now, the sight of it summoned childhood memories of being force-fed squash.

Using an airless sprayer, he planned to blast all the walls with white paint. But first he'd do the ceiling in black, and hang cheap but effective industrial light fixtures. He glanced down at the red-and-black diamond-patterned linoleum floor he'd unearthed. It was cool, in a retro sort of way.

A large iron floor grate along the back wall—part of some long-gone heating system—caught his eye. He'd have to find a better cover. He could imagine the big bucks lawsuit after some society dame caught her high heel and sprained an ankle. He nudged the heavy grate, it rattled. Deep down in the duct, a scraping noise echoed, followed by rodentlike scrabbling sounds.

"Mice," he muttered, making a mental note to buy some traps. The sound grew louder.

"Rats. Big, damn rats." Jake suppressed a shudder. He'd faced down his share of nasty creatures in his day, but damn, he hated rats. He upgraded from traps to a professional exterminator on the spot.

"*Ssshhh,* this way." The sound—so soft that at first he thought he'd imagined it—drifted up from the grate. Up from *his* basement.

"I'm being quiet. *You* be quiet!"

"Talking rats."

He'd heard those voices before. Each evening, he was subjected to what was either playtime or an evil howling contest. And every morning, he was tortured by their dog-whistle-shrill voices as they woke their mother.

"Little talking neighbor rats. Sneakiest kind."

ROWAN'S PAL Melanie strutted down the shop's narrow center aisle. Shoulders thrown back and cheeks sucked in to parody that underfed model look, she did a perfect runway turn.

"This is incredible, Rowan. I've spent my entire adult life trying to hide these," she gestured down at her generous hips and bustline, "and you make me look, well, sexy." She spoke the last word with reverent awe.

"You are sexy. I'm just showing you off." The sleek golden fabric of the dress clung lovingly to Melanie's breasts and then flowed to the floor. Rowan cocked her head and examined the effect. "Greek goddess is what I had in mind. Does it work?"

"Does it ever! Dan's going to fall over when he sees me in this. I wanted something really special for our party.

It's the fanciest bash we've ever thrown." She gazed at herself in a mirrored armoire door. "This is perfect."

Eyes bright with speculation, she swung around to face Rowan. "You know, our house is going to be crawling with bank-loan officers."

Rowan burst out laughing. "And I thought I was the only one who put bankers in a league with vermin." She'd tried the small-business loan route twice. Despite a business plan the bankers had loved, she'd been turned down. Not enough experience, they'd said. And no collateral.

Melanie gave a good-natured smile. "So they all can't be as perfect as my Dan. But really, Rowan, you ought to come on over. Some of those bankers are single. Two birds with one stone, and all that." Before Rowan could shape the words, her friend heaved a sigh of disgust. "I know, I know—Boy Vacation. How's it going, anyway?"

"Piece of cake," she fibbed.

"Seen that hunky man lately?"

She gave the news unwillingly. "Today, actually."

"Do tell?"

Rowan manufactured a casual shrug. She didn't need the Melanie McConnell Dating Service to know that she'd been wavering in her resolve. And after only a week, too. "Not much to tell. He said hi to me on the street this morning."

"That's a start," said the starry-eyed optimist.

"Then the UPS guy and I must be having one hot romance because he says hi to me every day."

Melanie wasn't deterred. "I'll give you two weeks, three at most, and mark my words, you'll be dating."

Rowan grinned. "Give it up, McConnell, and go on up to my apartment and get changed. You're a little overdressed, you know."

After Melanie left, Rowan stepped into the back room to see what the twins were up to. She pulled aside the curtain that cordoned off their play area from the rest of the storage room. Two coloring books lay open on a small table. Stubby crayon remnants were scattered around, including the obligatory few on the floor, but the twins were…gone, of course.

Rowan sprinted out the back door of the shop, over to the small landing area and upstairs to their apartment.

"All right, guys," she called as she climbed. "You're in trouble now."

She swung open the apartment door and was greeted by silence. "Abby? Mac? Are you in here?"

They weren't. She pounded downstairs and into the shop. "Kids, if this is your idea of a game, Mom's not playing." Panic had a firm hold, squeezing the air from her lungs. "Get out here *now!*"

She looked behind crates and peered down the basement steps. "This is *not* funny," she called, praying they could hear her.

"We're out *heee-re,*" Mac's singsong voice came from the front of the shop.

Rowan stalked back into the room. "This is getting really old, guys. Where have you been?"

Abby gave her most angelic smile. The effect was diminished by the streaks of grime across her face and the cobwebs tangled in her hair. "We were playin' hide and seek, and you were 'it.'"

"I can't be 'it' unless I know I'm playing."

"We heard you say this wasn't a game, so we came out." Mac's T-shirt was torn and his face even dirtier than Abby's.

"Out from where?"

Mac and Abby briefly touched hands, silent twin communication. They could have entire conversations without speaking a word, conspire with a simple touch. Now they were in accord. Abby nodded her head, freeing a fat dust bunny from her wild tangle of curls.

She pointed to a set of oak head- and footboards leaning against the wall. "Behind those beds over there."

Rowan ran her fingers through Abby's mop to dislodge whatever other creatures might be hiding in there. "You're going to tell me you got this dirty just crawling back there?"

"Yeah, you better clean up before Auntie Celeste comes back or she's gonna be *m-a-a-a-d,*" Mac said.

"I don't suppose that you'd like to tell me the truth?"

The gazed at her guilelessly. "That is the truth, Mommy."

"Mmm-hmm, sure it is."

JAKE STOOD in the middle of his basement, which was not his favorite room to begin with. He preferred places with more…air. And maybe a little more space so that he couldn't actually see the walls closing in on him. He dragged in a ragged breath and began a mental recitation of the usual platitudes.

Gut it out. Be a man. Control the circumstances, don't let them control you.

Better…sort of. Since he wasn't a fan of the "big picture," Jake focused on the details of his surroundings. The bare bulb hanging from the ceiling gave enough light that he could see the dozen boxes he still had to unpack, and the stacks of ancient magazines and piles of junk left by a former tenant. It didn't shed any light on where the little rats were hiding.

He knew they were still down there. There was no way out other than the stairs. Although, come to think of it, that was also the only way in. Down the narrow, dirty stairway from his own back room. He shook his head. He had let two maniac midgets slip in the back door without even hearing them.

Of course, he'd also failed to snag them the other day when they'd coated his apartment doorknob with peanut butter. Not to mention when they'd booby-trapped his mailbox with rubber snakes.

Even without their guerilla approach to welcoming the new neighbor, he wouldn't have had much use for them. Kids' litanies of questions were like fingernails down a blackboard. And he wasn't especially picky, but the way their hands and faces were always glopped up with whatever they'd eaten or rolled in really distracted him. He didn't know what to do with kids—except maybe haul 'em back to their mom, in this case.

"You might as well come on out. You're trapped, you know." He heard nothing, didn't even feel that primal tingle that let him know someone was watching him. "So much for jungle instinct," he muttered.

He dragged aside boxes, nudged piles of stuff with his foot. "You're in here. You have to be. Come on out, I won't hurt you. Hell, I mean, heck, I won't even yell at you."

He took a step backward and almost sprawled over a three-legged chair that lay on the ground behind him. Only flailing arms and an outstanding sense of balance stopped him from an ignominious landing on his butt.

As he righted himself, he knew without a doubt that he was alone. After all, no self-respecting kid could watch a grown-up make a fool of himself without laughing. Jake pulled together the shreds of his dignity. He forced himself to take the steps to freedom at a calm, nonclaustrophobic pace.

"Their voices must have carried through from the other side, that's all," he said aloud for any potential listeners over in Lindsay-land, while his jungle instinct weighed in with its silent opinion: *They were here, buddy. You know it!*

Sooner or later, he'd snare those sneaks, and he'd do it on his own turf.

4

IT WAS ONE OF THOSE glorious days where three things combined to create perfection: Indian summer, a sidewalk café and a best friend. Leaning back in her chair, Rowan indulged in a moment of people watching before answering Melanie's latest question. It had been over a week since they'd seen each other, and they had tons of catching up to do.

"I didn't say I've given up completely on my own shop, Mel—just that it looks like Royal Oak's out of the question. I've spent a week making calls and chasing down leads, and come up with nothing," she said, holding out empty hands. "Let's face it, Aunt Celeste's space was probably the last fixer-upper left in town."

"Well, there has to be a way to pull this off! You're too good and too young to put your dreams away."

Rowan felt warmed not just by the lazy fall sun, but by her friend's ardent support. Melanie was an awesome one-person cheering section. It felt as if they'd known each other forever, instead of the eleven months Rowan had been back in Michigan.

"I'm not putting my dreams away…just on hold for a while. Besides, the timing's not right. Aunt Celeste called last night and asked if I'd mind tending the store for just a few extra weeks. How could I say no?" Rowan shrugged, masking her disappointment by taking a long sip of her iced tea. Setting the glass back down, she added, "Anyway, I figure with the hours I'm putting in at the store, and the overtime keeping up with Abby and Mac's latest mischief campaign, I've got enough to handle."

Melanie leaned forward, her mouth curving into the amused smile that everyone but Rowan seemed to wear when there was a twin tale to tell. "Abby and Mac? What are they up to now?"

"Let me put it this way—Houdini and David Copperfield got nothin' on those two."

"Don't tell me they disappeared again!"

"Four times this week alone," Rowan replied. "But I know they're still somewhere in the store, or they couldn't get back to me so quickly. Still..." She hesitated when a shadow came over the table, then lingered. At Melanie's low, murmured sound of approval, she glanced up.

There, in all his glory, stood Mr. Gorgeous. Rowan's heart did a slow dance at the sight of him. He was so wonderfully disreputable looking. Only the humorous sparkle in his brown eyes saved him from a total tough guy appearance. Even then, he was close enough to the real thing that a dollop of hesitance mixed in with those libidinous urges she was feeling.

Broad, sun-darkened hands braced on the railing that separated the café from the rest of the busy street, he smiled at her. "Hey, supersleuth."

"H-hi," Rowan returned, wincing at the way her nervous stammer made her sound as if she were panting. Not that it was so far from the truth.

"Are you on some sort of mission, or actually enjoying the day?"

"I'm off work right now." Rowan spared a glance at Melanie, whose grin held a touch too much mischief for

Rowan's peace of mind. She gave her friend a warning nudge under the table, then launched into the formalities. "Melanie, I'd like you to meet—"

Pausing, Rowan glanced at Mr. Gorgeous. She knew a lot about the way his eyes crinkled when he smiled and what a fine behind he had. What she didn't know was his name. Arching her brows into an inquisitive curve, she waited for him to fill in the blank.

After an uncomfortable silence, he did. "Jake…Jake Miller," he answered, seeming to stumble over the name.

Now who was stammering? "Jake, this is Melanie McConnell."

Apparently recovered, he smiled an easy greeting at Melanie. "Hey, Melanie, great to meet you. Maybe you can clear up a little mystery for me."

"Such as?"

"Our friend's name. I've been captured by her kids and caught her spying, but she's never told me her name."

"Rowan! This is Rowan Lindsay. She's twenty-five, single and would love to—" Melanie finished with a yelp when Rowan planted a sincerely meant kick on her shin.

"Enough, Mel."

"Just trying to be helpful, that's all."

"Then stick with name, rank and serial number," she ordered, more embarrassed than actually angry.

Melanie batted her eyelashes. "Gee, I thought I did."

Jake the Gorgeous grinned down at Rowan, making her feel all warm and nervous and thrilled. "How about dinner tonight?"

"I can't—" The words slipped out automatically even as her heart finished another roller-coaster loop.

"I'll watch the kids," Melanie cut in. "That way you

don't have to worry about scraping up the money for a sitter."

For just an instant, Jake's smile looked a little frosty around the edges, but Rowan didn't take the time to consider why he might look that way. She had her own emotional stew simmering.

She pulled her gaze downward. This would be much less painful if she didn't actually look at what she was passing up. She had to turn him down.

She'd decided on a Boy Vacation to gain time to rebuild her confidence, and to get the twins well in hand before she lost out on a man she really cared about. Intuition shouted that Jake was going to fall into that category. She wasn't ready.

Not quite yet.

"I'm not dating right now," Rowan said with as much certainty as she could muster.

His smile was definitely back, and very persuasive. "Then don't consider it a date, call it reconnaissance. We'll have dinner at that Italian joint across from the neighbor you're so curious about, and you can do some spying."

"Really, I'm not interested," she said, knowing she'd never sounded less sincere in her life. And she knew that her interest had nothing to do with checking up on the wacky next-door neighbor.

"No pressure," Jake answered in that deep and sexy voice that could probably talk her into pulling a Lady Godiva act down Main Street. "Tell you what, I'll be there at seven tonight—the table right in the front window. And who knows, you just might pass by and feel like a bite to eat and a little company. At least, I'm hoping you will." He strolled off, leaving Rowan no time to answer.

In a superhuman feat of restraint, Melanie managed to hold her peace right up until a teenaged flower-shop clerk, blazing-green apron and all, came up to the table.

"You Rowan Lindsay?"

When Rowan nodded, he thrust a long, narrow box in her face. "This is for you," he said, then ambled back down the sidewalk.

"Go on, open it!" Melanie squealed. "What do you think it is?"

Rowan rolled her eyes and pretended to be cool when, in fact, she was nowhere near relaxed. "Gee, Mel, I don't know, maybe it's a brand-new candy-apple-red Porsche." Her fingers trembled as she slid the bow from the box and lifted the lid.

One rose, slender and silvery lavender—her favorite color—lay inside. Amazing, and just enough to send a tingle shimmering through her. She gently lifted the flower from its bed of pale pink tissue, took in its delicious scent, and settled it back into the box.

A tiny card nestled in one corner. Rowan laughed as she read the note. "No pressure," it said.

"Either you go to dinner with him, or I am!" Melanie announced, still giving the rose a covetous look.

"Uh, Mel, I don't think Dan would be real hot on that."

"Then you'd just better get yourself all fixed up and hustle your butt over to that restaurant tonight. If you don't, Rowan Lindsay, it's just, well, criminal!" Melanie finished in a voice loud enough to call the cops.

Rowan winced. "Keep it down. You're scaring everyone," she said, gesturing at the café patrons, who watched them with undisguised interest.

"I'm trying to scare you out of this rut you're in. I hate

to say it, kiddo, but you're in danger of becoming dull, and I mean with a capital *D!*''

Rowan slumped back in her chair. Melanie had honed in on her greatest secret fear. It was no cakewalk being the only parent and pretty much the only provider for two kids. It took planning, ritual, a schedule! So maybe she had become a bit rigid in her thinking. But *dull?* Rowan could feel it creeping up behind her in its drab, rusted four-door sedan and pure polyester clothes. *Dull.*

No way!

"Pick up the kids at four," Rowan commanded. The battle lines had been drawn. Dull was about to take it square in the teeth!

OR MAYBE NOT. Rowan gazed at the antique Regulator clock hanging on her living-room wall—6:55 p.m. She parted flowery drapes just enough to peek across the street at the stuccoed facade of La Bella Italia. A man of his word, that Jake. Framed in the restaurant's front window, he lounged at a table for two. The other empty chair beckoned to her.

Rowan yanked the drapes shut. She would have flung herself onto the sofa if she didn't fear getting goosed by one of the kids' action figures reaching up from between the cushions. She wished for the thousandth time she hadn't let Melanie give her that last little nudge into her current state of craziness. Now here she stood, all painted and perfumed in a dress that did a lot for her figure but nothing at all for her level of comfort. She gave one more nervous tug at the vee in front. A fine state of nerves she had herself in, over something that wasn't even a date!

She wanted to be at the movies with Melanie and the

twins. Mel would probably stuff them full of buttery pop-corn and those monster-size boxes of candy. Lucky kids.

Instead she stood in her own apartment, all bold thoughts, but still too scared to reach for a little fun. Or maybe a lot of it. Right across the street. It shouldn't be this hard, going out for a simple dinner. It shouldn't be this hard to open her life to someone else…to trust some-one. But it was. Chip, that cheating louse with his blue-blooded Back Bay breeding, had seen to that.

The antique clock behind her whirred, clicked, then be-gan its rusty chime to the count of seven. Human nature being what it is, Rowan turned to double-check the time. Mesmerized, she followed the arc of the clock's filigreed pendulum.

Jake…Chip. Jake…Chip. With each ticktock of the clock, *Jake…Chip.*

Opposite sides of the pendulum swing, for sure. She'd had enough of Chip's sort to last her a lifetime. And Jake? Rowan's emotions whirled—nerves and excitement and something really bright and shiny that she'd never felt warm her before. She straightened, picked up her purse and marched out of the apartment. Boy Vacation had of-ficially ended.

IT'S NO BIG DEAL, Jake tried to tell himself as Rowan walked in the restaurant door. *So maybe you didn't think she'd wear a little red dress that's snug in exactly the right places. Maybe you had no idea that she'd have that gotta-sink-my-fingers-into-it hair when it wasn't pulled back into a ponytail. Just play it cool, guy.*

He went to push back his chair and stand to greet her when he realized he was already on his feet. So much for cool. "Glad you're here," he said. The less words the better.

"Thanks," she replied as he held out her chair and she slipped into it. He'd barely gotten into his own seat before she launched into a speed-of-light monologue he was too distracted to keep up with. "But I want you to know that just because I showed up doesn't make this a date or anything. I mean, there are a thousand different reasons I could have decided to have dinner out. Maybe I'm hungry, or maybe I just need a night away from the kids, or...or—"

He lifted his hands in mock surrender. "Hey, I didn't say it was a date. In fact, I didn't say much of anything. Let's take this from the beginning, nice and slow and easy." He extended one hand across the table and patiently waited for Rowan to extend hers. When she did, he was careful not to hold it too long. He didn't plan to give her an excuse to run from the restaurant—which was exactly what she looked like she wanted to do.

Then he tried out some of the harmless and easy-to-remember semifiction he'd been rehearsing all afternoon. "My name's Jake Miller. I'm a welder—when I can find work—and I'm thirty years old. There, now we're even. You have my name, rank and serial number, too," he said.

She smiled. A knockout of a smile, to top it off, dammit. Jake could feel his heartbeat rev up to cruising speed. He subtly rubbed his palms against his khaki-covered knees. He hadn't had sweaty palms since he was sixteen years old and in the back seat of an old Chevy with Brandi Johnston and her tissue-stuffed bra.

So why now? It couldn't be the insignificant little lies he'd told, could it? Not possible. After all, no one was going to get hurt in this game. Just a little fun for both players. *Except Rowan doesn't know she's playing, you jerk*, his conscience snarled.

"Want some wine?" he offered, trying to drown out howling moral indignation.

"Sure, a little," she said. "I don't drink very much."

Jake poured a splash from the bottle of house Chianti sitting on the table. "So tell me, Sherlock, seen that neighbor of yours yet?"

She shot a narrow-eyed look across the street to the J. Albreight Gallery's covered windows. "I haven't seen him, but I've sure heard enough from him. But hey, I don't want to spoil my dinner thinking about that weirdo."

Weirdo? Maybe he was doing too good of a job spicing up her life. "Okay, let's try this. When you're not chasing your kids or working in that antique shop, what do you do for fun?"

She blinked at him oddly, as if he were speaking a foreign language. "Fun? I sew."

"Sew?"

"Yeah. I made this." She gestured shyly at the dress he'd almost riveted his eyeballs to when she'd come into the restaurant.

"It's...great," he finished lamely, thinking that a confession of a need to peel off the outfit with his teeth wasn't going to score any points.

"Thanks. I'm trying to start up my own business, but the banks won't touch me, and I don't happen to have any rich old grandmas lurking or mystery benefactors waiting in the wings. You wouldn't happen to know of any, would you?"

Thankful for the crisp white tablecloth hiding him, Jake wiped another sheen of sweat from his palms. Panic, this time. It was unfair of him to react this way. He knew it and couldn't stop himself. Rowan didn't—*and wouldn't*—know about his money.

"Nope, me and all my buddies are paycheck to paycheck. You don't play the lotto, huh?" he asked in a casual voice.

"That's like throwing cash out the car window. Every spare penny I have goes into the vacation fund. I figured if I start saving now, I'll be able to get Abby and Mac down to Florida to see the Mouse right before they're too old to care. And I don't even want to think about the cost of college. I'm hoping for some big, fat scholarships for them, or—"

He had to cut this off before he had some sort of anxiety attack. "How about their dad? Wouldn't he help out?"

"Chip?"

"Chip? Your husband's name was *Chip?*" He'd been handed the mother of all distractions. Jake knew there were countless preppy Chips, Treys and Trips in this world, but not in a million years could he imagine Rowan actually married to one. She was as far from the conservative silk dress, single strand of pearls women in a Chip's world as he could picture. With her gypsy hair and exotic clothes, she must have had a rotten time fitting in.

She frowned. "Yes, his name was Chip. And, no, he won't be helping out." She snapped open the menu that the waiter had just shown the perfect timing to present.

End of topic. Good thing, too. He knew all he needed to about her dismal finances. And she knew all she needed to about his. Zippo. Jake opened his menu and checked to see if weasel was one of the selections, because that voice inside kept telling him he was one king weasel.

"I'm sorry, I shouldn't have been so abrupt."

She was apologizing? Jake put down his menu. "Look, it's none of my business. I just kind of wondered about…"

"Their dad?" Her nose twitched as though she smelled something unpleasant. "We might as well get that out of the way, too. He's a lawyer, and a lot older than I am. I met him when he came to recruit for his law firm on campus at U of M."

Jake gave a low whistle. "You went to the University of Michigan? Pretty impressive stuff."

She shrugged. "Went, but didn't graduate. I met Chip and we started a long-distance romance. He'd fly into town from Boston every few weekends. Everything was great for the days we were together." She paused, and looking as if she really needed it, took a sip of her wine. "But before I married him, I should have asked what he was doing on those days we were apart. You see, I have a pretty low tolerance for liars."

Jake didn't suppose he should ask her to define "pretty low."

She started toying with the silverware, arranging it to suit her instead of convention. She didn't look up as she finished her story. "Chip wasn't much for fidelity. It didn't work out."

Out-and-out cheating from the old Chipster. Jake tried to imagine the man who'd be stupid enough to cheat on a woman like Rowan. One thing was for sure: By comparison, the jerk had left Jake looking a lot closer to a saint than a sinner.

"I'm sorry you had to go through that," he said, mentally adding that he wasn't sorry in the least that she'd ended up living in Royal Oak. He relaxed for the rest of the meal and enjoyed their conversation. She was brave and funny and smart, and his "nondate" was slipping by way too quickly.

IT WASN'T MIDNIGHT, but as she and Jake finished the last of their after-dinner coffees, Rowan began to feel a definite connection with Cinderella. Very soon, she'd have to rush home, hang up her hot red dress and return to everyday life.

She wanted a little more time with her prince of a welder. And if she was learning one thing, it was that you can't have something unless you ask for it. "Would you like to take a walk around town? It's warm enough that I'll bet some of the street musicians are still out."

"Can't think of anything I'd rather do," he said. Then Jake gave her a slow-and-sexy smile that had Rowan imagining a thing or two she'd like to do with this guy. A thing or two she hadn't done in so long, she was shocked when the image blazed through her mind.

Rowan pushed back from the table. "Then let's go," she said in a quavery voice. She stood and hung her art-deco beaded bag over her shoulder. Maybe under the streetlights her blush wouldn't show so much. Then again, she might just glow in the dark.

As they strolled down Main Street with its row of cafés and restaurants, Rowan pretended that her heart wasn't pumping a million miles an hour, all over the feel of Jake's large hand wrapped around hers. They chatted about the wares displayed in the art galleries and about the wild mix of hairstyles on the teenagers who hung out on the corners.

When he led her down a side street toward a grassy area where several people stood listening to a trio playing slow, jazzy music, Rowan smiled. "You must live around here. Not many people know where to find these guys."

"I live in the area," he answered as they stood at the back of the group.

Rowan liked that thought, knowing he was close by. "Me, too. Right upstairs from the antique shop."

Jake nodded absently. "Convenient," he said, then led her away from the small crowd and onto the grass. "Dance with me."

"Here?" she squeaked.

"Here," he replied in a low, firm voice. Drawing her into his arms, Jake gave her no time to consider whether she was really the sort of woman who'd dance on a patch of grass with no other couples to camouflage her nervousness. It was a blessing, because Rowan feared she wasn't the sort. But she wanted to be.

He was a good dancer. It felt natural to move with him in time to the slow sway of the music. One song slipped into the next and she scarcely noticed when other couples joined them on the makeshift dance floor. Only Jake mattered.

She looked up at him. In the dim light, he seemed even more dangerous than usual, and definitely delicious. His eyes shone dark and hot as he returned her gaze. Rowan thought she heard him mutter a soft curse, then didn't think at all as his mouth came down over hers.

She froze. Simply froze. Eyes wide-open, heart suspended somewhere between beats. When was the last time a man had kissed her? She couldn't recall. What was she supposed to do? She couldn't recall that, either.

Then as his lips moved firm, insistent and persuasive over hers, it all came back to Rowan—everything she knew, and a few moves she was pretty sure she hadn't known before.

Her eyes slipped closed. She pulled nearer and felt her heart start a mad waltz as one broad hand swept up and down her back. She opened her mouth wider. At the first sure sweep of his tongue tasting her, tasting of coffee and sweet liqueur, Rowan felt her knees give way and clutched even closer to his strong, hard body.

She would never know how long they stood there, both hearts pounding, both of them unwilling to be the first to end this wonderful madness.

Long enough for the music to stop.

Long enough for a smattering of applause to draw them back to reality.

Long enough to end the kiss, turn and realize that the applause was for *them!*

She ducked her crimson face against Jake's chest. His low laughter vibrated pleasantly against her burning cheek. "I feel like I've just awakened Sleeping Beauty," he murmured, and then gave her a brief, reassuring hug.

Wrong fairy tale, she wanted to say. *I'm one scared Cinderella and the clock's about to chime.*

"I think it's time I get home," she said instead. "Melanie's probably been back with the kids for ages." It bothered Rowan, using the twins as a way to cover the shock that held her, but it beat announcing the truth.

Melanie had been right. Jake Miller was no boy. And Rowan had no idea how to hold her heart safe from this man.

JAKE STOOD with Rowan outside her apartment. She had already unlocked the door and was poised to flee. He wanted to kiss her again. Actually, he wanted to start kissing her and never stop. Not when the sun came up. Not when he was ninety years old and needed a walker to keep standing.

Better not to start at all, especially when she looked so vulnerable, her eyes wide, face pale and mouth rosy from their earlier kiss. Kiss, hell! That had been some sort of hot, wild, hammered-over-the-head miracle, not a mere kiss.

"I need to see you again," he said. "Tomorrow."

She blinked, then shook her head as if she were coming out of a dream. "Abby and Mac—"

The words dropped like a roadblock in front of him.

"Lunch, then. They do go to school, right?" *Or Juvie Hall,* he added silently, recalling the tiny plastic building blocks scattered on the back steps that he'd about broken his leg on earlier tonight.

"Full-day kindergarten, but I have to work."

He was pushing too fast for both of them, but he couldn't help himself. He'd figure out this whole money-less Miller/rich Albreight two-guys-in-one mess later. After he saw her again.

"I'll bring the food to you."

"Jake—"

"Don't say no. Just lunch. No pressure," he wheedled.

Her answering smile was a little lopsided. "I think I've heard that somewhere before."

"And look what it got me—dinner with the prettiest woman in town."

She looked startled at his words, as though it had never occurred to her that she was pretty. More than ever, he wanted to bring some happiness into her life.

"Just lunch," she finally said.

He never thought he could feel so stupidly joyful. "Great."

"Well, see you tomorrow, then. I need to get some sleep." With that she slipped inside her apartment.

Jake turned and pulled out the keys to his own place. He was about to unlock his own door and hit the sack when two very obvious problems smacked him. First, sound carried through the old building with incredible ease. To have him open his squeaky apartment door, then rattle around inside mere seconds after he'd dropped off Rowan was a dumb move.

The second problem was sleep. Even if he tiptoed, he'd still hear Rowan on her side of the wall. It had taken only a night or two to figure out that her bed was one thin bit of wood and plaster away from his. He'd already spent enough time imagining her on that bed. Tonight's kiss had filled in a few more blanks in the picture.

No, sleep wasn't in the cards for hours to come. Not until he was too wiped out to remember that lush mouth, the feel of her under his hands, that little sound she made when he touched his tongue against hers for the first time. That, Jake admitted, might take forever.

With a sigh, he trudged down the stairs and made his way back to Main Street. A little music with his pals at Sonny's Bar sounded just right because, baby, Jake Albreight...Miller—*whoever the heck he was*—wanted to sing the Found-the-Right-Girl-and-Screwed-It-All-Up Blues.

5

"WATCH OUT, BROADWAY. Here come Abby and Mac!" Rowan proclaimed over the twins' enthusiastic, if slightly off-key, rendition of a Disney song they'd heard with Melanie at the movies the night before.

"Top this, Albreight," she added just under her breath before grabbing a spoon to bang against the pot she waved in her left hand. She pounded out a hot beat, maybe not as funky as what her neighbor could produce, but not half-bad for kitchen music at seven in the morning.

Good old J. Albreight had come in late, at 1:29 a.m., to be exact. And Rowan could be exact. She'd been tossing and turning at that hour, replaying for the zillionth time her kiss with Jake. Over Mr. J-stands-for-Jerk Albreight's wailing harmonica blues, she'd told herself that her reaction to Jake's kiss was natural. To be expected, even. After all, it had been a long time—a *very* long time—since she'd experienced anything other than the five-year-old, jam-sticky variety of smooch.

Rowan rolled her eyes. What a weenie excuse! As much to scold herself as to wake the bluesman next door, she smacked the spoon against the pot, making an extraloud clang. She knew that it wasn't the end of the kissing drought that had brought her to total meltdown. Nope, that complete loss of time and place had been for one man—

Jake Miller. And this morning, she found that thought as petrifying as she had last night.

It was one thing to make a minor exception to her self-declared break from dating. It was something else again to have gone head over heels the instant Jake's mouth touched hers. She hardly knew the guy! Chemistry was a quirky—and scary—thing.

"Mommy, are you okay?"

Rowan shook off her reverie. Abby and Mac were gazing up at her, their little foreheads creased with concern.

"We stopped singing a long time ago, and you've just been standing there looking all goofy," Mac said.

All goofy. That was a pretty sharp assessment of her emotional state. "Just woolgathering," she said.

"I don't see any sheep," Abby pointed out. "You're not gonna get much wool that way."

Rowan grinned. There was no creature more literal than a child. "Good point, kiddo. Okay, one round of 'It's a Small World,' then it'll be time to eat." The twins launched into the song wholeheartedly. As they sang, Rowan set her pot/instrument back on the stove, reached for the oatmeal, put herself on autopilot and threw together breakfast.

What should she do about Jake? Despite what he thought, she wasn't much of a risk taker, and putting her heart up for grabs was the biggest risk she could imagine. She also didn't like playing games, with the possible exception of evening the score with her neighbor. Rowan turned up the flame beneath the oatmeal and absently stirred the pot's contents. All this uncertainty was making her crazy. She didn't know what Jake wanted from her, or what he expected of her.

She wasn't very clear on what she wanted from Jake,

either. Except maybe another one of those kisses. Just to find out if she'd imagined that whole skyrockets-and-string-music thing, of course.

Rowan winced at that little lie. She could almost see her mom, back in the apple-pie-scented kitchen of Rowan's childhood, waggling a finger and saying, "Honesty is the best policy, dear."

Okay, honesty. She wanted more than a kiss. She wanted hearts and flowers and long, romantic walks. She wanted someone to share her dreams with. She wanted solid, sexy Jake. But only if he understood that she was part of a package deal. Only if he was willing to accept Abby and Mac.

Maybe if she got all her worries out in the open, she'd be able to sleep at night. Maybe Jake could give her an honest response. That wasn't so much to ask from a man, was it? The twins' song reached a crescendo, then ended. Rowan heard the sound of applause from the next apartment.

"At least the guy believes in fair play," she murmured. She only hoped that Jake Miller did, too.

As JAKE NEARED Lindsay's Antique Emporium, he ran through a quick mental checklist he figured should be titled "How to Impress a Girl on the Cheap."

Another lavender rose, which wasn't cheap, but even if he was setting a bad precedent for himself with a rose a day, he wanted to pamper her. A little, at least.

A few pastries from the Greek bakery down the street to play up to her sweet tooth. He'd learned that it never hurt to present dessert first.

A couple of veggie sandwiches from the deli, since he'd noticed she hadn't ordered anything with meat last night.

Wouldn't want to offend her sensibilities if she happened to be a vegetarian.

And finally, some raspberry iced tea. He hoped it was caffeine laden. Three cups of coffee hadn't been enough to get him firing on all cylinders after Rowan's wake-up call. He grinned at the memory. The woman had spunk, all right. No notes under the door or threats to tell the landlord, just a get-even concert of her own.

About now, he'd kill for a bottle of supercharged cola, but women seemed to like that fussy tea stuff. At least, Victoria had. Then again, she had liked everything fancy and fussy, and the more expensive the better.

Jake stopped in his tracks. Rowan didn't seem to be about fancy and fussy. At least, not when she was with empty-pockets Jake Miller. Maybe some water or juice would be better. He retraced his steps to the deli and bought some of each, plus a turkey sandwich to be sure he had his bases covered.

When he reached the antique shop, he realized that he'd done such a good job of base covering that he didn't have a hand free to open the door. Leaning over, he jammed his elbow onto the top of the handle, trying to push the latch downward. Struggling to keep his load of bags and boxes from falling, he didn't notice that he had help until the door opened and he stumbled inside.

"We really need to talk," Rowan said, while herding him toward a dining table at the back of the store. "I didn't sleep much last night—"

"Me, neither," he muttered, but she didn't even slow to take a breath.

"—and I've been doing a lot of thinking today. I really need to know where we're headed. I mean, I don't want to sound pushy or anything, it's just that I have two kids—''

''I know,'' he managed to fit in as she tugged the parcels from his hands and put them on the table. It was hard to miss little rodents who spent their free time trying to sabotage him. While he'd been romancing their mom last night, they'd upped the ante from putting peanut butter on the doorknob. He'd come home from Sonny's to find that some green substance he didn't want to dwell on had been squeezed into his door's lock cylinder.

''—and I have to think of them before I think of myself. They've had a lot of disruption in their lives, and I'm trying to make a home for them. Someplace safe. Someplace stable. I like you a lot. Really. But I don't want to start something that—that—'' She paused long enough to draw a breath, then finished with, ''If you want to be just friends, that's okay by me...I guess.''

Well, damn.

Was this really the woman who'd given him that all-out kiss the night before? One and the same, though now she was wringing her hands instead of holding on to him as if she'd never let go. He tried for a pleasant smile, but it came out a little crooked. A little tense.

''Darlin', there hasn't been a man born yet who wants to be 'just friends.' In fact, we're genetically coded to bang our heads on a brick wall when a woman uses those words on us.'' He moved toward her, and she backed away. Keeping his voice calm and low, he edged nearer, testing her limits, waiting to see how close she'd let him come. ''You know, I'm beginning to sense a pattern here.''

Her eyes narrowed. ''A pattern? We haven't known each other long enough to have a pattern.''

''Sure we have. You're acting just like you did last night

at dinner. You come at me blazing away, making sure I can't get a word in edgewise. Making sure you get me as off balance as you appear to be feeling.'' He noticed that she was turning a cute shade of pink, whether out of embarrassment or because she heard the truth in what he was saying, he didn't know. ''It's my turn now. I don't know where we're headed, I haven't even thought about your kids, but I'm pretty sure about one thing…. You don't want to be 'just friends.'''

''I don't?''

''Nope.'' He moved close enough to grasp her elbows and draw her the rest of the way to him. ''Want me to prove it?''

She was staring at his mouth. ''No.''

''Liar,'' he said, then settled his lips over the pulse thrumming at her throat. Oh, she tasted good, all sweet and clean and sexy. She leaned into him and gave a sigh that did a lot for his self-confidence.

''Need more proof?'' he asked.

''Well, maybe just a little.''

It was the first time Jake could recall wanting to laugh and kiss a woman at the same time. But the urge to laugh disappeared the moment Rowan's lips touched his. In its place came the need to let his hands run everywhere his imagination had already visited, to find some big feather bed and sink into its depths with her. To…

Her tongue teased his, and she wrapped her arms around his neck. Still kissing her, Jake looked around the best he could for a bed, an armchair, anything soft. He backed her toward a sofa—well, not his idea of one, but some froufrou thing with a narrow seat and spindly legs.

She was small and light, and it was easy to settle her on the sofa, kneel next to her and keep on kissing. Definitely keep on kissing. He needed more, though. He caressed his way down to the vee of her throat and fumbled with the buttons on her shirt. He had to learn whether she was as smooth and silky as he'd imagined. He ran knuckles over the soft rises of flesh clasped by the lacy pink cups of her bra.

Warm...gorgeous...perfect.

He let his mouth follow the same trail, and felt his heart turn over when she whispered his name, then tugged at his shoulders to bring him even closer. He was pretty sure he knew where things were heading—where he wanted them to head. Then the bells on the front door chimed and reminded him exactly where they were.

"Hey, Rowan, I've got the names of three more women just dying for your dresses! Rowan...are you back there?" called a woman's voice from somewhere too close for comfort.

Rowan gasped, then sat up so fast that Jake ended up sprawled on his butt.

"Back here, Mel," she called while closing the buttons on her blouse. "Give me just a second. Get *up!*" she directed him, in a low, urgent voice.

Jake stood and tried to get a grip on his surroundings. Rowan had a way of making him forget *who* he was, let alone where. He flinched as the truth hammered him. He'd managed to screw up the "who" part all on his own.

He had to end this stupid game, and fast. He didn't have to tell her everything—especially not his bank balance—but he did have to tell her that he was the guy next door. While Jake didn't want to focus on exactly what she might mean to him, he knew she deserved better than what he was giving.

"You were right, we definitely gotta talk," he said.

"Later," she squeaked, then left the nook the taller furniture created around their couch, or whatever the hell it was.

"What's up?" he heard Rowan say in a voice that was suddenly about as high-pitched as her kids'.

Figuring there was no point in hiding, Jake stepped out to join her.

Rowan's pal looked him up and down with a knowing—and clearly pleased—smile. "Nothing as interesting as whatever you've got going on here."

"You remember Jake, don't you, Melanie?" Rowan asked, then winced. She was blushing again. Jake watched as the color rose from the collar of her—*oh, cripes, was he going to hear it later!*—misbuttoned shirt to paint its way across her cheeks. "Well, of course you do, since you just met him yesterday."

"Hey, Jake. Quite a difference a day can make," Melanie practically purred.

Since he couldn't come up with an answer that wouldn't embarrass Rowan more, he settled for a smile. He tried to angle himself between Rowan and her friend. Rowan gave him an annoyed look and stepped around him. He subtly tried to tug her back.

"Jake brought me lunch," Rowan was saying, waving her hand toward the still-unpacked food. "Just a friendly visit."

"Best of buddies," Melanie agreed, her eyes sparkling. "Well, I don't want to interrupt…things. I guess I'll take off. I'll tell you later about the new clients who are going to be lining up at your door. When you're not so… occupied." She gave a cheery wave and turned back toward the front of the store. Jake began to believe that he just might have escaped a bad scene.

Rowan's sigh of relief was audible.

Then, just before opening the front door, Melanie paused. She turned back toward them. "One thing. Normally, I wouldn't mention a tiny detail like this, but, Rowan, knowing what a stickler you are about fashion and all..." She hesitated, then said, "Your shirt."

"My shirt?"

She waggled her fingers toward Rowan's chest. "I don't think that's quite the, uh, statement you intended."

Rowan looked down, and with a gasp, yanked the two-button gap closed.

Melanie giggled, then added, "Then again, maybe it is. I'll let you two get back to lunch," she finished, giving the last word laughing emphasis.

After Melanie left, Rowan wheeled to him. "Why didn't you say something? Or do something?"

"I tried, but it's not like I had a whole lot of options. And I don't think it would have saved your dignity if I did this in front of your friend." He unbuttoned her shirt, then rebuttoned it to close the breach.

She swatted at his hands as he finished. "Let's just eat."

Since this wasn't exactly the moment to bring up the little joke he'd been playing on her—maybe *with her* had a better sound to it—Jake sat down and ate.

After they'd finished the meal and Rowan seemed calmer, Jake gathered his courage. No way to do this but get it all out. Like yanking a splinter. He scooted his chair from the table just far enough for a quick exit if she got really, really mad. "Have you ever started something, then not known how to finish it?"

Rowan smiled, and he stored away the sight of it, figuring it was the last one he'd get for some time. Maybe forever.

"Well, there's that quilt I made for my mom when I was ten. It's about as wide as a scarf and she still has it on the end of her bed. That kind of thing?"

He knew that he wasn't doing a good job of hiding the way he was squirming because the smile left her face.

"Are you talking about *us?*" she asked.

This was more like putting a knife through her heart than yanking out a sliver. Last night, Rowan had made it very clear that the one thing she wanted was honesty. But the one thing he wanted was her, and being honest wasn't going to win him the girl. He was screwing this up. Royally.

"No...no, of course I'm not talking about us," he reassured, stumbling over his words. Time for a tactical retreat. And to find some tact. He took a slug of his soda, then tried again. "How do you feel about practical jokes?"

She gave him a confused look. No shock, since he didn't have any clue where he was going with this. "You mean whoopee cushions and shaving cream under the door?"

"Maybe a little more sophisticated." But not a lot, he admitted to himself.

Her nose wrinkled, and she gave him a look of supreme distaste. "Not my style, and before you ask, I'm not much for Three Stooges humor, either."

Now that was a shame, because Jake had never felt like a bigger stooge.

"Yeah, well, that Three Stooges thing is one of those male-female conflicts that'll never be solved," he said. "Let me go at this another way—"

When the telephone rang, and Rowan asked him to hang on while she answered it, Jake couldn't decide whether to be annoyed or relieved. He was just going to have to spit it out. No dancing around the issue, he resolved as he tried not to eavesdrop on Rowan's conversation. When she returned, her mouth was drawn into a tense line.

"That was the twins' school. Mac fell on the playground at recess. The school nurse says it doesn't look like anything serious, just some good scrapes on the forehead. I know it might sound overprotective, but I still need to close up and get him to the doctor. You can never be too careful with head injuries." She sighed. "It's times like these I wish I had decent health insurance or a trust fund."

She was digging through her purse as she spoke, and Jake was glad she couldn't see him wince. Kids seemed to eat their way through money faster than even Victoria could. Keeping his net worth to himself was definitely the right choice. How else could he be sure Rowan wanted him for more than his investment account?

Assuming she chose to speak to him again.

Jake swallowed hard. He could feel a yellow stripe rolling down the middle of his back.

Rowan glanced up at him. "I'm really sorry about this, but it kind of comes with the mommy territory. Do you want to come with me? We can talk when we get back."

Talk in front of a kid who'd first tried to trap him in string, then with his sister, started a prank parade a mile long? He couldn't imagine what the kid would do if he saw his mom all upset. No thanks. Jake took the coward's way out.

"How about breakfast tomorrow instead—after you get the kids off to school?"

"Um, yeah…that might work," Rowan answered in a distracted way. "There they are," she muttered, pulling a set of keys from her purse. "Let me lock the front door. You can come out the back with me."

She hustled him out of the store in record time, then left him in the alley without even once looking back. Go figure. He'd been granted a reprieve courtesy of a miniature felon-in-training.

6

EYES STILL BLEARY with sleep, Rowan squinted at the school calendar on the fridge door. "Teachers' meetings...no school. *Yikes!*"

The day off had slipped her mind, but after yesterday's emotional roller-coaster ride, she wasn't all that surprised. Still, it was time for some major craft-project mojo to keep the kids occupied while she minded the store. Either that, or be ready for one of their infamous—and all too frequent—disappearing acts.

Rowan pushed her hair out of her eyes, yawned, then measured the coffee. Double extrastrong. The guy next door had worked well into the night. There had been lots of pounding and sawing and clanging from the space downstairs. Since it hadn't been directed at her, she didn't take that part of the interruption personally.

Even later, though, the music had come. He had moved to his bedroom, just a wall away from her. He'd been playing some sort of flute instrument. The sound was low and sexy, and even if it wasn't intentional, it had still worked its charms on her. As she slipped into sleep, Rowan's mind had strayed to Jake. For that, and for the delicious dreams that had followed, she supposed she should thank her neighbor.

Jake. Thinking of him brought the potent brew of excitement, confusion and downright hunger she'd come to expect. But it also left her with the nagging feeling there was something else she was supposed to do this morning. Something else...but she had no idea what.

Rowan fed Abby and Mac, gathered up a fresh stock of toys to take downstairs to the shop, showered, and pulled herself together. Twenty minutes later, the twins were settled in their storage-room play area. She was giving the silver a preopening polish when she heard a rapping at the front window.

Jake! *Breakfast with Jake!* Rowan yanked off the cleaning mitt and dropped it next to the tea caddy she'd been shining. She hustled to the front door and let him in.

"Hi," he said. He wore a dark leather jacket that showed plenty of scrapes and real wear, not one of those stiff, pretentious numbers. Jake Miller was the real thing. She wanted to snuggle up against him and kiss him and revel in his scent—all clean, honest male.

"Hi," she said, squaring her shoulders and standing a little more assertively to make up for the breathy, Marilyn Monroe-esque way she'd sounded.

"You forgot about breakfast, right?"

Rowan nodded. "Sorry. Yesterday was a little crazy," she said, fighting down a blush at the recollection of just how crazy it had been. "I also forgot that—"

"Hey Abby, look! It's the man we caught," Mac shouted.

"—the kids don't have school today."

The twins stood at his feet, gazing at him with an odd mix of rapture and speculation. He was looking at them as though they were miniature martians. Rowan said a prayer that they weren't about to launch into a round of the Daddy Game. Given his chilly expression, she was willing to bet that being drafted as Daddy du Jour by the twins would make Jake disappear faster than any magician could.

"Abby and Mac, this is Mr. Miller," Rowan said.

"Hi," they chimed. He returned the greeting. Abby started circling Jake, no doubt sizing him up as daddy material.

Rowan had to move quickly, before the kids could get started. Jake's surprise arrival meant she'd missed giving them her standard don't-upset-the-nice-man speech.

"It's okay if you want to skip breakfast," she said to Jake. "I've already eaten, anyway."

"You didn't eat, Mommy," Mac volunteered. "And you just gave us cereal. It was one of those yucky grown-up kinds, and me and Abby didn't eat much—"

She shot Mac a warning glance. "Really, Jake, I'm fine. No big deal. I'll eat when I close down the shop at lunch-time."

He ignored the escape route she'd given him. "There's this really great little place named Dave's down by the railroad tracks. Eat there once, and you're hooked. Come with me now. All of you," he added after a brief pause.

"Are you sure?" Rowan felt compelled to ask.

"Yeah," he said, but the look he was giving the twins said something else. He wasn't seeing just Abby and Mac. He looked as if he was seeing a table awash in orange juice, faces coated in jam and chubby hands dropping forks and spoons over and over.

The twins were bouncing up and down, as though they had springs in their shoes. "Can we, Mommy?"

Rowan knew she should play it safe and refuse Jake's offer. Then again, maybe it was time to see whether he could stand up to her children, or if like all the guys before him, he'd head hollering for the hills. "Okay."

"Yeah!" They shouted with high-pitched gusto, and Jake flinched at the sound.

"It won't be that bad," she consoled. "For five-year-olds, they're pretty civilized."

He still looked like a man sentenced to hang at dawn. "Civilized five-year-olds. What civilization are we talking about—a rampaging mongol horde?"

Rowan grinned. "Think more in terms of early renaissance. You know...the cutlery-optional era."

"No hope for modern times?" Jake called to her as she gathered up the twins' jackets.

"None at all," she answered, then laughed at his dramatic groan. A hunk with a sense of humor. She was beginning to feel like a very lucky woman, indeed.

ELBOW TO ELBOW, they sat upon their swivel stools at Dave's horseshoe-shaped counter. It was sticky and warm in the crowded diner, and the scents of coffee and freshly buttered toast made Rowan's taste buds jump to attention. The waitress chatted with the regulars, not stopping even when taking orders or delivering platters of fried eggs, ham slabs and heaps of hash browns. She wore dangling earrings shaped like dancing forks. Rowan watched with fascination as they waltzed back and forth in time to her relentless stream of conversation.

They had already ordered when the first train rumbled by. Mac and Abby slipped from their stools and ran to the front windows. Noses pressed to the plate glass, they watched as the train crossed the intersection. After it passed and the pedestrian gates raised, neither child moved. Rowan wasn't surprised, or especially thrilled, when they launched into their favorite game. It was time to play "find a daddy...any daddy."

"How about that one?" Abby asked.

"Nah, too old," Mac said. "But maybe him. He looks like he's fun."

"Yeah, but Mommy wouldn't like his hair. It's too pink and spiky."

Rowan bit back a laugh as a guy heavily into tattooing walked by the front window. Pink hair was the least of the drawbacks with that candidate.

Mac pointed at a business type. "Him, maybe?"

Jake nudged her elbow and gestured toward the twins. "Do I want to know what they're doing?"

"Probably not."

Abby whispered something to Mac, then they both turned and pinned Jake with an appraising stare. Apparently satisfied, they turned back to the window.

He gave a rueful shake of his head. "I'll take your word on that one."

It took no stretch of Rowan's maternal skills to know they were up to no good. She needed to sit them down for another discussion on why they couldn't rope a stranger into fatherhood.

Jake's hand rested on her forearm for a moment. "Can we talk while the two of them are busy?"

"Sure," she said, though the edgy tone to his voice made her stomach flutter.

"Well, I wanted to tell you this yesterday…. There's something we need to talk about. I'm—"

Lightning fast, the possibilities shot through Rowan's mind. An escapee from maximum security? Leaving town to go to clown college? *Married?*

He rubbed his hand over his eyes, muttered something under his breath, then started again. "Things are going fast between us. A lot faster than I thought they would, and I don't want to mess this up. You mean too much to me.''

The hum of conversation around them faded away as Jake's words sunk in. He truly cared about her! She wasn't alone in this whirlwind of emotion. Thank heaven it wasn't all hormones, and no heart! The only thing worse than no romance was a one-sided one. She'd already experienced that when she gave her love to Chip.

Jake's hand closed over hers. ''We should start out right, and to do that, I need someplace quiet to talk to you.''

Courtesy of her kids and her noisy neighbor, there was no such thing as a quiet place in Rowan's life. She trusted Jake enough to offer the closest thing. ''Why don't you come over tonight around nine? Mac and Abby are in bed by then.'' She hesitated, then pushing aside caution and common sense, added, ''Jake, I care about you, too. A lot.''

His dark eyes grew intense, as if he saw her, and only her. ''You're really someone special, you know that, don't you?''

Rowan's heart turned over. It had been so long since she'd been special to any man. If ever.

A hand tugged at the back of her sweater. ''Hey, Mommy, is he gonna kiss you or something?''

''What? Of course not, Abby.''

Clearly skeptical, her daughter rolled her eyes. ''Then why—''

''Oh, look, here comes your breakfast,'' Rowan announced, supremely grateful for the diversion. ''Time to sit down.''

The waitress unloaded a plate the size of a Thanksgiving turkey platter in front of Rowan. She gave a small shudder as she inventoried the fat cells about to take up residence on her hips. As the first forkful of buttery scrambled eggs met taste buds, though, she closed her eyes and sighed with bliss. For this, she would battle a legion of the little buggers.

She heard, or rather, felt, Jake chuckle, a low wavelength sound that rumbled across her nerve endings.

"That look of pure rapture over a plate of eggs?"

"They're good, that's all," she mumbled, trying not to sound as embarrassed as she was.

The smile he gave her was flagrantly sexual. "The possibilities are endless." Showing some mercy, he turned to his pancakes, and dug in.

After eating, Jake walked them back to the antique shop. Rowan unlocked the store, had Mac and Abby say their thanks, then shooed them inside.

"I'll see you tonight, then," she said to Jake.

He clasped his hand around her wrist. "Hang on a second. Don't run off on me." He moved toward her, his intent obvious in his expression.

A kiss. One simple, perfect kiss. Rowan leaned into him. As their mouths neared, she caught a motion out of the corner of her eye. Two little faces peered at them from the front window. Rowan moved just enough that Jake's lips brushed her cheek.

Chuckling, he drew back. "You missed."

She gestured toward the twins. "Spectators."

Jake grinned, lifted her hand to his mouth and kissed it. "Proper enough for the audience?"

"Proper enough for a crown princess," she said, then gave him a smile of her own. "See you tonight."

"Yeah, tonight." As he turned away she noticed that there wasn't even a ghost of his good cheer left.

At least tonight she'd learn what was bothering him. "It

better not be clown college," she murmured. Somebody somewhere owed her a happy ending, and she wanted it with Jake.

JUST AFTER NOON, Rowan knelt on the floor marking—for the fifth blasted time—the hem on Mrs. Hammacher's dress. There was no customer more finicky than a mother of the bride.

"No, no! Not *there*," Mrs. Hammacher said in annoyance. Rowan could relate. If Mrs. H. hadn't sent so many new clients her way, about now Rowan would be handing the woman some duct tape and suggesting a permanently adjustable hemline.

"I really think it needs to be a quarter-inch lower."

A mouthful of pins prevented Rowan from saying that was where they'd been two markings ago. She dutifully rolled the silvery rose fabric down.

Mrs. Hammacher sighed the sigh of a martyr. "Now it's too low."

Before her client could offer another opinion, Rowan edged the dress back to its original starting point, tacked it and marked it.

Unfortunately, Mrs. H.'s eyes had already strayed to her neckline. "Maybe a little lower on top." She glanced down at Rowan. "Did I ever mention I used to be a Vegas showgirl?" She gestured at her breasts, which were a bit more bountiful than Mother Nature usually provided. "I know time's done a number on me, but these—"

Just then, the guy next door kicked into a boogie-down tune on something that sounded like bellows attached to a calliope.

Mrs. H. forgot her finest assets. "What's that?"

"Music...more or less," Rowan said, as she slid the last straight pin back into its cushion.

Mrs. H. wiggled her shoulders in a little shimmy. "I like it."

Visions of Vegas high-kicking propelling her, Rowan shot to her feet. "That should do it for today, Mrs. Hammacher. We'll do some fine-tuning if you need it when you pick up the dress tomorrow."

Rowan fielded Mrs. H.'s questions about the mystery man next door in as few words as possible, and simultaneously hustled the twins out of the back room. She wanted Mrs. H. changed and out the door before she launched into a stage show not suited for five-year-old eyes.

Ten minutes later, the twins were back in their playroom surrounded by markers, construction paper and enough glue sticks to reassemble Humpty Dumpty. Or bond Aunt Celeste's mail into a leaning tower—a feat they'd accomplished before breakfast could even settle in their tummies.

Rowan got to work on the finishing touches for her three-o'clock fitting. As if sensing her need for peace, J. Albreight switched over to a softer, springlike tune. Time slipped by as she hummed along with the music.

It made her think of warm spring days when the scent of lilacs perfumed the farmhouse she'd grown up in. Home... She should make her weekly call to her mom and assure her that she hadn't succumbed to the lures of the big city. Rowan smiled, thinking of Jake. Well, at least not all of the lures. Tucking aside the silky pantsuit, she rose to gather the twins and call their grandma.

As she neared the back room, she heard words guaranteed to make any mom's hair stand on end: "Quiet, or she'll hear us," Abby hissed.

"No, she won't. She's busy with that dopey outfit."

Rowan raised a brow at that one. She hoped Mac wasn't destined to be a fashion critic. She peeked though the doorway just in time to see the twins disappear down the cellar steps.

At last, a chance to catch them in the act!

Rowan dashed to the front door, locked it and put up the Closed sign. She sprinted to the back room, then crept down the stairs. When she reached the bottom, a bare bulb in an ancient fixture shone down on a jumble of boxes, but no kids.

The building was almost one hundred years old, and she was willing to bet no one had dusted down there in all that time. Rubbing her nose and fighting the urge to sneeze, she tiptoed to the far side of the room. The ceiling was low. She instinctively ducked, even though she had plenty of clearance.

She came to a spot where it was obvious that some crates had been moved recently. Stacked one on top of the other, to be exact. Next to them, a grate of some sort leaned against the old brick wall. She looked up. Just beneath the point where the wall met the joists of the floor above was a large, dark hole. And from that hole came two little voices.

"A little more, and quit being such a chicken. I'm telling ya, there's no spiders in here."

"That's what you said last time!"

Pure instinct took over. Rowan shoved one of the crates off the stack, climbed onto the rest and peeked into the hole. It was dark, of course. Hoping Mac was right about the spiders, she took the braille approach and felt around. Metal. Solid, very heavy metal. Probably a duct or airway from some old heating system, she decided. And hopefully strong enough to hold her.

Rowan boosted herself up and wriggled into the opening. The passage was practically spacious for a five-year-old, but not so accommodating for her. She had visions of a cork lodged snugly into a bottle. Praying that the rounder, rear portion of her anatomy fit through the opening, she slithered in. So far, so good. No protesting moans from the duct. A few alarmed sounds from the twins, though, who probably thought the mutant queen of all spiders was on their tails.

She had scarcely elbowed into the tunnel when she reached a hard right angle. Muttering a few things she hoped the twins couldn't hear, she made the turn, her feet pedaling in the air behind her. After that, it was a mercifully short trip—no more than four body-lengths on an incline toward a light at the other end. Somehow, she had the feeling that this wasn't Paradise she traveled toward.

But it was forbidden territory. The neighbor's territory.

Getting out of the duct was easier than getting in, thank heaven. This end sloped down so that she was no more than a foot or two from the ground. Reaching her hands in front of her, Rowan dragged herself out.

She stood and brushed off her backside. "Hey, kids. Interesting way to visit the neighbor."

"*Ssshhh!*" they hissed, an instant before their faces settled into expressions of sheer surprise.

Rowan gestured at the duct, with its thick metal straps holding it to the wall. She winced when she realized that she was standing right where the monster of a furnace that was probably big enough to swallow a child, must have once been. "You two really got lucky. Do you have any idea—"

"Quiet, Mommy, or he'll hear us!" Mac scowled at her as if she were the wrongdoer, while he and his sister were out for nothing more than an afternoon's stroll.

"I wouldn't be worrying about him so much, kiddo. The real trouble's right here in front of you." Rowan cocked her head and listened to the music from above. Her neighbor had switched to some instrument that reminded her of a calypso steel drum. "Besides, it sounds like we're safe, so far."

"Let's go back." Abby and Mac scurried toward the opening.

"Not so fast, guys."

They froze in their tracks and slowly turned to face her.

"We're not going back...yet."

"What?" They stared at her with a satisfying mixture of shock and alarm.

"We're going upstairs so you can explain to our neighbor how you've been sneaking into his place."

Neither child moved.

"You're teasing, right, Mommy?" Abby finally asked.

"I've never been more serious." Rowan pointed to the stairs. "March. Now!"

As they climbed, Rowan did a quick mental rehearsal of what she'd say to her odd—no, strike that—*weird* neighbor. She'd offer an abject apology, and—holy bonus!—get a chance to take a peek at what the heck this guy was up to. Not a bad payoff for admitting that her kids were into breaking and entering. Corraling Mac and Abby in front of her, she pushed aside the curtain that hung in the doorway to the main room.

"Show time," she murmured as she cleared the drape.

And then Rowan saw she wouldn't be getting her happy ending, either.

7

"JAKE."

For the space of a heartbeat, Jake was plenty startled but even more glad to hear that sexy voice come from behind him. While the fact that Rowan wasn't supposed to be there registered somewhere in the fringes of his mind, it was the pleasure of hearing her that stood front and center.

Smiling, he turned to her. When he saw her expression—hurt and anger and something so fragile that it wrenched his heart—the weight of all his lies came crashing down. Asking how she'd appeared came in a cold second to covering his butt.

"I can explain—"

She held out a hand to stop him. "Don't bother. I think I can fill in the blanks myself."

She swiped at her eyes. Jake couldn't tell whether they were bothering her from the coating of dust she wore, or from something much worse, such as his stupid stunt.

"Did you have yourself a good laugh at my expense?" She stalked closer, but her kids just hung back by the curtain, their round, scared eyes making him feel even guiltier, if such a thing were possible. "Was it fun setting me up like this? Did you get your kicks?"

Helpless, he shook his head.

"Jake...Miller. Well, we can scratch the last name because I know that's Albreight, but did you even bother to give me your real first name? Did I even rate that?" Her voice quavered as she asked the last question, and he hated himself. Really hated himself.

"It's Jake."

She tugged back her shoulders and narrowed her gaze. Jake took an involuntary step backward.

"Well, good. Jake Albreight. At least I have a name to attach to that voodoo doll I'm going home to whip up. Why don't you be a sport and toss in a personal effect as a parting gift—a lock of hair or something?"

He winced at the bloodthirsty look in her eyes. He had a strong suspicion that the "something" she was thinking of wasn't quite as benign as a hair clipping. Her anger was good, though. At least it was easier for him to bear than the hurt.

"Rowan—"

"Don't! Just...don't." She looked him up and down, and he felt even smaller than her kids. "Don't call me, don't try to apologize and if you see me on the street, don't even think of trying to talk to me. Got it?"

The fist around his heart closed tighter. Not laugh with her? Not touch her? Never again? Not a damn chance!

"I can't promise that."

She laughed, but the sound was hollow. "I'm not interested in your word. You and the truth don't seem to be very tight, anyway." She held out her hands. "Come on, Mac and Abby, we're getting out of here." They scurried up to her, shooting worried looks at both him and their mother. "I mean it, Jake. Just leave us alone."

They exited through the front door. It slammed, leaving him surrounded by silence and smothering in guilt.

Jake sliced his fist through the empty air. "Dammit!"

He wanted to throw something, hit something. He wanted to rage at his own stupidity. And if there weren't the chance that Rowan was back on the other side of the wall to hear him, he just might have. But he didn't want another black mark in her book. Those pages must be looking pretty ugly already: *liar, irresponsible* and *self-centered* came to mind right off the bat. No point in adding *foul temper* to the list.

Jake swung a leg over the weight bench he kept in the corner, and sat. He thought of the way Rowan had said his name when she came in the room—part criminal indictment, and part identifying a truly vile plague. He'd gotten just what he wanted in the first place—distance. That sweet, sassy woman would step in front of a train to get out of his path. He thought of a curse he'd heard his stern, German grandfather once toss out: "May you get exactly what you ask for."

Granddad sure had known how to skewer an enemy. And he'd sure known how to skewer himself, Jake admitted with a weary sigh.

If he owned half a brain, he'd run from this embarrassing mess. It amazed him that he was the same guy who'd had the guts and the smarts to put together an award-winning business. The same guy who'd sold high and was ready to live easy.

"Half a brain," he grumbled. "Hell, it's gone altogether."

He wasn't going to back down from Rowan Lindsay. Not by a long shot. All he needed now was a game plan, and it had better be the best one of his life.

TWO WEEKS PASSED, and Rowan heard nothing from Jake, not the slightest sound from next door. This was the way she wanted it, she reminded herself as she wielded a mascara wand with more nerves than skill. She was better off without him.

"Sheesh!" Rowan grabbed a tissue, dampened it and wiped at the glob beneath her lower lashes. All she did was make the mess worse.

Abby giggled from the doorway. "You look like a crazy raccoon."

Rowan smiled. "You're right about the crazy part."

Tonight, she was going out to dinner with one of Melanie's legion of blind dates. The only reason she had agreed to go was that Melanie and her husband were joining them. Besides, it wasn't so much a date as a Jake antidote. She didn't want to sit in her apartment another night, straining to hear whether he was home and telling herself that she shouldn't care. Didn't care!

Okay, maybe she still cared, but it was like a virus or something. A few more days and she'd be over it. Rowan gave one more try with the mascara and botched that eye, too. Giving up, she grabbed a washcloth, scrubbed her face clean, then dabbed on moisturizer and just a touch of lipstick.

"Now you look pretty." Abby still stood in the doorway. Rowan wondered if her daughter was doing what she used to—watch her mom get ready for a special evening and imagine what a wonderful, magical thing it was to be grown-up.

She turned from the mirror and gathered Abby in her arms. "Thanks, sweetie. You're quite a looker, yourself." But don't grow up too quickly, she added silently. Those fairy-tale endings are tough to come by. She hugged her daughter tighter, and Abby squirmed away.

"Can we do finger paints with the baby-sitter?"

Rowan winced, imagining the resulting paint-fest. Catch Mom while she's down, that was the twins' theory.

"Crayons," she said, then hurried to answer the knock on the door. "Here's the baby-sitter now."

Rowan swung open the door. Instead of the fifteen-year-old, gum-chewing, green-nail-polished girl she expected, there was an enormous bunch of helium balloons anchored to a funny little sculpture of a tree. The balloons were clear. Each held a small, folded sheet of paper.

A gift for the twins? she wondered, as she reached down and slipped free an envelope peeking from beneath the sculpture. The card had only two words of explanation: "The Truth." And it was signed, "Jake." Rowan sighed, lifted the tree and its cargo, then carried it inside. The twins frolicked around the gift. Or more accurately, peace offering.

Rowan frowned and absently tapped the tip of her nail against one of the balloons. It would take more than this to work his way back into her good graces. Really, he was a rat, and not deserving of forgiveness just because he'd come up with some cute surprise. He'd lied to her and probably had been laughing at her all along. Even before all that, he'd stolen the store space that should have been hers. She tapped harder, and the balloon popped.

Rowan jumped back, hand against her pounding heart. The twins crowed at her startled cry.

"What do you think that is?" Mac asked, pointing at the folded slip of paper resting at his feet.

Rowan scooped it from the carpet, unfolded it and blinked. It was a birth certificate. Jake's birth certificate—full name...all the vital stats. Opening the antique silver brooch that she'd pinned to her top, she popped the next balloon.

"I never went to college, but I wish I had," read the message on a scrap of yellow paper. She wiped the back of her hand across her eyes. Something suspiciously like tears moistened her skin. Heaven help her, she was softening. She didn't want to, but knew she was fighting a losing battle. Rowan read so hungrily, she scarcely heard when the twins let the baby-sitter into the apartment.

By the time she'd finished off the last balloon, she held Jake's wishes and regrets in her hands. He used to own a landscaping business named Greenworks, but needed a break. Once, he didn't pay a parking ticket, but would never cheat on his taxes. His mother had died when he was eight, and he still talked to her in his dreams. He loved old rock and roll and new country music, and used to think that he'd make a pretty good lead guitarist. He'd never been in love, but there was someone he needed to see. Very much.

Setting aside the rest, Rowan took the final note, carefully folded it, and slipped it into her pocket. She gave the baby-sitter her last instructions and left for a dinner she had no interest in eating. At least she'd been smart enough to tell Melanie that she'd meet them at the restaurant.

Holding the rail with one hand, she tucked the other into her skirt pocket as she walked downstairs to the back lot. She shifted Jake's note between her fingers. She wished she could weigh it for truth, for kind intent, for all of the things she thought she'd found in Jake, but now was afraid to believe.

His voice rang out as she was jiggling the key in her stubborn car door.

"I miss you."

She looked up to see him leaning against the fender of his truck. He was parked right next to her. She couldn't believe that she'd been distracted enough to walk past him. Rowan swallowed, unable to say anything, not even sure what she'd say if she could.

"I messed up. I was going to tell you the truth that night. Really, I was."

"I believe you," she whispered. Not that it mattered. That he'd done this to her in the first place was what hurt.

He pushed away from the truck and walked toward her. "Can I have a few minutes?"

"No, I have someplace I'm supposed to be. A date," she added, then immediately regretted the vindictive little poke.

His mouth tightened. Even in the evening light, she could see the intensity in his dark eyes. "Well, I'd tell you to have a good time, but that would be a lie. I hope it's the pits. I hope you come home early. And when you tuck yourself into bed, I want you to remember that I'm just on the other side of the wall from you. I want you to think about me. I want you to think about us."

She shook the key again, and the lock finally gave. "There is no us." Her car door opened with a rusty, protesting groan. Jake frowned—maybe at the sound, maybe at her comment.

"I can fix that for you," he said, bracing his hands on the car door.

Rowan sighed and slipped into the car. "Maybe, but you can't fix everything."

He leaned down and brushed his fingers along the line of her jaw, then across her lips. Rowan shivered at his touch.

"But I can try, sweetheart. I sure as hell can try."

He stepped back and closed her car door. Rowan was still shaking when she pulled into the restaurant parking lot, a good three miles north of where she'd left Jake. Of where she was becoming increasingly afraid she'd left her heart.

THAT NIGHT, Rowan lay in bed trying her darnedest to think of anything but Jake. It was the old "don't think of giraffes" game. At every corner in her mind, he was there.

He'd been out to dinner with her, too. Though she couldn't see him, she could still feel his touch and hear his words. She'd left just after the meal finished, pleading a headache when Melanie suggested they all go dancing at the new hot spot in town. Her poor date, Simon, hadn't looked upset to see her go.

Rowan shifted so that she stared at the drab off-white wall next to her bed.

"*Don't* think of Jake… *Don't* think of Jake," she whispered to herself, then tried to mentally list the wives of Henry the Eighth. She got lost somewhere around Catherine Parr, and gave up.

As if Jake could sense her will slipping away, music began to drift through the wall. A low and seductive melody washed over her, pooled in her mind, one note sliding into the next, drawing her down a warm stream. Silken notes caressed her skin, curled about her limbs, calling her to him. The air was perfumed with spice. He was making love to her without once touching her. Then the music stopped, leaving her suspended.

"Think about us, Rowan," he called.

Rowan moaned and yanked the blanket over her head. As if she could think about anything else.

8

ROWAN PEEKED OUT her tiny kitchen window and heaved a sigh of relief. Jake's truck was gone. She'd been playing a jittery game of hide-and-seek for the past several days, ducking whenever she saw him. She planned to hold on to her heart—and her sanity—for as long as she could.

Jake seemed to understand her unspoken rules. He never approached her during the day, when she was captive in the antique shop. It was a blessing he'd decided to play fair since Aunt Celeste had shown no interest in returning to rescue her. Celeste couldn't bail her out when she really needed it, anyway.

The days were a snap compared to the nights. Every night Jake played for her, and every night Rowan tossed and turned and muffled her ears with her pillow. Not that it helped.

Now it was morning, and she didn't want to stew over anything more complicated than the fact that it was a crisp autumn Sunday, and she had two children who deserved a trip to the zoo. She threw together a picnic lunch and coaxed the twins into clothing that suited the weather.

One more glance out the back window. The coast was still clear. She hustled Mac and Abby downstairs and toward the car. Just when a clean getaway seemed a sure bet, she heard the grit of tires against gravel and the growl of a truck engine.

"Look, Mommy, it's Jake!" Abby made the announcement with such enthusiasm, you'd think she was seeing a movie star.

"That's nice, honey. Now get in the car." She tried to hurry Abby along, jam the picnic basket into the back seat and make sure that Mac was clear of Jake's truck all at the same time. Abby made it into the car, Mac was unscathed, but the picnic basket tumbled upside down onto the ground.

"Damn," Rowan muttered not quite far enough under her breath.

"I heard that," Mac called from the other side of the car in an uncanny imitation of her own voice.

"Just don't repeat it." Fingers thick and clumsy with nerves, she scrambled to stuff the peanut-butter-and-jelly sandwiches and carrot sticks back into the basket before Jake could climb out of his truck.

"Can I help with that?"

Too late.

He squatted down next to her and stilled her hand as she mangled the last PB&J.

"Thanks." She anchored her gaze in the basket's depths.

"Hi, Jake! We're going to the zoo. Wanna come?" Abby bounced up and down within the restraint of her seat belt and ignored a sizzling look of motherly reproach.

Mac ambled around the back of the car to add his voice to the invitation. "Yeah, it's lots of fun. Last time we went, we got to see the piranhas eat dead rats."

Rowan pulled herself to her feet, clutching the picnic basket. "I'm sure Mr. Albreight has a lot to do today, guys. With all of your sneaking around and breaking in, he's probably behind schedule for…well, for whatever it is he does.''

"I'd say I'm right on schedule,'' Jake replied with a grin. She knew he wasn't referring to his work.

He had obviously forgotten the rules: Sunup, no contact; sundown, be the sexiest pied piper in town. Rowan narrowed her eyes, trying for a tougher version of the look that had been such a failure with Abby.

"We don't want to throw a wrench in your day. Mac, get in the car.'' Both males ignored her.

"You should see those fish eat. It's really neat!''

"I think I'll do that, Mac. You hop in back, and I'll get up front with your mom.'' He grinned at Rowan. "Hand me that basket, and let's go see some piranhas.''

Rowan gave one last shot at shaking him. "I didn't pack any extra sandwiches.''

"That's all right, I saw how you mauled them. I won't be missing much.'' As they slid into the car, he continued in a lower voice, one he was probably naive enough to think wouldn't reach little ears. "I'm going to think you're a coward if you keep running. Where's all that spunk of yours? Afraid I'll kiss you again and—''

"You kissed mommy? Why'd you do that?'' Abby was mystified.

"Because it's fun,'' Jake equably replied.

"You mean like when I go down the twisty slide at the park?'' asked Mac. Rowan glanced at him in the rearview mirror. He was an unbeliever, clearly doubting that a kiss from Plain Old Mom could ever rate that high.

"Something like that,'' Jake said. "Only much, much better,'' he finished for her benefit. Rowan could feel his gaze and quelled the warm tingle that chased through her. She concentrated on the road, thankful that the Detroit Zoo was a mercifully short mile away. The sooner she could distract the children—and Jake—the better.

As it turned out, they didn't get to see the piranhas eat. The nasty little carnivores were off display. They did watch the seal and sea lion feeding which, for everyone but Mac, was a fine substitute. Afterward, they had their own picnic lunch of flattened PB&Js, and Rowan did her very best to pretend that Jake wasn't there. He wouldn't let her, though, sitting too close and watching her with dark amber eyes that reminded her of a jungle creature's when observing its next meal. Oblivious to her tension and Jake's hunger, the twins noisily discussed their favorite zoo critters.

"Piranhas are more fun to watch 'cause you can see the rats floating on top of the tank. They're all white fur with pink tails and skin. Those fish sure love 'em."

"Eww," said Abby.

Mac turned toward Jake. "Last time we visited, the man feeding the fish told me they keep a big bunch of rats in the freezer. I wanted to see 'em, but Mommy said no."

Rowan's PB&J was going down with even less ease than usual. "No more rat talk while we're eating."

"The seals are bigger and way smarter," Abby added.

"Yeah, but you can't watch them tear off chunks of—"

Rowan gave up on the sandwich as a lost cause. "Enough!"

Mac's brow furrowed. "What's wrong?"

"You need a little practice on your skills with the ladies," Jake said. "Rule one, never talk to a woman about rats."

Rowan bit back the obvious comment that Jake should be more concerned over being a rat than talking about one.

Mac, though, was glowing under this rare male attention. For that, she'd forgive Jake just about anything.

"What's rule two?"

"Sorry, buddy, you'll have to be a lot older before we go on to my other lessons. But when the time comes, I'll even let you know the secret handshake. Deal?"

"Deal!"

"And until then, how about you share a secret with me?" He leaned closer to the twins. Rowan figured the smile he gave them had more to do with wheedling information than affection. Either way, her kids were eating it up. "How'd you guys do it? How'd you get into my basement?"

Mac gave Abby a questioning glance, and she nodded her head. "We got a secret tunnel," Mac said.

Jake's brows rose. "A tunnel?"

"An old heating duct," Rowan clarified.

A genuine smile crept across his face. "And you fit through it, too?"

"A big, old duct, okay?" she said, feeling mildly disgruntled.

"I'm going to have to weigh the pros and cons of sealing that thing off. Seems to me there might be some benefit in leaving it open. You might feel free to sneak on over." He winked at Rowan.

"I'm not planning on making the trip again. And neither are they," she added with a nod toward the twins. They cast angelic looks heavenward. Rowan thought she heard Jake stifle a snicker.

Leanly muscled legs stretched in front of him, he settled back on his elbows in the shaggy grass. Apparently satisfied with the info he'd gotten from the twins, he centered his attention solely on her. "So, Mac likes the piranhas, Abby likes the seals, and their mom likes...?"

You. The word blazed through Rowan's mind with such startling clarity that she was scared she might have said it aloud. Still, he wasn't wearing that cocky grin that appeared every time her mouth got ahead of her common sense, so she must have kept the dangerous thought to herself.

"The butterfly castle," she quickly replied.

"The what?"

"That's what we call the Wildlife Interpretive Center."

He chuckled. "You're one dyed-in-the-wool romantic, aren't you?"

"I don't have time for romance." What a lie! She was starry-eyed enough to sit there, pestered by slow-moving bees readying for their winter's sleep, and by two five-year-olds in need of a nap, yet still find the setting idyllic because Jake was with her. And she'd be sunk if he knew any of this.

"Romance isn't a matter of time, it's a matter of perception. Now, let's go see that butterfly castle."

HEAD TIPPED BACK and eyes closed, Rowan stood in a small alcove off the butterfly castle's main path. She pretended she was alone in a tropical rain forest, with the sound of the fountain as her personal waterfall. The thick, humid air made her feel languid. Limbs and thoughts slowed as heat caressed her. If she tried hard enough, she could almost forget the hassles of everyday life.

"I'm not going to conveniently disappear." Jake stood very close behind her. She held her breath, hoping he might move on and give her a chance to relax. No such luck. He was a big cat let loose in paradise, and she was the only game in sight.

"Chicken."

Rowan swung around. "I am *not* a—" She stopped when she realized she was being baited.

One corner of his mouth curled up in a satisfied smile. "I knew you still had some fight in you. Right now, you look ready to feed me to Mac's piranhas."

"Too bad the exhibit is closed."

"I'll count myself lucky." He stalked closer, and she backed into the corner of her little nook. Jake was all she saw. Maybe all she wanted to see. "Rowan, I want you to give us a chance. Don't shut me out."

She had to think of her children, of their need for some constancy in life. She had to think of trust. She had to think of anything but the way he was looking at her, somehow apologetic and commanding at the same time.

Meaning to hold him off, she braced her palm on the middle of his chest. A mistake, she realized, once she felt the insistent rhythm of his heart under her hand. It would be better not to touch him at all. She needed to be safe from the brand of craziness that Jake Albreight brought with him.

As if sensing her scared thoughts, he changed his tack. "One kiss. A friendly little 'let's be pals' smack on the cheek, then I'll know we're going to be okay."

"Oh, no," she shook her head, "I'm not falling for that one. Not here, for the twins and all the world to see." She nodded to an elderly couple who had stopped to watch the show.

"So if I get you someplace private, you might fall for it?"

He was tripping her up with words. "I didn't mean it that way."

He cupped her face with one large hand. "They've been some good kisses, definitely worth an encore. And who knows, with a little practice, you might improve. You're a little rusty, that's all."

"Rusty?" She was insulted down to the very soles of her purple high-tops. *"Rusty?"*

"Now don't get all upset on me. I like you a lot better this way, though, ready to punch me in the nose, instead of running away."

"What, no sport to the hunt then?"

"None at all."

"You're just trying to annoy me."

"I'm trying to get your attention," he corrected. "If we were your kids' age, I'd be chasing you around the playground."

"You're exactly the type."

"You've got me there. I've always liked to find the prettiest girl and tease her. Or kiss her."

Just as Rowan felt herself starting to sway toward him, he pulled back. "So do I get another chance?"

"What?" Her thoughts were muddled. She couldn't get past the temptation of his kiss to even begin to answer his question.

"A chance? Let me make it up to you. Please."

There was no fighting it. She'd rather take the risk of getting hurt than spend the rest of her life wondering "what if?"

"Okay, let's give it another try."

"You won't be sorry," Jake whispered, then brushed a fleeting caress against her cheek. "Hold still for a minute."

She started to ask him why, then trailed off, watching

him. Still as a sculpture, he stood with one arm slightly extended. An enormous Blue Morpho butterfly that had been dancing around them, settled on his outstretched arm. Together, they gazed at it, all beauty and delicate magic. Then Jake raised his arm a fraction. The butterfly took flight.

"Is there anyone you can't charm?" Rowan wanted the question to come out light and joking. It didn't, though.

"You tell me."

Their gazes locked, and neither spoke for several moments. Then, looking almost frustrated, Jake shook his head. "Come on, let's go find those little terrors of yours before they decide to set all of the butterflies free."

FOUR O'CLOCK the next day, Jake strolled into Lindsay's Antique Emporium. The rodents scurried out of the back room and straight to him before he could say a word. He wondered whether they had some bizarre type of radar. Whatever caused them to target him like little heat-seeking missiles was definitely not inherited from their mother. Until they charged at him, Rowan hadn't even looked up from her sewing.

"Hi, Jake!" Shrill little voices squealed and grimy little hands waved in the air. Jake could feel that air growing thicker, harder to suck in. If he had to choose what rattled him most—kids or closed-in spaces—it would be a tough call.

"Hi, guys," he said, wishing they would go do whatever it was that kids did. He had a campaign to wage. Having the eyes of the eat-paste-for-lunch age group on him wasn't doing much to help his cause.

"Wanna play?"

"Nope." Not with them. "I'm here to see your mom."

"Hey, Jake." Rowan wore the same cautious expression he'd once received from a doe he came upon while hiking on his land up north. This second chance wasn't going to be a gimme.

"Hey, yourself."

He put the slow roll of his heart down to the fact that he hadn't slept well in days. His seduction by music had its cost, measured in restless dreams of Rowan. But with those dreams came one stone-cold reality. In the long run, Rowan was the sort of woman a guy married. A hypothetical guy, Jake amended. Not him personally.

"Any chance you can find someone to watch Mac and Abby tonight?" he asked.

"I don't know…money's kind of tight. They managed to shoot through another shoe size, and—"

Jake flipped on his mental off switch. He didn't want to be reminded about her lack of money. After Victoria made it clear she was only interested in his bank statement, he wanted to be sure Rowan wanted him for him. He switched back on when he heard her enthusiastic, "Hey! I'll give Melanie a call. She's been saying she wants to practice the mommy thing again."

He figured that was pretty much like learning to swim by jumping off a cliff into three feet of water. Since he wasn't a total fool, he kept his opinion to himself.

"Well, if you can get your pal to help out, I'd like you to come over to my gallery tonight. I know you've probably been a little…ah, curious about what I'm doing over there."

"Not really." He might have believed her, except for the laughter dancing in her eyes.

"You're not even a little interested in how I make all the noise?"

"Noise? What noise?"

He grinned. "And peeking in my front window and sneaking into the place was nothing more than—"

"A way to pass the time?" she offered, then laughed. "Actually, I'd love to see what you're up to."

"Good. I'll pick you up at seven. If you're running late, just pound on the wall."

THAT NIGHT, Jake told Rowan to choose any restaurant she wanted for dinner. He was pleased—and surprised—when she settled on a little family-run Chinese place. It was inexpensive, and the food was great. Still, Jake wondered whether she would have gone upscale if she knew how much money he had socked away. He felt crummy for even thinking about it.

After they ate, he took her back to his music-gallery-in-the-making. Unlike Victoria, who looked as if she'd swallowed something lethal when he'd told her his plans, Rowan told him he was doing the right thing, choosing a business that made him happy. He liked the sound of that. A lot.

It was obvious where her kids inherited their freewheeling curiosity, too. She darted around the room, brushing her fingers against windchime sculptures and toying with the instruments he'd made. He folded his arms across his chest and leaned one shoulder against the wall, waiting, watching and enjoying every minute of her pleasure. She made several attempts to produce more than a gasping wheeze with the didgeridoo, then finally seemed to remember that he was there.

"All right, what's the trick?"

"Unless you're trying to pass out, you can't just blow. Think about how trumpet players purse their lips." He eased away from the wall and moved toward her with one palm extended. "Hand it over."

She smiled and his heart immediately began to beat double-time. "Gladly," she said. "I might as well learn from a master. Back when you first moved in, you just about rattled me out of the bathtub with this thing." She laid the didgeridoo across his open, and now sweaty, palm. Oblivious to the effect of her words, she continued, "It was all I could do to catch my glass of wine before it spilled."

Tub...

Wine...

The words gathered with the unstoppable force of a tsunami and rolled at him. Jake closed his eyes as an image broke across his mind with enough force to make him forget where he was, what he was supposed to be doing.

Barenaked, gorgeous ivory skin...

"Jake?"

"Huh?"

She stared pointedly at the object in his hand. At least, that's where he hoped she was looking, given the other item in sudden prominence down in that vicinity. She motioned in the same, general, south-of-the-belt direction. His gaze traveled slowly downward to the didgeridoo he still held slackly.

"What? Oh, yeah."

He was supposed to be playing the thing. That, he knew, would require controlled breathing. Unfortunately, all of those basic bodily functions—air to lungs, blood through heart, the Big Guy at full mast—were not under his control.

"Any time now," she prompted.

It was a damn crying shame they weren't thinking about the same act. With a resigned nod, he set the long, hollowed-out tube to his mouth and made a short bleat of a sound.

She snickered, a poke at his male pride. "Is that the best you can do?"

He handed it back to her. "Can you do better?"

She did, then smiled. "Well that's one fantasy down. I've always wanted to play one of these."

Jake wondered whether any of his fantasies would be set free tonight. The way Rowan caressed each new object she encountered didn't help matters. He wanted to be next in line to be explored, touched, wondered over. Rolling his shoulders, he tried to loosen knotted muscles.

"So, ah…what do you think of the place?"

She hesitated, then said, "Pretty nice."

He found that just about as thrilling as a lukewarm glass of milk. Granted, with the distraction Rowan had proved to be, he was far from finished. Still, he thought his gallery deserved more than "pretty nice."

"Think you could have done better at this, too?" he teased.

He caught a flash of something—wistfulness? frustration?—in her eyes.

"I guess we'll never know."

"Okay, what am I missing here?"

Rowan was quiet long enough to make him wonder if she planned to answer. "I wanted this space for my own, a place to gain some independence. I used to sit next door at Aunt Celeste's and plan the layout for my shop, nothing fancy, but *mine*. Then along you came, and a wall was slapped up." She hitched her thumb toward the spot where the connecting archway once stood. "It's gone."

Another strike against him, Jake thought. He was going to be out of the game before it even started. "Did you ever mention to Celeste that you wanted to use the space?"

"Not in so many words," she said, studying her feet.

"Sign language, then?"

"Not even smoke signals. I didn't tell her, okay?"

"Hey, I'm sorry. She's a nice lady. I'm sure she would have helped you out."

Rowan rubbed at her arms as if she were cold. "I was afraid to ask. I didn't want to risk hearing no again. I've had too much of it… 'No, I don't love you. No, I don't care about our children. No, I don't—'" She stopped, and with an apologetic smile, said, "Sorry. Too much info, huh?"

Jake wanted to hold her. He wanted to make all kinds of crazy promises. Promises that had nothing to do with his new, "no commitments" approach to life. He kept his hands to himself.

"That's okay. But unless you ask, you won't hear yes, either."

"I know," she said, tucking a lock of hair behind her ear.

Temptation. He reached out and wrapped one glossy black curl around his finger. Even against his work-roughened hands, it felt like silk. "I'd like to say that I'm sorry I rented this space, but I'm not. After all, I got to meet you."

The tightness around her features eased, and she grinned. Jake suspected for the gift of her smile, he'd do just about anything.

"Well, ending up with you for a neighbor isn't all bad," she said. "After all, I've had the chance to be annoyed by more noises that most people hear in a lifetime. Not to mention crawling through walls. Few people can say they've done that.''

He couldn't help himself.

''And then there's this.'' He leaned forward and kissed her full lips. She tasted sweet, like strawberries and something more subtle, magical.

''There is that.''

''There is,'' he agreed, and kissed her again. He wanted to peel away her clothes, piece by piece, and make love to her for the rest of the night.

His own advice drifted back to him, *Unless you ask...* The words were a siren song, irresistible, and probably fatal, too. She still had to reconcile him with the image she'd created of the guy on the other side of the wall. She still had to get past his lies. He'd settle for one more kiss.

Jake pulled her closer. Her scent reminded him of a tropical breeze—exotic, lightly perfumed. She leaned against him, trusting when he'd done nothing to earn it. He could easily lose himself in her. His hands wandered from her narrow waist to the flair of hips below.

She was rich curves, not the sharp angles and jutting bones so many women starved themselves for. The difference was intoxicating. He cupped his fingers around her lush bottom as he sent his tongue to stroke hers. Rowan held fast, fingers kneading into his back, as though she wanted to make him part of herself. With that thought, he spun out of control.

She wore a long, silky top that seemed to somehow lace in back. As he kissed her, he fumbled with the fabric, his fingers hopelessly clumsy. The ties held snug at her waist. He put his mouth to the warm skin exposed by the vee at the front of her shirt. Why the hell couldn't she wear something normal, say with buttons or a zipper? Things that all red-blooded American males were trained on. Those, he could handle. This silky tangle? Well, damn. He gave up the hunt.

Rowan started laughing. The deep and throaty sound only made him hungrier. "Don't you like my design work? A little complex, maybe?"

Jake barreled on ahead. "I'm going to ask straight out if I can take you upstairs and make love to you tonight."

Her brows arched. "Not even a please?"

He winced, realizing what a total ass he'd just made of himself. He put it down to brain freeze, pure and simple. "I don't think a please would help...would it?"

She moved out of his reach. "I'll admit I'm new to all of this. I mean, I never dated much until I met Chip, and we married quickly. But I'm pretty sure it's supposed to be a bit more, ah...romantic. And even if you did manage to pull off the hearts-and-flowers thing, you've forgotten one—wait—make that two little issues. My children are right on the other side of that wall upstairs."

She was right, he hadn't thought of that. Right now, he wasn't thinking about much of anything other than uncovering curve after curve of soft, sleek skin. He tried for humor.

"How about if I promise to keep real quiet?"

She made a frustrated sound that seemed to be part sigh and part growl. "Jake, I've tried to explain this to you. I'm the only parent Abby and Mac have, and it's up to me to set an example for them. That doesn't include what—" she paused for a second, then finished in a rush "—well, what you're suggesting. I don't think you have a clue what it means to have responsibilities. Have you ever had to think of anyone besides yourself?"

"Try fifty employees, a paranoid banker and the IRS."

She waved off the comment. "They all went home at night. I'm talking about family obligations."

He stalked closer to her, and she backed toward the wall. "I started with one old lawn mower and a lot of sweat when I was sixteen, and I worked my butt off to make something of myself. I've done nothing but answer to people and be responsible for them." He was damn sick of people telling him what he was and what he should be. "This time and this place—they're for me. If you think I'm being selfish, you're right! But don't judge me until you know me, and don't mix your kids into something that's happening between us. They're not part of this."

"Not part of this?" Her voice rose, and he knew that with one thoughtless phrase, he'd dug himself a hole deep enough to reach the old salt mines under Detroit.

He ran a weary hand through his hair. "Rowan, I'm sorry, I didn't mean that the way it sounded." Her expression shifted a little, and for a second he took heart. "I acted like a jerk. It's just that you hit on something that's a sensitive point with me. All I meant was—"

She advanced on him. "Oh, I've got your rules down. Now you need to understand mine. I'm a mother. That fact affects every choice I make." One finger with its neat oval nail thumped the middle of his chest. "You see, I might think you're the best-looking guy I've ever seen, and I might think you're kind and funny, too. But until you prove to me that you can deal with Abby and Mac, I'm not going upstairs or anyplace else with you, buster! You need to grow up, and—and get a haircut!"

"A haircut?"

Her eyes narrowed. "You know what I mean!"

She swept out the front door. A minute later, he heard

the slam of the back door to the apartments above and the staccato tapping of very angry feet.

"And the batter strikes out."

Late that night, Jake showered and toweled off. His bare skin was damp and slightly chilled in the cool air of his bedroom. He sat down on the end of the spring-shot single bed and closed his eyes, transporting himself far from his small, drab apartment, with its mostly rented furnishings, devoid of color and spirit. He turned sideways, leaned against the rough wall, barely noticing its cold scrape against his skin, and began to play his *ney*—a low-pitched African flute—for Rowan.

He hated being separated from her—by all of this wall, by the issue of her children, by responsibilities he wasn't willing to assume. "Crawling through walls," she had said. It took all of his restraint not to claw his way through this one, to her. That feat would be one hell of a lot easier than dealing with the other things that kept them apart.

"Sleep well," Jake murmured, knowing he wouldn't sleep at all.

9

JAKE'S BREATH made white puffs in the cold morning air as he paced the parking lot behind Lindsay's. Like a locomotive gathering steam, he jammed his fists into the pockets of his worn leather bomber jacket. He measured off his strides—three, six, nine and back again. Soon Rowan would return from walking her kids to school. Soon, but not soon enough.

Patience had never been his strong suit. Still, he'd managed to hold off from seeing her for two whole days. He'd needed the time to untangle the knot of hunger and confusion that his last run-in with her had created.

He wasn't willing to give up. But he wasn't ready for a rose-bordered cottage with a pair of grungy guerillas lurking in the shrubs. He needed time, but she needed a sign that he was willing to bend. Hopefully, what he'd done would be enough.

Rowan rounded the corner, then stopped so suddenly that he was surprised she didn't land on her nose. Her cheeks were as rosy red as the cape she wore. Her hair, as usual, was flying wild. She stared at him, her mouth a round *O* of amazement—or maybe shock.

"Your hair! What have you done to your hair?"

He ran his fingers over his closely shorn head. "Like it?"

"No!"

Damned if she didn't look ready to cry. So much for his grand, symbolic gesture. While the barber's clippers were buzzing around his head, devouring hair like a swarm of locusts, Jake had imagined her reaction. She would laugh, or at worst shrug it off. But not cry, definitely not cry.

"Don't get upset, it's just hair."

"I know it's just hair! Why did you do it?"

Sometimes, dealing with a woman was like taking a school exam. The obvious questions usually were the trickiest. "Uh, because you told me to?"

"What?"

"You know, a couple of days ago…'get a haircut.'"

Her exasperated sigh said he was in the running for Dunce of the Year. "I meant it metaphorically!"

"Okay, so I did it metaphorically."

"Tell that to your hair. Do you even get the point I was trying to make?"

She didn't give him a chance to answer, not that he was ready to trot out any more multiple guess responses.

"It's not your hair that's the problem, it's where you are in life. You want to kick back and have a few laughs. I'm not saying you don't deserve to. But I'm making up for lost time, knocking myself out to support my children and build a career."

Jake felt his net worth hovering over him like a guillotine blade. He could give her the money she needed to push her business ahead. He could, but then he'd never know, was it him or the cash that she wanted?

Rowan gave an abrupt shake of her head. "I'm on an entirely different track."

"So we'll meet at the same station." Forgetting there was nothing but brown bristles left, he dragged a hand through his hair. Rowan's lower lip trembled, and he wondered whether she was really going to cry. He was about as useful as a sandbox in the Sahara around weepy women.

"Don't make this so hard," he urged, as much for his sake as hers.

"I'm trying to be a realist, that's all."

Jake was torn between laughter and frustration. He'd never know anyone more ill suited to be a cold realist than this woman. "Why would you want to do that?"

"One of us has to be."

"Why?"

She tipped her gaze down to the crumbling asphalt beneath her feet, then back to him. "That's just the way it has to be."

He wondered who had fed her that piece of propaganda. Old Chip, no doubt. "Let's both be dreamers, okay? And let's see what those dreams make of us."

She stood taller. "I won't pretend to be someone I'm not. And you're going to have to understand that Abby and Mac will always be part of my decisions—"

"Whoa, there. That news already sank in. Promise."

"—and I don't want you to try to be someone you're not, either. It never works, I should know. I tried to change everything about myself to please Chip."

Jake brushed his fingertips against her tender skin. "Chip was an ass. Please yourself, be who *you* want to be."

The corners of her mouth curved upward. "Don't worry about that, Albreight, I learned my lesson. I can even say I like myself now, and I'm pretty proud of what I've accomplished."

"You should be." He was proud, too, in a personal way he didn't want to examine very closely. "About my hair—

long, short, it really doesn't matter to me, so long as I can keep it out of my way. I grew it to tick off an old girlfriend." He shrugged, feeling a little sheepish. "I cut it off to let you know I'm willing to make some changes. But we've been getting ahead of ourselves."

He settled his hands on the soft red wool covering her shoulders. "You should be thinking about your kids. And I really do understand that." He paused, then gave her some of the honesty she put so much stock in. "That doesn't mean I'm willing to sign on the dotted line and become a dad. But maybe a little more time around them wouldn't hurt. Is it a deal?"

She was quiet a moment. As she looked at him, Jake got the feeling she was searching for even the smallest amount of fudging on his part.

"Deal," she eventually said.

"Do you think they'll try to tie me to the sidewalk again?"

She smiled. "You're safe. They only pull the same stunt once."

"And that's a good thing?" He had never told her about their subsequent rounds of sabotage, and didn't plan to. Besides, it had been at least a week since their last offering—little piles of chocolate-covered raisins hidden in the gallery corners like supermouse droppings.

"Really, once you spend some more time with Mac and Abby, you'll find them as special as I do. I know you will."

He nodded, at a loss for words. When he was a teenager, he had a girlfriend who baby-sat. Every now and then, he'd managed to sneak in to visit. Not the kids. The girl. Based on what he'd seen, he'd rather clean a nuclear reactor's core with an ice pick than supervise a pack of kids. Now he had no choice. At least none he was willing to make.

Rowan didn't seem to notice his discomfort. Her expression had grown wistful. "Your hair, I really liked it."

"Ah," he said, unable to stop a satisfied grin from splitting his face. "So you had a fantasy or two about it?"

"Don't let it go to your stubbly head."

"Ouch!" He took her hand. "Here, feel this," he said, running it over the top of his head. "I know it's not quite the same, but this might give you some ideas. It might be an interesting texture against sensitive skin—"

She tugged her hand free. "I get the picture."

"I think you do. But to make sure..." He grasped her wrist and drew her close. He knew she wanted to be kissed. Instead, Jake slowly smoothed her hair away from one ear, bent and whispered an image to her, one so intimate that his blood raced. He let his mouth linger a second longer, closed his eyes and savored her scent. Then with an awesome act of will, he stepped away.

"Think about that today," he said.

"You, too," Rowan shot back, then gave him a smile that was one-hundred-percent temptation. Before leaving she added, "And remember, two can play at that game."

"But we'll both win." He planned to make sure of it.

Two WILD, wonderful weeks whirled by—some of the best in Rowan's life. Jake joined them for dinners, playtime at the park and skating at Lindell ice arena. The twins were on their best behavior. In fact, Rowan began to wonder if the real Abby and Mac hadn't been beamed up to the mother ship, with bland impostors left in their place.

"Don't borrow trouble," she whispered to herself as she peeked in on the twins, who sat in their playroom building some sort of mutant clown from clay. She didn't have time for trouble, not with her client list growing and Aunt Celeste off in Seattle making noises about how good the coffee and bread were, and how she'd like to pitch a tent outside Pike Place Market and never come home.

Rowan pulled a chair up to the twins' table. "Nice...ah, clown."

Mac globbed one more rope of orange clay onto the creature's head. "It's not a clown. It's our real daddy."

"Your real daddy." She'd been told by family counselors that they'd have anger to work through, and she was smart enough to know their pranks were a way of "acting out." Making a squishable Chip was fairly benign.

Rowan sat silent for a moment, watching them. "Speaking of daddies, I have a question..."

"Uh-huh," they said in unison. Neither child looked up from the pea-size blue pellets they were shaping.

"Why haven't you played the daddy game with Jake?"

Mac played with the modeling clay for an ominously long time. "You told us not to," he finally said.

"I've told you not to do lots of things, but it doesn't usually stop you. Why listen now?"

"'Cause this is important," Abby said. "It's not like when you tell us not to color our faces with markers and stuff like that. We like Jake. He's neat."

Rowan pushed aside a flashback to the dreaded permanent marker incident. "Good. I think that he's neat, too. Still, you two have been acting pretty funny lately."

"We've just been bein' good," Mac said.

"That's what I mean. I know I told you Jake isn't used to being around kids, but that doesn't mean you have to act like robots. Act like you did when you first met him. Maybe not that very first day," she quickly amended.

Abby lined up her clay spheres in a tidy row. "We want him to like us. We don't want him to go away like Daddy did."

Straight to the heart, Rowan thought. "That was *not* your fault. Now, here's what I want you to do. Play fair with Jake. Let him get to know who you really are."

Mac stopped playing with the clay. "*Co-o-o-l.* Does that mean that we can—?"

Rowan raised one hand. "No, it doesn't mean that you can play the daddy game, tie him up, decorate his gallery or paint his truck. Just…be yourselves. Only with better manners, okay?"

"Okay."

The front bell chimed, and Rowan stood, wishing she had more time to talk about this. "That's probably my next client. I need you guys to cruise out of here so she can try on her dress. Why don't you go into the front room and play house?"

Mac and Abby mashed their squishable Chip, then led the way back into the shop.

ANNOYED, Jake squinted at the display rack he'd built. Even though he'd measured and remeasured, the unit ran downhill. More accurately, the floor beneath it did. He tilted his head, then wrestled the monster along the wall, looking for level ground. Finally, he found a spot that wasn't perfect, but good enough. After locating the studs, he set the rack's anchors with solid swings of his hammer, into the back wall.

His plan was beginning to take shape. Besides displaying his stuff, he'd agreed to showcase the work of four artists on a consignment basis. He was spending enough on this place without dumping money into inventory. Better to save his cash for a trip someplace warm—Mexico with his fishing buddies, maybe—and make sure cutting the strings with Rowan would be easy if he decided it was time to fly.

It seemed that those strings were getting tighter and tighter, too. Throughout the day he listened to the hum of her sewing machine, and when that fell silent, tantalizing bits and pieces of conversations with customers and her kids. He focused more on her than he did the work under his nose.

Jake shook his head. He might as well admit it. He'd been snared the moment he stepped into the web the twins had built outside their mother's front door.

"Will you make us something?"

With nothing but the shock of interruption registering, Jake smacked the hammer into his thumb, swore, then spun around on the balls of his feet.

The twins gazed up at him, all innocence. He pinned them with the meanest look he could muster, which wasn't much with his eyes watering and his thumb throbbing.

"Dammit, ah, I mean darn it, didn't anybody ever teach you not to sneak up on people?"

"Nope," Mac cheerfully replied.

"Well, I know you've been told not to break in here. That lesson sure as heck didn't stick, and I've got the chocolate-covered raisins to prove it."

"We didn't like those things, they were yucky. So, will you make us something?" Abby asked. "Mommy said you made her the tree that had the balloons on it. She keeps the tree right next to her bed. We like balloons."

Jake blinked, struggling to keep up with the free-form conversation, and at the same time feeling inordinately jazzed that something of his was that close to Rowan. "Uh, I didn't make the balloons."

"That's okay. We'll let you make us something, anyway."

Wasn't that generous of the kid?

Jake's heart slowed as the adrenaline burst passed. He set the hammer on the shelf, since it looked as if he'd be taking a break. He'd already learned there was no such thing as a short chat with the twins. One answer produced a dozen more questions.

"So why should I want to make you something?"

"Because if you do, we'll tell Mommy that we like you."

Nothing like a little bribery. "How about if I just haul you both back, and tell your mom what you've been up to?"

"You wouldn't do that." Abby spoke with absolute certainty, and Mac nodded his head in agreement.

"Why not?"

"It would make Mommy sad if she knew we were in our tunnel. And you like our mommy. You wouldn't want to make her sad," she said, then gave him a totally fake waiflike smile.

It bordered on blackmail, but Abby was right. He didn't want to bother Rowan, not even with something as minor as this. She seemed to be on the verge of putting her life back together, and he wanted her to get there.

For more reasons than his pleasure in her happiness, too.

For half a million mind-messing reasons sitting in his investment account, to be exact.

"Yeah," he agreed, "I like your mom." That, he admitted to himself, was an understatement on a massive scale. "So how did you sneak off, anyway?"

"She's been real busy, too busy to watch us. Lots of people are looking at Auntie Celeste's old stuff, and Mommy has another lady in underwear standing in our playroom."

Mac supplied this tidbit while sending his left hand on a subtle foray toward the hammer Jake had set down. Just as smoothly, and with an internal wince over the thought of Mac on the loose with a hammer, Jake slid it away.

Mac shrugged, and said, "This lady turned real red when she saw us, so we decided to give her some piracy."

"Piracy?"

Mac nodded. "Mommy said that ladies like piracy when they got their clothes off."

"I think she probably said *privacy*, Mac," Jake explained, choking back a laugh. "Sometimes people want to be alone—that's what privacy is all about."

"Oh. Like when you look to see where we are before you kiss Mommy."

Obviously, he hadn't been looking carefully enough. "Yeah, like that."

Miniature reflections of their mother, the twins started wandering around the gallery, snooping into stuff. When Mac began nudging Jake's favorite *ney* closer to the edge of the table it sat on, Jake bit his tongue. Literally.

Let 'em look. Let 'em touch, was his silent litany. *You promised you'd spend more time with 'em. So what if something gets smashed into a billion pieces? So what if it took you thirty hours to make that, and it's the best piece of ebony you've ever seen?*

The *ney* rolled from the table. Jake made a diving catch, and averted disaster at the price of a stumbling fall to the floor. He lay there, eyes shut, clutching the *ney* and once more telling his heart to slow.

"Since that lady needs privacy, can we play over here?"

Against his better judgment, he opened his eyes. The twins were looking down at him as though they were used to flat-on-the-butt heroic dives taking place around them all the time. And they probably were. He'd had about all the togetherness he could take.

"Today's not a good day. I've got a lot to do."

Abby spoke in a small, tight voice. "You don't have time for us. Neither did our daddy. Come on, Mac, let's go." As they headed toward the back room, Jake heard Mac say to Abby, "A real daddy would never be an awful meany like that."

"Damn," Jake muttered, hauling his sorry self up from the floor. He'd screwed up again. Those two were going to run next door and tell their mother what an "awful meany" he was. He needed to buy some peace.

"I'M GOING TO FIND YOU," Rowan called. She intentionally turned away from the giggles drifting from beneath a rolltop desk. "I know you're here somewhere."

When Mac and Abby had appeared and begged for a game of hide-and-seek, her first impulse had been to say no, as she had too often lately. She'd been stopped by the looks of resignation that settled on their faces before she could answer. Now, with hours of work looming in front of her, she crept around the store on tiptoe.

"Is that you under the sofa?" She dropped to her knees and stuck her head under the couch. She knew the twins were watching her. Her bottom waved in the air as, for show, she tried to scoot as much of herself as she could under the low piece. Just then, the entry bell chimed. With a rueful sigh, Rowan considered the fact that she was in direct view of the door. At least, half of her was.

"Haven't we done this before?"

Jake's voice, deep, sexy and rough with humor, sent a thrill chasing through her. She scrambled backward and clambered to her feet.

"I know. We have to stop meeting like this, right?" Rowan noticed that he carried something in one hand. He'd fallen into the habit of bringing her small gifts. Nothing fancy, just little luxuries like tiny, perfumed soaps that her budget couldn't bear. "So what's in the bag?"

"It's a surprise."

She darted toward it.

"Not for you," he added, holding the bag aloft and dancing a step backward. "Where are Abby and Mac?"

Rowan was startled. This was the first time he'd asked for them by name. Usually, it was "the twin terrors" or some other dubious term of endearment.

"Over there," she said.

They stood silently, watching him. Jake bridged the distance and crouched down in front of them.

"Hi, guys. I made you something." He reached into the bag. "They're called panpipes."

Mac's brows rose with obvious respect. "Like Peter Pan?"

"Among others."

They turned the pipes over and over in inquisitive hands, then brought them to their mouths with immediate, ear-splitting results. Side by side, they marched around the store.

Rowan clapped her hands over her ears. "Grandma toys," she muttered.

Jake looked at her with a bemused expression. "What?"

"That's what little toys that make big noises are called,"

she explained over the din. "Only someone who doesn't live with kids would give them a toy like that."

"I must have messed up when I put them together, they're not usually this loud. Really."

Suddenly, Rowan didn't mind the noise, considering what it meant. "You made them? Especially for the twins?"

He nodded, and Rowan thought he looked a little embarrassed. She liked him all the more for showing this sensitive side. And trusted him all the more, too. If Jake could come to accept Mac and Abby, she could free her feelings for him. Not that she was doing such a hot job of keeping them under rein, anyway. Impulsively, she wrapped her arms around his neck and pulled him down for a kiss.

"Hey!" His exclamation of surprise stopped when her lips touched his. It was a sweet kiss, brief, tender and filled with promise. When it ended, she nestled the side of her face against his chest, into his thick, scratchy wool sweater, and listened to the beat of his heart.

"Whatcha doin', Mommy?"

Rowan turned her face in the other direction to see Mac and Abby looking at her and Jake with the same anthropologists-in-training expressions they wore when watching the chimps at the zoo. She tried to pull away, but Jake wouldn't let her.

"I think they want some of that privacy," Mac said.

"Okay," answered Abby. On some cue only they could hear, the twins started weaving between chair and table, desk and sideboard, blowing into the pipes with all the breath they could muster.

Rowan gave Jake another nudge. "You can let me go any time now."

"Why? I like it just fine the way we are. Besides, Mac and Abby need to see they're not the only ones with a claim on you."

"A claim? So you're staking your turf?" Her nose wrinkled at the thought. "Yeech."

He laughed. "All I meant was maybe it's time they see that their mom is more than just a mom."

She poked him in the ribs, and he finally let her go. "Watch it with that 'just a mom' stuff, buddy. What's wrong with being a mom?"

"Man, I'm butchering my words today. I'd better get out of here before I talk myself straight into the doghouse."

It would take more than a few verbal slipups to land him in her bad graces. Especially when he'd finally thought of Mac and Abby with no prompting at all.

"Jake," she said softly as he turned to leave. "The twins were right—it's time we find ourselves some privacy."

He grinned. "Amen to that, lady."

Rowan let out a shaky breath. She'd committed herself now.

10

PRIVACY, ROWAN DECIDED as she nibbled on her eat-while-you-work breakfast of a warm "everything" bagel, was tougher to find than a good man. First, she'd considered driving the kids the two hundred miles to visit Grandma, but couldn't bear the thought of her mother's inquisition. Then she'd briefly pondered asking Melanie to take them for the night. But, no, that scene would be even worse. Rowan shuddered. She could almost see her pal's gloating victory dance.

She needed a solution with a little more dignity. A little more decorum. And she needed one fast.

"Do you have any more bright ideas?" she asked Jake, who lounged in the chair next to hers. The only solution he'd come up with was military school, though he conceded that the odds of finding one with a kindergarten class were pretty slim. Rowan was only half-convinced he'd been joking.

"A few," he said, after taking a leisurely sip of his coffee, then setting it back on the table. He ignored his bagel altogether.

Rowan stuck a napkin under his cup. She'd grown rabid about protecting her aunt's merchandise. "Anything you'd care to let me in on?"

"When the time is right."

"The time was right about a week ago," she grumbled.

He still wasn't eating his bagel, and it really bugged her. "You gonna eat that thing?"

He laughed and nudged it toward her. "Before I started bringing you goodies, what did you live on, stale bread and gruel?"

"I'm a stress eater, okay?"

"And you're stressed?"

She ripped off a chunk of the bagel. "Yeah, I'm stressed. I've made my bed, so to speak—"

He grinned. "And you can't wait to lie in it?"

She swatted him. "Pretty full of yourself, aren't you?"

"Maybe I have reason to be," he said, nudging her arm.

Which was exactly why Rowan was about to ascend to the title of Stress Queen. She had no basis to believe she had any aptitude for...well, *that*. She and Chip had never exactly set the bed afire. And though he'd just been teasing with his comment, Jake was as secure in his sexuality as she was scared. She just wanted to get it over with. Before she ran back home to the farm and tucked herself into her frilly pink canopy bed for the next decade or so.

"Hey, you all right over there?"

"What? Yeah...yeah, I'm fine."

"Don't try to kid a kidder." He rose from his chair and drew her into his arms. "It's going to be okay, you know. Better than okay."

Jake's mouth settled over hers, and Rowan thought he just might be right. When he pulled her closer, she was sure of it.

"It looks like you've been busy," commented a voice from the back of the room.

"Aunt Celeste!"

Rowan tried to untangle herself from Jake.

"The lady's got timing," he whispered before letting her go.

So much for dignity and decorum. She wanted to sink into the floor. Aunt Celeste's smug—practically victorious—expression was almost as cringe producing as Melanie's would be.

Aunt Celeste? Smug?

She picked up the scent of conspiracy.

"What, no greetings for the prodigal aunt?"

Rowan managed a wave.

"Hi, Celeste," Jake said, then gave her a lazy smile. "Have a good trip?"

"I had a great time, thanks. I'd ask what you two were doing, but I'm not so old that I can't recognize a good lovers' clinch."

"Yeah, well, you've probably had your share of 'em," Jake said with a chuckle.

Celeste strolled closer and brushed some bagel crumbs off the Stickley table. "So, Jake, what happened to your hair?"

"Sacrificed for the cause," he replied with a grin that made Rowan's fingers tingle with the urge to tug on what little mink-brown hair remained.

"I see." Aunt Celeste perched her glasses on the end of her nose and scrutinized Rowan. "It looks like you survived while I was gone. Maybe even thrived," she added with a flash of a grin.

"I did okay," Rowan said, studying the tips of her black granny boots.

"Just okay?" Jake asked. "I'll put that under the category of faint praise."

She could feel crimson heat rising up her throat and painting itself across her cheeks. "Okay, I'm great, Aunt

Celeste, just great, top of the world. And welcome back."
No call, no warning, though she supposed since it was
Aunt Celeste's store, warnings weren't strictly required.
Still, one would have been helpful.

Aunt Celeste was still wearing that told-you-so smile.
"Well, thanks for the entertaining welcoming scene. I'm
assuming Mac and Abby are at school learning new ways
to amaze and terrify."

Rowan nodded.

"You know, I missed those kids more than I thought I
would. I must be getting soft in my old age."

Fat chance, thought Rowan. Her aunt would find life in
a survivalist camp leisurely, and she was far from old,
anyway.

Celeste looked first at Rowan, then at Jake. "I think I'll
take the twins for the weekend. That should be enough to
cure me, don't you think? I'm sure you two can find something to do with yourselves." She gave Jake a pointed
smile, eyebrows arched as if challenging him to decline.

Jake grinned. "You're a real gem, Celeste." He turned
toward Rowan. "I've got to get back to work, sweetheart.
We'll make plans later."

Rowan waited until Jake had cleared the front door, and
a measure of her composure had returned. "So what brings
you home, anyway, Aunt Celeste?"

"Something told me that it might be time."

"Something? Aren't we talking more about a *someone*?"

"Well, I called Jake the other day, and he did mention—"

"You called Jake?" Rowan's voice danced up the scale
toward soprano.

"It was the first time I've done that, I swear. I just wanted to see how things were progressing."

"*Things?*" Now she was definitely in the upper ranges.

"His gallery, of course!"

Rowan managed to keep her answer down to a wry, "Of course."

"I didn't meddle."

Her aunt's unsolicited comment reminded Rowan of the time Mac had greeted her by saying that he hadn't cut Abby's hair. "Sure you didn't, Aunt Celeste."

"Okay, I'll admit I gave you a little push in the right direction before leaving town. But the rest of it, kiddo, that was up to you. And it looked to me like you knew what you were doing when I came into the shop." Celeste picked up a painted silk fan and waved it in front of her face as though she were a Southern belle. Not that Rowan imagined many of those genteel ladies had short silver hair that stood up in spikes, or a fondness for purple eyeliner. "This room is still humming with hormones.

"And I really did miss Abby and Mac, you know. I'd love to have them for a few days. Why don't you go on upstairs, take a long, hot soak in the tub and pamper yourself? And you might stop being so embarrassed, too. For a woman with two children, you're acting like you've never had a romantic night in your life."

"Close enough," Rowan said under her breath, then thanked her aunt and beat a hasty retreat to her apartment.

ONCE THE TWINS were packed and off for a weekend of spoiling with Aunt Celeste, Rowan knew there was no turning back. Hoping to bolster her courage, she slipped on her favorite dress. She marveled at the impulse that had whispered to her to create this sexy, almost magical thing.

Although new, the dark blue velvet possessed a patina of age and shone silvery when the light hit it at just the right angle.

She stood on tiptoe and examined herself in her dresser mirror. While cut very low, the bodice was sufficiently snug to stay put. Sleeves tight to the wrist and a flowing skirt only accentuated the bold neckline. Rowan loved the way the dress caressed her curves. She looked like a princess—a very naughty princess. But she still felt more frightened than anything.

They were to have dinner at Antoine's, a restaurant set in an old mansion not far from the Detroit River. From the reviews Rowan had read, it was intimate, expensive and incredibly romantic. She felt a little uncomfortable at how much their meal would set Jake back, but decided that it was a once-in-a-lifetime event. She shouldn't spoil it by worrying about money.

She gave herself one last glance in the mirror. Satisfied with her appearance, she turned to practical matters. She had borrowed an antique beaded bag from Aunt Celeste's shop. The purse was adorned with a silver-and-blue art-deco design, and closed with a clasp formed by two silver swans. Nervously, she inventoried the modern-day items she had packed into a space designed for simpler times: apartment key, lipstick, mascara, a small brush, her driver's license, a credit card and a small, but highly embarrassing package of condoms.

Rowan had never bought something like that before. Her education in such matters was woefully inadequate. After all, Chip had been her "one and only." Luckily, she had broader resources than her experience to rely upon. She might be a smidge behind the learning curve, but she wasn't clueless. She had read *Cosmo,* after all.

So now, the condoms waited in her purse, and she couldn't stop thinking about them. What if they didn't get put to good use tonight? She wondered where she would hide them from the twins. Not much escaped their notice in the cramped apartment. She couldn't see herself explaining, or evading explanation of these items with any particular skill.

And what if they did get put to good use? Jake would certainly understand why she had come prepared, but it all seemed so…premeditated. She paced the small living room. Who was she fooling? Of course this was planned. Tonight, she was going to make love with Jake Albreight.

She knew it.

He knew it.

Aunt Celeste damn well expected it.

ROWAN PUSHED her food from one side of the plate to the other. The beaded bag hung from its chain off the back of her chair. Out of sight, however, was not out of mind. Her neatly packaged friends called to her.

"Hey, it's a little stuffy in here."

She shifted restlessly in her seat, the velvet of her dress tugging against the brocade chair. As subtly as possible, she lifted her hips and wiggled the dress back down a bit.

"You okay?"

Rowan gave a little jump. "What? Oh, fine, just fine."

"Are you enjoying the food?"

"It's wonderful."

"How would you know? I don't think you've eaten any."

She looked down at her plate and winced. "Sorry, I guess I'm a little distracted."

He grinned. "You, sweetheart, are a *lot* distracted. Want to tell me what you're thinking about?"

"Not really."

"Are you worried about your kids?"

With a guilty start of conscience, she realized she'd barely given the twins a thought since leaving them with Aunt Celeste. Just as quickly, she saw that as good evidence she was making a life of her own.

"No," she said. "Aunt Celeste is a softy when it comes to Abby and Mac. I'm sure they're having the time of their lives."

"And you?"

"And me what?"

"Are you having the time of your life?"

"Not yet, pal." The beaded bag's passengers were muffled, but insistent.

"You're taking too long to answer," Jake said. "I'm going to have to work a little harder." He placed his napkin on the table. "Tell you what, if you're through pushing your food around the plate, why don't we dance?"

"Dance?" Rowan echoed.

"Oh my, you are out of practice, you poor thing. Just tuck yourself in real close to him, and—"

"I get the picture," Rowan muttered under her breath.

"Time's up. You're dancing." As he stood, one hand extended, Rowan gazed up at him. His dark, tailored suit—custom-made unless she missed her bet—showed off his athlete's build and made him look solid and sexy.

"I'll dance," she said. Jake grasped her hand and led her away from the table. Rowan smiled as she left her little cheering section behind.

Several couples were already on the small floor. Jake smoothly maneuvered between them and led her to a spot almost directly in the middle. Strong fingers curled around her waist and held her close. That hand, resting so easily against her, was all it took. What had been an abstract longing became real desire. Her mind filled with images of other, more intimate rhythms they would learn tonight.

"You're shivering. Are you cold?"

She gazed resolutely at Jake's shoulder. "No."

Another tremor passed through her and he pulled her even closer. She had never felt desire this elemental, almost frightening in its power.

"Rowan, look at me." His voice was soft, but the words carried the weight of a command. She forced herself to meet his eyes.

"Are you afraid of me?" The notion seemed to startle him. A slight frown creased his forehead, and not a hint of his usual teasing expression was evident. "Tonight doesn't have to be any more than this. We can take it as slowly as you like."

"That's not it." Her voice was barely above a whisper.

"What's wrong, then?"

"I wouldn't call it wrong, exactly, but I can't seem to stop shaking. I'm trying, but I just can't." She tried to laugh it off, but to her ears the sound was closer to desperation.

"Why?"

Her fingers tightened convulsively against the firm muscles of his back. "I keep thinking about what it will be like when we…"

She couldn't finish. The thought, the images it provoked, lured her. She was no longer afraid. Rowan leaned into him, wanting to feel the fire.

Jake jerked back slightly. "Hang on, I'm going to get us out of here." He wrapped one large hand around her wrist and drew her from the dance floor so quickly that she stumbled slightly, unaccustomed to wearing high heels.

Dancers cleared a path, and Jake wove through it with the single-minded intensity of a running back at the opposition's ten-yard line. Rowan ignored the soft laughter following in their wake. At least they were proving that romance was alive and well, if a bit steamed up.

"Slow down," she said, when he paused long enough to put a pile of money on their table and shove her purse into her hands.

"Not a good idea," he returned, then led her by the hand from the restaurant.

Neither spoke during the ride home. Even her little package of commentators remained silent, no doubt knowing that their encouragement was no longer needed.

Jake efficiently threaded through the traffic on I-75, not once letting go of Rowan's hand. She still shook. She forced herself to slow her breathing, to think of anything other than how she ached to feel his skin against hers.

When they pulled in behind the building, he switched off the ignition and said, "My place."

Rowan nodded and swallowed against the nerves that constricted her throat. She followed him upstairs, and was relieved to see that his hand shook as he unlocked his front door. At least she wasn't alone in this muddle of need and nervousness.

Jake led her into the living room. "I'll be right back."

He disappeared into what Rowan knew was his bedroom, where a wall divided his bed from hers. She thought of the nights she had lain in bed and listened to his music. She had imagined him, how he would look. She had dreamed of this night, dark entangled images from which she had awakened, body humming with desire. She thought of how she felt on the dance floor at Antoine's, bold and ready. Now that she was here, she was…scared silly.

She delivered herself a silent talking-to. *This is what you wanted. Now, relax!*

She thought of sex with Chip, how he had clung to order and routine even then. What a failure the whole dismal act had been. This time, she would do it her way. Shake things up, just a little. She set down her beaded bag on a large tapestry armchair, the sole piece of furniture that graced Jake's living room, other than a beautiful antique bookcase. It was enormous, but still not big enough to hold the collection of books that was stacked around it, too.

Biting her lower lip in concentration, Rowan slid the zipper of her dress down to the small of her back. Balancing precariously on one foot at a time, she slipped out of the dress, and laid it carefully over the back of the chair.

She felt a little chilled and a lot nervous, standing in the middle of a practically empty room wearing only a black demibra, stockings and matching lace panties too brief to be called skimpy. She loved the lingerie, a long-ago bridal shower gift. She had never worn it for Chip; he would have considered it tasteless. She'd bet that Jake was going to have a more liberal opinion. She drew in a deep breath, and squared her shoulders.

"Ready or not," she murmured at the exact same time she heard Jake's half-finished, "Do you—" trail into silence.

11

JAKE STOOD FROZEN in the bedroom doorway. Every fantasy he'd conjured, every hope he'd held, didn't come close to Rowan's reality. He'd had some idea she was hiding one delicious body under her clothes. What he hadn't known was that he'd find her expression—a mix of hesitance, desire and humor—every bit as staggering as her luminous white skin.

He didn't blink, didn't want to miss a millisecond of this incredible sight. He couldn't even begin to guess how long they stayed locked in each other's gaze.

He saw her throat work as she swallowed once, then said, "Do I what?"

"Uh… Do you what, what?"

She backed a step toward the chair. "You started to ask me something."

"I did?" Damned if he could remember.

She grabbed her dress off the chair and held it in front of herself. *Wa-a-a-y* too late for that. The image of her had already seared into his memory with all the force of a full solar eclipse. He rubbed a hand over his face and tried to pull himself together.

"Okay," she said, "you're beginning to make me nervous. I know I weigh a few more pounds than I should, and that I have a few stretch marks—well, more than a few—but you should try carrying twins full-term."

''No.'' Jake had already removed his jacket and tie. He began to work the buttons of his shirt as he closed the distance between them. He had to feel her skin against his.

Her eyes grew wider. ''No, what?''

''No, you don't weigh more than you should. You're perfect.'' He eased the dress from her hands and tossed it onto the chair. ''And, no, I don't want to carry twins.''

With one finger—dammit, one shaking finger—he touched the curve of her breast where it spilled over a sexy scrap of fabric that was supposed to be her bra. He drew in a sharp breath as he watched one scarcely covered nipple peak. It was all he could do not to bend down and cover it with his mouth. Damn, he'd be gasping like a racehorse in the homestretch if he didn't step back and slow down.

Step back and slow down? As if he could. He'd never felt like this. The world could grind to a complete halt and he'd still be impelled toward finishing this. Making her his. Slow down? He'd settle for not messing up, for ratcheting down on his need so at least he wasn't scaring her. Or himself.

He slipped the bra straps off her shoulders, then traced the line of her collarbone with his mouth. She was sweet, so sweet he could feast on her forever.

Rowan closed her eyes at the intensity of the sensations rushing through her. She felt his mouth against her—hot. And his hands against her—rough, yet gentle. It was all so new, being touched by another. He kissed her neck, then her breast, where his hand had lingered. He moved lower, his lips blazing a trail of unfurling heat. He ran his thumb across the line of her black panties low across her belly, and dipped it beneath the fabric for the briefest of touches. She was sure her knees were going to give out.

He began to roll first one stocking, then the next, down her thighs. She clutched his shoulders as he knelt before her and slipped off her shoes and the hose. His hands stroked the back of her legs from thigh to ankle, and she could feel each muscle in his path instinctively tighten in anticipation of his touch. He rested his lips on the tender flesh just below her navel, then gently nipped.

"Please." The word drifted from her lips. She wasn't exactly certain what she asked for, where these feelings would lead, but she had to know.

He stood again and led her into his bedroom. There, he had lit candles, and their entwined shadows danced against the walls. A single lavender rose in a slender bud vase sat on the nightstand beside a bottle of wine and two glasses. His simple gestures touched her. She was overemotional, she knew. Flooded with joy, fear, tenderness and desire so overwhelmingly, it left her weak yet thrillingly alive. Tears welled in her eyes, and she was helpless to stop them.

Jake kissed her gently, then paused when his thumb brushed against the moisture that had trailed down her cheek. "Oh, sweetheart, don't cry." His voice was gruff with emotion, and that made the tears flow faster.

"Do you need to sit down?" He sounded uneasy, probably afraid she was about to dissolve into a puddle on the floor. She gave a weepy laugh at the thought.

"No," she said, and wiped her fingertips under her eyes. "I need you to make love to me."

"What, no please?" he said, echoing her words of weeks before.

Rowan smiled, glad to play this little game and take the edge off her jitters. "Would it help?"

"A mom like you should know that manners are always

important,'' he answered with a slow smile that became hotter by the instant.

She slipped her hands into the opening of his shirt and rubbed her palms over the sleek furring she found there. His heart slammed against the wall of his chest. She liked knowing that he was holding himself back for her, taking his time. Rowan drifted closer, tracing the strong lines where his neck gave way to broad shoulders, testing her fingers against his short-cropped hair. Oh, she liked this, liked the spicy male scent of him, the heat of his body.

She twined her arms around his neck and nudged her hips against him. She felt her mouth curve into a smile of absolute female contentment as he groaned low in his chest.

"Pretty please," she whispered.

With a thoroughness that left no room for other matters, Jake kissed her. Flower, wine, candles, tears—all of it was forgotten in the delight of his mouth hard against hers. Gentleness and soft words were gone, devoured by relentless need. She didn't know precisely when or how they ended up on the bed, but reveled in the feeling of his solid body pinned against hers. Jake kissed her as if he tried to feed years of hungry wanting, not weeks.

Rowan stretched beneath him, and ran the bare toes of one foot over his still-clad leg. How decadent it felt to be practically naked while he was still clothed. How wonderful it was to press herself up against him, to rub against him like a cat. She arched her back, affording him access to the closure to her bra. Jake removed it, then knelt above her. He ran both hands over her breasts, down to her waist, then back up to cup her. The feel of his calloused fingers against sensitive skin made her gasp.

He pulled his hands away and asked, "Am I too rough?"

"No. Oh, definitely, no," she said, the earnestness of her response drawing a brief smile from him.

He slid off her black panties. Vulnerable in heart and body, she lay there. He knelt above her, and his eyes traveled from the rise of her breast to the vee of her thighs. She felt a jolt of something electric, more primal than fear.

"How about you?" Her voice came out a whisper, hoarse with passion. "Planning to get out of those clothes?"

"My turn, is it?"

Rowan's hands shook as she helped him undress, kissing newly exposed skin. To have this magnificent body hers to stroke, to touch, to taste, was the most incredible gift she had ever been given. She knelt behind him as he sat on the edge of the bed, then shucked his remaining garments down his legs and into a heap on the floor. Rowan ran her hands over his shoulders and pressed her breasts into the hot skin of his back. She settled her open mouth over the side of his neck, where she could see his pulse racing. Flicking her tongue against the tender spot, she tasted the slightly salty tang of his skin.

She urged him back on the bed, and over her. He shook his head and made a sound that was almost a laugh, but not quite.

"Not yet," he said.

He gave pleasure generously, and Rowan found that somehow she could accept without inhibition. "How does this feel?" he would ask. Or, "Tell me if you like this." She loved it all, demanded more and finally begged for completion.

"Not yet," he said again. "I've imagined this for too long."

He tasted her, touched her in ways she had never thought to experience, until her body rioted with sensations, a firestorm of pleasure so intense it almost seemed like pain. All that he left her was an emptiness begging to be filled.

When he pulled a packet from the nightstand drawer, she gave a passing thought to her little friends waiting in the beaded bag. Soon, they'd get their turns. Very soon.

When he entered her, she tensed in spite of herself. "It's been a long time," she said, cautiously bracing her hands against his chest.

He lowered his forehead to hers, and whispered, "I know, and I'll make it good for you. Trust me."

She did, and it was far, far beyond good.

ROWAN CURLED INTO Jake, her skin warm and damp against his. The mingled scents of her floral perfume and their lovemaking filled the small room. Her hair had come undone hours before and now wove a net around them. He was trapped all right, but for some reason that fact didn't trouble him. She stirred and wound her leg over his hips, drawing him closer. Trapped and happy—a new combination.

"It was never like this before," she said, her voice low and languid. He didn't like to think that she had experienced a "before." Admittedly irrational, since she was the mother of two. Trapped, happy and an idiot.

For an answer, he kissed the top of her head, then ran his hand along the valley of her waist and up the rise of her hips. He couldn't come up with words to describe how it had felt to lose himself in her. At least, not words he could share with Rowan. He didn't want to put a name to what they had, or even to think about it anymore.

The word *love* flitted forward from his subconscious, and he brutally shoved it back. It scared the hell out of him. He had never used the *L*-word. Ever. Even the stupid little heart stamps at the post office gave him sweaty palms.

He wouldn't give the word to Rowan until it unquestionably fit. He owed her that much honesty. As it was, she had been lured to him by something less than the truth.

Jake winced at his own thought: *Something less than the truth.* What a low-down way to get around the fact that he'd taken the easy—and dishonest—route.

He had seen her face the day he gave the twins their panpipes. He'd watched the doubts recede, and her green eyes glimmer with hope. He was the worst kind of manipulator not to have told her the truth right then and there: His gifts to the twins had been nothing more than a bargaining chip for peace.

It was one sticky situation all the way around. The twins would never tell her the truth, not when it meant admitting that they had been up to—or in this case, tunneling to—no good. And if he told her, there would be hell to pay.

Jake closed his eyes as the weight of his decision rolled over him. He'd change what he could about himself, and the rest he'd just have to confess to. Starting now.

He drew in a breath, then let 'er roll. "The topic never came up before, but I think you should know that I have money. Lots of it."

She propped herself up on one elbow and pushed the hair out of her face. "You're rich?"

He tried to gauge her expression, but couldn't. "Yeah."

"Like 'I can buy both Park Place and Boardwalk rich' or 'I won't have to eat cat food when I'm ninety rich?' "

"Kind of in the middle."

"Really?" She sat upright, dragging the sheet with her. "Was there any particular reason you weren't sharing this with me?"

"Uh...no?" He sounded like a dirty-dog liar even to his own ears.

She switched on the bedside lamp. Since he was still stretched out on the bed, the light nailed him square in the eyes. He knew the inquisition had begun.

"So you're rich," she said in a voice just sweet enough to let him know she was really, really ticked.

Jake sat up to avoid the bare-bulb effect of the lamp, and to give himself some height advantage over his inquisitor. "I like to think of it as comfortable."

She snorted. "You can think of your money however you want, but it doesn't change the fact that you hid it from me. You had plenty of opportunity to tell me, like when you took me around the gallery for the first time." She paused and shook her head. "I was so dense. I guess this explains how you could afford the suit you were wearing tonight. I know hand-tailored when I see it, and I also know how much it costs."

He tried to toss in a couple of words before she got on a roll. "I got a deal on it—"

"And you know what bugs me most of all? It's that you assumed I'd care whether you had a dollar or ten billion of 'em stashed away. What made you decide I was some sort of gold digger? Did I do something I've forgotten, like demand diamonds with my bagel this morning? Or maybe it was the time we went to the movie at night, instead of paying matinee prices."

"Rowan—"

She yanked the sheet off the bed and stood, leaving him naked and feeling pretty damn dumb.

"I'm not done yet, buster," she said as she wrapped the sheet like a toga around her. "Don't you ever—and I mean *ever*—assume I want a single dollar from you. When I was married to Chip, he used his money like a weapon. I hated what he did—*hated* it! He'd 'forget' to put money in the household checking account if I said the wrong thing at a country-club dinner, then shower it on me when I was his 'good girl.' I'm never going to be anyone's 'good girl' again. I'm going to stand on my own, and accept love only when it's given honestly and freely."

Jake stood and looked around the room for something he could pull on. Half his clothes were heaped in a pile on the other side of the bed. He almost went to dig out his underwear, then decided not to. As long as they were baring their souls, he might as well keep the rest of him that way, too. He sat on the edge of the bed and watched Rowan pace back and forth.

"I swore when I started my design business, I'd do it myself. Taking a bank's money is a business proposition, but taking a friend's...or a lover's..."

He smiled at the color climbing above the top edge of her makeshift toga, up her throat and to her cheeks. It floored him to think they could have made love the way they just did, and she'd still be innocent enough to blush when using the word *lover*.

She cleared her throat before speaking again. "Well, that's never going to happen. And it really hurts to know you thought I might be trying to use you."

Jake sighed, then patted the bed next to him. It was still warm from the combined heat of their bodies—something he hoped he'd be able to feel again, one day. "Come sit down."

She did, but left a big space between them.

"I never thought you were trying to use me. And what I'm going to tell you isn't an excuse for what I did—"

"Good thing."

"—it's more an explanation." Jake took a second to pull his thoughts together. He'd never been good at eating a fat slice of humble pie, but now he was ready.

"I had this girlfriend for a really long time, one of those hotshot, cell-phone-toting business types. I think at first she kind of got a kick out of being with a guy who wasn't college educated and all smooth manners like her other friends. After a while, I learned to play their game, but it always felt wrong to me...like I'd somehow fallen into someone else's life."

"I know what you mean." Her brief smile gave him hope. Maybe she'd forgive him...eventually.

"Anyway, my business took off. Pretty soon I had money to spare, and Victoria decided it was her personal mission to spend it. We bought a house together on Orchard Lake. It was a 1960s-style ranch, one of the last original houses sitting smack in the middle of all these mansions. The neighborhood was a little rich for my blood, but I loved the thought of being on the water, and I knew it was a good investment.

"We'd barely closed on the place when she had bull-dozers out there to tear the house down. It didn't make the right statement, she said. I felt like I'd been royally ma-nipulated, but I was too stressed with other stuff to get into it with her. She built a showcase. I found myself missing that old ranch house. And feeling buried under mortgage payments that were more than I used to make in a year."

The stress he thought he'd left behind dug its claws into his temples. He rubbed at the ache before continuing.

"We lasted maybe another year together. I felt like my life was killing me, and when I tried to talk to Victoria about it, she got all ticked off and stormed out."

Rowan scooted closer. She took his hand and wove her fingers through his. Comfort seeped into his bones as she said, "You don't have to finish this."

"Yeah, I do. Anyway, I needed to scale back and take my life where I wanted it, instead of being led by my, ah, bills. I called one of my competitors who'd been angling to buy my business. When I told Victoria what I planned to do, she had the locks changed on the house."

He drew in a breath, then spoke the humbling, warts-and-all truth. "All she wanted was my money. During the time we were together, I was never more than a plaything and a walking checkbook. It really stunk to realize what my life had become. I signed over my portion of the house and moved in with a friend. A few months later, the business sold, and I told myself I'd never look back."

He stared down at his hand and Rowan's. "So, now here we sit, and I find that I've been looking back all along. Once—just once—I wanted to know that someone wanted me, for *me*."

"I want you, for *you*," she whispered. "I promise."

And he wanted her more than he'd ever wanted anyone. He should tell her that, but the thought still scared him. Instead, he pulled her closer. "Think I can talk you out of that sheet?"

Later, after he'd made love to her again, Jake watched Rowan sleep. For her, he thought while stroking her smooth skin, he'd do whatever it took. He'd change. Really change. He'd try to adjust to her kids and the endless bligations that came with them. He had no idea how he'd choke down the parental responsibility—both financial and emotional—when he wanted none, but he'd do it. He'd become her home-and-hearth, settled-down family man. Or die trying.

12

ROWAN WASN'T SURE if it was her prophetic Scots blood or just the cumulative effect of watching Jake's expression grow more strained the longer he was around the twins, but she had a bad feeling. A very bad feeling.

"So why shouldn't we take the kids to Papa's Pizza Palace for dinner?" Jake asked again. "They can run off a little steam."

Papa's was no place for an amateur, and for all his recent effort, Jake scarcely qualified for that status. Even Rowan felt chilled at the thought of Papa's. Legions of shrieking children ran, crawled and slithered through a giant elevated maze of plastic tubes and slides. It looked like a chemistry experiment gone wrong, spewing out a stream of wild, howling offspring. The kids stopped only to slug down gallons of sugary soda, gnaw on cold pizza crusts and beg game tokens.

"Have you ever actually been to Papa's?"

"Come on, how bad can it be?" he scoffed.

"You don't want to know."

"Sure I do," Jake said, lifting the twins' jackets from their hooks by the back door. "Are you wimping out on me? Maybe sprouting a few chicken feathers?"

The same Scots heritage that brought premonitions also carried the inability to turn down a challenge. Rowan tugged on her coat. "Just remember, you asked for it."

OKAY, SO HE'D asked for it. Jake wanted to press his palms to his skull and howl. No one would hear him if he did. Back in his head-banging days, he'd been to quieter heavy-metal concerts.

Rowan was off ordering pizza and buying more game tokens. He hadn't seen much of the twins, not that he'd be able to distinguish them from the rest of the wild-haired mob stampeding through the joint. Yeah, this place had a lot in common with those concerts of old. Only now he felt just that. Old.

Rowan slid into the seat next to him. "The pizza will be up in a few minutes. Just watch for our number on the monitor. I got pepperoni, if that's okay."

"Aspirin would have been better."

"Come on, it hasn't been that bad. We just might make it out of here in one piece."

"Not a chance. I've already left a good part of my hearing behind."

She laughed. "Here's some incentive to make sure the rest of you gets out. Melanie has tickets to a live show down at the Fox Theatre tomorrow and plans to take the twins. We have the afternoon to ourselves. The whole afternoon...all alone."

Now that was something to live for. Between the twins and Rowan's hours spent sketching and sewing, they hadn't managed any private time since that weekend when he'd set himself down the path to pizza hell. He figured he was about due for some undivided attention.

"Don't you have work to get done?" he asked.

"Nothing that can't be finished later. And I don't know about you, but I'm tired of waiting."

Satisfied that soon he'd have more, Jake brushed a quick kiss against her mouth. "I'll second that, sweetheart."

She looked adorably embarrassed as she glanced to see

if they'd caught anybody's attention. Not a chance in this bedlam.

"Hey, the pizza's ready," she said. "Why don't I go find the kids and you get the dinner?"

"Nah, I'll corral 'em." One kiss and he felt as though there was nothing he couldn't handle.

Almost nothing, he decided a few moments later. He stood at the base of an enormous yellow playscape and squinted upward, trying to sort Rowan's kids from the thousand or so others that clung to it. He didn't stand a chance. He couldn't even remember what Mac and Abby were wearing. There was no telling them apart by voice, either. His ears rang with high-pitched squeals and an intermittent sirenlike scream that punctuated the noise.

A hand tugged at his. "Jake, Jake! Abby's up at the top and she's scared to come down! These big boys keep pushing her."

That explained the scream. "Let me go get your mom."

"No, that'll take too long! You go get her. Now! She's really scared." Mac's eyes welled. "C'mon, Jake."

He was a sucker for tears, all right. "Okay, Mac. Point to where she is."

"Right in the middle. See?"

Great. Right in the middle. Jake spotted a little head with the same wild dark waves as Rowan's. He moved to where he had a clearer view.

"Abby, can you climb down to me?" he called.

"No!"

"Just put your feet on the rope netting and back down. I'll be right here."

Mac tugged at him again. "She doesn't like that stuff. She's scared she'll fall through."

"Great," he muttered. He turned his attention back to

Abby. "How about the slide in the big tube? Just keep moving forward."

"*No-o-o-o!* Those mean boys are waiting at the bottom."

"I'll go scare them off."

"You *ca-a-a-n't!*"

Jake knew a loser of a situation when he saw one. He bit back the words he wanted to use and settled for a groan instead.

"Stay put, Abby. I'll be right there," he called.

Ignoring the "Hey mister, go play with kids your own size" comments, Jake worked his way up the outside of the giant rat maze. It wasn't the fastest way to Abby, but it was the surest. The tubes and tunnels looked to be a pretty tight squeeze, and he didn't want to risk bumping into any kids, anyway.

And there was the tiny, almost insignificant, additional fact that he broke into a cold sweat followed by a red-hot panic whenever he was confined to a small space. That, though, was his little secret.

He glanced up at Abby. She clung to a post at the mouth of the slide. Her eyes were squeezed shut, but at least she'd stopped screaming.

"I'm getting closer," he said in his most reassuring voice.

She nodded and clutched the post tighter. "Hurry."

He angled around a corner, asking kids to move aside so he could reach Rowan's daughter. One more platform and he'd be to her.

One more platform and she was nowhere in sight.

"Abby!" The other children glared at him, then went back to playing. Well, he'd been played. For a fool.

No way was he going down the tunnel/slide that Abby must have finally taken. As he retraced his path, he worked up the first parental lecture of his life. That little scam artist was going to get it with both barrels.

He reached the bottom and stalked around the structure. When he finished, he was zero-for-two in twin-finding. Jake hustled to the doorway of the dining room. Rowan sat at the table alone. He pulled up short. He could hardly tell her that he'd misplaced her kids.

He checked out the video game area, the art barn, the play farm and the bathrooms. Annoyance gave way to fear. His skin was clammier than it had been the time he got stuck between floors in an elevator. He double-checked the playscape. Not a sign of them. His heart pounded faster and faster as he considered the possibilities.

A hand grasped the crook of his elbow from behind. He spun around.

Rowan let go and stepped back. He wondered if he looked as terrified as he felt. "Jake, are you okay?"

"Uh…"

"I told Mac and Abby they had to wait for you before they ate."

"They're—" he managed to get past air-starved lungs.

"Hungry," she said, then took his hand and led him toward their table. "You're really looking weird. Want to tell me what happened?"

He rubbed his free hand across his forehead. "I, uh…lost them. I went to rescue Abby from the top of the playscape, but she was gone by the time I got there. Then both of 'em disappeared."

"Abby said the boys who were bothering her went away. I'm sure you just missed each other in the crowd after that. It is a scary feeling, though, isn't it? Once, I lost her in a department store. She was hiding in a clothes rack about three feet from where I stood. Anyway, just when I was ready to scream for Security, the police and whomever else I could holler up, she decided to come out. Not the best of memories, but it comes with the territory."

He was beginning to see that the territory was even more rugged than he'd imagined. And the responsibilities were, too. He wondered how a single parent on the planet ever managed to sleep at night, what with all the unnamed dangers just waiting out there to grab a kid. This was serious business, for serious players only.

He could feel those chicken feathers he'd accused Rowan of having begin to pop out on him faster than a case of poison ivy. This was the Big League, and he wasn't even fit to sit on the bench. Just what had he gotten himself into?

Aunt Celeste stood, hands on hips, amidst the most recent shipment from her Seattle buying spree.

"That was the fourth trip upstairs you've made to answer your phone this morning," she said to Rowan. "Why don't you just give your customers the number down here? It beats the heck out of making that mad dash every time the phone rings."

"I didn't want to use the number without asking you first. Besides, I need the exercise." With a rueful smile, she patted her bottom.

"So join a gym and give your clients the number down here."

Rowan laughed. "It's a deal. But I want you to know that no matter how busy I get, I'll always be around to help you out," she added, while sorting through a box brimming with tarnished silver flatware.

"I don't expect you to work here forever. When it's time for you to move on, I'll plant one foot in the middle of that behind of yours and send you out the door."

Rowan gave a burst of shocked laughter. "Aunt Celeste!"

"Don't take it the wrong way. I love you like you were my daughter." She waggled one index finger. "But there's a big world out there, and you've hidden yourself away from it for too long."

"It's been a tough haul," Rowan agreed. "Since Chi—"

Her aunt waved a sugar bowl as if it were a bulb of garlic in front of a vampire. "Don't say that name—you'd be invoking evil spirits."

Rowan grinned. "Okay, since that name I won't mention has been out of my life, I've felt like a recovering amnesia victim. I'm finally beginning to remember who I am, but it's still a bit fuzzy around the edges." The muffled ring of the phone sounded from upstairs. "Oops, gotta run," she said, dropping a fistful of salad forks back into their box.

After scheduling two more fittings, Rowan trailed into the shop. Aunt Celeste had made quite a dent in the unpacking, but Rowan suspected more was on the way.

"Here, let me give you a hand." Costume jewelry and the real stuff, old and new, were jumbled together in a shoe box. Knotted necklaces snaked through the entire mess, binding it tightly together. "Just couldn't help yourself, could you?"

Celeste chuckled. "Never can. You never know when you're going to find that perfect gem hiding in so much junk. Besides, the more time passes, the more the portable end of the business appeals to me. I stayed away from furniture this trip. As the store clears out, I won't jam it so full."

It didn't take a flashing neon sign for Rowan to recognize a second chance. She'd learned so much about herself over the past several weeks, including the fact that sometimes she was her own worst enemy. This time she didn't hesitate.

"Would it be all right if I filled in some of the empty space? I'd really love to have a place to display a few of my pieces down here. You know, a few holiday dresses now, some really short and sexy things around Valentine's Day. I won't take up much room, and you'll have final approval on anything I want to put out. I wouldn't want to offend you. If you say no, I'll understand—"

"Or you could stop talking long enough to let me say yes."

ROWAN EXECUTED an exuberant twirl in the middle of Jake's gallery. "The most absolutely, wonderfully marvelous thing just happened! Try to guess!"

His mouth tilted up in a teasing smile. "You finally realized that I can do no wrong?"

Rowan planted a quick kiss on the corner of that smile, then spun away. "Arrogance, Albreight. Sheer arrogance. Aunt Celeste has agreed to give me some floor space!"

"All right!" he crowed. "I knew you could do it!" He pulled her back into his arms and kissed her long and hard.

When he finally let go, Rowan kept her arms twined around his waist and leaned back to look at him. Like everything, this new opportunity was going to come at a cost.

"This is going to make things even harder on us, you know. I'll be lucky to find a spare twenty minutes in the next month."

He cupped her face with one broad palm. "I know, sweetheart. It's okay." He gently drew his thumb along the line of her jaw. Rowan felt so tender and cherished. "When you find that spare twenty minutes, I'll be here."

Joy unfurled until she wondered how her heart could expand to hold it all. She did know one way she wanted to share it, though. "Speaking of spare minutes, do you have a few for me right now?" she asked, her voice thick with emotion.

Jake gave her a cautious look. "You're not going to cry all over me, are you?"

"No," she said over a watery smile. "I promise I won't. I just want us to have some time...together."

Jake immediately understood. He took her by the hand. "You know, lately I've been having these thoughts involving you and that chair in my living room."

Rowan felt rosy heat color her face as she took in his intense expression. Her blush wasn't from embarrassment; it was made of pure desire. Given her past, it had never occurred to her that making love could be fun. She might be a little late in coming to the party, but she intended to make up for lost time.

"Now that you mention it, I've been doing a little thinking myself," Rowan said, then smiled as his hand tightened over hers.

AFTER THEY'D TURNED their thoughts to hot and sweet action, then tested the capacity of Jake's bathtub, Rowan got ready to go back to work. She brushed her hair at the bathroom mirror. Jake stood behind her, watching.

"The big day is Friday, you know," she said.

"What big day?"

"Halloween, of course."

"Oh, that." His eyes narrowed. "You're not one of those people who gets all done up in some ridiculous costume, are you?"

"And if I were?" Maybe now wasn't the best time to tell him all about her Anne Boleyn costume, made to represent poor Anne before she and her head parted ways, naturally.

"I'd tell you there's no way you'll ever get me dressed up." His jaw jutted at a stubborn angle. Rowan couldn't help but smile at the sight.

"Based on the way you're looking at me now, I'd say slap on a spiked collar and you could pass as a bulldog."

"Don't even think of it," he growled.

Laughing, she turned to face him. "Don't worry, you're off the hook. It takes ages to get Abby and Mac all done up, anyway. But if I can't get you dressed up, will you at least come trick-or-treating with us?"

"I don't think that's such a hot idea."

"It would only be for an hour or so. Come on, we'll have fun."

He took a backward step. "Really, no."

"Why not?"

"Rowan, I lost them once in pizza hell—"

"I've told you that wasn't your fault," she interrupted. "I shouldn't have left you alone for so long."

He shook his head. "I'd have to be crazy to go out on the one night of the year that they can blend in with thousands more of their kind. Talk about a nightmare."

She gave the half smile that his forced attempt at humor deserved. "I understand."

Unfortunately, she really did. The bottom line was that she wanted Jake to act like a part of her family, when he wasn't. He still saw her as a divided entity: Rowan the lover, and Rowan the mother. His half. Their half. His time. Their time. She had hoped the passing days would close the rift. That didn't seem to be happening; if anything, he was drawing back. It would do her no good to push him along. When they handed out awards for mule headedness, Jake Albreight would be standing front and center.

"If you change your mind, just let me know," she said in the cheeriest voice she could muster. She walked into the living room, and he followed.

"I won't."

"Have it your way, Albreight. Be a sour old Scrooge," she teased, trying to set aside her disappointment. "Don't worry, I'll love you, anyway."

Rowan's heart suspended midbeat when she realized what she had said. *Joke, it was just a joke!* she wanted to cry. Suddenly, she recalled her freshman Intro Psych course and how Freud, that old goat, had believed there was no such thing as a joke. It was just possible the guy had a point. What she had said wasn't a joke; it was the truth. She had no idea how she'd missed it when it had come rumbling at her with all the stealth and subtlety of a freight train.

She loved Jake. It was so clear now, so obvious that she couldn't believe it had taken her this long to understand. To accept. Jake encouraged her dreams, praised her, comforted her. He'd never laugh at her, or intentionally hurt her as Chip had.

Of course she loved Jake. And, of course, she never should have blurted it out like that. Those were the last words he'd want to hear. To cover the moment—and to avoid seeing his expression—Rowan fussed with her clothes.

"Wrong holiday," he finally answered in a voice that sounded just the tiniest bit thin.

"Well, you get the idea," she said, stumbling in her haste to get the heck out of there. "I've gotta run...right off the nearest cliff," she finished as she closed his apartment door behind her.

No doubt about it, she still was her own worst enemy.

13

JAKE STOOD exactly where Rowan had left him. He felt as if he were in one of those old sci-fi movies, where time stretched and slowed until it stopped entirely. He could still see her mouth shaping each syllable of that terrifying statement. He imagined himself running toward her in slow motion, shouting a drawn-out *"N-o-o-o!"*

Life was closing in on him, and he didn't like it one damn bit. This was supposed to be his time to do what he wanted, when he wanted and with whom he wanted. He wasn't kidding himself on one count: He wanted Rowan. He got a real kick out of her sassiness, the way she didn't back down when he teased her. And even when he wasn't with her, he spent a lot of time thinking about her, imagining what she was doing on the other side of that wall. Still, he couldn't shake the selfish feeling that his hard-won freedom was slipping away. Everything was becoming so serious. So adult. So permanent.

Jake clasped his hands behind his neck and stared at the ceiling. Maybe he was overreacting. Maybe he was reading too much into this. He eased into his chair, then sprung up as if it was a trap closing on him. The very spot where he'd just made love to her wasn't the place to be sorting out this mess.

"'I'll love you...'" Pacing the room, he shook his head

and repeated the words again. Not as definite as a flat-out "I love you," but not very short of the mark, either.

"I *will* love you," he tried on for size. He paused, then nodded his head. Okay, somehow that was easier to swallow. Someday in a far-off, hazy future he didn't need to think about, Rowan would love him. For now, she could just…like him one whole helluva lot. That, he could live with. Almost.

Jake looked around his apartment and scowled. The close quarters seemed even tighter. Maybe if he brought some of the outside in. He was tugging at a jammed window and flinging language hot enough to melt glass when he realized just how tightly he was strung. He needed a breather—a few days to get his head on straight. It was either that or lose it altogether.

Jake picked up the phone and dialed Joe, the friend he'd roomed with before moving here to Claustrophobia Central. An hour later, he was geared to party hard with his single, ready-to-roll pal.

ROWAN SAT with her feet propped up on her least favorite umbrella stand. She and Melanie had set up camp for a chocofest in the back of the antique shop.

"You think he would have told me he was leaving town. A phone call, a note under the door, morse code on the blasted bedroom wall…it wouldn't have taken much," Rowan said, then bit another corner off the candy bar she'd liberated from the twins' Halloween stash. Mac and Abby had raked in so much stuff that they'd never miss a pound or two. Good thing, too, because Melanie and she must have chowed that much already.

"And I have no idea where he is. I mean, what if something happens to him? What if something already has? His truck's been in the back lot all this time. What if he's really over there—you know, slipped and fell, or something? Maybe I should go next door and check.''

"Tsk, tsk." Melanie gave her a sympathetic pat on the hand. "You've got it bad, don't you?"

"Got what bad?"

"The love bug," her friend replied, while dredging a packet of chocolate-covered pretzels from the grinning orange jack-o'-lantern bucket.

Rowan didn't bother to deny the nature of her disease, though she did hope it was caffeine and chocolate—not love—making her this squirrelly. "Okay, I know he's probably not over there, but I can't help worrying."

Melanie munched on a few pretzels, then said, "I thought he was working on getting that gallery of his open. Why'd he take off now?"

"I might have made him a little nervous. I, uh, told him I loved him."

"What?"

"It's not like I threw myself at his feet or anything, but he could have inferred it from a little joke I made."

"Well, I guess he picked up the signal, since he blew town." Melanie gave a rueful shake of her head. "Take it from the voice of experience, you gotta break that kind of news slowly."

"Or not at all," Rowan said glumly. "Good thing I've had this place to keep me busy or I would have spent the last week kicking myself on the butt."

The days had passed in a wild blur, as, by some vision only Aunt Celeste could see, she reorganized her store. In the end, a space had magically appeared. Rowan's space. She was now the proud renter of half the front window— complete with three mannequins—and a small salon area with an antique settee for customers to sit on as they flipped though her portfolio.

"Just play it calm and cool with Jake the next time you see him. No apologies, no explanations," Melanie advised. "Maybe he's already forgotten. Guys have notoriously short memories. My Dan can't even remember where the laundry hamper is."

Rowan smiled. "That's selective, not short."

"Well, you get the point. Just cruise on down the road like you never hit that little pothole."

It had felt more like a bottomless crater to Rowan, but otherwise Melanie was right. Rowan sighed, then finished off her latest candy victim.

She'd already spent too much time bludgeoning Jake over the head with every little reason why their relationship would never work. Now she recognized her behavior for what it was—her form of self-protection. Her form of self-fulfilling prophesy. If she could just relax, maybe everything would be okay. As she considered how one went about pretending that an admission of love had never occurred, she was interrupted by the chime of the front bells.

Melanie nudged her. "Here's your big chance, Ms. Cool." She grabbed a couple of caramels from the jack-o'-lantern, said "Gotta run!" then did.

Rowan looked at the candy wrappers littering the table and winced. She called a semi-alarmed "hi" to Jake, and began jamming evidence of gluttony first into the bucket, then into her pockets. Love and chocolate consumption—those were two of the many things that a guy just didn't need to know about.

Jake brushed a kiss against her lips, then took her hands in his. "Guess you wonder where I've been."

A really snippy, sugar-fired "Not at all" came to mind,

but Rowan bit it back. There was no point in hiding her anxiety behind bluster.

"I've missed you," she said instead, hoping that "missing" didn't fall into the same forbidden category as "loving."

He stroked his thumbs over the tops of her hands. "I missed you, too."

She could feel herself leaning toward him, drawn into the temptation of his touch. How was she supposed to play it calm and cool when he made her feel so hot and confused?

"I went up to Manistee for some end-of-the-season fishing. Nothing but buddies, boats and fish guts for a week."

Now there was something a woman just didn't need to know about. Rowan pulled back a bit and wrinkled her nose. "Not even a shower?"

He grinned. "One. Right when I got home."

"Nice."

"I'm kidding," he said, hauling her closer. "But I wasn't kidding about missing you." He led her over to a sofa and sat with her. "I probably should have mentioned that I was leaving—"

"It's no big deal," she interrupted. "It's not like we're married or anything." She winced as she realized what word had slipped out. To Jake, *married* had to be even more toxic than *love*. "What I mean is—"

He stopped her. "It's okay. No, we aren't married, but we are something. What, I haven't quite got my finger on," he added with a half smile. "I'm going to ask you to trust me, and let me get this figured out in my own head. I don't want to talk about what you said before I left town. I want to take it slow and easy. Just…give me a chance to get used to this, okay?"

Rowan shifted on the sofa and looked down at her nibbled fingernails. She didn't like this. As much as she wanted to be that perfectly calm-and-cool person, she wasn't. It bothered her the way tension had settled over Jake's features, drawing his mouth tight and shadowing his eyes. If she didn't speak now, it was going to be like picking her way through a minefield, deciding what she could and couldn't say to him.

Then again, better to walk on tiptoe than to blow sky-high, she reminded herself. If all he wanted was some time, she should be able to give it to him. It was the price she'd have to pay for her mouth getting ahead of his heart.

"Okay. But I really think—"

Jake cupped her face between his strong hands and kissed her. "Think all you want, sweetheart. Just keep those thoughts to yourself for a while, huh?"

Rowan gasped. It was a good thing she loved him, or she'd have his hide for a comment like that. "You're walking mighty close to a dangerous edge, pal."

Jake's mouth flirted with hers, tugging at her lower lip before getting down to real business. He was buying her silence with kisses, and doing a hot job of it, too. Feeling only the slightest twinge of conscience, she curled closer to him. Later, she'd give him a talking-to about his underhanded tactics. Much, much later, after the kissing was done.

"RELATIONSHIPS," Jake muttered aloud, then shook his head in outright disgust. He picked up his jacket from the end of his bed and gave a frustrated growl. Two weeks ago he'd been flying high when he'd managed to delay all talk of the future. And of obligations. And responsibilities.

Man, those words made him feel like he was whistling

his way through a graveyard. But his and Rowan's pact of silence had only let the issues come to life. Now they followed him everywhere, dragging their chains and moaning his name. The beasts were closing ground, and he knew he couldn't outrun them much longer.

Tonight he'd get it all cleared up, he thought, while making sure he had his wallet and keys. He'd tell Rowan they could go steady or something for a while, then maybe, just maybe work their way toward something more formal.

Go steady? He paused and cocked his head at the thought. Not quite what he was looking for. Going steady sounded as though he'd have to give her his letter jacket or high school ring to wear. Way too juvenile. Besides, he'd never bought a class ring and had lost his letter jacket years ago. He'd have to come up with the adult equivalent, and have it ready to offer up after the twins were stowed for the night.

It was shaping up to be one tough evening all the way around. Before he would even have the chance to talk to Rowan, he'd have to survive the Emerson Elementary School Thanksgiving play. When Rowan had asked him to come watch Mac and Abby with her, there was no way he could have turned her down—not after the way he'd teased her about the hokey corn costumes she'd made for the kids. And not after skipping out on Halloween, either.

He figured he'd pretty much traded up one costumed disaster for another. With all the enthusiasm of a doomed man, he grabbed his camera, switched off the last light and closed the apartment door.

NERVES. It had to be nerves. Rowan's heart fluttered against the wall of her chest like a captured bird. She couldn't seem to stop talking, either. "You two are the sweetest, most wonderful ears of corn I have ever seen. Mac, let me straighten your cornsilk, and, Abby, remember to smile." She adjusted Abby's tasseled cap for good measure, too. "Do you both remember what you're supposed to do?"

"Rowan—"

"And don't let the audience frighten you." She wiped at a smudge of chocolate frosting that still clung to Mac's cheek. "You're going to have a great time. Once you get up on stage, just think about—"

"Rowan!"

"For heaven's sake, what, Jake?" She stopped fussing with Abby's hair long enough to look at him. He was wearing one of those aren't-mothers-the-most-embarrassing-people sympathetic grins. Abby and Mac were giving it right back to him.

"The kids have to get backstage." He paused for a brief comedic downbeat before adding, "Quit talking their ears off."

Rowan rolled her eyes. "Very funny. How long have you been saving up that terrible pun?"

"Too corny, huh?"

She gave him a nudge. "Stop it!" She turned back to Mac and Abby. "Now scoot, guys. Jake and I will get seats as close to the front as we can. You just have a wonderful time, and don't forget your lines."

"They don't have any lines."

"What? Oh, right. I'm just so nerv—um, excited."

Jake patted them each on the shoulder. "Go on guys, make a break for it before your mom starts talking again. And as they say in showbiz—break a leg. Or in this case would it be an ear?"

Rowan groaned, and the twins giggled.

"See you after the play," she called as they waddled to the backstage area. Watching them, Rowan frowned. She should have given more thought to mobility and less to realism when she put together their costumes. She took a step toward them.

Laughing, Jake hauled her back. "Don't even think of it."

"I just want to fix their costumes."

His brows arched. "Now? Why not wait ten minutes and go on stage with them?"

"Sorry, I guess I'm a little wound up."

He took her hand and wove his fingers through hers. "I hadn't noticed," he said, clearly in a tongue-in-cheek sort of way. "They're going to be okay, you know."

She sighed and clasped his hand tighter. "I do."

He smiled. "Let's go find a spot where this camera of mine will do some good."

Once they were seated, Rowan crossed her left leg over her right, switched to right over left, and back again. At Jake's resigned sigh, she jiggled her foot to keep from bouncing in her seat.

He settled his free hand on Rowan's leg. "Sweetheart, relax. All they have to do is walk on stage and back off. What can go wrong?"

"I don't know. But with Mac and Abby, it's always big."

"Good point."

"Hey, you're supposed to be reassuring me."

"Given the subject matter, I'm doing the best I can," he whispered, then just as the lights dimmed, gave her a quick kiss.

When Abby and Mac appeared as part of the Thanksgiving feast, it was obvious they had decided to milk their moment of glory. Turkeys, pumpkins and gourds took their bows and exited. The twins still stood center stage. Abby used her best Miss America wave, and Mac bowed more times than an assemblage of foreign dignitaries. By the time their teacher gave up whispering from the wings and stepped on stage to corral them, the audience roared with laughter. Rowan and Jake, too.

After the play, she and Jake went to gather up the twins in their classroom. Their teacher rushed to greet them.

"Weren't they adorable? I was a little worried we'd never get them off the stage, but they were the hit of the show! You must be so proud!"

Rowan smiled and was about to speak when Mac and Abby flung themselves at her. She bent down to take them in her arms. "You two are something else," she whispered, then wrapped them in an enormous hug.

"Careful, Mom, or you'll pop us," Abby said with a giggle. "Pop...corn.... See, we can make silly jokes, too! But we gotta get going now."

"Really fast," Mac added, wriggling within her grip.

The teacher's attention landed on Jake. "You must be Mac and Abby's new father. With all they talk about you, I'd know you anywhere. I can't wait to see the shop you're opening. The twins tell me it will be any day now."

New father?

First, her slipups over love and marriage, and now this? Rowan's arms dropped to her sides, and the twins stared at their shoes. She felt as if the air had been knocked out of her, leaving a gaping vacuum. Uncertain she could stand, Rowan kept kneeling. She closed her eyes and focused on a silent plea.

Please let him see that they didn't mean anything by it. Please let him understand.

After an endless silence, Jake cleared his throat and answered a toneless, ''Yeah, any day now.''

Rowan's shoulders slumped. That was not the voice of understanding she'd just heard. When she looked up at him, he held out a hand. ''We should get going.''

As Jake helped her to her feet, she tried to read his eyes, to assess the extent of the damage, but he looked away. Knowing that now was neither the time nor the place to discuss this, she left him to retrieve the twins' jackets.

Mac and Abby's teacher stopped Rowan and asked if she had said something wrong. Rowan assured her that she hadn't, and promised to stop by school a few minutes early in the morning and explain their family situation.

She took as long as she possibly could bundling up the twins. Jake would need a few minutes to come to his senses, to recognize Mac and Abby's tales for what they were—wishful thinking. He couldn't blame them for dreaming of a real father. At their age, the line between dreams and reality often blurred. But they understood they had done wrong. It was obvious by their pale, pinched faces, and by their rare silence.

The drive home was the longest five-block trip Rowan could recall. In that time, her mix of fright and regret boiled down to anger—at Jake. How could he act this way, blowing something so far out of proportion? Her children weren't the only ones who needed to do a little growing up.

Rowan's hand shook as she opened the apartment door. Feeling as fierce as a lioness protecting her cubs, she drew Mac and Abby inside. Jake followed.

She pointed at the timeworn couch. ''Wait there,'' she said, then took the twins to tuck them in bed.

JAKE UNZIPPED his jacket, but didn't bother taking it off. He wasn't staying long. He leaned back against the couch and closed his eyes for a second. One word from his high school baseball career kept coming back to him: *Choke*.

That teacher's words had flown at him, and he'd frozen, just stood there not even able to blink. He wasn't sure he'd thawed yet. And he was even less certain that he wanted to.

Rowan came back into the room and looked him up and down like he was some mess the kids had forgotten to clean up.

He stood. "I'm sorry."

Her expression softened. "Sorry?"

"I thought I could do this, could adjust to kids, to changing my plans—"

Whatever softness he'd seen was gone. "Who asked you to change? I sure didn't. In fact, I recall saying directly the opposite. You knew from the first time we met that I have children." Her arms clasped around her midsection, she stepped away from him. "I haven't asked you to give up anything for them or for me."

He inclined his head in acknowledgment of her words, but didn't say anything. It was hard to argue with the truth.

"The twins were just engaging in a little fantasy. They know that telling those stories to their teacher was wrong, and they feel terrible. But they yearn for a father. It's only natural."

Jake swallowed hard, still feeling those fingers of panic tightening around his throat. "It isn't just what they said to their teacher. It's...well, it's a lot of things, and I don't really want to sort it all out."

"You could try, you know. You owe me that much."

"You're right. I do owe you at least that...and I'm really sorry, but I can't." He raised his hands palms out, a gesture of total surrender. "I can't commit to what you need. I can't...tie myself down like this. I'm sorry," he repeated.

"I know you're sorry, and I am, too. I'm not going to make a scene, or beg you to reconsider. You're a grown man, and by now you should know what you're capable of." Her eyes shone with something that looked and felt like sympathy. Jake shifted uneasily, somehow feeling smaller than her kids. "The funny thing is that you don't. Let's just end it here, okay?"

The choking sensation slipped lower and squeezed his heart. "Can I stop by and visit sometime?"

"No!" She paused and seemed to gather herself. "It would be too much for Mac and Abby."

"I wasn't thinking about them."

Rowan opened the apartment door and gestured to the hall-way beyond. "No," she said, "I don't suppose you were."

The door closed solidly behind him. It was the most final sound Jake had ever heard.

HOURS LATER, Rowan stared dry-eyed into the smothering darkness of her bedroom. The twins' explanation had broken her heart.

"We weren't playing the Daddy Game, Mommy. We weren't! We wanted it to be real this time."

She had wanted it to be real, too.

Rowan refused to cry. The silence on the other side of the wall was oppressive, overwhelming. She knew Jake was there, though. She could feel his presence as surely as she ever could. And she could feel his pain. Well, let him hurt a little.

There was plenty to go around.

"THANKSGIVING DAY." Jake spoke to the haggard reflection in his bathroom mirror. "Now there's a concept rich with irony." He squinted at his three days' worth of beard and gave a shrug. No point in shaving when no one would see him. No point in pretending he was anything other than miserable, either.

He had heard them leave last night, speaking in hushed tones so their voices wouldn't carry. He hated knowing she felt as if she had to creep about in her own home. Part of him resented it, too. He had grown accustomed to the twins' high-pitched voices and Rowan's soothing tones. He had come to enjoy the thumping noises of Mac and Abby as they ran through their apartment, bumping walls, banging chairs. Unfair, but he felt on some level as though Rowan had chosen to punish him, intentionally deprive him of those comforts. It was so quiet now, so bleak.

Jake paced the confines of his living room, then stopped to pick up a book. Maybe some Greeley would do the job. Then again, where did he plan to read? Over in the chair, or how about his bed? No memories there, right? He set the book back on the nearest pile.

Maybe he should go downstairs to the gallery and finish things up. It didn't look as though any Thanksgiving invitations were forthcoming. Not that he'd expected any.

Jake was halfway down the back stairs when the realization hit him. He spat an obscenity, one he seldom used, and listened to it echo down the narrow stairwell. He stood frozen for a moment, then sat down hard on the steps. There was no escaping the monumental mistake he had made.

For weeks now, he'd done nothing but hide from himself. He wanted independence, no commitments. He had been so damned sure his feelings couldn't have changed, that he never stopped to ask himself whether they might have. Now, it was a meaningless question. He was alone. He didn't have a commitment in the world.

He hated it.

"Choice." He said the word softly.

He repeated it louder. "Choice."

His goal hadn't been freedom from commitment. It had been the power to choose. And he had had that power all along. He had chosen to pursue Rowan. He had chosen to change for her. And he had chosen to push her away.

The only thing he hadn't chosen to do was love her. But sometime between his first peek at her backing out from under a table in the antique shop, and that last when he left her alone and hurt, it had happened anyway. He loved Rowan, and it was too late to do a damn thing about it.

He scrubbed his hand over his face. She deserved far better than him, anyway. Mac and Abby, too. He'd been an ass. She would never take him back now, and he couldn't blame her.

14

CHRISTMAS-SHOPPING season arrived with a vengeance. Every soul in the Detroit area wanted either the perfect holiday dress or the perfect antique whatnot for their collection, and was bent on buying it from one of the two Lindsays. Rowan's patience was at an end. Her smile was as artificial as the shop's lopsided plastic Christmas tree, and her nerves stretched as thin as the tinsel adorning it.

"Sit down and rest," Aunt Celeste commanded. "There's no reason to pace like a caged tiger for the thirteen seconds we have the place to ourselves." A veteran of countless holiday campaigns, she reclined on a plump goosedown-stuffed fainting couch.

"Good point." Rowan settled into an armchair. No sooner had her bottom touched the cushion than the door chimed again.

"No, stay. It's just the mail."

Rowan leaned back until the wooden trim at the top of the old chair nudged her head. "'Sit, stay,'" she mimicked. "I'm beginning to feel like I'm in obedience school."

"This time of year, it's more like boot camp." Celeste flipped through the stack of mail. She stopped, opened something, then frowned.

She tossed a large, square envelope onto Rowan's lap. "What should I do about this?"

Sticking diagonally out of the envelope was a thick white card imprinted in black script. Rowan slid it out and read. It was an invitation to a party celebrating the opening of the J. Albreight Gallery. She checked the envelope as an afterthought. Only Celeste had been invited.

Tears burned at Rowan's eyes. She angrily wiped them away. It was crazy to feel this pain over being excluded. After all, she had flat-out told Jake she didn't want to see him again. Even if he had invited her, she wouldn't go, would she?

She missed him so much. She missed the teasing, the laughter and intimacy of having someone to share her dreams with.

Rowan scowled at the invitation. She was forgetting one crucial element: Jake didn't want to share her life. He had made that agonizingly clear last week. She had wanted a man who would tell her the truth, and boy, had she gotten one.

She tucked the card back into the envelope and handed it to her aunt. "You should go."

Celeste toyed with her glasses, frowning down at them as if they offended her. "I couldn't possibly, not with things the way they are between the two of you. Besides, his party is the same night as Winter Walk."

"Winter Walk?"

"That's the annual costumed celebration hosted by the downtown merchants. You got here too late for it last year. The streets will be packed past midnight with shoppers."

"I'll keep the store open. You go to his party."

"If you're uncomfortable—"

Rowan raised one hand. "No, I'm going to be an adult about this. Jake's your tenant, and more than that, the son of an old friend. Of course you'll go." She worked up a smile. "Besides, we need a Lindsay in attendance to show him what he's missing."

Her aunt looked downright misty-eyed. "You're turning into one spectacular woman, you know that?"

Actually, she felt like one weepy woman, and something as unthinkable as Aunt Celeste crying was about to push her over the edge. Rowan bounced out of the chair. "Would you mind if I went for a little walk? I need to clear my head."

"I can do better than that. I'll pick up the twins from school. You make yourself scarce for the day. Take a walk, do your shopping, go read a book...okay?"

Rowan didn't need to be asked twice. She gave her aunt a hug. "Are you sure you're not really my fairy god-mother?"

"Only if a fairy godmother can listen to Santana and enjoy a good shot of single malt Scotch every now and then."

"Works for me," Rowan said, then wrapped herself in her coat and grabbed her purse. "I'll be back by dinner."

She stepped out the front door of Lindsay's, braced her-self against the bite in the air, then turned right, toward Jake's place. Since they had broken up, she always averted her eyes when she walked by—silly, since the windows were covered. Today, she'd force herself to look, to prove that she could get by fine without him.

Rowan jammed her hands deep into her coat pockets. Head to the ground, she took the five steps needed to place herself smack in the middle of Jake territory. On the count of three, she told herself, she would turn and face him square on. It was a coward's dare, anyway. All she'd be looking at was Jake's white butcher paper, not the man himself. No big deal.

One...Two...Three!

Yikes! No paper. Nothing but plate [...] self and...*Jake.*

She wanted to duck her head and run. She was [...] running, she knew. After all, she had hightailed it all [...] way back to Michigan from Massachusetts. She had given up a house and hard-won friends she loved rather than face the humiliation of seeing Chip and his new wife.

Not this time.

She focused on Jake with determined eyes. He stood mannequin still, looking directly at her. She'd been fooling herself. She'd get by without him, but it wouldn't be *fine.* Not for a very, very long time.

Even in his gray T-shirt and sweats, he looked beautiful. She knew how it felt to be held in those strong arms. She knew the taste of his skin, the heat of his mouth against hers. And he knew how good they were together. He knew and he'd thrown it all away. *Big, brick-headed mule of a man!*

Rowan tipped her chin up a notch, then narrowed her eyes and challenged him as though this was a child's staring match. He gave her a flat look, but she could see something brewing in his dark eyes. It couldn't have been more than a few seconds before the emotions cascaded across his face—regret, desire and finally, absolute frustration.

She was so pleased to be an annoyance, to work her way under his skin. He scowled, and in a lightning strike of inspiration—or maybe insanity—she stuck out her tongue. Jake's eyebrows shot up, and he jumped backward. Laughing for the first time in days, she flew down the sidewalk. She'd had enough of heartbreak; it was time for some fun.

ℝ THAT AFTERNOON, Celeste Lindsay picked up the ℝphone. Before dialing, she looked down at Abby and ℝac. "No point in being a fairy godmother if you can't shake things up, right?"

They nodded.

"And you two promise that you're absolutely positive you can pull off this plan."

"Sure," Mac said. "We're the sneakiest people we know."

Smiling, Celeste dialed the phone, then waited. "Hello, Melanie? This is Celeste Lindsay, Rowan's aunt. The twins and I have come up with a little surprise for Rowan, and we need your help...."

DELUGED BY holiday shoppers and drowning in work, Rowan managed to pretend that Jake's party wasn't even going to happen. She was good at that sort of thing. While in labor with the twins, she had spent every breath between contractions telling the nurses this couldn't possibly be the real thing, and that they should have her doctor send her home. Ignoring a stupid little party was a breeze compared to that.

She maintained her heavenly state of self-delusion until the night of the bash. When Aunt Celeste announced she was leaving early to get "done up," rain began to fall on the rosy world Rowan had created. Luckily, Melanie was there to lend her a hankie and some moral support.

"Looks like it's just us, Cinderella," Melanie said. "But if you've been left home from the ball and I'm with you, that must make me one of those mice. Yeech!"

Rowan managed a tiny smile at her friend's appalled expression. "Actually, Mac and Abby are more the mouse types." She walked to the armoire where she'd tucked away some Winter Walk costumes and pulled one out. "You can be Cinderella's little-known twin sister, who just happens to be a bawdy tavern wench."

Melanie grabbed the clothes. "Cool! I'll be right back." She hustled off to the back room.

After Melanie returned and Rowan took a moment to be sure her pal remained "G-rated," it was Rowan's turn. She slipped into a long and sheer black lace dress from her collection—Cinderella in mourning—then pinned her hair into a cascade of curls. She pasted on her best yuletide smile and rejoined Melanie and the twins.

Mac walked a circle around her. "Wow, Mommy, you should go next door and show Jake how pretty you look."

Rowan had thought she was cried out, but apparently she wasn't. Melanie handed her a box of tissues. "Just carry it with you," she advised. "We're in for a bumpy ride."

Before Rowan could even begin to recover, Winter Walk was in full swing. A juggler in a crimson-and-gold velvet Renaissance costume visited, and a black-caped magician stopped by to perform some sleight of hand. Mac and Abby hovered by the front door, plates of cookies in hand, offering a paltry few, and jamming the rest in their mouths.

Through it all, Rowan and Melanie helped a steady stream of customers. Rowan's hair was beginning to tumble loose and she lived for the moment that she could take off her 1940s heels, which were so high, she was risking a nosebleed.

During one of the few quiet times, she flopped onto a couch against the inside wall. From the other side she could hear laughter and music. She scooted closer to try to home in on familiar voices—Jake's, for instance. No luck. Rowan knelt; cupping her ear, she leaned against the wall. Ah, much clearer. Though she couldn't hear Jake, she did pick up what sounded to be a bevy of females. She grabbed a tissue from her box. What had he done, gone and gotten himself a harem?

JAKE LEANED against the wall and bit back a sigh. This was supposed to be fun, right? He'd loaded up his guest list with good-looking women who had lots of bucks, and the night was going exactly as planned. Plenty of money spent, plenty of laughs had. Plenty of invitations to come find a sprig of mistletoe, too. Those had been easy to turn down. The only woman he wanted to kiss wasn't there. Jake tried to block the noise of his party and listen for Rowan, just some small hint of what she was doing.

Celeste walked up and settled her hand on his shoulder. "She isn't any happier than you are."

He tried playing dumb. "Who isn't?"

"Really, Jake, you can do better than that," Celeste said after taking a sip of her wine, a move which Jake suspected she'd used to hide a smile. "If you're going to try to pretend that you're not thinking of Rowan, the least you can do is move away from that wall."

He shrugged. "Okay, so you caught me." The real trick was to catch him when he wasn't thinking of Rowan. Heck, he'd spent the better part of a week replaying that scene in his front window, trying to decide if it meant something good that she'd stuck out her tongue at him like a bratty schoolgirl. He'd concluded that she'd done it to drive him crazy. And it had worked.

"Why don't you go next door and ask her to come over? I'll mind the cash register and keep the party going."

He'd never noticed before, but Celeste's eyes were the

same true green as Rowan's. And like Rowan's, they could hold a world of sympathy and kindness, neither of which he deserved.

"I think I'll just stick around here."

Celeste shook her head. "Your choice, and not a very good one. At least go mingle for a while. You can't stand here and sulk all night."

Sulking sounded like a plan to him.

JUST AFTER ten o'clock, the true craziness started. Late-dinner goers had just finished their meals and joined the crush of people on the streets. As a compromise between mommyhood and work, Rowan had gotten the twins changed into their footed pajamas and brought them back down to the shop. At least when she closed up, she could put them straight to bed. That was assuming it ever got quiet enough for sleep to be a possibility. Jake had started some sort of wild jam session next door, and the noise reverberated like distant jungle drums whispering of trouble to come.

Abby tugged on her hand. "Listen to the music, Mommy."

"How could I miss it?" Rowan snapped, then immediately apologized. "I'm sorry, I shouldn't have yelled at you."

"It's okay," she consoled. "Auntie Celeste told us you were really sad, and that we should be extra good. You'll be better tomorrow. I promise."

Her daughter was mothering her. The thought was sweet and depressing all at the same time. "Don't worry about me, baby. I'm just fine. Go have some fun before it's bedtime, okay?"

With one last concerned glance over her shoulder, Abby

padded off. Rowan wished for a pair of footed pj's of her own, and a hot chocolate for a nightcap. And some earplugs. Instead, she found herself surrounded by a group of women, each of whom wanted a dress for New Year's Eve. Business was business, no matter how much her feet—and heart—ached.

Rowan pulled out her portfolio, sat down at a dining table and started discussing options. The more she talked, the more women clustered around her. She was sure at least two of them would be returning, and had one just about hooked when Melanie approached.

"Uh, Rowan…we seem to have one tiny problem."

Louder now, the drums next door pounded out their warning. Melanie wrung her hands.

"Now don't get panicked or anything—"

Boom-a-dah-dah…boom-a-dah-dah-boom-a-dah-dah…

"—but the twins are—"

"Gone," Rowan finished.

15

ROWAN STOOD at the top of the cellar steps, teetering on heels that were going down in her personal record book as the worst footwear choice ever. "Mac...Abby, I know you're there," she called.

They hadn't been in the apartment, where she'd hoped against hope that she'd find them tucked safely in bed. No, nothing so conventional from her children. Instead, she'd sprinted downstairs as fast as her wobbly ankles would carry her. She'd flung open the cellar door and found that Mac and Abby had ever-so-nicely left a trail of toys, and a light shining like a beacon at the bottom of the steps.

Hiking up the hem of her dress with one hand and gripping the rail with the other, she closed in on her kids.

"So what happened to being 'extra good' like you promised Aunt Celeste?" she asked, knowing she wouldn't get an answer out of either of them.

Rowan hit Ground Zero and saw exactly what she figured she would—no one. The instant she'd seen the Hansel and Gretel trail, she had known that this was to be the prank of all pranks. Mac and Abby wouldn't be satisfied with ending their little game in the cellar, not when there was music, laughter and—most tempting of all—Jake on the other side of the wall.

She navigated between boxes to the duct she should

have been bright enough to seal off weeks before. Next to the crates stacked by the opening was one of the panpipes Jake had made for the twins. Subtlety was an art they had yet to master.

Rowan looked down at her delicate lace dress, black stockings and high-altitude shoes. She definitely wasn't dressed for kid mining.

"Don't make me come in there after you." She winced. The words had come out sounding more like a plea than a threat. She cleared her throat and tried again. "Get out...*now*. Really, guys, I mean it!"

She squeezed her eyes shut and launched a silent prayer, *Please, oh, please, oh, please, don't make me do this...*

She picked up a faint scrabbling sound and the whistle of the other set of pipes. The sound was unnervingly distant, just thin enough to be coming from Jake's cellar.

Rowan swallowed hard, slipped off her shoes and hauled her dress up to her hips. "Okay, if that's the way it's going to be..."

STILL A SPECTATOR at his own party, Jake watched as Rowan's pal Melanie—dressed as if she'd just gotten off work at the Brazen Mermaid Tavern—scurried in the front door and up to Celeste Lindsay. Celeste's eyes grew wider and wider as she took in whatever was being said to her. Melanie pointed frantically upward, whispered something more, then both women turned and pinned Jake with a wild-eyed stare. He took an involuntary step backward.

As Rowan's friend ran out the door, Celeste shot through the crowd to him. Jake debated the merits of turning tail and running himself, but he knew it wouldn't do any good. Once she got her sights set, Celeste was as single-minded as a bloodhound.

Her hand latched onto his arm. "The twins have crawled into their tunnel and won't come out until they've talked to you."

Half-amused and half-annoyed, he drawled, "Well, isn't that special?" Then the full meaning of her words hit him. "Did you say *in* the tunnel, as in the tunnel to my place?"

She waved away the question. "They're smack in the middle of the duct, and won't come out. Melanie said that Rowan has been trying to coax them, but they won't budge." She started tugging at him. Damn, she was strong. "Did you know that those poor little angels think this whole disaster between you and Rowan is their fault? They scarcely sleep at night."

"That makes three of us," Jake muttered as he quickly gave in to the inevitable. It wasn't right to let the kids think that they'd messed up, when it was his fault. One hundred percent his. And much as it pained him to admit it, he genuinely cared for the little monsters.

"You're going to fix this," Celeste ordered, as she hauled him through the crowd and to the back room.

Jake opened the cellar door and switched on the light. They had to choose this route, didn't they? Why knock on the door when there were so many more entertaining places to be? Say, the dark, confining pits-of-hell cellar...leading to the tomb-of-death tunnel. A horror story designed with just his personal...ah...*nonpreference* in mind. He swallowed once, or maybe gulped, based on Celeste's odd expression.

"Hurry," she urged. "I'll keep your guests busy."

Jake squinted down into the dim underworld, then back at her. There was nothing to be done but descend. "Okay," he said, then dawdled at the top step. "Just do me a favor and keep this door open."

"Fine, just move it!"

Easier said than done, Jake thought, then step by step got ready to live his worst nightmare. As he closed in on his tomb, he focused on what he'd say to the kids, how he could explain the mess he'd made of things. How he could get them out of there before he turned into a sweaty, shaking mess. Laughter drifted down to him. He fought the impulse to look over his shoulder and see if everyone had gathered at the top of the steps to watch him make a fool of himself.

Jake tugged at the base of the duct. Just his luck they'd built things to last back when this beast had been put in. It could hold his weight with ease. He bent into the opening to see if he'd fit. If he angled his shoulders, he would...unfortunately.

He heard a child's giggle and some scraping sounds.

Damn, he'd rather face a tank full of those piranhas Mac liked so much, than this. He drew a deep breath and felt the added rush of air zing into his system and send his gut for an extra tumble. Maybe hyperventilation wasn't so bad after all. A little less oxygen to the brain, and he just might not remember this...if he survived.

"Okay, here goes..." he said under his breath, then stuck his head into total, suffocating darkness.

ROWAN COULD hear Mac and Abby's distant, happy laughter. They sounded as though they thought this was an event second only to eating their way through a chocolate cake. When she got to the other side of this blasted tunnel, she'd give them a thing or two to think about. That is, if she got to the other side of the tunnel. She seemed to have put on a pound or two in all the wrong locations since the last time she'd made the trip. No more Christmas cookies, she promised herself.

Of all the places she didn't want to be crawling, Jake's duct was tops on the list. As she felt her stockings snag, then shred on a metal seam, Rowan reconsidered the military school option Jake had mentioned. It was either that, or a time-out until the twins were twenty.

Heaven help them if she actually had to see the man. She paused in her slow wriggle and waved at the cobwebs tickling the tip of her nose. Heaven help her if she *didn't* see him. No more crying, she reminded herself. And no more pretending that Jake cared about her.

JAKE WEDGED himself a little farther into the duct. He could hear the kids whispering somewhere just ahead, almost within reach. And just far enough away that this freakin' piece of metal was going to swallow him whole. *Think wide open places, the rolling prairie, an endless stretch of beach. Think...I'm gonna be sick.* He closed his eyes and saw a pattern of flashing lights he'd last seen when he'd fallen from a tree—right as the earth knocked him unconscious.

Of all the color-me-stupid moments of his life! He'd be damned if he was going to faint. Girls fainted. Guys toughed it out. And, man, did he want out! It was time to start some pretty convincing chat. He dragged in a breath of musty air, and shaped his mouth to form Mac's name.

"M-muh-muh..." he wheezed, then exhausted his air supply. Sparks shot around him like Fourth of July sparklers. Jake wiped at his forehead. He needed to conserve his energy or he'd smother in here, and lose the pleasure of killing the twins over this little stunt.

Only he had to find 'em first. Giving himself up for

dead, Jake pushed off with the foot he'd left connected to freedom. Do or die. Be a man.

IT COULDN'T be much farther, Rowan thought, feeling the way in front of her. She rounded the corner. The kids' whispers and giggles sounded louder, if not clearer. A cheery thought occurred to her. Maybe they'd stopped short of committing breaking and entering. It was possible they were right in front of her. She sent her hand on a braille dance across the duct floor.

"Huh?" Her hand closed on a small, rectangular object...buttons...a dial...a faint vibration under her fingers—a cassette recorder chattering the night away! She clenched the thing tighter, wishing it was one of the twins' collars.

"*Aaaiiiee!*" she yelped, as a sweaty male hand closed over hers.

"Rowan?" She knew that voice, even if it did sound like a black leather glove was slowly squeezing the life from it.

"Jake, what are you doing in here?"

"Dying," he croaked.

Events spun out fast and furious after that. In fact, that blazing moment of epiphany—the realization that she'd been conned by her own kids—came too late. Over Jake's gasped-out stream of salty language she heard the slam of metal and the grinding of heavy objects across a concrete floor. Or two concrete floors.

"We've got you trapped," Aunt Celeste called from in front of her.

"And we're not letting you lovebirds out," came Melanie's laughter-filled voice from behind.

"So kiss and make up," the twins chorused.

Other than crying, Rowan did the only thing she could. She laughed.

"I DON'T SEE what's so funny," Jake growled as he wrapped his hand around Rowan's wrist and tugged just enough to bring her closer. She was a lifeline, even if she was too busy laughing to realize it.

"Nothing...everything," she forced out between peals of laughter.

"Can you stop that? You're using up all of the air."

"There's plenty of air going through here. Well, maybe a little less since they did whatever it is they did to close us in here." She paused as if considering the matter. "Still, I'm pretty sure they'll let us out before we suffocate."

Something cold and clammy raced up the back of his neck. "*Pretty* sure?"

"Okay, positive."

Her other hand reached out and traced his features. He closed his eyes and took what comfort he could from her touch.

"Jake, what's going on here? You feel like a dead fish."

"Romantic of you to notice," he muttered. "I've got a little problem with...ah...tight spaces. And a really big one with tight, dark ones," he added.

"Aunt Celeste, let us out of here!" she screamed.

Jake covered an ear with his free hand.

"Not until you two have straightened things out," her aunt called back.

"But Jake's panicking or something. What if he faints?"

He cringed at that girlie word.

"He's probably just playing possum. He's a wiley thing, you know."

Rowan hesitated. "And if he's not faking?"

"Then we'll haul his carcass out of there...after he's fainted!"

Since passing out remained a distinct—and humiliating—possibility, Jake grasped Rowan's hand tighter, dragged in what air he could, then let the truth free.

"Look, I crawled into this tomb because Celeste told me that the kids were upset over us and wouldn't come out. But if this hadn't happened, I would have found another way to you. Maybe not underground and through a wall, but I swear I would have gotten there, Rowan.

"I love you. I want to wake up every day for the rest of my life seeing you, loving you, and knowing that together, we're better than we'll ever be apart. It's taken me a while to admit this to myself, let alone another person, but I'm just a responsible sort of guy. I don't want to keep my options open. I want to be here. With you, and Mac and Abby, and maybe a kid or two of our own...if you're willing."

He was out of wind, out of words and surviving on nothing more substantial than hope.

"Rowan?"

He could feel her moving toward him. "Sweetheart, come on, say something...anything."

After hazarding their way across his cheek and chin, her lips met his. If he'd had the strength left, he would have shouted with joy.

Rowan did it for him. "He says he loves me," she yelled. "You can let us go, Aunt Celeste!"

Cheers echoed from both ends of the tunnel, followed by the rattle and clank of heavy objects. Jake slipped bonelessly back toward freedom. Once out, he sat against the wall trying to adjust to liberty like a prisoner of war escapee in one of those old Lee Marvin movies. He squinted at one of his former captors.

"Thanks," he said to Celeste over a mouthful of sarcasm.

The woman had the nerve to laugh. "Think nothing of it."

He didn't have the time to tell her exactly what he did think, because Rowan appeared and flung herself at him.

"You didn't say all that just to get out of there, did you? Because if you did, I swear I'll just stuff you back into that duct myself. And it's not like it was my idea or anything. I mean, I was as surprised as you were. But really, if—"

He could tell by the glint in her eyes that she was really on a roll. Jake did the only thing he could.

He kissed her...and it was a forever kind of kiss.

HARLEQUIN®

Duets™

C'mon back to Paxton, Texas!

The Hometown Heartthrobs have returned to delight their fans with a second double Duets volume from author Liz Jarrett!

Chase and Nathan got their stories in Duets #71 in March 2002...

Now it's brother-and-sister time, as Trent and Leigh finally find their own matches and true love not far behind, amidst the all-around wackiness of their neighbors and small-town life!

Look for this exciting volume,
Duets #87, in November 2002,
as we find out who's...
Meant for Trent and that
Leigh's for Me.

Yahoo x 2!

HARLEQUIN®
Makes any time special ®

The holidays have descended on

COOPER'S CORNER

providing a touch of seasonal magic!

Coming in November 2002...
MY CHRISTMAS COWBOY
by Kate Hoffmann

Check-in: Bah humbug! That's what single mom
Grace Penrose felt about Christmas this year. All her plans
for the Cooper's Corner Christmas Festival are going wrong—
and now she finds out she has an unexpected houseguest!

Checkout: But sexy cowboy Tucker McCabe is no ordinary
houseguest, and Grace feels her spirits start to lift. Suddenly
she has the craziest urge to stand under the mistletoe...forever!

HARLEQUIN®

Makes any time special ®

Visit us at www.cooperscorner.com

CC-CNM4

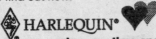